The Songbird Setup
Maggie Linn Sharpe

eBook Edition ISBN-13: 979-8-9923370-2-0

Paperback ISBN-13: 979-8-9923370-0-6
www.maggielinnsharpe.com

Cover design by Maggie Linn Sharpe.

Also by Maggie

The Songbird Cafe Series

The Songbird Setup (Leena & Bailey)

The Boss Boycott (Annie & Eric)

To anyone who still isn't sure what they want to be when they grow up. You don't have to have it all figured out. It's never too late to find and follow your passion.

Don't give up!

She's imperfect, but she tries

She is good, but she lies

She is hard on herself

She is broken and won't ask for help

She is messy, but she's kind

She is lonely most of the time

She is all of this mixed up

And baked in a beautiful pie

She is gone, but she used to be mine

Sara Bareilles

Contents

Chapter One

Leena

"I LOVE TO SING sad songs. For anyone who doesn't know me: I'm Leena, the owner of the Songbird Cafe and Bar. For those who are already familiar, this is old news, but for anyone new to our open mic night, I like to kick things off with this disclaimer." I laugh softly into the microphone.

The crowd chuckles, and some shake their heads, but they humor me. They know that if I perform at my cafe's open mic night, nine times out of ten, I will choose a slow, sad ballad.

Some of the most interesting songs to sing happen to be slow, heart-wrenching melodies, and I've always gravitated towards them. This is why going to karaoke nights with friends causes problems for me. Karaoke has this fun, crazy vibe, and nothing can kill the vibe faster than belting about lost love or singing a mournful song about heartbreak.

"My love of sad songs is exactly why, when I opened Songbird, I started open mic nights. I was tired of feeling left out at karaoke and just wanted to sing what I wanted to sing." I go on to detail the rules of our open mic nights.

"Rule #1: We do not tolerate heckling or booing of any kind. This is a safe space for anyone to perform whatever they want. Art is subjective. If you don't like someone's performance, use that time to visit the bar or the bathroom. It's the in-person equivalent of 'just keep scrolling.' Leave the mean comments for your social media feeds." I give the crowd a quick, serious-faced stare to make certain they understand that even though I'm cracking jokes, I'm dead serious about the rules, and in case there is anyone who thinks I'm kidding, I go on.

"Rule #2: We reserve the right to boot your ass if you break rule #1." I raise my eyebrows and make eye contact with a table of twenty-something guys that I haven't seen before. They nod their understanding and a couple of them hold up their hands in an expression of innocence, letting me know that they'll behave.

"Finally, rule #3: Have fun. This isn't life or death. Everyone will move on with their lives, whether you give the performance of a lifetime or completely forget every line of your new slam poem." I smile and the crowd chuckles. I sit down at the keyboard and lower the mic with me. "My final warning is that we do a lot of Broadway numbers here, and while you're welcome to do whatever you like for your turn—I'll never turn down anyone who wants to cover some Taylor Swift classics—show tunes are my jam and I play what I want!" I shrug my shoulders as I play the intro for "Burn" from *Hamilton*. Someone near the back whoops and I laugh into the microphone.

"Sounds like we've got some Lin-Manuel Miranda fans in the back," I sweep my gaze around the room, "Or maybe this is just the 'I've been cheated on and it sucks' anthem."

The laughter of the crowd gives me the same rush it always does. Laughter and applause are the best medicine and performing always helps me to become lighter and less haunted. I give myself over to that emotion as I launch into the song, wishing I could feel this free all the time rather than my default settings of melancholy and sarcastic.

The lift performing gives me is one of the main reasons that I often open and close the open mic night lineup. I like to give my speech about the rules and what to expect. I also like to say goodnight to the loyal customers who drank with us all night. Plus, I have very little social life, so the twice-a-week open mic nights get me out of my small apartment above the cafe and out of my head for a little while.

The Songbird Cafe and Bar is a large open rectangular room. The bar runs along the right side of the room with open back barstools along the front. Seating is a mix of cozy chairs and couches, with high-top tables scattered throughout the room. I wanted to create a place for anyone to hang out, no matter the time of day. We even have a few racks of donated new and used books that operate like a little free library along the left side of the room, for anyone looking for something to read while they relax in our comfy vibe.

Towards the back of the bar, we have a barista station that handles all the morning cafe drinks with a pastry case that we fill from local bakeries. A mirrored wall displays an assortment of liquor and mixers, and we offer a selection of local beers on tap for our evening crowd. Most people will bring takeout since we don't have a full kitchen.

The stage, complete with microphone, electric keyboard, and speaker system, sits in the left corner for our open mic nights. I bought a gently used karaoke setup from a bar that was going out of business to add options for open mic nights.

I started open mic nights about two months after opening Songbird. Morning coffee and pastry sales were good, but I wanted a reason for people to come out in the evening. I had the idea one weekend after some friends dragged me out for karaoke and I couldn't sing what I wanted without bringing down the entire room. In the year since, they've become increasingly popular and we always have a full crowd.

As I come to the end of "Burn," I let myself get a little lost in the lyrics and the thoughts of the past bubble up. It's been two years since my life blew up, but somehow the wounds are still fresh when I'm performing like this. However, there is something cathartic—like I'm working through some of the damage—when I get lost in the song lyrics.

After playing the final notes, the crowd applauds, and whoops and my spirit lifts. I take just a second to enjoy the moment and then I put the past back in the box in the back of my mind where it belongs.

"Thank you, everyone!" I say, hoping the sincerity in my voice is perceived by the crowd. "Next up we've got Stella and Ian to entertain us with their acoustic stylings." The singer-songwriter duo that's always popular with the crowd takes the stage and gets set up with their acoustic guitars. They start with a really cool cover of *NSYNC's "Bye Bye Bye" before launching into some of their original pieces. I hang out at the bar to listen for a little while and then continue on with my Tuesday night.

LATER THAT WEEK, I'M helping Cass tend the bar before the start of open mic. For a Friday night in early January, we're super busy. We've had an unseasonably warm week and more people are here without the snow and ice encouraging them to stay home. On top of that, we're short-handed tonight since our weekend bartender, Alaina, is out with the flu.

Cass is Songbird's full-time general manager and has been with me from the start. She is a total rock star when it comes to running the business side. We met in my junior year of college when she was a freshman. Cass and I hit it off right away back then, and she's become one of my best friends now that we're running Songbird together.

We reconnected after Cass finished her MBA from Ohio State. After she graduated, I asked if she wanted to help me open my own place. She grew up working in her family's restaurant in West Virginia and it gave her the perfect experience for running a cafe and bar. I prefer to focus more on the creative side of the business like fun events and the ambiance of the space.

Cass and I have only gotten closer during the year she's worked for me. Our personalities mesh perfectly and there's no one else I would want running my business. We're both snarky and fluent in sarcasm and inappropriate jokes. We like to joke that we are twins separated at birth, although we look nothing alike.

In appearance, we're total opposites, with her tall willowy frame and dark straight hair that is cut into a short, smooth bob framing her face perfectly. I'm several inches shorter with curves for days. I usually pull my unruly auburn curls up into a bun or Dutch braid to keep them out of my way.

"What depressing ballad are you kicking off open mic with tonight?" Cass murmurs with a smirk. She is not a fan of my penchant for sad songs and likes to remind me of that fact often. If Cass gets up to sing, she usually goes with something fun and upbeat—she has no problems fitting in at karaoke—although she loves show tunes as much as I do.

"I'm thinking it's a Sara Bareilles sort of night," I smirk as she rolls her eyes and sighs.

"Whatever floats your boat, boss-lady!"

"Thank you so much for your support." I snark back at her and laugh as I stroll up to the piano. I sit down and sigh, with tiredness weighing on my body.

A recurring nightmare featuring my asshole of an ex made for a night of shitty sleep. I woke up in a pool of sweat with my heart pounding. It took me a while to shake off the panic and rush of adrenaline. I had a hard time sleeping after that so I'm exhausted, emotionally drained, and downcast today. Sara Bareilles's songs are like my performance security blanket, always there when I need to let the emotions flow.

I run through my usual welcome speech with the rules of open mic night and start playing "Gravity" which is one of my absolute favorites. This song has carried me through several heartbreaks and always feels relevant. I hear the door open as I start the second verse, but I don't bother looking up. People come and go a lot through open mic night and I prefer to let myself get lost in the lyrics.

As I come to the bridge, a chill runs up my spine, and I can sense someone watching from near the door. We dim the lights in the bar so I can't see him very well, only his very tall frame standing watching me sing. The hairs on my arm stand on end and my heart rate picks up. It reminds me a little of the adrenaline I experienced after my nightmare, but this time I'm not scared. I'm intrigued. I have never in my life been so aware of someone's physical presence in my life and I silently hope the tall stranger will stick around so I can figure out why. Maybe I know him?

After I finish my number and hand off the mic to the next act, I pop behind the bar to help Cass manage the crowd that has built up. I'm so focused on running drinks that when I look up and find the mystery man sitting at the bar in front of me, I'm almost startled. Not just because of the reaction my body seems to have to his presence, but also because he is stunning.

His dark wavy hair is close-cropped on the sides and worn a little longer on top. He has the perfect amount of scruff covering his chiseled jaw, somewhere between a five o'clock shadow and a full beard. His dark brown eyes have a spark of humor in them and follow me as I approach. Even sitting on the bar stool, I have to look up at him to get his order.

"Hi there! What can I get you?" I chirp, trying not to let on how his presence is affecting me. If he knew me at all, he'd see right through me. Most of my regulars are used to me being grumpy or snarky with them. I rarely do the upbeat customer service voice but something about him makes me nervous.

He takes a glance at our beer list. "I'll take the Wolf's Ridge lager on tap, thanks," he answers with a smooth, deep voice and a smile.

"Be right back with that!" I take off to pour his drink at the other end of the bar with my hands shaking.

What the hell is wrong with me? He hasn't even said anything real, just ordered a beer, but my heart is beating like he asked me to marry him.

Whoa.. marry him? Where the actual fuck did that thought come from? I berate myself as I pour his beer. I'm not sure I believe in marriage anymore. I'm certainly not in the habit of imagining strangers proposing to me.

As soon as the thought crosses my mind, I picture it. This beautiful man, down on one knee, holding my hand and looking up at me in adoration. It's enough to make my stomach churn and I'm even more nervous as I head back towards him. I set the glass on a coaster in front of him as he slides a twenty across the bar.

"I'll just be right back with your change!" I slowly slide away as I'm talking. I want to both be near him and get as far away as possible at the same time, and it's scrambling my brain a bit.

"Nah, keep the change. " He gives me a small smile and my stomach bottoms out while my heart rate climbs.

"Oh! Thank you!" I give him a genuine smile despite my unease. Cass is saving up for a down payment on a new car and generous tippers are always welcome at my bar. I glance around for the next customer when I realize the line is slowing down and everyone has been helped. I start to walk away when the handsome stranger stops me.

"Wait! I ... uh ... I actually came over here to talk to you," he says in a rush. I raise my eyebrows at that and wait for him to elaborate. "I was walking past and heard you singing and I just had to find out where that voice was coming from." He finishes quickly, seeming mildly embarrassed by the confession.

"Well, I'll be damned," I quip. "I guess I owe some cartoon fairytale writers an apology!" The snarky comment makes me feel a little more like myself. My cheeks are blushing from his compliment, but I can't keep the sarcasm from flying out of my mouth.

"What do you mean?" He asks and I laugh while rolling my eyes before launching into one of my favorite tirades.

"Fairy tales completely set me up for disappointment when all the boys growing up didn't give two shits about my singing voice." I realize I'm about to confess an old insecurity, but I'm not able to stop myself. "For a chubby, awkward teenager who was way too into musical theater, the promise that my prince charming just needed to hear me sing to be interested definitely did not pan out the way I hoped." I laugh and only just barely keep the bitterness out of my voice.

The gorgeous stranger chuckles kindly and takes a slow up-and-down glance at my body that sets my skin tingling. After years of work on my self-esteem, I love—or at least feel some neutrality about—my mid-size curvy body. I no longer beat myself up about my pant size having double digits and I refuse to even own a scale.

But in the gaze of this stunning man, I'm feeling self-conscious. What is he seeing when he looks at me? I think I'm detecting a hint of heat in his eyes, and that makes me blush all over again. I'm sure he notices my cheeks burning but is nice enough not to mention it.

"Do you think your manager would mind if I bought you a drink?" He asks with a smile. He clearly missed the part of my welcome speech where I mentioned that I'm the owner of the bar. So I play along and pour myself a gin and Sprite.

"I don't think she would mind at all," I smirk as I sip the drink. He's just about to say something when the alarm on my phone goes off, making me jump. I look down at my watch to see that it's almost nine and time for my weekly FaceTime with Annie.

My two best friends and I have been a tight-knit trio since we met in the seventh grade. For years, it was Annie, Jessie, and me. We did everything together, all the way through college at Ohio State, before going our separate ways.

Jessie and I have found our way back to Fort Starling, but Annie moved to Chicago a few years ago and her job keeps her crazy busy. We've taken to scheduling our FaceTimes to make sure we stay in touch. I miss her big time, so I am not in the habit of bailing on our calls, but the handsome guy in front of me makes it tempting.

"Oh shit, I have a phone call I have to take!" I say apologetically.

That I even for a second considered blowing off Annie for this guy makes my stomach drop. What am I even doing? I'm not interested in dating anyone. I don't want a relationship. What is even the point of staying here chatting with him when I'm not interested in it going any further than a drink in my bar? He nods like he isn't sure whether I'm telling the truth or blowing him off, and for some reason, I can't stop myself from continuing our exchange.

"Will you be around for a while? I'll be back down to close out open mic at midnight." I hear the pleading tone in my voice that low-key embarrasses me, but can't quite make it stop. He checks his phone and shrugs a bit.

"I've got kind of an early morning, so I'm not sure if I can stick around," he says regretfully.

"Oh okay. Well... it was really nice to meet you!" I say too loudly and spin around. I take off through the door to the kitchen so he doesn't see the disappointment and confusion blazing across my face.

It's only as I'm climbing the stairs to my apartment over the bar that I realize we didn't even exchange names. He's still a mystery and that's probably for the best. I actually hope he's not there when I go back down to the bar. For the most part, I believe my own lies.

Chapter Two

Leena

"WHAT'S WRONG WITH YOU?" Annie asks as the call connects. She knows me so well. Why do we live hours away from each other? As always I feel the familiar pang of missing having our heart-to-hearts in person instead of on FaceTime. Her light brown hair hangs to her shoulders and I can see the freckles across her nose move as she narrows her eyes, assessing me.

"I have no idea," I groan. "I think I just flirted with a handsome stranger and then ran." I run my hands down my face. I'm so confused by my body's reaction to the hot guy from the bar and how much it conflicts with the way I usually shut down any attraction.

"You think you flirted?" her voice drips with sarcasm. "Do you not know what flirting is anymore? Have you completely lost that skill with lack of use?"

I huff a laugh because she isn't too far off the mark. I avoid any romantic situations. Ever since my five-year relationship and subsequent engagement imploded a couple of years ago, I decided I am just fine on my own and I don't need to waste energy pursuing the "happily ever after" that likely isn't coming.

"You know I haven't been interested in anyone since things ended with Adam," I grumble. This is a point of contention with Annie and Jessie. They insist that I just need to get back out there. I don't see any point in dumping time and energy into a relationship that will just blow up in my face and leave me even more broken than I already am.

"Leena, I know, but I really think it would be good for you to at least consider dating again. You're only 30. Are you planning on just being alone for the rest of your life?" I shrug my shoulders. Better alone and healing like I am now than alone and shattered all over again. I'm better off this way.

"I don't miss being in a relationship," which is only half a lie. Overall, I really don't miss being in a relationship. There were more downsides to being in a relationship, in my experience, so I'm not really interested in going through the hassle all over again.

Every so often, I miss the companionship of having someone know me so well that they could predict exactly what I'd like to do on a random Tuesday evening. Of course, when someone knows you that well, they know exactly how to cut you down and manipulate you.

Even more rarely I miss the regular sex, but I have a battery-operated buddy and a fabulously fancy shower head to help out with that. And let me just say, my vibrator doesn't guilt me into putting out when I'm not in the mood. I don't need to worry about disappointing it or finding out it's been looking for some action on the side.

"That's because your only serious relationship was with that twat-waffle!" Exasperated from having to repeat this sentiment every time we broach the subject of my dating life, she practically yells at the screen. "Not every guy is as awful as Adam, Leena. There are some good men still out there!" I raise my eyebrows at her vehemence. That was one line of reasoning that I hadn't heard from her before.

"Are you seeing someone?" I ask, my voice full of suspicion and curiosity. "You haven't mentioned anyone since that guy last fall!" I bounce my eyebrows at her suggestively and I can see her blushing through the screen. I'm not interested in a relationship for myself, but I have no qualms about living vicariously through my friends' dating adventures. I consider dating a spectator sport and I'm happy to cheer on my besties.

"Umm... it's new... hey! We were talking about your love life, not mine!" she scolds. I bark a laugh and roll my eyes again.

"A. there is no love life. I had one mildly flirty interaction with a gorgeous guy and then panicked and ran before I even got his name. He's probably already gone and I'll never see him again, so it really isn't worth discussing. Now, how's work in that fancy high rise office of yours?"

We keep the conversation light from there. She knows when I've hit my limit for being scolded about my singledom. As we're chatting, my mind wanders to the very handsome stranger and I can't shake the confusion and anxious feeling that I may be missing something after all.

AFTER CHATTING WITH ANNIE, I wander into my small kitchen to grab a snack. Part of me wants to run back down to the bar to see if the mystery man is still there, but the part of me that wants to protect my heart and my closely guarded walls keeps me upstairs. As I slice up a Honeycrisp apple, I wonder why this guy even affected me so much.

There are attractive men in the bar all the time, but I'd never had such an instant reaction to anyone. I am not a fan of this sensation—like

I'm losing control of the tight rein I usually hold on every aspect of my emotions. This control is how I've survived the last couple of years. I am not about to let loose now just because a pretty face smiled at me.

As I munch on my apple and peanut butter, I hear my phone buzz. I glance down to find a text from Jessie, the other third of our trio and a wannabe matchmaker. I immediately groan loudly and roll my eyes as I read it.

Jessie:

> Hey babes! I told Bailey you'd meet him at that new wine bistro on Main at 7. Do you want me to help you get ready?!

Dammit. I completely forgot that I agreed—after months of dodging and avoiding—to be set up on a blind date. Jessie has been up my ass for the better part of a year about meeting one of her husband's teammates.

Dan and Jessie got together at the beginning of our freshman year of college and have been together ever since. They got married shortly after we graduated and I think she's tired of being the only one in our trio of friends that's married, so she likes to play matchmaker. Dan is the starting catcher for the Ft. Starling Flash—the major league baseball team based here—and Jessie has been dying to set me up with one of their pitchers.

For a long time, I was able to put her off, but she is so fucking stubborn. A few weeks ago, after a few too many glasses of wine, I agreed to a single blind date. I completely forgot about the conversation until now. I'm pretty sure Jessie got me drunk that night just so she could trick me into this.

Me:

> Ugh, do I really have to go? I was tipsy when I agreed to it, so I don't think it should count!

Jessie:

> Yes!! You have to go!!! I promise you're going to like him so much. You're perfect for each other, if you would just GIVE HIM A CHANCE!!! I SWEAR TO GOD YOU BETTER SHOW UP TOMORROW OR I WILL BE KICKING YOUR ASS INTO NEXT WEEK, MISSY!!!!!!

Me:

> Geez, fine! You don't need to yell! I'll be there.

I sigh deeply, suddenly so tired of her matchmaking and annoyed with myself that I even agreed to her crazy setup plan. Perfect for each other? Yeah, unlikely. I'll go on her ridiculous date but I am not putting in anything other than minimal effort and then I can come home and read the new Meghan Quinn book that's releasing tomorrow like I had originally planned.

A quick glance at the clock tells me it's time to make my way downstairs to finish out open mic. As I pop out into the bar, Cass catches my eye, so I make my way over to her. I take a quick peek around the room to see if the cute guy from earlier was still around, but I don't see him.

"Looking for someone?" Cass asks expectantly, making me jump.

"Nope, just seeing what kind of crowd is still around," I lie with a shrug as I avoid eye contact. I'm not the best liar and Cass knows me way too well to buy my bullshit.

"Are you sure you're not looking for that hunk of a man you were chatting with earlier?" she raises her eyebrows like she knows she caught me fibbing. I laugh and shake my head.

"If you thought he was so hunky, why don't you go after him?" I snipe back at her. "I'm not looking to start anything right now. Or ever." She just laughs at me.

"He was almost too pretty for me. You know I like 'em a bit more rough around the edges. That man was a little too clean-cut for me." I roll my eyes at her as I pour myself a glass of water to get ready to sing. "So what are you singing for closing, still in a depressed Sara Bareilles mood?"

"I'm still feeling Sara, but I'll at least give you a more upbeat one this time!" I say with a saucy wink. Approaching the stage, a new comedian finishes his set. He's pretty good and I could see him making it at the comedy clubs soon. We have a few comedians that like our open mic nights for trying out new material. It always makes for a fun break in the music and adds some variety to the lineup. As he finishes up his set, I stroll up to the mic while cueing up my song and connecting my phone to the Bluetooth speaker.

"Alright folks, it's rolling up on midnight, which means our open mic night is coming to a close. We'll have another next Tuesday if you haven't had enough. I'm still feeling Sara Bareilles tonight, but I thought I'd give you a peppier number for once." Wiggling my eyebrows at the crowd, I continue. "I'm a decent piano player, but for songs that move a little quicker, I need some help from technology. So here's 'When He Sees Me' from *Waitress the Musical*."

I dive into the fast-paced, funny song and put on my best Southern accent. My current mood is surprisingly cheerful, despite my earlier gloomy attitude. I'm almost done with the song when the hair stands up on the back of my neck again. I scan the crowd and the back of the room. Sure enough, as I reach the last few lines of the song, the mystery man himself steps out from behind one of the taller display shelves of books.

Our eyes lock as I finish the song, and I seriously start sweating. I can feel my cheeks heat as he holds my gaze for a beat longer. He shoots me a quick smile and a wink and ducks out the door.

What the fuck was that?

I don't know how a wink from a stranger can leave me this flustered. I leave the stage, still thinking about the smile he gave me as he left. Why hadn't he stayed to at least give me his name? Did he even know my name? Why on earth did I even care? And that's the question that echoes through my mind as I drag myself upstairs to bed.

I ARRIVE EARLY AT the restaurant, already regretting this blind date. I wanted to get the lay of the land before the guy that Jessie insists is my "soulmate" shows up. She's been begging me to meet this guy for the better part of a year.

For a long time, she begrudgingly accepted my excuse that I was still heartbroken over what had happened with Adam and losing my Gram a few months later. But in the last few months, I think she knew I was using them as an excuse.

I may have decided relationships aren't something I'm interested in anymore, but I don't still have the raw heartache that plagued me for that first year. And as much as I hate it, I'm learning to cope in a world without my Gram.

I brought a book with me, so I let the hostess seat me. I meant what I said about not putting in an effort for this date, so I'm wearing comfy leggings, an oversized sweatshirt, and slip-on sneakers. My hair's down and I at least attempted to tame the curls a bit, but I didn't do anything special. I dabbed on a little makeup, but that is just because people ask me if I'm sick if I skip makeup altogether. My habit of being practically nocturnal only accentuates the dark circles that are always present under my eyes.

I order my usual gin and Sprite and get to reading. My goal is 200 books this year and while I'm on pace to making it; I like to read any chance I get. The spicy romance I'm devouring is just getting to the good part. The waitress brings my drink right as the main characters start to lose their clothing and I thank her and take a sip.

I have a low-key superpower of keeping a completely straight face while reading spicy scenes in public. I could sit across from my Gram reading a downright filthy scene, and no one would be the wiser. The thought of Gram gives me another sharp pang, but I push it down like I always do and keep reading. I'm deeply immersed in the action of my book and I completely lose track of my surroundings. I'm startled when I hear someone clearing their throat and a deep voice saying my name.

"Leena?"

I jump in my seat and look up, then up some more because he's so tall that he towers over me. My jaw drops as I recognize him. The handsome stranger I met at my bar grins down at me.

"B-bailey?" I stutter, not quite believing he's there.

"That's me. It's nice to see you again," he says with a smirk.

"You've got to be fucking kidding me."

Chapter Three

Bailey

THE LOOK ON LEENA'S face is a cross between bewilderment and murderous rage.

"You've got to be fucking kidding me," she grumbles, and I do my best to stifle my laugh.

Jessie warned me that there was a good chance that Leena wouldn't be all that happy to be on this date. I'm doing this to appease Jessie, not being able to take any more of her pleading that I meet her friend. But after stumbling into Leena's bar by accident last night, and the brief conversation we had, I'll admit that I'm more than a little intrigued. All day today, I found myself looking forward to this date.

"It's nice to officially meet you!" I say, pouring on my signature charm and taking the seat next to her. I'm known for my ability to charm anyone but this standoffish bar owner who doesn't want to be on a blind date with me may be the exception.

She frowns even harder and I can't get over how cute she is when frowning. It makes me determined to see her smile. She smiled a little during our conversation at her bar, but I want to see an actual smile on her beautiful face. Even more, I want to be the one to put it there.

Her red curly hair is down around her shoulders and I have to fight the urge to run my fingers through it to see if it's as soft as it looks. She narrows her gorgeous hazel eyes at me, and her adorable scrunched nose highlights the freckles across her nose and cheeks. She eyes me with intense suspicion.

"Did you know who I was yesterday?! Were you there to spy on me?" she asks forcefully, furrowing her brow. I can't help but chuckle at her suspicious tone.

"No, I figured it out after you went upstairs. I overheard your bar manager tell someone that you'd be back down later and when I learned your name, I pieced it together from what Jessie told me about you." She looks a little less hostile at that, but still disgruntled. "What I said about following your voice into the bar was true."

I was walking in the neighborhood considering ordering a car to take me back to my apartment when the door of her cafe opened in front of me as someone left and I heard her singing. Something clenched in my chest and I couldn't have walked away if I wanted to. I had to see whose voice I was hearing. I stood transfixed as she poured her heart into the music. She was so beautiful and sad. Something in me wanted to cheer her up. Make her feel better. The snark she showed off when she brought me my drink only made me more interested.

I was disappointed when she left to take a phone call, and I wondered who she was talking to. A boyfriend? Her mother? It was clearly important enough for her to duck out of work. However, once I heard the bar manager mention Leena's name, all the pieces clicked together, and I realized who she was.

My buddy's wife Jessie was trying to set me up with Leena forever. She swore up and down that we were perfect for each other. I told her over and over that I wasn't looking for a relationship and it wouldn't be fair to go on a date with her friend. Finally, after months of putting her off, Dan brought it up while we were out for drinks one night.

"Dude, just take Leena out and then we'll all be done hearing about this. I can almost guarantee that Leena doesn't want a relationship any more than you do." He rolled his eyes and took a drink of his beer. "Jessie is worried about her, so she's trying to push this on her, but I've heard Leena say she's not interested in dating. Just have a meal with the woman and this will all be over."

Dan had been right on the money. Leena still hasn't put her book away, just holds her finger between the pages like she doesn't want to lose her place while I distract her. She's wearing leggings and a baggy sweatshirt that I think are supposed to show that she isn't happy about being on a date. It feels like a challenge to change her mind. I never can turn down a challenge.

I lean towards her as I give her my most winning smile. Somehow, she frowns even harder. She's really going to make me work for it, but I'm sure I can win her over.

"What are you reading? You seemed really into it when I walked up."

"Oh.. uh... it's just a romance novel." She blushes, and it's obvious that it must not be a PG sort of book. I can't resist teasing her.

"So basically porn in book form?" I bounce my eyebrows and she blushes even more.

"I wouldn't say that. The romances I like have a good story with compelling characters. Do I know exactly how they will end with a happily ever after? Yes. Are there a good amount of spicy sex scenes? You bet your ass there are. That doesn't make them porn and there is nothing shameful about reading and enjoying romances!" By the end of her rant, her face is red, and she's breathing hard. Her eyes flash with a stunningly gorgeous fire. It is fascinating to watch the fiery temper build as she speaks, but now I decide it might be a good idea to backpedal a bit before she throws her drink in my face or storms out.

"I'm sorry. I didn't mean to imply that there's anything wrong with reading romance." I shrug my shoulders. "And I happen to enjoy porn on occasion. I wasn't throwing shade." She stares me down for a minute and then seems to find my apology satisfactory as she shakes her head a bit and takes a sip of her drink.

"Well then, fine." She slides the book into her bag and picks up her menu. "Have you eaten here before? What are you having?" She asks.

"I haven't, but the pimento cheeseburger looks kind of good," I respond as I look over the menu.

"Oooh, I love pimento cheese!" The enthusiasm in her voice catches me off guard since she's been so snarky and standoffish until now. "Hmm, but a Reuben sounds good too!" It's looking like food may be the way to her heart, or at least around her grumpy exterior, because she's practically bouncing in her seat as we discuss the menu.

"Why don't I order the burger and you order the Reuben and then we can split them?" That did it. I finally get a full smile from her and I swear to God my heart skips a beat. She is so beautiful. It makes me want to keep making her smile forever. I immediately tamp down the thought. Forever is not something I've entertained in the past and I don't have time to start something now as I'm focusing on finishing out my career strong.

I'm about to start my eighth season playing for the Ft. Starling Flash and I likely only have a few good years left. Thirty-two might be young in general, but in baseball years, I'm getting up there, especially as a pitcher. A fact that my body likes to routinely remind me of after a hard workout. I do not need to be making any lasting commitments right now, since I don't know what the next few years will look like. I can settle down once I'm comfortably retired.

The waitress takes our orders for the burger and Reuben with curly fries for her and onion rings for me, which we will also be splitting. I order a beer and ask Leena to tell me about the book she was reading.

"It's a fake relationship romance, or really more of a rom-com because it has a lot of humor and fun side characters. Fake relationship is one of my favorite tropes." She explains with a similar enthusiasm as she does when discussing food.

"Fake relationship?"

"Yeah, like when the main characters are pretending to be in a relationship for some XYZ reason, but of course they fall in love once they have to spend all this time together. And then they live happily ever after." She nods like a happily ever after is the most obvious thing in the world.

"Jessie said you aren't really into relationships, but you seem to love that happily ever after." I smile at her. She blushes again and squirms in her seat.

"I'm not interested in chasing that particular pipe dream myself. Real life is too messy and relationships don't last. People grow apart or they turn on each other in the end. This is fiction." And she's back to scowling at me. Relationships are definitely a sore spot for her. So, what do I do? Do I drop it and change the subject? Of course not. I've never been one to walk on eggshells.

"Okay, I get that. A lasting relationship seems to be a rare thing. But I do think they exist. My parents have been together for close to 40 years and I'm 100% sure they are still in love with each other. They're difficult to watch sometimes because they enjoy their PDA." I roll my eyes and chuckle, thinking about my parents and missing home a little.

My parents still live in the small town outside of Portland, Oregon, where I grew up and I only get to see them a few times a year for the holidays or if they travel to see me pitch. They gave me and my brother an idyllic childhood and have been my biggest supporters my whole life. When I set my sights on playing baseball professionally they did everything in their power to help me achieve my goals. Fuck, I miss them. I shake away the homesickness and focus back in on the lovely woman in front of me.

"Alright, I'll concede that it is possible. But they're the exception, not the rule." She takes a big gulp of her drink. "And I don't believe in them for myself. I'd rather be alone than deal with the hassle of a relationship."

"That's fair," I say, nodding. After all, I'm not looking for a relationship either, but something about the certainty of her tone makes me want to challenge her again. Find a way through the high walls she's built around her heart. "What about your parents? Are they still together?"

She stares at me for a beat. "Technically, they are. They died in a car accident when I was two. My Gram raised me."

Christ. I'm regretting not asking Jessie and Dan for Leena's backstory.

"I'm sorry. That must have been hard."

She shrugs and takes a long drink. "I don't really remember them. And Gram was amazing to grow up with. She was strict, but still fun. Somehow, she has a way of blending being a parent and a grandparent."

"She sounds awesome," I reply with a smile.

A strange look crosses her face, but I can't quite pinpoint it before it disappears.

"She is."

Our food arrives and we're quiet as we dig in. We split both entrees and Leena becomes even more animated. As she's focused on the food, I steal glances at her. She really is stunning, especially since the food seems to have lowered her guard a bit. I decide to take my life in my hands and bring Jessie's matchmaking back into the conversation.

"So. Jessie really wanted us to meet each other," I say cautiously. She rolls her eyes hard and scoffs.

"Jessie means well, but I've told her I'm not interested in a relationship." She raises her eyebrows, waiting for my response.

"I told her the same thing. I've been pretty clear I wanted to focus on my career." It's still the truth, despite how enchanted I am by Leena. I cannot let anything distract me this season while I'm still pitching at my best. These are my last few years to make a name for myself before I retire. The tension leaves her shoulders, and she smiles at me, more at ease than she's been up to this point.

"Alright then. We can be friends." She reaches out her slender hand and I take it in mine. Her hand feels tiny engulfed in my larger one. I force myself to drop her hand and ignore the spark of lightning that raced up my arm at her touch.

"Friends," I agree, ignoring how the word tastes sour in my mouth. It's for the best that we got this out of the way early on. Now we can just enjoy the evening and get to know each other. As friends.

"You did not!" Leena exclaims and wipes tears from the corner of her eyes as she cracks up, laughing.

"I did! Me and like five other guys on the team, lost a bet and had to run the bases naked." I shake my head, remembering the hijinks of my college ball days.

"Oh my god, what was the bet?!"

"You know, I can't for the life of me remember! There may have been beer pong involved."

"Ah, college," she says wistfully. She chuckles as she turns her phone over to check the time. "Whoa, we've been here for three hours. I'm pretty sure our server hates us right now!"

"Don't worry, I'll leave a big tip and she'll forgive us." I make eye contact with the server for the check. When she brings it, Leena tries to grab it from the table, but I'm too quick. "I don't think so, Sunshine! It's on me!"

"Sunshine?" she scoffs. "I don't think anyone would claim I have a sunny disposition." She quirks her eyebrow at me, waiting for an explanation.

"That's why it's the perfect nickname for you. Sarcastic, just like you." She rolls her eyes again and I smirk. I'm enjoying pushing her buttons.

"Ha Ha." she deadpans. "Why don't we at least split it? Neither of us wanted to be here, so it's not really fair for you to pay!"

"Nope, my treat!" I smirk, "Maybe I'll let you pay next time."

"There won't be a next time! We just agreed not to date a couple of hours ago!" she whines.

"Exactly." I wink at her and hand the waitress my card.

"Cheater!" she huffs, but I can tell she's entertained by my shenanigans. Over the last few hours, she's let the grumpy mask fall just a little and while she was still sarcastic, the hostility did lower several notches. Actually, it's one of the best dates I'd ever been on, even if we aren't counting it as an real date.

"So, what are we telling Jessie about tonight? We can't let her know we agreed to not date." I point out. "She'll never let it go if she thinks we didn't give it a real try."

Leena sighs and places her chin in her hand. "Ugh, you're right. We need some sort of cover story. Jessie's so convinced that we would live happily ever after if we just got to know each other." She rolls her eyes so hard I think one of these times they might get stuck. "She will definitely call and text me tonight to get the scoop on how madly in love I am with you."

"If Jessie doesn't try texting me tonight, I will for sure see Dan at the gym tomorrow and you know she'll have twisted his arm into asking for info." I laugh to myself, picturing Dan begrudgingly asking about the date in the locker room.

"Why don't we tell her that there was just no spark? Jessie loves to talk about the spark that she felt when she met Dan. She's been going on about it for the last 12 years." Leena laughs and shakes her head.

"Yep, even I have heard that story more than once and I don't hang out with Jessie that much." Jessie is one of the most talkative people I know. I'm pretty sure she could make friends with literally anyone and they would know her life story by the end of the night. "The spark thing might work. We'll both say it so it's mutual and then push the 'I wasn't interested in a relationship anyway' reminder so that she doesn't start getting ideas of other people to set us up with."

"Oh, good call! I could see her doing that! She won't rest until everyone she knows is happily coupled up." We both laugh.

"She's a sweetheart, but misguided when it comes to the two of us." I say with a smirk.

"That she is." Leena stands and gathers her things. "Well, thank you for dinner. I guess I'll see you around."

I finish signing the credit card slip and place a hundred-dollar bill on the table.

"Hang on, I'll walk you to your car." I stand and grab my jacket.

"Oh, that's okay. I didn't have to park very far." She replies as she shrugs into her coat.

"I'm pretty sure my mother could feel me neglecting everything she taught me about being a gentleman all the way from Portland if I let you walk alone at night."

She laughs and shakes her head, but doesn't argue. We leave the restaurant and walk a couple of blocks to where she had parked her car, a newer-looking SUV. She turns to say goodnight, and I instinctively open my arms for a hug. She follows my lead and wraps her arms around my waist.

"I had a nice time tonight. Thank you," she says in a quiet tone. She leans back to look up at me, her hazel eyes shining in the dim glow of the streetlight. Her lips are shiny and lush and just for a second, I think about kissing her. Then the moment is over and she is stepping back and climbing into the driver's seat of her car.

"I had a nice time, too. Drive safe!" She smiles as she starts the car and gives me a little wave. I watch her drive away and hope I can be convincing when I tell Jessie and Dan lies about not feeling a spark.

"So you really weren't into her?" Dan at least waited until after our workout to start the interrogation. He strikes up the conversation as we're changing out of our sweaty workout gear and bundling up to face the January cold.

"Nah, man. I mean, she's pretty, and we got along okay, but there just wasn't any spark." I deliver my prepared line with a nonchalance that I don't feel. Especially after I tossed and turned all night and couldn't get Leena out of my head. But I won't go back on what we agreed, so I give Dan the "no spark" excuse.

"Damn. Jessie's gonna be bummed. She was so sure she had you two set up perfectly."

I shrug my shoulders and sit to untie my sneakers and pull my socks off.

"I could see us being decent friends. It wasn't a terrible night, just not magical." I keep my gaze focused on my shoes so that I can avoid looking him in the eyes. I know that if he senses I'm bullshitting him, he'll tell Jessie, and we'd never hear the end.

"I guess it's good that it wasn't terrible. You kind of never know what you'll get with Leena these days." He shrugs and moves to pull his shirt over his head.

"What do you mean?"

"Leena's just had a rough couple of years. Her grandmother who raised her got sick a few years after they graduated college, so Leena moved home to care for her and her shitty ex-fiancé was a total douche about it. He was one of those assholes that comes off charming but is super controlling and dickish behind closed doors. Then once her Gram passed, the guy said some heinous stuff to Leena, and she finally broke things off." Dan unloads Leena's history like he hasn't just dropped an emotional bomb on me. So many things about her refusal to believe in happily ever after make sense.

"Wow. I had no idea. We talked for like three hours last night and none of that came up." I'm amazed at how she's able to keep from talking about it all. She must be good at compartmentalizing all of that in her head. "She talked a bit about her Gram, but it was mostly good things from her childhood. I don't think I even realized the woman wasn't alive."

"Yeah, Leena keeps her cards close to her chest. I only know all of that because Jessie tells me everything. I've never actually heard Leena discuss any of it." He looks me in the eye to make sure I'm listening. "Don't tell either of them I told you that stuff. Jessie told me not to, but I thought you might want to know."

I hold his gaze for a moment and then nod. "Of course, man. I won't say anything." He nods and walks towards the shower as I sit and replay everything he told me about Leena.

I want to call her. I want to hug her and tell her everything is going to be alright. That she is safe with me. I want to beat the shit out of her ex. But I can't do any of that because we agreed to be friends and I'm not supposed to know about any of it. Instead, I swallow down my frustration and stalk off to take a scalding hot shower.

SINCE I DIDN'T SLEEP well the night before, I crash hard when I get home, but even my subconscious can't get enough of Leena. In my dream, I walk her to her car and open my arms for a hug, just like I did. But this time, in that moment when I thought about kissing her, I gave in to the impulse.

Instead of slapping me like the real Leena surely would have, dream Leena melts into my arms as I kiss her. Her lips are soft and she comes alive under my touch. I thread my fingers through the fiery curls of her hair and use them to tilt her head to me as I slant my mouth over hers, deepening the kiss.

"What are we doing?" she murmurs between kisses and soft gasps.

"Whatever you want to do," I mumble back. Remembering for a second that we agreed to be friends, I have to make sure she's okay with where this is heading. "Do you want me to stop?"

"I really don't," she says, sounding mildly surprised at herself. The kiss builds as I lick along the seam of her mouth and she opens for me. She clutches my shirt as I pull her to me. She lets out a soft moan as she presses her hips against my growing bulge. Fire races through my veins, and I have to have her here and now.

"I need you," she breathes as if she's reading my mind and saying what I'm thinking. She opens the door to the back seat of her SUV and we clamber in. I pull her onto my lap with her legs straddling my hips. She moans as she swivels her hips to grind herself against my erection that is trying to bust its way through my jeans.

I slide my hands up her sides under the baggy sweatshirt she wears. I reach behind her and unclasp her bra in a quick motion. My hands cup her perfectly round tits and find her nipples already hard and puckered. I break off the kiss to lower my head and run my tongue all around her nipples. She lets out the most adorable gasps and moans as I alternate between sucking and gently biting my way back and forth between her tits.

As I finally reach my hand down the front of her leggings, I wake with a start. I'm drenched in sweat with a raging hard-on from the not-so-friend like dream. I reach down to take my swollen cock in my hands.

With a pang of guilt that I quickly push aside, I stroke myself and let my mind imagine what would happen next. I imagine moving my hand down into her leggings and panties and finding her soaking wet pussy waiting for me. The tip of my finger would circle her clit before I would slide one and then two digits inside. I would encourage her to ride my hand until she was coming all over it.

After she came once on my hand, we would get rid of her leggings and underwear and free my dick from trying to bust a hole through my jeans. She would slowly lower herself down onto my aching cock until I was buried inside her. As I imagine her tight, wet pussy pulsing around me, I pump my fist over my erection before finally exploding all over my stomach.

I clean up in the bathroom and avoid looking myself in the eyes, as if my reflection would scold me for the very dirty dream and thoughts I just had about my new friend. I shake myself and head back to bed.

It was just because you were talking to Dan about her. She's on your mind and things will go back to normal now. I tell myself, as I try to settle back into sleep, but I can't shake the feeling that everything has changed.

Chapter Four

Leena

"WHAT DO YOU MEAN there was no spark?!" I ducked Jessie's calls and texts for two days before she finally tracks me down at the cafe around lunchtime. Since we don't have a full kitchen, lunchtime tends to be when there's a lull between our morning coffee crowd and our evening drinkers.

I stand behind the bar drying glasses. I shrug and avoid all eye contact. I'm not a great liar, especially with Jessie who has known me since middle school and knows all my tells. And I am so lying to her now. There was a spark with Bailey, but there is no way in hell that I'm admitting it. Spark or not, it doesn't change anything. I don't want a relationship and neither does he. I roll my eyes in annoyance, as even my thoughts sound like a broken record. Maybe a few more hundred times and I'll believe it.

"Yeah, I mean, he's attractive for sure. I'm not blind. But I just wasn't feeling that spark. I think we'll be good friends though, so thanks for introducing us." I hope that thanking her for my new friend will distract her from her insistence that we are soul mates. It does not.

"I so don't believe you!" she huffs. "Did you even try?" She crosses her arms and glares. I roll my eyes and glare back before letting out a deep sigh. I'm so fucking tired of arguing with her about my lack of a dating life.

"Jess, we had a perfectly lovely conversation. We ate an entire meal together. We agreed we'd be better off as friends. I don't know what else you want me to do here?" She doesn't say anything for a long minute and I think I have her convinced. Hopefully now she will leave me in peace and focus her matchmaking attempts on someone else. I raise my eyebrows and wait for her to respond as she stares me down.

"No." She says sharply.

"No?"

"No. I know I'm right and that you two belong together." She grabs her bag off the bar and stalks to the door. Once she's gone, the tension leaves my body all at once and I slump onto one of the bar stools.

"What's she all fired up about?" Cass asks as she comes out from the back room.

"How much did you hear?"

"Just the tail end. Was she trying to set you up again?" Cass knows all about Jessie's obsession with trying to get me paired up.

"Yup. I finally caved and went on a date she set up and now she's pissed because there wasn't a spark." I roll my eyes and hope Cass won't zero in on the lie. But Cass knows me incredibly well and can smell bullshit from a mile away. She stays silent and studies my face for a minute. I squirm in my seat under her scrutiny, but don't say anything.

"Was there no spark?" She says it casually, but I can tell she knows I'm trying to evade the point. I shrug and she raises her eyebrows, waiting for me to say something. I try to stay silent as I stare at a spot on the bar, but Cass is always way more stubborn than me and has a way of drawing the truth out of me. Annie and Jessie have known me longer, but I tend to be more open with Cass. Probably because Cass is the embodiment of the "we listen, we don't judge" mentality.

"There might have been a little, tiny spark," I mumble, still staring at the bar top.

"So why are we lying to Jessie about this?" She asks curiously.

"Ugh, just because there was some mild interest does not mean I want to date him." I huff. "I don't want a relationship. Just because this guy was attractive and funny and nice to talk to and smelled good, does not mean I am going to change everything about how I want to live my life!" I'm fired up by the time I reach the end of my rant, but Cass just stares silently for a moment before nodding.

"If you're sure, then you do you." She shrugs and goes back to getting the bar ready for the evening rush.

I am sure. But even in my head, it doesn't quite ring true. There was one moment right as I was getting into my car when I thought Bailey might kiss me and I don't think I would have objected. There was a part of me that wanted to kiss him. But what would be the point? I'm not interested in a one-night stand either.

With a deep sigh, I return to the inventory I had been working on when Jessie stormed in. My thoughts return to the dreamy guy I am definitely sure that I'm not interested in as more than a friend.

"So I talked to Jessie..." Annie starts.

I groan and put my head down. This is so not the way I wanted to start our FaceTime. They're about to gang up on me when it comes to Bailey and giving love a chance. Fucking hell.

"Leens, she's just worried about you. We all are. It's like you've detached from life and we want to see you happy and thriving."

"And that's lovely, but why am I required to date some guy for that?" I may have come a long way from the shattered version of myself that I was two years ago, but I'm still pretty damaged and we all know it.

"You don't. But we're not exactly seeing you making any progress in living your life in any other way. And we ..."

"I'm pretty sure I own a thriving business that ..." I cut her off.

"That Cass runs!" she interrupts me right back. "Jessie thinks that you and Bailey would be good for each other, so why not give that a chance?" Her pleading tone makes me feel low-key guilty for being so annoyed with my friends. They have my best interests at heart.

"Well, we decided to be friends. That'll need to be enough. But hey, when was the last time I made a new friend, huh? I'd call that progress!" I put on a fake cheerful tone but Annie just shakes her head, seeing right through it.

"Okay, Leens. I'll let it go for now, but I don't think you're going to get Jess to drop it that easily. I'm actually kind of worried about her, too. She's so fixated on this, I wonder if something is going on with her?"

"Now that you mention it, that makes sense. I'll be honest, I've been avoiding her a bit lately. Every conversation for the last few months has turned into her crusade to get me into a relationship, but I probably need to be checking in on her."

"It's times like these that I hate living so far away from you guys. I wish I could be there for you both. In person, not just through my phone screen." She complains.

"I know, A. but you couldn't pass up your dream job!" Annie shrugs and her eyes don't meet the camera. My stomach knots at the sight. Shit. Should we be concerned about all three of us? "How's the job going these days?"

"It's really good." She throws me a fake smile and I can instantly tell she's lying. "We're insanely busy and I've been working a shit ton of hours, but it's good. I should have some vacation coming up..."

"That's good. I'm glad you'll get some time off soon! What about the dating front? Last week you said there was something new happening?" She does another fake smile and shrug and I'm seriously starting to worry about her.

"Eh, it didn't go anywhere. Not even worth discussing!"

"Seriously? No details for me?" I whine, hoping to get her to open up a bit more. This secretive, question-dodging Annie is so not her. We usually tell each other everything. A pang of guilt shoots through me at the thought. I'm not telling her everything about how Bailey affects me. I should just let her keep her secrets for now.

"Nope, nothing to report! Did Jessie tell you what Dan said to her the other day?" And just like that, the subject is changed to us gossiping about the married couple in our lives in order to avoid talking about ourselves. I'm not entirely sure how Annie and I got to this secret-keeping place in our relationship and it weighs on my heart. But I just don't possess the energy tonight to get into it with her.

Soon. Next time we FaceTime, I'll bring it up. I tell myself, but deep down I'm sure I'll avoid the conversation because the second I call her out

on keeping things from me, I'll need to own up to the omissions I've made
and I'm not ready to go there.

"I'M NOT SURE IF you all will recognize this one. It's a little more obscure
in the Broadway catalog, but it's one of my favorites." The room is full for
our Friday night open mic, so I love giving them a sample of sad Broadway
songs they may not be familiar with. "Anyone that can tell me what musical
this is from—without looking it up—will get a free drink!"

I play the slow piano intro for "When I Look at You" from *The Scarlet
Pimpernel*. I scan the crowd to see if anyone recognizes it. We get a few
Broadway fans that like to come to open mic, so there's a possibility, but it
doesn't look like it's ringing any bells for anyone. As usual, I let myself get
carried away in the lyrics and do my best to not get choked up by emotion.
When I'm done, I smirk at the crowd.

"Anyone?" I look around, but no one seems to have the answer.
"Looks like I won this round of guess that tune! Up next is a Songbird
staple. It's everyone's favorite grandpa, Fred!"

The 75-year-old grandfather of seven is known in the cafe for loving
80s and 90s rap. It should be absurd when he gets up to perform, but it's so
entertaining that he's become a crowd favorite. He and his wife were good
friends of Gram's and I've known Fred my whole life. It's like he's my own
grandpa.

As I walk to the bar, I hear him launch into Sir Mix-A-Lot's "Baby
Got Back" and chuckle to myself. I love this one. The crowd always gets

particularly wild when he thrusts his hips on the line about his "anaconda" and you can tell he loves the energy of the rowdy crowd. I think in another life he must have been a rock star rather than an awesome accountant who's helped me with my taxes since I was old enough to file.

Cass and Alaina have the bar under control, so I pop into the back to check my phone and find a text message from Jessie.

Jessie:

> Leens! It feels like we haven't hung out in forever! What are you doing this Sunday?

Me:

> I'd have to check my schedule! What's up?

I know I don't have anything on my schedule, but I'm not about to commit to anything until I know what she's up to. I can never tell what Jessie will get me into these days.

Jessie:

> We're having people over to watch the Bengals game since they're in the playoffs. I know you don't care about football, but we'll have a bunch of food and we can hang out! I think Dan told people to show up around 6 so we can hang out and eat before the game starts.

A football get-together sounds chill enough so I don't mind giving her this one. Things have been a little tense between us and a normal Sunday of hanging out while Dan and his friends watch football may help to get us back to our usual comfort level.

Me:

Ok! Want me to bring anything?

Jessie:

If there's anything in particular that you want to drink. Maybe a side or dessert? Dan's smoking a brisket and I'm making some cheesy potatoes, so we have the main dishes covered!

Me:

Sounds good. See you Sunday!

I put the event on my calendar for Sunday and start thinking of what dish I could make. I don't do a lot of cooking but I enjoy trying different dessert recipes. After making a mental note to do some Pinterest research tomorrow, I head back out to the bar to enjoy some open mic. I'm feeling lighter now that Jessie and I are getting back to normal.

I'M CARRYING MY DESSERT slowly as I walk down the sidewalk to Jessie and Dan's house. A layered trifle is what I landed on for my football party contribution. I love how trifles have so many variations and how decorative they look once they're done. In honor of the Bengals, I added some orange food coloring when I made the pound cake and used a dark chocolate pudding so it looks a little like tiger stripes. I may be grumpy and cynical most of the time, but I do love a good themed party. I'm even wearing a Bengals tee shirt I own for these exact occasions.

"Hey Leena, wait up!"

I hear a deep, familiar voice behind me say. It's been a week since our blind date and I forgot how sexy his smooth voice is. A chill runs down my spine as Bailey comes up beside me holding a large bag with the Raising Cane's logo.

"Hi there, Sunshine." He says, smirking down at me. I roll my eyes, but I smile back up at him.

"Hey Bailey, I didn't know you were going to be here!" I may not love Jessie's attempts at matchmaking, but I can't deny that I'm happy to see him. I motion toward the bag he's holding. "Did you bring Cane's or are you recycling a bag?"

His low chuckle sends goosebumps down my arms. "No, I brought Cane's. I know Dan's doing a brisket, but I was in a chicken mood." He shrugs his shoulders.

"Just chicken?" I say with raised eyebrows. He grins, reading my mind.

"Of course not. I got a bunch of toast and Cane's sauce too." He assures me.

"Good. The chicken's good and all, but the toast is where it's at."

"Agreed."

As we approach the walkway, I see Dan's brother, Andy, and his wife, Jen, up ahead. They turn towards us on the porch landing as we climb the four steps. Jen and I exchange a quick hug as Andy rings the doorbell.

"Hi, Leena! It's great to see you!" She smiles warmly at me and then looks up at Bailey and I see the question cross her face. "Oh! I didn't know you guys were together!" I chuckle, shake my head, and glance at Bailey, who is smirking.

"Nah, we just happened to walk up at the same time," I tell her, as Jen looks puzzled.

"But I thought this was a couple's party?" She glances up at Andy and he nods to confirm. "Jessie was adamant that we both come because they were only inviting couples. We even got a babysitter since she was so insistent."

I can feel the color draining from my face as I quickly realize that this isn't just another casual football party. This is another fucking setup. Bailey looks at me with confusion in his eyes. He also doesn't seem to be aware of the couples-only policy.

"Are you sure?" He asks Jen.

"Very sure. I wanted to stay home since I don't care that much about football and I had a busy week at work, but Jessie begged."

My blood starts to boil as the rage takes over. I am so fucking sick of Jessie and her meddling that I start to see red. As Dan opens the door and we all file in, I glare at him and sharply ask.

"Where. Is. Your. Wife?"

Chapter Five

Bailey

"WHERE. IS. YOUR. WIFE?" Leena asks in a clipped tone as we shed coats and put down our food on the dining room table. I can practically see the steam coming out of her ears. Sensing her mood, Dan points her toward the kitchen and she storms off. I follow closely behind in case I need to help prevent a murder. I'm a bit irritated Jessie pulled another setup, but I'd be lying if I said I wasn't glad to see Leena.

"Jessalyn Marie Chase!" Leena seethes. Jessie pops out of the pantry door with a guilty look on her face.

"Oh good, you and Bailey found each other! I totally forgot to tell you he was going to be here!" Her tone is bright, but I can see the wariness in her eyes as she notices how angry Leena is.

"Don't fucking act like this isn't a setup. Andy and Jen told us about you insisting this be a couple's party." Leena snaps. Jessie's bright demeanor drops and I can see the irritation build in her expression as she puts her hands on her hips.

"Well, what do you expect?! I told you I wasn't accepting your bullshit excuse of not having a spark. I don't believe either of you with that nonsense." She shrugs and goes back to stirring something in a crock pot.

"I don't care what you believe. I told you I didn't want to date. I showed up for the date you insisted I go on. We decided to be friends.

That's the fucking end of it!" Leena snaps, fighting to keep her voice down. The tension in her body is visible from across the room as she stands stiff, hands in fists at her sides.

"It's not the end of it!" Jessie yells back, her face turning red. "Don't you realize how worried we've been about you? You've completely stopped living, and I understood during the first few months, but it's been two years!" I can see the moment when Leena finally loses her cool, rage filling her eyes.

"It's not up to you to understand. This is how I'm living my life. I don't need to be in a relationship to be living. I'm doing just fine!" Leena yells.

"YOU'RE NOT FINE!" Jessie practically screams. I notice Dan comes up alongside me waiting in case we'll need to jump in to mediate. "You're living a half-life. All you do is hang out at your bar or in your apartment. You don't socialize unless one of us begs. You have no interest in getting out and meeting people. This isn't you!"

"This is me now! This is the way I want to live my life." Leena screams back. "People change, Jessie. It's none of your business!"

"You are my business! You're my best friend." Jessie takes a deep breath, trying to calm down. "Gram would hate the way you're living."

Jessie says it quietly, but Leena's head snaps back as if Jessie had slapped her. I can see the tears filling her eyes as she glares at Jessie, stunned. The entire house has gone silent during their fight. Leena shakes her head and turns to walk out the back door. It slams behind her, and Jessie bursts into tears.

Dan goes to comfort Jessie, but I can see the "I told you so" lingering in his eyes. Through the window over the sink, I can see that Leena has dropped into the swing that Dan and Jessie have in their backyard. I turn back to the dining room to grab both of our coats and slip out the front door.

I walk around the side of the house, grateful that the snow has held off as I crunch through the frozen grass. Leena and I may have agreed to just be friends, but I feel drawn to her. I want to pull her into my arms and comfort her. As a friend. I'm just hoping that she'll let me.

I approach the bench swing slowly to make sure Leena hears me coming. She glances up and tries to wipe the tears off her face, but I can still see them streaming out as she sniffs.

"I brought your coat," I say gently. "I figured you might be cold out here."

"Thanks." Her voice is small and sad. Nothing like her usual bold and snarky self. She pulls her coat over her arms, drapes it over her body, and scrunches down into the swing. I sit next to her and enjoy the quiet of the dark winter night. I wait for her to speak since she still seems pretty upset. The silence is comfortable between us.

"I'm sorry you had to see that," she says finally.

"That's alright. Are you okay?" I ask. She lets out a long sigh and stares up at the sky.

"Not really. I can't remember the last time Jessie and I fought like that. I'm pretty sure we were teenagers." Her head gives a slow shake. "I just finally snapped and couldn't take her meddling anymore."

"I get that. She has been persistent. I get the feeling that bringing up your Gram crossed the line?" Leena makes a choked-up noise and I instantly regret bringing it back up. "I'm sorry. I shouldn't have asked that."

"No, it's okay. It's a valid question. She definitely crossed a line, and that was the first time I've ever considered punching my best friend in the face." She huffs out a humorless laugh. "Do you want to know the worst part, though?"

"What?"

"She might be right. Gram would not love me being a hermit living over my bar and only coming out when they need help or to sing for open mic." Her eyes water again and she shakes her head sadly. "She would not be pleased at all." Leena wipes away the tears sliding down her cheek and I take a chance and put my arm around her, offering her both warmth and comfort. She snuggles into me and we sit in companionable silence for a few moments.

"Ugh, I really do not want to go back in there," she says finally with a sigh.

"Then don't." I shrug and squeeze her shoulders. "Let Jessie stress about you leaving, at least for tonight."

"I would, but my purse is still inside. I can't order an Uber without my phone," she grumbles.

"I'll get it and tell them I'm giving you a ride home." I offer as an idea is taking shape in my mind. "Why don't we go grab something to eat before I take you home, though?"

"You really don't have to do that," she says in such a quiet voice that it's clear she's not actually trying to dissuade me.

"I know. That's what makes me so nice."

"Did...did you just quote *Wicked*?" she asks with a timid smile. I shoot her a proud grin. I was sure that would cheer her up.

"Yep. You started it. Now come on, you can come sit in my truck while it warms up." We stand from the bench swing and she adjusts her coat, putting it on the right way. As we walk around the side yard, I return my arm to its spot around her shoulders. She walks stiffly at first, but after a second I feel her slide her arm around my waist, gripping my side. I smile to myself, enjoying the feel of her holding onto me for support.

Wait, what is happening?

I'm starting to like this girl—and not just as a friend—which is a problem, considering she adamantly doesn't want to date me.

Shit. I'm in trouble.

After getting Leena situated in my truck with the heat blasting, I pop back into Dan and Jessie's to grab her bag. Dan sees me come through the door, but Jessie is nowhere in sight. He follows me to the dining room, where I quickly locate Leena's purse. Dan shoves his hands in the pockets of his jeans.

"Hey man, sorry about all that earlier with Jessie." The awkward tension is palpable. I want to tell him it's not *his* fault, but I don't want him to think I'm mad at Jessie. I'm annoyed that she can't seem to mind her own business, but I sort of get where she's coming from in looking out for Leena.

"It's alright. Leena's still pretty upset, so I'm going to give her a ride home." I try to stay casual with my tone, but Dan tilts his head to the side and stares me down. He doesn't say anything, but nods his head and runs his hand through his hair. He lets out a deep sigh.

"I'll tell Jessie you guys left. She's still upset too and went upstairs to lie down." He shakes his head. "I'm sure when she cools down she'll want to apologize, though. It wasn't her best night."

"Thanks, man." We share an awkward nod as I gather Leena's things and head back out the door. When I reach the truck, she faces the window, her head resting on the glass. Even from a few feet away, I can see the defeated expression on her face. I decide right then that I'm not taking her home until I cheer her up. I slide into the driver's seat of my truck, rubbing my hands together to warm up and turn on my heated seat.

"Fuck, it's cold tonight." She doesn't say anything, just nods her head in agreement. "Alright, now what sounds good to eat?"

"I'm not really that hungry. You can just take me back to Songbird." It's like she's lost all spark. This is not the sassy girl I met a few weeks ago. She may have been snarky and on the grumpy side, but this Leena sounds hollow.

"Yeah, that's not an option." She looks over at me with her eyebrows raised. "I'm not dropping you off like this. I insist on turning this night around before I take you home."

"I'm not sure you can turn this night around. We should probably just call time of death on it," she grumbles.

"Nope. I'm afraid I'm not taking no for an answer on this. So what do you like to eat when you need cheering up?" She stares at me for a moment and just when I'm sure she's going to insist that I take her home, she shrugs her shoulders.

"Carbs."

"Carbs?"

"Yeah, bread, pasta, cake... something like that." She sounds no more animated, but at least she gave me an answer, which sparks an idea that already has my stomach growling. Thank god it's the off-season and I haven't started back on my stricter diet yet.

"Would you totally judge me if I suggested Olive Garden right now?" I meet her gaze at her with eyebrows raised and, shockingly enough, a small smile appears on her face. Damn, she's pretty when she smiles.

"I know it gets a lot of shade, but Olive Garden is actually one of my favorite restaurants."

"Yeah?" I ask, encouraging her to elaborate.

"Yeah." I think she's going to leave it at that, but her soft voice continues. "When I was younger, there weren't as many options in Ft. Starling, so Olive Garden was our go-to for any kind of celebration. Gram and I went there on pretty much any special occasion."

The thought of her and her Gram hitting up the OG on special days makes me smile, and it seems to have cheered her up a little as well. Enough to push me to ask my next question.

"You know, when we were out on that first date, you talked about Gram in the present tense. I had no idea that she had passed away until Dan told me. Why didn't you mention it?" She shrugs and looks back out the window. I know I probably shouldn't have pushed the topic, but I just need to know where her head's at. Did she not mention it because she doesn't like to talk about it or because she didn't trust me with the information?

"I do that sometimes, especially with people who didn't know Gram. It lets me forget for just a little while that she's gone." She admits sadly.

"I get that," I say softly. God, I want to pull over my truck and wrap her in a hug, but I don't think she'd appreciate that, so I just reach over and put my hand on her thigh and give her a gentle squeeze. I know I should take my hand back, but I don't.

Her hand moves and I'm afraid for a second she's going to lift my hand off her leg, but she doesn't. Instead, she grabs my hand and holds on as she looks back out the window. I feel a rush of butterflies and I have to remind myself that this isn't a romantic thing. This is just a friendly handhold for comfort on a rough night.

I park the truck outside of Olive Garden and give her leg another squeeze. I look over at her and give her my most charming smile. "Are you ready to eat our weight in salad, breadsticks, and pasta?"

"Let's do it." She grins back at me and damn if my heart doesn't flip over in my chest at the sight.

IT TURNS OUT, THERE'S a big difference between Leena on a blind date she was coerced into and Leena willingly having dinner with a friend. On our date, she made polite conversation and had pleasant things to say about the food. Tonight she's way more animated. It's like we've broken down a barrier between us.

And man, is she enjoying the hell out of her food. I won't lie, eating with her—it's incredibly hot. The first time she let out a moan as she put a breadstick in her mouth, my cock jerked to life in my pants, and it has been paying attention the whole meal. I've barely been able to notice my food as I try to contain the constant semi I've been sporting.

"Oh my god, this cheesecake is so good." She lets out what can only be described as a whimper and I grit my teeth, trying to keep my erection under control.

"The tiramisu is fantastic, too."

"Thanks for this." She gives me a soft smile. "I needed a fun night after that blowup at Jessie's house."

"No problem. It was super intense there."

"Yeah, sorry about that." Her shoulders droop. I hate that the conversation has brought her back down, but I have an idea that I'm working up to sharing.

"You really don't need to apologize. I know it's Jessie who's pushing this." I run my hand over my face. "I doubt she's going to let it go. Dan seemed to think she wouldn't."

"Ugh... I don't know what to say to her to get her to drop it." She puts her face in her hands and rubs her eyes.

"I might have an idea." I wait for her to look up at me. When those hazel irises connect with mine, my heart beats faster and I swallow hard before continuing. "We could let her think we're together."

"Let her think we're together?" Her forehead creases, like she's trying to puzzle out what I'm suggesting.

"Like that book trope thing you were talking about? A fake re-lationship to get her to leave us alone. She can't keep pushing and hounding us if she thinks we're already dating."

"This isn't a romance novel, Bailey. This is real life and she would never buy it."

The more I think about it, the more I want her to say yes. I don't look too closely at those feelings as I try to convince her that my plan will work.

"We can totally pull it off," I assure her.

"You know she's going to want to go on a double date. And she'll find it super weird when we're not touching each other."

"So we may have to do some light PDA." I shrug, trying not to get excited at the thought of PDA with Leena. Christ, this is a terrible plan, but I can't seem to stop myself. "Just think of it like you're in a play. Don't tell me that with your love of Broadway, you've never acted before."

"This is different, though. With acting, you have a script telling you what to do or say."

"So this leans a little more towards improv," I say with a laugh. I can tell she's hesitant, but she's not dismissing the idea either. "Why don't we take the night to think about it? We can grab lunch tomorrow and discuss the pros and cons?"

"I guess that would work." She nods her head and fiddles with the straw in her drink. She looks so unsure and vulnerable that I want to take her in my arms and protect her from the world. I nod and put on a nonchalant attitude that I don't feel.

"Okay then, tomorrow I'll pick you up around one?" She nods as I finish signing the credit card slip. "Why don't I take you home now so you can get some rest?"

We bundle into our coats and make our way back out to my truck. Neither of us speaks on the short ride to the bar, but the silence isn't uncomfortable. I pull up to the curb in front of the bar and throw my hazards on so I can walk her to her door.

"You didn't need to walk me to the door."

"Yes, I did. Fake dating or not, my mom raised a gentleman." She gives me a soft smile and meets my gaze.

"Thank you again for tonight. I appreciate you being there for me." I pull her into a hug. With a quick kiss to her hair, I murmur.

"Anytime, Sunshine." She melts into my embrace for just a second before she pulls away and heads inside the bar. The urge to follow her in and stay by her side is so strong that I have to bite the inside of my cheek. She turns before she ducks into the back room and gives me a small wave.

I'm pretty sure this fake dating idea is a horrible plan given my ever-growing attraction to this woman, but God, do I fucking hope she says yes.

Chapter Six

Leena

I PACE THE FLOOR behind the bar as I wait for Bailey to pick me up for lunch. I'd like to say I went back and forth on accepting his offer, but I know I'm going to say yes. I was sure last night when he suggested it. Something inside of me wants to spend more time with Bailey, but I won't be admitting that to anyone, least of all Bailey himself. I'm barely admitting it to myself.

Cass watches me warily all morning but hasn't said anything as I've paced and anxiously fiddled with bottles behind the bar. I sigh and sink onto a stool, trying to chill out before Bailey shows up.

"You want to tell me what's going on with you?" I can see the concern in her eyes. As usual, Cass can take one glance at me and judge my mood.

"Not really." She just raises her eyebrows and waits. I let out an enormous sigh. "I'm going to lunch with Bailey."

"Ah, that tracks. So Jessie's matchmaking attempts finally got through, huh?" She smirks at me, enjoying my distress.

"Um, not exactly."

"What do you mean?" I glance around the bar to make sure no one is listening to our conversation. I fill her in on all of the drama that went down last night at Jessie's party and the dinner I had with Bailey after.

"Bailey suggested we should just let Jessie—well, actually, I guess everyone—think that we're dating, so that Jessie leaves us alone." She stays silent and keeps staring at me. "It'll work."

"Uh-huh. So he wants to hang out with you but doesn't want any real commitment to you?" She says incredulously. I shrug my shoulders.

"It's not like I want a commitment. That's kind of the whole point of it being fake. There are no strings for either of us."

"What about the Flash Floozies? Is he going to stop sleeping with the cleat chasers that follow all those guys around?" Damn. She kind of has a point. It's not like Jessie won't notice if he's still going out with other girls.

The Flash Floozies are well known around Ft. Starling for always being at Flash games and being ready and willing to visit their bedrooms. I'm pretty sure they even have their own Facebook group to share info on players. They're also notorious for seeing if they can sleep with as many guys on the roster as they can.

Jessie loves to complain about them showing up at the hotels where the guys were staying for away games. She says the other wives and girl-friends can't stand the Floozies. This is, of course, hearsay since I've never actually met a Floozy myself.

"Okay, that may be a valid point. I didn't agree to the fake relationship idea yet so I'll add that to the list of questions to ask him at lunch." I may have a notebook in my purse with a list of things that I want to know before I agree to this scheme.

"Just be careful, alright? I don't want to see you get hurt."

I nod, but I don't point out again that avoiding getting hurt is the purpose of it being a fake relationship instead of a real one.

"I'll make sure we lay down some ground rules."

"If you're sure."

"Yeah, it'll be fine!" I see Bailey's truck pull up, so I grab my purse and head out through the doors. "See you later, Cass!"

I hop up into Bailey's truck before he can get out. He flashes me an annoyed glance.

"I would have gotten the door for you." He practically growls. Oof, his deep voice is extremely sexy when it has a gruff, irritated tone to it.

"It's not a big deal!" I say with a shrug. He freezes for a second and looks me in the eye. A chill goes down my spine with the eye contact.

"You being treated with the respect you deserve is absolutely a big deal." Oh fuck. I can tell from the serious expression on his face that he means it. He isn't giving me a cheesy line, and it's making me all swoony and hot. I'm pretty sure my panties have dissolved altogether.

What the hell?

I realize he's waiting for some sort of answer, so I give him a shaky nod. He nods back and flashes a quick smile at me as he puts the truck in gear. I spend the drive to the restaurant getting my heart rate back under control and trying to figure out what the fuck this guy is doing to me.

WE DECIDE TO HIT Ft. Starling's fifties-style diner, The Main Bite, for lunch. Since it's a Monday and a little later in the afternoon, we missed most of the lunch rush. We're seated in a booth with a view out the front window of Main Street. We put our orders in and once our waitress brings our drinks, I pull out my notebook.

"I didn't realize we were having an official meeting," Bailey smirks at me, his dark eyes sparkling with humor. "I left my notes at home."

"Hilarious. There are just some details we should iron out before I agree to this whole fake dating thing. I wanted to make sure I didn't forget," I explain.

"Fair enough, ask away!" He smiles at me and I swear my heart stutters a bit. He's so fucking gorgeous. It's distracting. This is exactly why I wrote down my questions.

"Okay, why do you even want to do this? Why don't you just date someone for real? I'm sure some Flash Floozies are lining up for a shot." He stares me down for a moment and then clears his throat.

"The Floozies haven't been my scene for a while. They were fun to... hang out with in my first few years, but it got old pretty fast." He takes a deep breath before continuing. "I'm considering moving back to the West Coast to be closer to my parents. It doesn't make sense to start something with someone here when I might be gone in a few months. Plus, I hadn't planned on settling down until after I retire, anyway."

I don't love the sinking feeling I get in my stomach. He's leaving. That should make me more comfortable with the ruse since there will be a built-in end date, but it just makes me sad. I'm enjoying Bailey's company and I don't love the thought of him not being around.

"Oh, so are you retiring, or are you switching teams?" I ask.

"Switching teams?" he barks out a laugh.

"I don't know the lingo! I'm not a sports person!" I exclaim. He laughs and shakes his head at me.

"My agent has been talking to a few different teams about potential trades. I'm not sure where or if it will even happen." He shrugs his shoulders a bit and looks visibly uncomfortable with the idea. "I probably have a few years left. I'm only 32, but that's on the older side for a pitcher. My parents are getting up there in years and I want to help if they need it. My brother and his family live in Pennsylvania, so my parents are pretty much on their own. Plus, I'd like them to be able to come to more of my games while I'm still able to pitch."

"That makes sense. I moved back to Ft. Starling to take care of my Gram when she needed me. It wasn't even a question." I get where he's coming from. It was only an hour and a half drive to get to Gram, but it was still difficult for me to help her out before I moved home. I can't imagine being across the country from your family. I could see why he would want to move home. So why did the idea of him leaving leave a sour feeling in my stomach? "So, are you for sure moving?"

"I really have no idea. My contract is technically up with the Flash so it's all about who offers me what kind of deal. There's a decent deal on the table from them, but my agent is shopping around to some teams that would be closer to my parents.

I nod my head and take in this information. If he moves, it'll be easy for us to call it quits on our pretending, but if he doesn't—what happens then?

"So if for some reason you don't move, there wouldn't be a built-in end-date for our fake dating?"

"I guess not. But we can always choose when to end things and go back to being just friends." He says.

I nod and take a drink of my pop.

"Okay. I'm pretty sure we can do this, but we need some ground rules." I say as I turn to a fresh page of my notebook. At the top of the page, I write "Bailey and Leena's Fake Dating Rules," in big letters.

"What kind of rules?" He asks with his eyebrows raised.

"Just things to keep us from giving away that it's fake or getting confused," I explain. "Rule number one, no... dating anyone else. I'm pretty sure Jessie would notice if either of us got caught ...dating other people."

"You mean no sleeping with other people, don't you?" He asks with a smirk.

"I was trying to be polite. Didn't want to make assumptions about your sex life!" I say as I feel my cheeks turning red. "Umm... is that going to be a problem?"

"I haven't been with anyone in a while. I'm not really into hook-ups these days. I can handle it." He says with a smile. "What about you?"

I bark out a laugh. "No. Not gonna be an issue."

He raises his eyebrows, but I don't elaborate on the fact that it's been over two years since I've slept with anyone.

"Okay, then. What's your next rule?"

"Rule number two... no sex with each other." I write in the rule slowly before I look up at him. His eyebrows shoot up to his hairline. He clears his throat.

"I didn't realize that was even an option." He says sarcastically.

"It's not. That's why it's a rule." I say, feeling my face turning even more red.

"I meant, I thought that was an unspoken thing." He explains.

"I just think it's better to put it on the list in case either of us gets confused... I mean... we'll probably need to do some PDA and we should be clear that it's not going to... lead anywhere." I stammer my explanation out as I start to sweat in earnest. He nods and stares at me for a long beat.

"Alright, no sex. Rule number three? We don't tell anyone we're faking it." He suggests.

"Cass already knows because I was acting weird before you picked me up and I can't lie to her for some reason, but I agree we don't tell anyone else," I reply.

"Sounds good. Any other rules?" He asks.

"We split the cost of any dates we end up on," I suggest, but he snatches the pen out of my hand before I can write it down.

"Gonna veto that one. I'll be paying if we're on a date. I don't care if it's fake." He declares.

"But it's not fair that you would always pay for me. I have money of my own. I can contribute." I argue.

"Nope. Not happening." He says firmly. I can see I'm not going to change his mind on this one, so I drop it.

"Ugh, fine! Any other rules you want to add?" I ask.

"Rule four, we stay friends after the fake breakup. I enjoy spending time with you and don't want to cut off contact." He says as he hands me my pen back. I smile at him and quickly add it to the list.

"Hmm. A list of four seems like a weird number. We need one more to round it out."

"How about for rule number five, we put honesty? We're going to be lying to a bunch of people, but we shouldn't lie to each other." He suggests quietly.

"That sounds like a good rule. So we're doing this?" I ask just to confirm.

"Yeah. We're doing this. You've got yourself a fake boyfriend, Sunshine." He says, smirking. I smile at him and try to tamp down the sense of foreboding that this was a bad idea. It's too late now, we're in this so hopefully, it doesn't blow up in our faces.

"Leena!" Jessie's voice rings out through the cafe a couple of days later. She's discovered that tracking me down during the lunchtime lull works better than calling or texting. I refused to answer a single one of her texts or calls after the nonsense she pulled the other night.

"Hey, Jess. What's up?" I say flatly, not quite ready to forgive her for the things she said at her house.

"You've been avoiding my calls and won't respond to my texts!" She doesn't seem mad, just kind of defeated. "And honestly, I guess I can't blame you." She lets out a deep sigh as my eyebrows shoot up to my hairline.

"What do you mean?" I ask cautiously.

"I've been informed that I pushed you too hard to jump into dating and that you'll pursue a relationship when you're ready. And what I did with the sneaky game night setup wasn't cool. It crossed the line with what I said about Gram, too." I take a deep breath to steady myself. I don't want to keep fighting with Jessie. Especially now that Bailey and I have our agreement.

"Annie?" I ask with a wary smile. She sighs again and meets my gaze. She looks genuinely sorry for pushing, but I'm having trouble believing that she would just let it go.

"And Dan, and also maybe my therapist."

"Oh my god, you talked about my dating life in therapy?" I huff out a laugh.

"I'm just concerned about you. And as my therapist pointed out, I may have also been projecting some of my own stuff onto you." She gives me a soft smile and a shrug. "I'm sorry, Leens. I haven't been the easiest to live with lately."

She seems so sad that I quickly come around the bar and wrap her in a hug. This is the Jessie that I've been missing.

"It's really alright." I take a deep breath to steady myself as I prepare to drop the biggest lie I've ever told her. "Actually... I have something I need to tell you."

She looks up at my tone and raises her eyebrows. I'm hoping that if any guilt is showing on my expression over the lie, she reads it as simple nerves.

"It turns out you were right." I look at the bar top and scrub at an imaginary stain.

"Right about what?" She definitely does not know where I'm going with this, so I'm going to have to actually say it.

"Well, after I stormed out the other night, Bailey found me and we got to talking even more than we did on our date. And I don't know if we were just both nervous and weird that first night, but something clicked this time. We're going out again this weekend." Jessie's jaw drops. She sits stunned for a moment and I start to sweat, thinking she might not believe me until she lets out an ear-piercing squeal and grabs me in a tight hug.

"I knew it, I knew it, I knew it!" She practically screams. "I told you! Ah, I fucking told you!" I knew she'd have no problem gloating once she bought my story.

"Yeah, you told me. I didn't want to date anyone, but I don't know... there's just something about Bailey." I shrug and smile at her. At least now I'm not lying to her. The thought makes my stomach plummet. When did I start to actually like Bailey? Have I always liked him? Well shit, that shouldn't complicate our fake relationship at all.

"Oh, I'm so happy for you guys!" She glances down at her watch and grabs her purse from where she dropped it on the bar top. "Shit, I gotta go. My lunch break is almost over, but I'll need to hear EVERYTHING about your date! Love you!" She lets out another squeal and vanishes out the door before I can even respond.

That went surprisingly well. And while I don't love lying to her, it is nice to have regular Jessie back. I stare at the door after her, trying to push aside the guilt when Cass drops a box on the bar top next to me.

"Shit, you scared me!" My hand goes to my chest to keep my heart from bursting through.

"Sorry," she says, but the amused smirk on her face tells me she's not really sorry. "So you and Bailey are going through with the fake relationship thing, huh?" She gives me an unblinking stare as she tries to decide what to think of our plan. I fix my gaze on the glass I'm pretending to clean as I feel her eyes studying me. I finally risk a glance at her and she lifts her eyebrows.

"What?!" I practically shout as my cool officially runs out.

"You're sure this is a good idea?"

Probably not.

"Yeah, it'll be fine!" I give her another shrug, even though I know she sees straight through my attempt at nonchalance.

"Fine. If you're sure." She takes off for the back to finish the prep work for the afternoon and the tension in my shoulders finally eases. Not completely, but a little, as I think over Cass's question.

Am I sure this is a good idea? No, probably not, but there's no going back now that I've already told Jessie. Would I even want to back out? I don't think so. While I wouldn't admit it out loud, there's a part of me that is looking forward to spending some time with Bailey. And that fact is what scares me the most about this arrangement. I'm finally in a place where I don't feel quite so broken by my past and I don't think I'd survive, my heart being shattered again now that I've finally glued all the pieces back together.

"It'll be fine. We're just friends." I say out loud to the almost empty bar, glad there's no one else around to hear me lying to myself.

Chapter Seven

Bailey

LEENA'S BAR IS MORE crowded than I expected at dinner time, considering they don't serve food. One glance around the dim room tells me I'm not the only one who grabbed food before coming over to the Songbird. Most tables have pizza or takeout containers open and Cass is busy pouring drinks. I walk towards the bar and set my pizza boxes down so I can retrieve my phone. I'm about to text Leena that I'm here when Cass stops in front of me.

"Oh, hey! Cass... right? I'm Bailey Tu—"

"I know who you are," she says flatly.

"Oh, right..." I tug on the back of my neck as the awkwardness intensifies. "I'm just here to see Leena."

"I know." Same flat tone, same blank stare. I'm considering my original plan of texting when Leena pops out from the back kitchen area.

Thank Christ.

"Hey, have you been here long?" She gives me a big smile and my heart skips a bit. Her auburn curls cascade around her shoulders, and black mascara coats her eyelashes, giving her hazel eyes a smoky look. Her tight long sleeve shirt, which is tucked into her skintight jeans, cuts just low enough on her chest to show off a hint of cleavage.

I gulp as I take in just how gorgeous this woman is. Not for the first time, and probably not for the last time, I'm regretting my suggestion of a fake relationship. There's nothing fake about my attraction to Leena. She raises an eyebrow as I realize she asked a question. I clear my throat and try to shake some of the lust out of my gaze.

"No, I just got here. I was just having a fascinating conversation with Cass!" I shoot Cass a big grin that earns me an eye roll as she huffs away. Leena watches as Cass moves back down the bar and gives her an eye roll of her own.

"Come on up!" she says as she waves me behind the bar.

"See you later, Cass!" I shout as I pass the end of the bar, giving her a big smile and wave as she glares at me. Leena shakes her head with a chuckle as she leads me to the staircase along the back wall of the small kitchen.

"I don't think Cass likes me very much."

"It's not you... she may not be the biggest fan of our fake dating plan." She shrugs her shoulders and continues up the stairs. I follow her up and make the mistake of focusing on her perfect, round ass as she walks up the flight. My cock twitches to life and I swallow hard. I calculate some batting stats in my head and picture my grandmother to fight back the wave of lust.

What the fuck was I thinking when I suggested we fake date? My balls are going to be an intense shade of blue by the time this is all over. I, for sure, will need a cold shower later tonight. As I walk into Leena's apartment, I'm hit in the face with her sweet scent. Hints of vanilla and coconut fill my lungs as I walk into the small space.

Yeah, I'm fucked.

Her apartment is one cozy rectangular room with a door on one wall that I assume leads to the bathroom. A kitchenette is in the corner to the left of the door with a tiny round cafe table and two chairs. The table sits close enough that I could reach the countertop while seated.

In the corner across from the kitchen, she has a flat-screen TV mounted on the wall opposite a plush couch. Her king-size bed is in the corner along the back wall, covered in a plush comforter with a colorful floral print. I avert my eyes quickly from the bed and try not to think about how close it is. Leena clears her throat and I realize what she was saying before I was distracted by her ass.

"Why doesn't Cass approve?" She shrugs her shoulders as she crosses to the fridge.

"She's just being protective. She'll get over it! Beer?" She explains as she offers me a bottle of Yuengling lager. I nod and grab the cold bottle from her.

"I guess that makes sense," I say, still not happy that Cass seems to be against our plan.

"I'm sure she'll come around. And Cass will keep it to herself since she doesn't hang out with Jessie, so we're good there."

She grabs a bottle of Diet Coke for herself and a bowl of salad before she pulls out the chair at the small table and takes a seat. She already had the table set with plates, silverware, and napkins. I take the chair across from her and open the pizza box. She glances at the pie covered with feta cheese, green olives, and bacon and then looks up at me in surprise.

"What made you pick these toppings?!"

"I asked Jessie what your favorite pizza toppings are." I shrug and pull on the back of my neck as she studies me.

"Thank you," she murmurs. I shrug again and feel my cheeks blush a bit at her sincere thanks.

"It's not a big deal. I like these toppings, too." I stab some salad on my fork.

"It's a big deal to me." She stares at her plate for a minute before adding. "I'm not used to someone being so considerate. So, thank you." I get the feeling that there is more to the story, and I'm guessing it has to do with the asshole ex Dan mentioned but it's like a wall has come up behind her eyes. I know I won't get any more information on the subject tonight.

"Well, you're welcome." I smile at her and hold her gaze for a beat before I go back to eating my salad. It's quiet while we're focused on our food, but it's not an awkward quiet. Once we've demolished the pizza and salad, I clear plates and get started on dishes.

"Oh, I can take care of that later!"

"I'm sure you can, but you won't need to." I don't leave any room for argument as I run the hot water into the sink. She leans against the counter a few feet away with her arms crossed and stares me down. I make a heroic effort to keep from glancing at her cleavage that she's pushed up. She huffs a laugh.

"You might be the best fake boyfriend I've ever had." I quirk an eyebrow her way.

"How many fake boyfriends have you had?"

"Don't worry, you're my first," she says with a laugh.

"I'm glad I have the pleasure of taking your fake relationship virginity," I say with an exaggerated wink that makes her throw her head back and laugh. My heart skips in my chest and leaves an ache that has me considering making it my new life goal to get a real Leena laugh as often as possible.

As she stops laughing, she realizes I'm still staring, and the air around us thickens. Her gaze connects with mine. She takes a small step towards me and my body heats as I lean her way, like she has some sort of gravitational pull on me. Maybe she does. Just as I'm about to take a step to bring her close enough to gather in my arms, a loud alarm on her phone snaps her attention away. I'm not sure if I'm disappointed or relieved.

It's clear there's some intense chemistry between us, but we have our rules to stick to. Leena glances in the mirror she has by the front door and I take the moment while she's occupied to rearrange my half-hard dick that hasn't gotten the memo about keeping things uncomplicated and following the rules.

"Ready for open mic?" she says with a smile.

"By ready, you mean ready to listen, right? I have way too much stage fright to sing in front of other people." Her eyes spark with a dare.

"You play baseball in front of thousands of people, but you can't sing in front of like twenty in a dinky bar?" She asks in a teasing tone.

"That is accurate," I confirm.

"We'll work on it!" she says with a wink and leads the way out of the apartment to the bar below. Something deep in my gut tells me I'd do just about anything for this woman and that thought is fucking terrifying.

THIS WAS A MISTAKE. A big mistake. I should have known that hearing Leena sing again was only going to complicate my feelings more. I should have avoided it at all costs. I don't know what it is, but I've always been insanely attracted to girls who can sing. In high school, I joined choir just so I could be around them. Hell, the night I met Leena, I literally followed her voice into this bar, so I really should have known better.

Leena leans into the microphone and smiles as she sings a haunting melody. She said it was a song by Sara Bareilles, but I don't know this one, so it must not have had much radio play. It's clearly a breakup song and I can almost see the heartbreak lingering in Leena's gaze.

Fuck, she's gorgeous. I'm in serious trouble. I'm developing a crush on my fake girlfriend and I don't think there's anything I can do to stop it. She finishes the sad song and comes over to sit next to me at the bar.

"Hey Cass, can you pour me a diet coke?" She smiles at Cass, and surprisingly enough, Cass smiles back. I didn't know she knew how to smile. She pours Leena's drink and as her gaze shifts to me her smile falls. So much for that.

"You want anything?" Cass deadpans.

"Nah, I'm good," I say, holding up my half-full beer. She nods and sets the pop in front of Leena, who then turns on her stool to look at me.

"So, what did you think of that one?" She sips her drink, but I can see the nerves she's trying to hide. I don't know why she's nervous about feedback with a voice like that.

"You were fantastic! What was the name of that song?" I make sure she's looking me in the eye so she knows I'm not blowing smoke up her ass. "Your voice is fucking incredible." She blushes a pretty shade of pink and I wonder what else could make her blush like that.

"Thanks," she gives me a soft smile as her cheeks go pink. "That was one of my favorite Sara Bareilles songs called 'Between The Lines.' I've always loved singing and performing, so I started open mic nights pretty soon after I opened the cafe."

"I didn't know that you started the cafe yourself. So this wasn't here before? For some reason, I thought it was passed down to you from your Gram?"

"Nope. The building was a dive bar at one point, and I used the money that Gram left to me to turn it into Songbird, but I started pretty much from scratch. The bar top was the only salvageable thing."

"That is damn impressive, Sunshine." She blushes some more and shrugs her shoulders as she downs her pop. "You don't like compliments, do you?"

"I'm just not used to getting them." Her gaze trains on the floor and I really would like to punch the asshole from her past that made her so self-conscious.

"Well, get used to them. As long as you're my girl, you'll hear all about your good qualities any chance I get." She stares at me for a long beat. The air thickens between us again and even though we're sitting in a crowded bar, it's like we're alone. I swallow hard and lean towards her.

A glass being placed on the bar with a thunk breaks the spell and we both look up to find Cass putting down another Diet Coke for Leena. Cass smirks as she walks away, knowing she interrupted a moment. Leena shakes her head and sips the fresh drink, choosing to move past my declaration.

"So, what's on the agenda now?" I ask, "Do you sing again?"

"I usually just do the opener and the closer, so we've got some time to kill. We can hang out and listen. Some of my favorite regulars are here tonight."

"Sounds like a plan to me, Sunshine." I settle in and scoot my stool a little closer to Leena so there's not a gap between us and rest my knee along hers. With my back leaning against the bar, my shoulder rubs against hers any time one of us moves. I hold my breath, waiting for her to scoot away, but she stays right where she is.

"Hey, were you planning to go to Jessie and Dan's Super Bowl party?" she asks. "I thought that might be a good first friend group appearance for us."

I nod my head and take a sip of my beer.

"That sounds good. I was planning on going anyway," I say.

"I went last year, and it was pretty fun. I'm actually surprised we weren't introduced then, or were you not there?" She asks.

"No, I was actually at the game last year."

Her eyes widen in surprise. "Wow! That's awesome. I'm not really into football that much, but I do think it would be fun to go to the Super Bowl someday."

"It was incredible! One perk of being a pro athlete. We get invited to all kinds of things like that for publicity." I explain.

"I low-key forgot that you're a big famous athlete. You seem so normal." She huffs out a laugh.

"Thank you?" I say with a laugh.

"No, I mean. I always half expect pro ball players to be more like the stereotypical arrogant jock, but that doesn't seem to be you." She shrugs her shoulders and I shoot her a grin.

"I know what you mean. I shift into jock mode when I'm on the field, but I like to think I stay pretty down to earth everywhere else."

"You do a good job." She smiles up at me and holds my gaze for a moment before clearing her throat and turning her attention to the group of college guys that have taken the stage at the back of the room. She may look back at the stage, but she didn't move away from me. I do my best to pay attention to the boy band instead of her arm resting against mine and ignore the urge to put my arm around her. It's gonna be a long-ass fake relationship.

"WHERE DO YOU THINK Fred learned how to twerk?" I ask, still laughing at the memory of the old man's performance. "Do you think he had his grandkids teach him?"

Leena laughs and shakes her head as she finishes wiping down the tables. We're the only people left in the bar after closing.

"I asked him once, and he just smirked at me and told me it was a natural talent. I'm not sure I believe him though, since I saw his youngest granddaughter teaching him how to search on YouTube when he brought her by for a smoothie."

"I would love to see that man's search history." I laugh again as I help Leena stack the chairs on top of the tables. Once we're done, Leena looks around the room like she's ticking tasks off a mental to-do list. Finally, she nods and wipes her hands on a dish towel.

"Thanks for your help. You didn't have to stay past closing."

"I wanted to help. Plus, I was having fun." I shrug, trying not to give away just how much fun I've been having. I don't want to spook her into giving up on the fake relationship plan. Not before I get to spend a little more time with her.

"Well, thank you," she hesitates for just a moment before adding, "I had fun tonight too."

I give her a grin as I grab my coat from behind the bar and head towards the door. She follows me so she can lock up after I'm gone. Right before I get to the door, I pause. It doesn't feel right to not kiss her goodnight, but I don't want to freak her out either. A light bulb goes off in my brain as I come up with the perfect excuse.

"You know, our friends are probably going to expect some PDA on Sunday." She goes still and holds my gaze. After a second's thought, she nods.

"You're probably right." Her gaze tracks to the floor as if she's embarrassed. "Is that going to be okay with you?"

This woman. She doesn't understand just how appealing she is. I close the space between us and lift her chin so she meets my eye. Tucking a stray strand of hair behind her ear, I lean in. I can see the indecision and worry in her eyes.

"That will be more than okay for me." I pause with my lips hovering just above hers. I wait to see if she'll close the space between us. Just as I'm about to give up and take a step back, she raises up on her toes and brushes her soft lips against mine. Her hands go to my waist and I can't resist threading my hands into her soft curls as I angle her head and slant my mouth over hers.

I deepen the kiss, running my tongue along the seam of her lips. She opens with a gasp and I take the opportunity to explore. My hands roam down her back and I band my arms around her and pull her tighter against me. She lets out a whimper and we both seem to realize at the same time that our practice kiss has gotten out of hand and pull back. She takes a step and our gazes lock.

"Wow," she murmurs as her hand comes up to touch her lips. Wow, is fucking right. That kiss, arguably the best kiss of my life, only confirms what I was already suspecting. I'm developing real feelings for my fake girlfriend.

Fuck me.

Chapter Eight

Leena

I FIDGET WITH MY hair in the mirror by the door for the millionth time. Bailey will be here any minute to pick me up for Jessie and Dan's Super Bowl party and I am a hot mess of nerves. Somehow, I'm both eager to spend more time with Bailey and terrified by that fact. That fucking kiss. I felt it in every nerve ending of my body when he pulled me into him and I about melted into a puddle with the heat between us.

We said it was a practice kiss, knowing our friends would expect some affection at the party, but there was nothing about that kiss that felt fake. Especially since I've replayed it in my mind constantly since Friday and my vibrator has seen more action in the last few days than it has in the whole past year.

I meet my eyes in the mirror and take a deep breath to calm my racing heart. God, he's not even here yet and my body is on high alert.

"It's just a physical reaction," I tell my reflection sternly. "It's just a normal response to an objectively gorgeous man." The fact that I haven't had an orgasm that wasn't self-made in a couple of years isn't helping matters either. I take a few more deep breaths before a knock sounds at my door. I pull the door open to find Bailey smiling on the other side.

"Hey, ready to go?" he leans in and kisses my cheek. I blush from the contact and swallow hard as I turn away to grab my coat.

"Yeah, let me grab the dessert I made from the fridge." I grab the plastic-wrapped dish and turn back towards him. He studies my outfit with a smirk.

"Are you a big Seahawks fan?" I chuckle and shake my head.

"Nope! I'm not really a fan of any sports teams."

"Ouch," he puts a hand to his heart like I've wounded him. I laugh again and shake my head.

"Except the Flash, of course. I can't get enough of baseball," I deadpan.

"Yeah, yeah. So if you're not a big Seahawks fan, what with the getup?"

His question makes sense. I'm decked out head to toe in Seattle colors. I have a bow in my hair with the Seahawks logo, and I even painted my nails to match.

"I don't care about specific sports teams per se, but I love dressing up for a good theme party," I say, shrugging. "It's basically a football costume party." Bailey studies my face for a long moment but doesn't say anything. "What?"

"I can't decide if that's infuriating or adorable," he says matter-of-factly. My cheeks heat at the almost compliment before I fully process what he said.

"Wait.. why infuriating?" He shakes his head and unzips his coat to show a Seattle jersey. "Oooh, so you're a real Seahawks fan."

"Yeah, I grew up watching the games with my dad."

"Got it. Well, at least I picked the right team!" I start to put my coat on, but Bailey—the constant gentleman—grabs it out of my hands to hold it open for me.

"Do I even want to know how you picked which team to root for?" I give him an exaggerated guilty look with my eyes widened and my lips pursed.

"I, uh, I picked it based on the team colors." He runs his hand over his mouth in frustration as he's trying not to smile. "How else was I supposed to pick?!"

"Team record? Stats? Projections for this game?" I let out a big laugh and shake my head.

"You want me to learn something about sports?" I tease. He chuckles and shakes his head as we head out the door. I lock up my apartment and walk across the landing to the stairwell.

"Don't worry Sunshine, I'll teach you." I almost trip down the stairs as my heart rate kicks up. My mind went to a very dirty place just now, and I'm sure there are several things this man could teach me. Thank god I'm leading the way down the steps so that he can't see my very red face and try to take deep breaths to dispel the thought of Bailey in my bed. I'll save that image for later on tonight when I'm alone with my battery-operated friend.

THE ACHE THAT STARTED from my inadvertent dirty thoughts in the stairwell has only gotten worse during this party. Even though Jessie and Dan's living room is huge, this party is crowded, and there isn't a ton of seating. I find myself perched on Bailey's lap for most of the first quarter. Every so often, he leans in and talks softly in my ear. Mostly about the football game—explaining all the rules that usually go right over my head—but the contact has me clenching my thighs and squirming. I keep reminding myself that we have rules for a reason.

"Sunshine. You gotta stop moving." I freeze. I'm not used to sitting on anyone's lap and I know I'm not the lightest weight girl in the world.

"I'm sorry. Am I too heavy? I can find another seat!" I move to get off Bailey's lap, but his large hand grips my hip to hold me in place.

"Don't get up. I don't need the entire room to get an eye-full," he hisses in my ear. I stay seated but reposition myself so that I'm not putting as much pressure on the impressive bulge that I have suddenly noticed digging into my ass.

"Ah, I see." I've maneuvered our positions so that I can whisper in his ear for once. "It's your own fault, you know." His eyebrows shoot up as he looks down at me and waits for me to continue.

Thanks to Jessie stocking a full bar for this party, I'm just tipsy enough to be bold and flirty, so I lean in close so that my lips are against the bottom of his ear. "All the soft talking into my ear was having a similar effect on me, hence the squirming."

His hands tighten on my hips as he mutters a string of profanity under his breath. My cheeks heat and my core throbs again. Jessie is smirking over at us and typing on her phone. I'm not at all surprised when my phone buzzes in my lap.

Jessie:

Are you two going to make it through the game or do you need to go get a room?

I huff out a laugh and show Bailey the text. He chuckles and leans in to whisper in my ear again. "Looks like we're doing a good job acting like two people who want to fuck each other's brains out." A shiver rolls down my spine. The wave of lust for my fake boyfriend that hits me with those words is very much real. At that moment, I decide to throw our rules and all caution out the window. I pull back so that I can hold eye contact and whisper.

"Oh, are we supposed to be acting?" His eyes darken as we hold each other's gaze. After only a few seconds, which seem to last forever, we're moving. In one fluid motion, Bailey has us both on our feet and heading out of the room.

"Where are we going?" I murmur as he grabs my hand.

"We're watching the rest of the game at my place."

I wave a quick goodbye to Jessie, who has a very smug look on her face. She's really fucking pleased with herself and I will not hear the end of it, but I don't care about that at all right this minute.

Is it a good idea to sleep with my fake boyfriend? Definitely not. Is it already breaking one of the rules we set for this arrangement? Yes, it is. Am I going to do it, anyway? Fuck yes.

BAILEY PARKS HIS TRUCK in a large garage and cuts the engine. He gets out quickly and opens my door before I can even get my seat belt undone.

He helps me down from my seat and we quickly head inside a door that opens into a large kitchen.

Bailey barely has the door closed before we're colliding. This is no soft, sweet goodnight kiss like last week. Our mouths crash together as we explore each other with tongues, teeth, and hands.

His large hands grip my ass as he lifts me off my feet. I wrap my legs around his waist and thread my hands into his hair. He spins us around and presses me into the door we just walked through. Holding me up with one arm, he uses the other to pull at my top. He tosses it to the floor, then leans down to take my nipple into his mouth, fabric and all. I let out a moan as he sucks hard through the bright green lace.

"Oh god, yes." I moan and hold his head to my chest.

"Hang on, Sunshine," he says as he carries me over to the giant island in the middle of the kitchen and sets me on the edge. I reach around to unclasp my bra and he slides the straps down my arms, unleashing my breasts. Bailey takes a moment to have a good look before taking them in both hands. My moans get louder as he pinches and rolls my hardened nubs.

Traveling his mouth from mine down the side of my neck, he softly nips at the sensitive skin and then leaves soothing kisses, causing goose-bumps to break out along my arm. He takes his time making his way down my body, spending what seems like hours licking and sucking each breast and working me into a frenzy. I have never felt so worshipped and frustrated at the same time.

He continues his painstaking process down my belly and grabs the waistband of the leggings I'm wearing. With a questioning glance, he meets my eyes and pauses waiting for me to confirm that I want this. I give him an emphatic nod and he strips me out of the leggings, taking my panties with them. I'm laid completely bare on the island. He stops to study me from head to toe, his eyes getting impossibly darker.

"You are so fucking gorgeous." He practically whispers.

"And you have way too many clothes on," I respond. He grabs the back of the jersey and pulls it off, tossing it to join my clothes on the floor. "Holy shit," I practically squeak as I take in his ripped torso.

I knew he would be fit. He is a professional athlete, after all, but the man is in incredible shape. My mouth waters as I imagine running my tongue over each of his eight abs and down that delicious v-cut at his hips. I reach for the button of his jeans and he pulls away.

"Not yet, Sunshine. We're not moving on until I've tasted every inch of your beautiful body." He presses gently at my chest, pushing me to lie back on the island as he resumes kissing down my belly. "Are you wet for me?"

"Soaked," I manage to moan out as he licks and nips his way down my hips and along the sensitive skin of my inner thighs. He teases me, never quite landing where I want him. I arch my hips towards him, seeking contact. He chuckles softly and the vibration so close to my core has me moaning louder. Finally, his talented tongue finds my wet slit and swirls around my entrance. "Oh god, more. I need more."

He laughs again but thankfully gives me exactly what I need as he finds my clit and latches on the bundle of nerves. He holds my thighs open as I try to thrash and squirm. His tongue flicks at the sensitive bundle of nerves as he slides his long finger inside of me. He works me higher and higher, adding a second finger and curling them inward to find that perfect spot that makes me lose my mind.

My whole body clenches and trembles as the fireworks explode behind my eyes and I ride out into the most intense orgasm of my life. As I slowly come down, I hear Bailey finally undoing his jeans.

I lean up on my elbows to take in the sight of him losing the jeans and boxer briefs. His cock bobs as it comes free of the underwear, already glistening at the tip. He kicks his pants away and tears open the foil packet of the condom that he produced from his wallet. Once he's sheathed, he fists his cock as he slowly peruses my body again. He takes his time and my patience runs out.

"Please," I pant. "I need you inside of me." A desperate growl-like sounds rips from his throat as he surges toward me. His large hands grip my hips and pull me to the edge of the counter, and rubs his tip along my folds. He enters me slowly, inch by inch, until he is fully inside. I gasp at the sensation of fullness as he gives me a moment to get used to his size before he starts rocking in and out. He starts slowly, but quickly picks up the pace as my inner walls clench around him.

"Oh god, Leena, you feel amazing," he groans. He pulls me up so that he can crash his lips into mine and swallow my gasps and moans. "I'm not going to last long, Sunshine."

"I'm right there!" I breathe. "Oh god, Bailey, I'm so close. More."

He pistons his hips into mine, never breaking his rhythm as my legs start to shake and I feel my core clench around his hard length. I scream his name as my next orgasm hits me and takes me over the edge. I spoke way too soon when I said the last one was the most intense of my life. The second orgasm comes in waves as he thrusts impossibly faster chasing his own release. Finally, he stills and lets out a loud groan with his face buried in the side of my neck as clutches my hips.

We both stay locked in a tight embrace as we catch our breath. He leans his forehead against mine as his dark brown eyes find mine. I can't hold back the utterly satisfied grin on my face. He smiles back down at me before dropping a sweet kiss on my lips.

He cups my cheek as he stares into my eyes and I suddenly realize just how much trouble this man is going to be. The chances of me leaving this fake relationship with my heart intact are dwindling quickly.

I should throw my walls back up and take a step back. I should ask him to take me home. Instead, I lean in for another long and slow kiss, throwing all caution and smart decisions right the fuck out the window.

Chapter Nine

Bailey

I COULD NOT HAVE foreseen this happening. When I picked Leena up for the Super Bowl party, I was excited to spend some time with her. Maybe get to know her a little better. I did not allow myself to imagine the possibility of spending time inside of her. I pull back from the slow kiss she just started.

"I gotta get rid of the condom." I give her another quick kiss on the forehead and point toward the first door in the hallway across the living room. "There's a bathroom there if you want to clean up a bit. Be right back."

She gives me a soft smile as I help her down from the counter. I'll have to remember to sanitize it before any of my teammates come over for dinner. Although, no amount of sanitizer will remove the image of Leena naked and ready for me. I will probably see her coming on my tongue and fingers anytime I look at that island for the foreseeable future.

I'm not exactly sure where we go from here. We broke one of our rules in a big way. Are we still in a fake relationship? A real one? We'll have to have that conversation, but I could see the insecurity and indecision flicker through her eyes before she kissed me.

She's not ready to have a serious relationship talk and I don't want to push her. She's been burned before, and although most of what I know is hearsay from Dan, she didn't fight Jessie on being set up for no reason. If I want something real with her, I'm going to have to tread carefully.

That thought hits me like a freight train. *Shit. I want something real with her.*

Until now, I hadn't met anyone that made the idea of balancing my baseball career and a relationship seem worth it, but Leena does. I ditch the condom and pull on a fresh pair of boxer briefs from my dresser. As I'm washing my hands, I study myself in the mirror and give myself a pep talk about taking the relationship talk slow. I don't want her running for the door before we explore what's going on between us.

When I peek back into the open concept kitchen and living room, I find Leena picking up her clothes. At first, I think she's going to get dressed and bolt and a flicker of dread rolls through me, but as I come fully into the room, I see that she's put on my Seahawks jersey. She deposits her clothing in a pile and is filling a glass with water from my fridge when she notices me watching.

My jersey fits like a dress on her petite body. I catch a pop of bright green from the bench by the door where she'd ditched her purse and clothes. Which means she's wearing only my jersey and nothing else under it. I feel my cock twitch at the thought. Round two is not far off, but first I need to eat something. We didn't end up eating much at the party, and I'm starving after that workout. She hands me the glass of ice water after she takes a long gulp herself.

"Thanks," I say, suddenly realizing just how parched I am. "You hungry?"

"Starving!" She grins as I hand the water glass back to her and open the fridge.

"I'm sure the wait times for takeout are insane with the game still going, and I don't have much here. Grilled cheese?" I ask.

"Sounds perfect! Should we turn the game on?"

"We can if you want?" I say with a shrug.

"I'm literally wearing your Seahawks jersey. You don't care how the game's going?" She questions.

I huff out a laugh as I set the bread on the counter next to the stove. I stalk closer to her and reach out to play with the hem of my jersey. "Oh, I definitely noticed that you're wearing my jersey. In fact, the sight of you in that jersey makes me really not give a shit about the game." I run my hand up the side of her bare hip to grab her supple ass. "I'd be dragging you into my bedroom for another round right now if I thought I'd survive it without eating something first." I give her a light swat and a quick kiss and get back to making sandwiches.

"Who says there's going to be another round?" She says with a mischievous smirk on her face.

"You did when you put on my jersey and left your panties over there by the door where I can see them." I waggle my eyebrows at her and she laughs. "Now make yourself useful and grab me the butter out of the fridge."

"Yes, sir!" she says with mock seriousness. I close my eyes to get my dick under control.

"Woman. If you don't stop turning me on, we'll never eat." She laughs and shakes her head as she starts to butter the bread. We work in companionable silence to get food together. I open a bag of salt and vinegar chips that we snack on as the sandwiches are cooking. When they're done, we take our plates and water to the plush couch in my living room.

"I think I will put the game on while we eat," I say as I grab the remote to the TV.

She chuckles and shakes her head. "I knew you couldn't resist!"

"It is my team in the Super Bowl!" I shrug and smile as I turn on the massive TV that is the focal point of the room. The game is in the third quarter and I'm pleased to see that the Seahawks are ahead by 14.

Leena laughs and murmurs. "I guess you're not the only one scoring tonight."

Thank fuck for that.

WE KEPT WATCHING THE game after we'd inhaled our sandwiches. The food combined with the countertop sex made Leena drowsy, and as the game went on, she cuddled into my side. By the time we hit the fourth quarter, she was fast asleep in my arms and I was just fine with that development.

Our relationship shifted tonight and I'm determined to make sure that Leena sees it that way too. This fake relationship became real the minute we left Jessie's party. I know she's skittish about relationships, but I'll make her realize we deserve to give this a real shot.

When the game ends, I shake her awake gently. "Sunshine, the game's over." She sits up with a start and blinks adorably at the TV.

"Did we win?" She asks sleepily.

"Yeah, we won," I say with a smirk.

"Oh, good." She nods and tries to lie back down on the couch to go back to sleep.

"Leena? Hey, do you want me to drive you home or do you want to stay here?" I ask without letting on how much I want her to stay.

"Hmmm. I want to stay here." She snuggles against me some more and even though I know she's half asleep, her easy affection gives me hope.

"Okay, Sunshine. Why don't I get you something more comfortable to sleep in and we can go to bed?" I murmur into her hair with a quick kiss on her head.

"Mmmhhmmm." She nods with her eyes still closed but doesn't move to get off the couch.

I chuckle and shake my head. I slide one arm under her legs and wrap the other around her back to carry her to my bedroom. She slides her arms up around my neck and snuggles into my chest. For someone who started so standoffish, she's turning out to be super affectionate. I'm not mad about it.

I set her on the edge of my bed and go to the dresser to grab her a shirt that will be more comfortable than my jersey. She has already curled herself to the side by the time I get back, so I lift her back to sitting.

"Come on sleepyhead! You can go back to sleep in just a minute." She squints her eyes at me, but doesn't say anything as she lifts her arms. My chest squeezes at the thought of how vulnerable and innocent she looks at this moment. I slide the jersey off and quickly pull an old Ft. Starling Flash tee shirt over her head. I avert my eyes as I help her into the shirt so my dick doesn't get any ideas. I tuck her under the covers, then go back out to lock up the house and turn out the lights.

I slide into bed and Leena rolls to find me like a heat-seeking missile. As she snuggles into my chest and I start to drift towards sleep, it hits me just how natural this feels. I'm not usually one for cuddling or even overnight stays. But this feeling right here? I could get used to this.

Chapter Ten

Leena

I WAKE DISORIENTED TO bright sunlight, and it takes me a second to remember where I am. Bailey's bedroom doesn't have blackout curtains like I installed in my apartment and the morning sunlight is startling in a way I'm not used to yet. In the week since Jessie's Super Bowl party, we've spent most of our nights together either here or at my apartment when I'm running open mic.

I didn't know it could be like this. This week with Bailey is truly eye-opening to how lacking my previous relationships had been. Being with him has been all-consuming. And the sex. The Sex. I haven't had as many man-made orgasms in my entire life as I have this week. Bailey knows exactly what he's doing in the bedroom. And the kitchen. And the living room. And the edge of his hot tub.

It's not just the sex though. Bailey is affectionate and sweet. You wouldn't think a man that gorgeous would be so perceptive or interested in knowing me better, but that's exactly what this week has been like. My mind is sending me loud alarm bells warning me that if I'm not careful, I'll forget that what we're doing here is fake. It's temporary. It may feel right and wonderful now, but that won't last and it will only shatter my barely healed heart.

Bailey has his muscular arm tossed over my waist, his large body fitting to my back. His slow, rhythmic breaths tell me he's still asleep as I take in the moment. We haven't discussed what we're doing or the fact that we completely threw rule number two right out the window. Neither of us has brought it up, but with spring training looming next week, we'll need to have a discussion. The idea of starting that conversation sends pure panic through my system.

"I can hear you thinking." Bailey groans behind me. He slides over and pulls me flat to the mattress so that he can look into my eyes. "What's on your mind, Sunshine?"

"Nothing." I shrug and glance away, but Bailey isn't fooled for a second. He raises one eyebrow and waits me out. I huff out an exasperated breath. "Ugh fine. I was just wondering what we're doing. We've completely ignored one of our rules, so do they still apply? And what is spring training going to be like? Not for you. I know what you'll be doing, but more for ... us."

Bailey meets my gaze and searches my eyes for a moment before he asks, "What do you want us to be doing?"

Of course, he's going to leave it up to me. He knows how against a relationship I was—am. My mind races, trying to decide if I'm going to take a risk or play it safe. Part of me wants to take the leap and see where this can go, but the idea terrifies me too much to give it a voice.

"Um, I guess we should keep things casual. That way, when we fake break up, neither of us is getting hurt." Fuck. Play it safe it is. He nods, but I can almost feel the disappointment rolling off of him.

"Yeah, okay. Still exclusive though, right?" He asks.

"Right. The other rules still apply. We can be exclusive but casual. Kind of like friends with benefits?" I shrug my shoulders as I dig even deeper into self-preservation. Avoiding his gaze, I launch myself from the bed and glance at my phone. I continue to babble nonsense as I pull on my clothes.

"Oh shoot. I told Cass I'd help her with the inventory today. Better get going. I'll ... um, text you later!"

With that, I make a break for the front door before he can even get out of bed. I'm being a coward here, but it's for the best. If we made this an actual relationship, there's no way my heart would make it out unbroken. As it is, there's still a pretty strong chance of it being severely bruised at the end, but I can't bring myself to cut things off with Bailey yet. So friends with benefits it is.

As I drive back to the cafe, I remind myself over and over that this is for the best as I try to get Bailey's disappointed expression out of my mind.

"CATHLEEN ELIZABETH MITCHELL!!" RINGS out as Cass spots me trying to sneak up to my apartment. Dammit, busted. I slink over to the bar, where she's waiting with her arms crossed.

"Oh, hey Cass!" I give her an awkward wave. "How's it going?" She rolls her eyes hard and fixes me with another glare.

"Where the hell have you been? I haven't seen you in days!" she huffs angrily.

"Um, I've been around. Been busy." I shrug and pour myself a glass of ice water to avoid looking at her.

"Busy doing what?" She asks with heavy suspicion in her voice. I'm not sure what she knows yet, so I don't elaborate that I've been spending most of my free time in Bailey's bed. I give her another casual shrug.

"You know, working, hanging out, the usual," I say.

"Your usual is spending 99% of your time in this building. Also, Jessie mentioned that you and Bailey were looking pretty hot and heavy when you left her party early." She raises an eyebrow as if she's asked a question.

"You talked to Jessie? I thought you guys hated each other?" I ask skeptically.

"We don't hate each other... we're just ... very different people. Anyway, don't change the subject, missy! Is there anything you'd like to tell me?" She demands.

I let out an amused scoff. "What are you, my mother?"

She lets out a gigantic sigh, like I've exhausted her with my refusal to answer her questions. "I'm just worried about you," she says seriously.

Fucking hell. She had to get all sincere and caring on me. I slump onto a bar stool and fill her in on the last week, as well as the conversation Bailey and I had before I fled from his house.

"So, you're not fake dating anymore?" She asks.

"No, we are. As far as anyone but you is concerned, we're in a relationship and have been since the big blow-up at Jessie's last month." I explain.

"But you're actually dating him now?" She asks, confused.

"No. We're friends with benefits. It's a casual fling that will end when the fake relationship has run its course. He's hoping to move back closer to his parents, so it makes sense that we would end things when that happens." I elaborate.

I ignore the stabbing pain in my gut that happens every time I think about Bailey moving across the country and not being in my life anymore. This is just casual, I remind myself.

Casual.

Casual.

Casual.

I wonder how many times it will take before I believe it.

"WE'RE GOING TO MIX it up a bit tonight! You regulars know I love my sad songs, but I'm in the mood for something a little different tonight!" Out of the corner of my eye, I can see Cass's eyebrows shoot up. She's going to have something snarky to say when I'm done, but I don't care. "If we have any Swifties in the house tonight, you may remember this one from her Red era."

A couple of girls that look about my age let out some whoops from the side of the crowd and I start playing "Begin Again." It's not one of Taylor's best-known songs, but I've always loved its hopeful lyrics. I can see Cass holding up her phone and taking a video. She's probably getting evidence of the time I sang something not depressing.

Just as I'm playing the last few notes, I notice the door open and in walks Bailey. I catch myself and tone down my automatic smile as I remind myself to play it cool. I don't think it's working, though, because Bailey smirks and winks at me as he makes his way to the bar. Christ, just a wink from the man has my cheeks going hot. I'm so in trouble.

"Alright folks, now we have a crowd favorite with our friend Fred and his rendition of..." I glance at the sign-up slip in my hand and look up at Fred, who's already grinning. He usually goes with 80s and 90s songs, but he's chosen something a little more modern this time and it caught me off guard.

I looked up to confirm I was reading the right thing, but now seeing Fred decked out in head-to-toe flamboyant cowboy gear gave me all the confirmation I need. I clear my throat a bit and continue, "Welcome Fred and his rendition of 'Old Town Road'!"

The crowd goes wild for Fred as he sings and shakes his fringe-covered ass. I laugh as I make my way over to Bailey, who is clapping and whistling for Fred. He spots me coming towards him and gives me a heart-stopping full smile. I trip a little over my own feet and I can sense Cass watching with her eagle eyes. I'm looking at another well-meaning but super annoying lecture for sure.

"Hey Sunshine, sorry I missed your song," Bailey says, with a kiss to my cheek that is immediately blushing both from his proximity and from being glad he missed me singing about love starting over.

"No big deal!" I say with a wave of my hand.

"What'd you sing?" he asks.

"Oh, just a Taylor Swift song," I say, being intentionally vague. This is casual, after all. I don't want him reading into my song choices and thinking I'm turning into a clingy Flash Floozy. "I didn't know you were coming over tonight." Despite my friends with benefits declaration last week, we've still been spending most nights together, but I knew he was finishing getting packed up to leave for spring training in the morning.

"I wanted to see you before I have to leave tomorrow," he whispers in my ear. I meet his eyes and lose my breath for a minute. I will never get over just how handsome he is. I clear my throat and drop my gaze. If I keep staring into his eyes, I'm never going to get my "casual casual casual" mantra to stick.

"Plus, I got tired of packing. I've unpacked and re-packed a ton of stuff several times, so it was time to step away." He complains.

"Haven't you been doing this for decades? You should have it down to a science." I tease.

A low chuckle rumbles in his chest, making chills run down my spine. He rolls his eyes with amusement before correcting me. "Decade singular. I had a couple of years in the minors and this is my eighth year in the majors, thank you very much. And yes, I should have figured out how to pack for this but I always change things and then get a couple of weeks into training and wish I'd brought different stuff and then I end up going out and buying clothes I don't need because I have the same thing at home."

"Aww, you poor pitiful pro athlete," I coo mockingly. "You have to go and spend some of that measly salary you earn," Bailey barks out a laugh and shakes his head.

"Yeah, yeah, I know. I can afford it. It just feels wasteful, that's all." He gives me a sheepish smile. Bailey Turner is the complete package. Not only is he gorgeous beyond all fairness, but he's also a good man. As I study his earnest expression, an idea hits me.

"You know, you could always auction off the duplicates at the end of training. You could make an entire campaign out of it on socials and then donate the money to a charity. Or start a foundation or something."

He stares dumbfounded for a beat and then breaks into a huge smile. "You're a fucking genius, Sunshine. That is such a good idea!"

I can feel my cheeks heating at his compliment and the use of my nickname. Our gazes meet and hold for a long moment. As I get lost in his dark chocolate eyes, my entire body heats. I'm just about to suggest that we head up to my apartment when I hear a polite cough behind me. I turn to see Fred sliding onto the barstool next to me.

"Leena, could I trouble you for a glass of ice water? Cass looks to be in the weeds and I don't want to interrupt her." I glance over to Cass to see that she has a line forming for drinks at her end of the bar and I hop up to get Fred a water.

"Here you go, Fred!" I say as I set the cold glass in front of him.

"Thank you, dear," he replies before he takes a long gulp. "I worked up quite a sweat with that number." He exclaims. I chuckle under my breath.

"It was a showstopper for sure! What I need to know is if you already owned this cowboy getup or if you bought it for this song?" I raise my eyebrows at the old man with a smirk.

"Well, as soon as I first saw the video of Billy Ray and that Lil Nas fella, I thought I should get a western suit of my own. My wife had the grandkids get it for me for Christmas, so I've been practicing since then." He beams.

"Gail is a treasure. Tell her we appreciated her styling you for our stage." I give the old man that I've known all of my life a warm smile. "I'm gonna help Cass out for a bit. Be right back."

I shoot Bailey a wink and pop over to help Cass get caught up. As I feel his gaze follow me across the bar, I shiver, knowing I'll be dragging that handsome man up to my apartment at the soonest possible opportunity.

Chapter Eleven

Bailey

My heated gaze follows Leena as she goes to help Cass, but I soon realize Fred is studying me and I drop my eyes to the glass of water in front of me. I clear my throat and shoot a glance at the old man in a cowboy costume to find him still staring my way. I give him a polite smile and head nod that finally seems to give him permission to chat.

"You've been spending a lot of time with our Leena, huh?"

"Yes, sir." It feels like he's gearing up for a protective relative lecture, so I do my best to take him seriously despite how crazy he looks in the fringe covered and bedazzled cowboy costume.

"Did you know I've known her since the day she was born?" he asks. "My wife was sorority sisters with her Gram, Lizzie. They always kept in touch, even when we didn't live in the area. We moved back here when Leena was around 12."

"I didn't know that," I say with a shake of the head. "Leena tends to be pretty tight-lipped about the past."

"Yeah. She keeps her cards close to the vest now." He says sadly and takes a large drink of his water.

"What do you mean now?" I feel a little guilty asking for information, but if it helps me get to know Leena better, I'll take all the help I can get.

Fred lets out a big sigh and glances around to find Leena at the bar, like he doesn't want to get caught talking about her.

"She wasn't always so closed off, but after everything that rat bastard of an ex put her through, and with losing Lizzie. Well... she kind of shut down and decided not to let anyone else in. Even those of us who have known her forever. She keeps everyone at arm's length." He gives a sad shrug and I nod.

"So I shouldn't take it personally?" I say with a smirk. Fred chuckles and shakes his head.

"No, you shouldn't take it personally. And I'd appreciate you taking care to not make it worse." He looks me in the eye with a serious expression. "You're the first man she's been willing to spend time with, so if you hurt her, she may not open her heart again ever."

Fred's stare is intense and genuine. I can tell he's legitimately afraid of how Leena would react to being hurt. I swallow hard as the weight of everything he's said lands on my shoulders.

"I wouldn't hurt her," I assure him. "But I think you're overestimating how much she cares about me. She's pretty adamant about keeping things casual between us." Fred studies me for a minute. He finishes his glass of water.

"That may be. But I haven't seen her light up the way she did talking to you in a very long time." He pats me on the shoulder and stands from the bar stool. "Now, if you'll excuse me, I do believe my wife will enjoy helping me out of this cowboy costume." He smirks and throws me a wink. I shake my head and watch him leave. I'm torn between wanting to gag and hoping I'm exactly like him in forty years.

As I finish my water, I watch Leena pour drinks and chat with Cass as I replay my conversation with Fred. It was Leena's idea to do the whole friends-with-benefits thing. And fuck if it didn't sting. The minute she said it, I realized just how much I want to be so much more with her. Fred's words echo in my head and give me hope we can move beyond casual.

"Hey, sorry! We got so busy all of a sudden. Did Fred leave?" Leena asks looking around the bar for him.

"Yeah, he said his wife would be waiting to help him take off his cowboy costume." I deadpan. She scrunches her nose.

"Oh gross. You did not have to pass along that info." She sticks her tongue out and gags a little. "Blegh, they're like an extra set of grandparents." She shudders and shakes her head. I can't hold back my laugh.

"I didn't think I should have to suffer that image alone!" I laugh. She pushes at my shoulder and I poke her side, sending her into a fit of giggles. I wrap my arm around her waist and she rests her head on my shoulder as she threads her arms around my neck. She lets out a soft sigh as she relaxes against me.

"Rude," she says with a scoff, but I can sense her smiling against my arm. She clears her throat gently. "Cass is going to close out open mic so we can go if you want?" I smile down at her as she lifts her head but keeps her arms around my shoulders.

"Oh yeah? Where are we going?" I meet her eyes and smirk as her gaze instantly heats.

"Your place." She steps away and grabs my hand as she pulls me towards the door, her bag already looped over her shoulder. Once we're out on the quiet street, she turns and raises her eyebrows with a devious look. "There are way too many people here for us to go up to my apartment."

"Really? Why is that?" I feign ignorance.

"I don't want to worry about staying quiet." She declares and her words go straight to my cock. If I wasn't already half hard, that would have done it.

"You know, I think you made the right choice."

"Oh, really?" She smirks back at me. "What do you have in mind? I was clearly talking about listening to some loud music. Maybe doing some tap dancing."

I pull her hand to slow her walking and grab both of her hips. I tug her gently until her body is flush against mine and I can whisper in her ear.

"I was planning on doing my best to make you come so hard that you're screaming my name over and over." She lets out a soft gasp as she holds my gaze. Her body slowly melts into mine. I take a step back and shrug. "But we can always just listen to some music if that's what you want."

She stares at me for a beat and then quickly grabs my hand and practically pulls me towards my truck as I chuckle behind her. She hops up into the passenger seat of my truck and almost closes the door on me. I wedge my body between her seat and the door so that we're face to face. I lean in and kiss her long and slow.

"Are you in some kind of hurry?" I tease. She huffs a laugh and gives my chest a push before taking another slow kiss.

"Shut up and take me home."

My chest squeezes at the thought of her calling my house home, so I hurry to do exactly as she says. I take my girl home.

THE TENSION IN THE air between us is palpable as I drive us to my house. We both steal glances, and the closer we get, the thicker the atmosphere grows in the truck. At a red light about a minute away from my neighborhood, Leena throws up the center console of the truck and buckles herself into the center seat so that her body is pressing against mine. Her hand is on my thigh, and every so often, she turns and presses small kisses into my shoulder.

The zipper of my jeans threatens to leave a lasting mark as my erection tries to push free. As soon as I have the truck parked in my garage and the ignition off, we're all over each other. She swings her leg over my lap and I slide to the center seat so the steering wheel isn't digging into her back.

The long skirt she's wearing rides up her thighs and I move it higher. I run my hand along the outside of her panties and am answered with a moan.

"God, you're so wet for me I can feel it through your panties." She lets out a whimper as I push her damp underwear to the side and run my finger along her slit. "So fucking wet for me, Sunshine."

She reaches for my belt buckle and deftly unbuttons my jeans. Without hesitation, she plunges her hand into my jeans and frees my throbbing cock. She pumps me a few times before I grab her wrist to slow her down.

We need to get in the house before I blow my load all over her like a teenager parked at a scenic outlook.

"Leena, slow down. I don't have any condoms in the truck." She stills and meets my eyes. Her teeth clench on her bottom lip as she searches my face.

"I'm on birth control. I have the implant. And you're the only person I've been with since I was last tested." All the breath leaves my body as I realize she's suggesting that I take her bare.

"I just had my pre-season workup. I'm good too." Now it's my turn to study her eyes. "Are you sure?"

"Yes. I need you inside me. I want to feel you with nothing between us." Her voice is small and vulnerable, but there's a fire in her eyes. I help her remove her panties and she repositions herself over me. She runs the head of my cock along her slit and circles her clit a few times before bringing me to her entrance. She meets my gaze as she slowly lowers herself down and takes me all the way in.

Once I'm seated fully, she rocks her hips and moans softly. I hold her hips steady but let her control the movement as she chases her pleasure.

"That's it, Leena. Use my cock. Ride me."

I drive my hips upward and I'm rewarded with a sharp gasp and a long moan. Her movements get more frantic as I help her lift and drop back down onto my cock.

"Oh god, you're so deep this way."

"Fuck Sunshine. I'm not gonna last much longer." I groan into her open mouth as I try to hold back my orgasm. My balls are tightening and the lightning zinging up my spine tells me I'm close. I drop my hand between us and find her clit. A few quick swipes of that sensitive bundle of nerves and she shatters in my arms. Her pussy squeezes me like a vise as she continues to rock her hips. She lets out a long, gasping moan as she calls my name.

Her orgasm triggers my own and I let out a loud groan as I come harder than I ever have and pour into her over and over. She slumps against my shoulder as we catch our breath. I let out a tired laugh and think back to when steaming up the windows of a car with Leena was just a fantasy I felt guilty about.

"Well, I definitely didn't have car sex on my bingo card for tonight, but I'm not mad about it." She sits up and graces me with a perfect full smile. My chest squeezes and my breath hitches.

I would be perfectly content with spending my whole life making her smile like that.

I WAKE UP SUPER early the next morning but I don't move from my position wrapped around Leena's still-sleeping body. I take a deep breath, loving the smell of my shampoo in her hair. Once we dragged ourselves out of my truck last night, we spent some time in my shower where we went for round two before collapsing, exhausted, in my bed.

Fuck, I'm going to miss her while I'm at spring training. I've never been in a relationship during those weeks before and the anxiety of being away from her is already rising. We're amazing together, but she's so in her head about being in a relationship that she still won't let us label this thing we're doing as anything more than friends with benefits.

What will happen when I'm gone for two months and our only contact is texting and FaceTime? Is she going to pull away and use this time as an excuse to call it quits, or will she miss me as much as I'll miss her?

Leena starts to stir and stretch. I move my hand under the hem of my tee shirt she wore to bed. She lets out a soft hum and presses her ass into my quickly growing erection. I press against her slowly, trailing my hand up to gently pinch her already hard nipple, causing her to let out a low moan. She slept without underwear, so I drift my hand down to find her warm and wet pussy ready for me.

"Mmm, this is a much nicer way to wake up." She murmurs. I let out a chuckle and swipe my fingers through her soaking folds and find her clit.

"I completely agree. God, you're always ready for me." I say in a hushed tone.

"Bailey, please." She gasps.

"Please what?" I tease.

"I need you. Now."

I hitch her leg up and slowly enter her from behind. She gasps and grinds her hips back to meet my painstakingly slow thrusts. I bring my hand back up to toy with her nipples and I gently nip at her earlobe with my teeth. In a steady rhythm, I work her higher and higher until her pussy starts to spasm. I find her clit again and within a few swirls of my fingers on the sensitive nerves, she clenches tight around my cock and comes apart with a low moan.

I don't give her much time to come down as I pull out and move her down to her back. I quickly thrust back home and lock eyes with her.

"Oh god. It's so good. How is it always so good?" She gasps again as I continue to pull almost all the way out and then drive back into her as deep as I can. I hold her gaze as I pick up momentum. The tingle at the base of my spine tells me that my orgasm is on its way, but I fight to tamp it down. I need her to come one more time before we part ways. Her second release is almost there as she's squeezing my cock tight. She closes her eyes as the ecstasy takes over.

"Leena, eyes on me, Sunshine. I want to look into your eyes as we both come." Her eyes pop open and hold mine as we both shatter together.

"Oh fuck, Bailey." She all but whispers, never taking her eyes from mine. We stay connected, searching each other's faces. We share a slow sensual kiss before I pull out and collapse back onto the bed beside her. I pull her over onto my chest and we hold each other in silence for a few long minutes before my alarm blares from my nightstand.

"Ugh, I don't want to get up." She whines into my chest. I let out a low chuckle.

"If I could stay right here with you forever, I would." Her soft gasp tells me she hears the sincerity in my voice. She doesn't say anything in response, but she places a soft kiss on my chest and snuggles further into me. I'll take it as a win that my use of the word forever didn't send her running out of the bedroom.

When my alarm goes off again, I groan and head to the bathroom to start getting ready. I need to drop Leena off at the cafe before I meet up with Dan to catch a ride to the airport. On my way back to bed, where

Leena is still dozing, the small box I'd left on my nightstand catches my eye. I decide to give Leena her present now while she's still recovering from a couple of orgasms. I sit back down on the bed facing her and set the small box between us.

"I have something for you." Her eyebrows wing upwards and suspicion takes over her face.

"What is it?" She asks.

"Just open the box, Sunshine," I say with a roll of my eyes.

She pops the lid and pulls out a delicate enamel key chain with a single key on the ring. The enamel is an image of a microphone and has the words, 'She sings the lyrics that are written on her heart' in script on a scroll of music staff that's flowing around the microphone.

"When I saw the key chain online, it seemed so perfectly you I just had to buy it for you." She nods and smiles softly.

"And the key?" She murmurs. This was the part where I knew I'd have to tread carefully so I don't scare her off.

"The key is to my house." She searches my eyes, trying to uncover a hidden meaning in my gift. "I thought it would be good for you to have a key while I'm gone. You're welcome here anytime. So if you want to use the hot tub or, you know, wear my hoodie and sleep in my bed because you miss me so much, you can make that happen." I nudge her with my elbow, trying to lighten the serious expression on her face. She smirks back at me.

"So I can throw a big rager and test the limits of that fancy built-in sound system of yours?" I bark out a laugh, half in humor and half in relief that she's not freaking out about me giving her a key.

"If you want to." I shrug. "Or you can throw it into the bottom of that suitcase you call a purse, never to be seen again. It's completely up to you." I lean forward and give her a soft kiss before hopping out of bed again to head to my closet.

"Bailey?" she calls after me.

"Yeah?"

"Thank you. I love the key chain... and I'll think about using the key." It's no declaration of love or a promise of forever, but it sure as fuck feels like a step in the right direction. I'll take it.

Chapter Twelve

Leena

I CAN SEE CASS taking another video on her phone out of the corner of my eye. I'm getting suspicious since she's been doing this randomly in the three weeks that Bailey's been away at spring training. She gives me vague non-answers every time I bring it up, so I'm gonna have to do some investigating to find out what she's up to.

I sing the last notes of Christina Perri's "Arms" and turn the mic over to the fraternity boy band that has become a regular at open mic. Tonight they're going with "I Want It That Way" and I appreciate how they don't pick sides in the Backstreet Boys vs. *NSYNC battle since they did the song from the third Trolls movie last week.

I pop behind the bar, ready to take another crack at questioning Cass, when I hear my name from further down the bar. Jessie is waving at me impatiently, so I make a mental note to check in with Cass later and head down to chat with my frantic friend.

"Do you never check your phone?! I've been texting you." She exclaims.

"Hi Jessie, it's nice to see you too," I deadpan.

"Yeah, yeah, yeah. Did you get my text earlier?" She asks urgently.

"No, we've been a bit busy, and I left my phone upstairs to charge. What's up?" She huffs a frustrated breath and rolls her eyes at my nonplussed response.

"What are you doing this weekend?" She demands.

"Umm, probably just hanging around here. There's a new Lucy Score book coming out on Thursday, so that will keep me busy for a day or two!"

It's exactly the way I've spent weekends for the past couple of years, but it suddenly feels empty and lonely. I guess in the short time we've been fake together, I've gotten used to Bailey filling my time in more exciting... and satisfying ways.

She shakes her head and waves me off. "You can read on the plane!"

"Jessie. What plane? What the fuck are you talking about?"

"We're going to go visit the boys in Arizona!" She states with a big grin.

"Jess, I'm not sure that's a good idea," I say cautiously.

"Why not?"

"Well, for one, Bailey didn't invite me!" I exclaim. "He never mentioned me coming to visit him during training."

Jessie gives me a flat stare. "If he had asked you, would you have freaked out about a long-distance visit seeming too serious?"

I blink at her for a long beat. "You know, it's really fucking annoying how well you know me." Jessie laughs and rolls her eyes.

"Bailey knows you too. He wouldn't have wanted to send you spiraling right before he left town for two months! I'm still shocked he gave you the key. And that you've used it. That was a big step, Leena!" She beams at me proudly, and I roll my eyes again. I'm going to have a headache if she doesn't leave soon. I never should have told her I went over to Bailey's house last week. I was missing him and he got a kick out of me FaceTiming him from his bed while wearing very little clothing.

"Ugh fine. I'll ask how he feels about me visiting. Let me just go get my ph—"

"NO!" she practically screams at me. "We're surprising them!"

"Jessie, you have got to be joking. I can't show up unannounced! That's crazy Floozy behavior!" Jessie shakes her head emphatically.

"Girl. No. This is a tradition with the wives and girlfriends of the team! We pick a weekend where we can go to a spring game but also have a day off with the guys and we all fly down. We don't tell them we're coming, so they get a delightful surprise!" She explains excitedly. "I mean, they probably all realize we're coming this weekend because of the game schedule, but it'll still be so much fun!"

"I don't know Jess... Bailey and I are still so new." I say nervously. "What if he doesn't want me there?"

"Have you guys been keeping in touch while he's been gone?" She asks seriously.

"Uh yeah. We text and sometimes call or FaceTime." I don't admit that we text all day long whenever he has a free moment and that we've talked every night since he's been gone.

"So he'll be thrilled to see you in person. Trust me. Plus...I already bought your ticket!" She gives me a devious smile.

"Jessie!" I scold and press my hand to my forehead.

"Babes, I'm not taking no for an answer!" She glances at her phone and hops off her bar stool. "I gotta run, but I'll text you all the details for

Friday! Love you, bye!" I watch as she bounces her way out the door and I feel Cass sidle up next to me.

"What was that all about?" she questions as I let out a deep sigh.

"Apparently, I'm going to Arizona this weekend." Cass gives me a smirk and heads back down the bar to take an order as I make my way to my apartment to mull over our surprise trip. While I'm nervous about showing up uninvited, I can't deny that a big part of me is excited to visit Bailey. I didn't realize just how much I was enjoying his company until he was away for a bit.

What will happen if he gets the trade he wants and moves away? Dread fills me and my stomach drops. How much will I miss his company when this is all over? I'm not sure I want the answer to that question.

FOR ALL MY INDECISION, on Friday afternoon I find myself sitting at the airport gate with five other Ft. Starling Flash wives and girlfriends. Jessie even forced me into a matching Flash WAG shirt to make sure I fit in with the rest of the group. I was pretty sure she would physically put it on me herself, so I complied after only a few minutes of arguing with her. Now I'm trying to distract myself from my nerves by losing myself in reading.

"Hey, girl! Whatcha reading?" one WAG—I think her name is Leslie—asks me as she plops into the seat next to me and pulls out her own Kindle.

"Um, I'm finishing up the Lucy Score book that came out yesterday," I say timidly.

"Girl, me too!" She holds up her Kindle to show me her screen and sure enough, we're reading the same book and that's really all it takes for me to consider her a new friend.

"I love Lucy. She's one of my absolute favorites!" I say excitedly.

"Same! Are you in her Facebook group?!" she asks.

"Oh yeah. I have been for years." I respond, smiling at Leslie.

"Well, it's nice to meet a fellow BRA in the wild." She grins back at me. "You're Bailey's girlfriend, right?"

"Uh yeah. It's still kind of new, so I feel a little awkward surprising him like this." I'm not sure why I confide in her, having just met her, but she has that kind of open and non-judgmental vibe.

"He'll be happy to see you. Just the fact that he's dating you says a lot about how he feels!" She says casually.

"What do you mean?" I ask suddenly on guard.

"He's always said he didn't want to be in a relationship until he retired." She shrugs. "He wanted to focus on his career and didn't think it was fair to whoever he dated. As far as I know, he hasn't had a girlfriend while he's been in the majors."

"Huh. I didn't know that." I mumble with my brow furrowed.

"Guess he just didn't meet the right person before, eh?" She smiles and settles in with her Kindle. I smile back at her and turn my attention back to mine, but I'm not reading. I'm replaying everything she just said about Bailey and relationships.

He suggested the whole fake dating thing. We've been acting like we're in a real relationship. We've said we're actually just friends with benefits, but we definitely talk more than any other friends I have, benefits or not.

Why is he putting in all the effort of a boyfriend if he doesn't date? He said in the beginning that he wasn't interested in a relationship. Did that change?

"Leena!" Jessie's voice pulls me out of my mental spiral and it's pretty clear she's said my name a few times and I didn't hear her. "You okay, babes?"

"Yeah, I'm fine." I wave her off and smile at her, but Jessie knows me well enough to know I'm freaking out. She raises a delicate blond eyebrow and gives me a suspicious glance but doesn't push further, thank god.

We board our plane and get situated in first class as the Flight Attendants pass out champagne. It's not my favorite drink, but the bubbles and dry flavor help to ease some of the nerves bouncing around my stomach.

Leslie gave me a lot to think about on this flight and I spend almost every minute of the four hours considering my non-relationship with Bailey. I'm already in too deep. Should I dive deeper or get out altogether? What happens if I'm in deeper than he is? Am I setting myself up to drown?

When we land, I'm no closer to answering those questions, so I push them from my mind and focus on getting through the next few days. Maybe spending time with Bailey will help to answer some of them.

OUR UBER LETS US out at a small but very nice-looking condo complex. I'm surprised when all the WAGs pile out.

"Do all the guys live here?" I ask.

"They have these three condos here," Jessie explains, pointing to the condo row we're standing in front of. "They're all two bedrooms so they each have their own room, but it's kind of like college all living together during training."

"Oh. That's kind of fun!" I say with a nod. I was aware Bailey was living with Dan during training, but I didn't know his other teammates were their neighbors.

"It definitely is. You'll get to meet everyone this weekend." She smiles and squeezes my arm. Jessie knows I haven't been big on making new friends since I closed myself off after Gram died. But perhaps it's time to try. "Alright ladies. We have about an hour to freshen up and then reconvene here to head over to the bar."

The ladies all nod and start walking towards their respective condos as I follow Jessie to the condo on the left-hand side of the row.

"What bar, Jess?" I ask realizing that I didn't ask many questions about how this weekend would go. "Are the guys not here?"

"Nope, they're in the eighth inning of the game they had today." She grins at me. "Remember, they're not supposed to know we're in town. And you should download their game schedule." She bumps me with her hip playfully.

"I haven't had a reason to until now! I usually just talk to Bailey at night before bed." I say with a shrug, suddenly insecure about being a bad fake girlfriend. I should know his game schedule, shouldn't I?

"Before bed or in bed?" Jessie asks as she waggles her eyebrows.

"I'm not sure what you're implying," I say with a sniff. Of course, I know exactly what she's implying, but I'm not discussing mine and Bailey's virtual sex life with her.

"Sure you don't." She shoots me a wink as she unlocks the condo door.

The guys have a sparsely decorated open-concept living room and they clearly haven't spent time adding personal touches. There's a large TV mounted along one wall with a big plush sectional facing it. A couple of end tables are holding mismatched lamps and there's a coffee table in front of the couch. The furniture's mismatched styles show it definitely wasn't bought as a set, and the walls are bare. There's a long dining table near the kitchen area that seats eight but has no other embellishments. The kitchen counters are bare other than a coffeemaker and a tub of protein powder.

Jessie huffs out a laugh as she takes in the condo. "You can tell they didn't do any more decorating than they had to." She rolls her eyes as she looks around. "Would it have killed them to at least get an area rug?"

I laugh as she echoes my thoughts about the spartan decor. "I can't imagine they care about any of it. Although it's a little surprising since Bailey's house is put together so nicely."

"He probably hired a designer when he bought the house." She explains. "That's what most of the single guys do."

"I didn't think of that." I nod my head and follow Jessie as she climbs the stairs. A full bathroom is in the center of the landing, with a bedroom on either side of it. She points to the room on the right side.

"That's Bailey's room. Dan's over here." She says as she walks towards Dan's room.

"Have you been here?" I ask. She seemed surprised by the lack of decor in the living room, but she knows her way around.

"Not this condo specifically, but they've rented in this complex for the last four years and they always choose the same room setup." She shakes her head and gives me a big smile. "I'm really glad you came with us, Leena. This weekend is going to be so much fun!"

"Well, you didn't give me much choice... but I'm glad I'm here too." I startle myself with that surprising truth. "Now we just hope Bailey is happy I'm here."

"He will be. I'm gonna freshen up a bit and then you can have the bathroom. We'll meet the other girls outside in about 45 minutes."

"Okay. Should I change clothes?" I glance down at myself. I opted for cozy joggers for the flight and I'm wearing the WAG tee shirt Jessie gave me. It's cute with glitter letters for the Flash logo and the v-neckline gives just a peek of cleavage. The back has Bailey's name and number and to be honest, it gives me a bit of a thrill to wear it.

"We're all wearing the shirts to the game tomorrow, so maybe change into something else!" she says quickly. "The bar's pretty casual, so jeans and a cute top with your sparkly Adidas would be good."

I roll my eyes at her uncanny ability to predict what I packed and head into Bailey's room to raid my suitcase. I set my bag down and take a look around the room. Bailey's done a little more decorating up here, but not much. He has a king bed with a soft grey comforter against one wall and another TV mounted in the corner. A long dresser fills the wall next to a decent-sized closet. On the top of the dresser, he's placed an assortment of picture frames.

I study each picture and I find shots of him and his parents, a couple of frames with photos of a young Bailey with people that look like grandparents, and a few photos of him with different teammates in various uniforms with their arms around each other's shoulders and beaming smiles. The nightstand has a frame and when I see the photo, my breath catches in my throat. It's a picture of us from the week before he left. He insisted on taking selfies and it's pretty clear he was planning all along to print one to bring with him.

Why though? He didn't need to keep up the fake boyfriend appearance here in his room. He didn't know that I'd be here. If anything, he would have known this would throw me for a loop. More questions to add to my growing mental list. I shake my head and move to get my clothes ready to head out.

I pull out my favorite boyfriend jeans, a fun peplum top in a cobalt blue that makes my waist look tiny, and of course my sparkly Adidas sneakers. I also grab the new bright pink lacy underwear set that I may have bought when Jessie informed me of this trip and set it out with the other clothes.

"I like where your head's at! The bathroom's all yours!" Jessie cheers from the doorway and I feel my cheeks go red. I grab my pile of clothes and push past her.

"Shut up!" I exclaim as I close the bathroom door, and I can hear her cackling through.

"Thirty minutes, babes!" Jessie yells through the door, still laughing. I take a deep breath and stare at my reflection for a moment.

Okay. Time to get ready for Bailey. I can't quite help the smile that creeps onto my face at the thought.

Chapter Thirteen

Bailey

I CLOSE MY EYES as the Uber bumps into the parking lot of the bar we're hitting after the game. I don't particularly want to be here, but Dan insisted I couldn't bail on the team after our win. While I didn't pitch today, I'm feeling like I'm hitting my prime this season. But tonight I'm in a foul mood. Probably because these bastards are giddy about their women meeting us at the bar tonight.

The ladies like to pretend that it's a surprise trip, but every one of these guys has been counting down the days until their wives or girlfriends visit. It's no surprise that I'm salty knowing they'll all get to spend the weekend with their girls and I'll be stuck just texting and FaceTiming mine. Shit. Mine isn't even really mine. Friends with fucking benefits and a side of fake relationship.

I lean my head on the window next to me. I should probably skip our call tonight, so I don't take this mood out on her. She's trying to protect herself, but Christ, I'm getting tired of not knowing where I stand with her. We talk every night and we text a bunch during the day when my schedule allows it. Does she really still think we're just friends with benefits? This kind of inner turmoil is exactly why I've avoided relationships until now.

The Uber comes to a stop and we pile out. Dan pats me on the shoulder and shakes me a bit.

"Cheer up, man! We won and now we get to go celebrate!" Dan practically yells.

"Thanks, man. I'm just tired." I shrug, hoping he doesn't catch on to why I'm not feeling going out tonight.

"Bullshit. You didn't even pitch today. You're pouting because it's WAG weekend and you don't think Leena's gonna be here." He teases.

I tense at his weird wording and stop to stare him down for a moment.

"Why would Leena be here? Wait. Do you know something?" He shrugs and heads into the bar. I shake my head and follow him. Leena won't even admit to us being more than friends. She wouldn't fly across the country just to see me. Would she?

As we enter, I let my gaze wander around the large bar space. This place kind of reminds me of Leena's cafe and I smile as I see the small stage with a keyboard and microphone set up.

"Jessie baby!" Dan booms out next to me as he takes off towards the corner of the bar. He lifts her off her feet in an enormous hug before lowering her to her feet so he can kiss the shit out of her. I glance around the group of women searching for a particular head of red curls, and my heart sinks. I'm gonna punch Dan for getting my goddamn hopes up.

As I head towards one of the empty chairs, a soft hand grabs mine. I look down and my heart skips a damn beat as I see the gorgeous hazel eyes that I've been missing looking up at me.

"Hey, Bailey." She smiles at me shyly. "I hope it's okay that I'm here."

I pull her into my arms and hold her tight for a long moment so I can breathe in her vanilla and coconut scent.

"Sunshine! Are you kidding me?! It's fucking awesome that you're here!" My heart pounds as I lock my lips to hers and her body melts into mine. When she finally breaks away, I grin down at her and study the beautiful face I've missed so much over the last month.

"I've missed you." I almost don't hear her as she takes the words right out of my fucking mouth.

"God, Leena, I've missed you too. I'm so happy you're here!" I grab her hand and we head over to the table with my teammates and their partners.

"Well, Jessie didn't give me much of a choice, but I'm happy I'm here too!"

Jessie is getting a big bouquet of expensive flowers from me once this weekend is done, that's for sure. Jessie wanders over to us.

"Surprised?" she smirks at me.

"Definitely!" I exclaim.

"Well, that's not the only surprise for the night!" She zeros in on Leena. "It's open mic night!" She waggles her eyebrows and flounces back to take her seat next to Dan. Leena lets out a big laugh and I turn to her.

"Looks like you're doing some singing tonight!" I smile down at her, just so happy to have her next to me.

"Yeah, we'll see if audiences still like me when I don't own the bar." She chuckles.

"They'll love you." *As much as I do.*

Shit. I almost said the second half out loud and I'm not surprised to find that it's true. I love this woman. But she's nowhere near ready to hear it. Will she ever be? Or am I setting myself up for a big heartbreak?

LEENA IS RADIANT AS she takes the stage. She sits down at the keyboard and adjusts the microphone so she can play and sing.

"Hi there everyone! So this is strange for me since I own a bar that also does open mic nights, but that's in Ohio and I'm here in Arizona, so we'll make it work!" She smiles and glances around the crowd. She has such an amazing presence, and the audience has taken notice before she's even sung a note. "This song is one of my favorites by Demi Lovato, and I hope you love it too."

She smiles and stares at the keyboard for a second, taking a moment to breathe and concentrate. When she plays a catchy tune, I realize just how much I've missed being at her open mic nights and hearing her beautiful voice.

Then I listen to the words of the song she's singing, and I freeze in my seat. She's so into the song that she closes her eyes as she plays it. Leena, the woman who, until this point in our situationship, has been completely anti-commitment, is singing about falling in love. Granted, the song is about being terrified of how she feels. The lyric is literally "please don't catch me" and it feels like she's singing it directly to me even though her eyes are closed. She sings the ending line about letting go and giving in to the feelings. She pauses for a beat before her eyes snap open.

Her gaze focuses in on me and a look of panic crosses her face as her cheeks go pink. If I didn't know any better, she low-key forgot I was here listening to her sing those words.

Holy shit. Is this how she feels?

Her terrified expression vanishes, replaced by her usual unbothered poker face. But for the first time, real hope blooms in my chest. Before this weekend I would have sworn that my feelings were one-sided, now I'm not too sure. She flew across the country to see me and now she's singing about love.

I know her well enough to know I need to tread lightly here. If we're going to discuss anything about the lyrics she just sang, it needs to be later when we're alone. She comes back over to the table and I stand up to give her a quick hug.

"You were so great, Sunshine!"

"Thank you," she murmurs shyly, studying my face to see if I'm going to say any more. We take our seats and she downs half her glass of water nervously. Once she realizes that I'm not going to question her about her song choice, she starts to relax and enjoy chatting with the group.

"That was so amazing!" Austin's wife, Leslie, exclaims. "We totally have to do a WAG night at your bar when we get home!"

"We can make that happen!" Leena responds with a smile. "We could even work on a group number. It would be fun, plus we get a lot of Flash fans that hang out on non-game nights so they'd enjoy seeing the team's better halves." She shoots me a wink and smiles. I stay relatively quiet, just enjoying her presence. She fits here so perfectly. It's like she's the puzzle piece I didn't even know was missing.

I catch Jessie's eye across the table, and she gives me a knowing look and a wink. Christ, if Leena and I end up together, Jessie will never let us forget that she's the one who orchestrated it. I smile at her and shake my head. She can gloat all she wants. All I'll ever be is grateful for her matchmaking and meddling.

WE DON'T STAY AT the bar late since we have a game tomorrow, plus any of the guys that have visitors are pretty eager to get them back to their beds for some non-sleep activities. Leena and I share an Uber with Dan and Jessie, who are snuggled up in the backseat with Leena while I sit shotgun. I can't help myself from glancing back at Leena, still so surprised and grateful that she came all this way to see me.

When we get to our condo, Jessie and Dan make a break for his room. Leena and I share a knowing laugh at how quickly they yell goodnight and run for his bedroom.

"Well, I think we know what they're doing. How thick are the walls on these condos?" Leena asks with a chuckle.

"If I remember correctly from last year, not thick enough." I laugh. Suddenly, we hear Dan's TV turn on loudly with the sound of the theme song for The Office and we both burst into laughter. I go to the fridge and grab a bottle of water for me and a sprite for Leena. I hand her the pop and head towards the stairs while she pauses, staring at the bottle.

"Did you want something different, Sunshine?" I ask, realizing that I didn't even ask what she wanted for bedtime.

"No, that is exactly what I want." She says with a note of confusion in her voice. She shakes her head quickly and smiles at me. "You just surprised me by reading my mind."

Her stunned expression makes me laugh. She's so cute when she's caught off-guard. I've noticed that she genuinely seems surprised anytime I show how well I know her. Like I haven't been paying attention to every little drop of information she gives me.

"Well, we did spend a bunch of nights together before training started. You always wanted something fizzy at bedtime, so I just assumed." I shrug. Her gaze meets mine and instantly heats as thoughts of those nights we spent together flood our brains. I take a few steps to where she's standing by the counter, place both of our drinks on the surface, and take her in my arms. "I missed you so much, Leena."

I swallow her gasp as I take her lips in a long, hard kiss. When we come up for air a few minutes later, I rest my forehead against hers.

"Take me upstairs, Bailey." Her gaze burns into mine, and I quickly duck down and toss her over my shoulder. She lets out a yelp as I grab the drink bottles with my free hand and take off for the stairs. "This is not what I meant!" She squeals as she smacks my ass from her upside-down perch.

I drop the drinks on the nightstand so I can give her ass a swat that makes her let out another laughing yelp. I toss her down onto my bed and she's still giggling as she bounces.

"Seemed easier that way!" I shrug and smile down at her. Since the heat of the moment has cooled a bit, I decide to take my life into my own hands and ask about the song lyrics. "So, that song tonight..."

"What about it?" She says evasively while getting up and walking towards her suitcase that is already taking over a corner of my room.

"I don't think I've heard it before. It was a different style for you." She shrugs and busies herself digging in her suitcase.

"Yeah, it's one of Demi's older ones. I heard it on a playlist a couple of weeks ago and decided to get it into shape for open mic." She's trying to act nonchalant about it but she's not making eye contact with me. "I'm going to run to the bathroom really quick."

When she said "run to the bathroom" she meant it as she practically sprints out of my room. I cross my arms, plant my legs, and wait until she comes back so we can continue this conversation. Once she crosses back into my room, she pauses as she sees my unmoving posture.

"What's up?" she says with raised eyebrows, like we weren't in the middle of something.

"The song?" I remind her.

"What song?" she says coyly as she removes her shirt to put a hot pink lacy bra on display. The color is bold, but the lace is sheer enough that I can see her already hard nipples through the fabric. Shit.

"Are you trying to distract me?" I ask warily. She flips the button on her jeans open and slides them down at a painstakingly slow rate.

"Is it working?" She asks with a smirk. She removes her jeans with her shoes and socks and then the little minx turns and bends at the waist under the guise of picking up her discarded clothing. I practically growl at her with her gorgeous curvy ass on display encased in matching hot pink sheer lace boyshorts. My resistance snaps as I grab her at the hips and pull her round ass into my quickly growing erection.

"Yes. But only because it's been weeks since I've been inside you." I whisper along the side of her neck. "My hand doesn't measure up."

Leena turns in my arms and presses up on her toes to give me a hard kiss. She pulls back a bit to give me a devious smile.

"My shower head doesn't measure up to you either." She breathes out. My willpower is completely gone now and I lift her into my arms as I crash my lips down onto hers. I lay her out on my bed and take a beat to memorize the way she looks here. I grab my shirt at the nape of my neck and yank it over my head. I get rid of my belt and jeans but leave my boxer briefs for now.

"I need to taste you." Her only reply is a soft whimper as I slowly peel off the lace panties and toss them to the floor. I kiss my way from the inside of her ankle to her inner thighs. She giggles and squirms as my scruff tickles the sensitive skin of her legs. The giggles quickly turn to gasps and panting breaths as I flatten my tongue and swipe it through her folds.

I find her clit immediately but circle it with my tongue never quite giving her the pressure she needs. Her hips buck, searching for the friction she's craving. I slowly slide a finger into her wet heat.

"So sweet." I murmur into her pussy as I go back to flicking her clit with my tongue. I add another finger as the spasms start to take over. Leena tangles her fingers into my hair as she moans and writhes beneath my mouth and fingers. "That's it, Sunshine, I want to taste you coming on my tongue."

I keep up a steady rhythm, fucking her slowly with my fingers. I latch onto her clit and suck as she shatters. Her pussy clenches down on my fingers so tight it makes my cock harden even more in anticipation.

"Oh god, Bailey. How does it get better every time?!" She gasps. I chuckle and kiss her inner thigh again before meeting her eyes.

"I guess practice makes perfect," I smirk up at her. She smiles back at me.

"In that case, I can think of something else we better practice."

"Is that so?" I ask raising one eyebrow.

"Might as well, right?" She shrugs a shoulder and smirks at me.

I lift away from my position between her thighs and move to remove my boxer briefs to let my cock bounce free. Leena bites her lip as she watches me approach.

"On all fours, Sunshine," I order, and her eyes glaze as she moves to comply. I wouldn't have guessed that my independent, stubborn girl would enjoy taking orders, but I've learned quickly in our time together that she does. "Do you think I should give you a spanking for implying that I need practice giving you my cock?"

She moans softly and pushes her round ass against the hand I have resting on her cheek. I lift my hand and give her ass a loud smack. She moans louder and grinds back into me.

"Did you like that, Leena?" I ask as I rub the area that's turning a gorgeous pink color on her creamy cheek. She whimpers low. "Use your words, Sunshine. Did you like me spanking you?"

"Yes. Please. I need more." She moans out. I give her another slap on the opposite cheek so it matches the pretty pink of the other. I gently push a hand between her shoulder blades to lower her chest to the bed with her ass up in the air as I line myself up to her entrance. I give her ass another hard slap and enter her completely with one thrust. Leena moans loud and her core is already clenching around me.

"Oh, fuck. I'm not gonna last." I groan as I pick up the pace with my thrusts.

"Good. I'm so close." She groans into the pillow under her. I piston my hips faster and periodically give her a sharp swat. Every time my hand connects with her ass her pussy clenches hard around me. My release is right there and I can feel my balls tightening, so I reach around and find her clit with my fingertips. I barely make contact before she explodes beneath me, screaming into the pillow she's pulled into her face. Her orgasm sets mine loose and I pour into her with a loud groan.

We both collapse to the bed to catch our breath. As she recovers, she pushes up onto an elbow to look at me.

"I guess you didn't really need to practice." She grins and pats my stomach. "Be right back."

She leans in to give me a quick kiss, throws my shirt on, and pops out to the bathroom.

We may not need to, but fuck if I don't want to practice with her for the rest of my life.

Chapter Fourteen

Leena

THE MOOD IN OUR Uber on the way to the game the next day is subdued. We're running a bit late so it's just Jessie and I sitting in the back seat staring out our respective windows. I keep playing the night before over in my head. Just how happy I was to see Bailey. How good it felt to be back with him. My accidental musical confession. The way he knows exactly what to do to make my body come apart. My surprising enjoyment of some light spanking. How amazing it was to wake up with him in the morning. My mind is spinning, thinking about it all.

I glance at Jessie as she stares out her window. I know why I'm not feeling super chatty, but it's totally out of personality for her to be so quiet.

"You okay, Jess?" I ask softly. She lets out a deep sigh and shrugs her shoulders.

"Just tired I guess." She says.

"You sure that's it?" I press. Something is going on with her. She meets my eyes and I see hers fill with tears. I reach across the seat and squeeze her hand. "Jessie, what's wrong?"

"Ugh, it's stupid," she sniffs and wipes at her eyes. "Dan and I had a big fight this morning, and I can't quite shake it."

"What was the fight about?" I ask.

"He brought up trying for a baby," she mumbles, avoiding my gaze.

"Isn't that something you've always wanted? Does he not want to?" I ask carefully. As long as I've known her, Jessie has wanted kids. I'm frankly surprised they haven't already been trying. I'm instantly hit with a wave of guilt for not checking in on my friend as much these last couple of years. She huffs out an angry breath.

"Oh, he wants to. He thinks we should start trying now so that the baby would be born in the off-season. Which makes sense, but then I made the mistake of asking if that means he'll be retiring at the end of this season. You know, like he promised he would two fucking years ago when we started having this argument."

"I take it he doesn't want to retire?" I ask gently.

"No. He wants to keep playing and leave me alone with a baby for half the year. There are plenty of baseball wives that are fine with that setup, but it's not what I want! I want us to have a baby together, not just with both of our DNA." She swipes angrily at the tears running down her face.

At a red light, I switch to the middle seat so I can hug her while we drive. I suspected something was up with her and Dan when she was so obnoxiously involved in getting me and Bailey together, but I didn't realize just how intense things were.

"I'm sorry, Jess," I murmur soothingly. "I'm sure he'll come around soon. It's probably just hard for him to let go of playing."

"I guess. I'm just tired of having the same fight." She shakes her head and digs through her purse for her compact to refresh her makeup. "Okay, no more of that! Let's go cheer on our men!"

Our men. Bailey feels like mine, but is he? I made such a big deal about us being casual to protect my own heart, but what if that's why he was willing to keep this going? Maybe a casual fling is exactly what he wants. Leslie made it pretty clear that he hadn't done relationships before, so maybe this really is a friends-with-benefits fake relationship.

That's what I said I wanted. I thought I did. But what if I do want more, after all? My stomach drops to my toes at the thought that I may have set myself up for the exact heartbreak I was trying to avoid.

As our car pulls up to the stadium, I resolve to put on a happy face and cheer for Bailey. I'll be here to support my man while he's still mine and try not to worry about a time when he won't be.

THE VIBE IN THE stadium is surprisingly electric, considering this game isn't even part of their actual season. I look over at Jessie, who's heckling the other team's batter as she snacks on some popcorn.

"I didn't expect this game to be so intense!" I exclaim as our section yells at the umpire for calling the last pitch a ball.

"Oh, come on, Ump! That was a strike!" Jessie screams before smirking back at me. "It's because we're playing Charlotte. The rivalry always gets people riled up!"

"Ah. Got it." I nod, but all my focus is on the handsome man on the pitcher's mound. Bailey looks so serious and imposing as he stares down the batter. His body moves with fluid precision as he winds up and sends the pitch flying straight into the catcher's mitt.

"Strike three. Out!" the umpire declares, signaling the change of the inning. We cheer loudly for Bailey's strikeout. We're seated with the other wives and girlfriends right near the dugout, and as he makes his way over, Bailey finds me in the crowd and smiles. I give him a wave and he shoots me back a wink that makes my heart flutter.

Oh man, I'm in trouble here. Somehow, in a matter of a couple of months, I've gone from being adamantly against being set up to having full-on butterflies when the man winks at me. The thought is overwhelming, and suddenly the crowd around me feels oppressive. I need to escape for a bit.

I clear my throat and tell Jessie I'm going to pop to the bathroom. After taking care of my business in the closed stall, I take just a few minutes to breathe and take in the relative quiet of the bathroom. I hear a couple of feminine voices coming from the sinks, but I'm not paying them any attention until I hear a familiar name.

"Bailey Turner has a girl wearing his name in the WAG section. Did you see her?" The first voice says.

"Oh yeah. Red hair, she's pretty. She's sitting with Dan Chase's wife." Voice two responds.

"Pretty. Pretty lucky. God, he's so fucking hot. Didn't you sleep with him?" My heart catches in my throat as I listen intently for voice one's answer. It couldn't have been recently, right? Bailey wouldn't do that. Luckily voice one puts me out of my misery quickly as she chuckles.

"Yeah, but that was like six years ago. I let him know I was interested in some fun when I ran into him last season, but he told me he wasn't doing the one-night stand thing anymore, so I'm not surprised he's got a girlfriend now." Voice one says.

Through the crack in the stall, I can see her fixing her bold red lipstick. Her long dark hair flows down her back over the Flash jersey that she has tied at her waist over her short denim shorts.

"Damn, the hot ones always want to settle down, eventually." Voice two responds. She's got platinum blonde hair and is wearing a similar outfit as her friend, but with a cute flippy athletic skort instead of shorts. "Luckily, they bring up some new options from the minors every year."

The brunette chuckles and adjusts her boobs in the mirror. "That rookie is a looker. I wouldn't mind giving him some Floozy experience." Her friend laughs as they exit the bathroom.

Once the door closes, I exit the stall and move over to wash my hands. As I'm adjusting my ponytail, the brunette pops back into the bathroom and seems startled to see me.

"Oh! I … uh, left my bag." She murmurs as she grabs her clutch from the edge of the counter. She goes to leave and then changes her mind and turns towards me. "So … um … I'm sorry if you heard what we were saying. We've been Floozies for a while, so we know most of the guys. I swear I haven't even spoken to Bailey since last summer!"

I give her a soft smile. "No worries. He and I have only been seeing each other for a couple of months." I shrug. "I know he wasn't a monk before I came along."

She barks out a laugh. "No, he wasn't, but he was never the biggest man whore on the team either."

"Good to know." I chuckle.

"Thanks for being cool." She says with a smile. "Some WAGs can be really bitchy when they come across Floozies, but most of us would never go after the players that are in relationships. The ones that do just give us all a bad name!"

"I'm new to the WAG club, but I'll pass that info along," I say with a smirk and a shrug. I refuse to judge her for choosing a no-strings approach to the players on the team. It's not that different from the relationship boycott I was living with before Bailey, except that she's getting regular orgasms from professional athletes.

"We all like fucking baseball players, so we at least have that in common," I say with a devious smile. The Floozy's jaw drops for a second before she throws her head back laughing. She's absolutely gorgeous, and I wonder why Bailey turned her down last year. I'm pretty sure I wouldn't kick her out of bed and I'm not into women.

"Omg, that's hilarious. I'm Sabrina, by the way." She holds out her hand to shake mine.

"I'm Leena. It's nice to meet you." We head out of the bathroom and back towards the stands. We part ways when I get to my section. Our guys are still in the dugout as I sit back down next to Jessie, still smirking from my bathroom encounter.

"What?" Jessie asks.

"Oh, I think I just made friends with one of the Floozies in the bathroom. Apparently, Bailey spent some... quality time with her a few years ago," I respond casually.

"WHAT?!" she practically yells in my ear.

"She didn't know I was in the stall and was talking to her friend." I shrug. "She seems nice. Says Bailey turned her down last season because, and I quote 'he wasn't doing the one-night stand thing anymore' so it's not like she's any kind of threat."

"I do believe I tried setting you up with him earlier and you wouldn't let me!" Jessie reminds me. "I knew he was getting ready to settle down." I roll my eyes at her unending gloating.

I shrug my shoulders but think back to when Bailey and I started this whole thing. He told me he wasn't looking for a relationship when Jessie was trying to set us up and what Leslie said seems to track with that. He was hoping to be traded to a team that was closer to his parents. But both Jessie and Sabrina seem to think that he is ready to settle down. The mixed messages are flying.

The big problem here is that none of them know that our relationship is fake and that the whole thing was his idea in the first place. I've been so focused on keeping things casual that I failed to realize that Bailey has never once asked for more. What we're doing seems like a relationship, but when I declared us friends with benefits, he didn't fight to have a more official relationship.

My mind is spinning in circles throughout the rest of the game. I'm not sure what I want out of this thing we're doing. I'm *really* not sure what Bailey wants, but there's no way in hell that I'm asking him until I figure out where I stand.

Jessie's voice brings me out of my mental spiral as she's screaming at the umpire again. She plops back down in her seat.

"So wait, did you say you made friends with the Floozy?" She asks with a sneer, bringing me back to our conversation.

"Yeah. She was perfectly pleasant. Although I get the impression she hasn't had the nicest interactions with player's wives and girl-friends." I reply pointedly.

Jessie scoffs, "Well, yeah. We don't want them all over our guys," she says with disdain. I shrug my shoulders at her and take a sip of my Diet Coke.

"She said most of the Floozies stay away from the players that are in relationships and the ones that don't give the rest a bad name. She was totally cool, Jess." I insist. I'm not sure why I'm hell-bent on defending a woman I just met, but it's important to me. "Just because she'd rather hop into bed with the players instead of marry them doesn't make her a bad person."

"Okay, girl, I get your drift. We shouldn't be slut-shaming the Floozies just because they don't want to settle down." Jessie finally concedes. "We should organize something with them. I'm pretty sure they have their own Facebook group. A charity softball game could be fun. WAGs vs. Floozies!"

"Oh yeah! And the single players could be their coaches while the locked down guys would be ours." I add, getting into the planning of the hypothetical softball game. "I bet I could swing it so that the Songbird is a sponsor!"

We spend the rest of the game throwing out ideas for how we could work with the Floozies. It's fun to just hang out with Jessie without the strife and heaviness of my relationship drama and her issues with Dan weighing us down. Now, if only Annie were with us, it would be a perfect afternoon.

After the game, we meet the guys at a bar to celebrate their win. When I see Bailey from across the room, my heart stutters and all of my insecurities and relationship questions from earlier come flooding back. The joy rushing through me at seeing him smiling at me is laced with a heavy dose of fear. If I let myself want him for real, there's no guarantee that he'll want me back. And I'm just not sure that my heart can take another hit.

I'm not sure of anything.

Chapter Fifteen

Bailey

SHE'S PULLING AWAY. I can feel it. As we're sitting in a bar after our game surrounded by my teammates and their women, she's gone quiet, like she's trying to work out a problem in her head. When I first spotted her across the room, she gave me a sparkling smile, but as I watched her walk towards me, her expression shifted to confusion and panic before going blank. She's smiling and talking but it seems robotic, like all the life has gone out of her.

I'm not sure what happened in those two seconds, but I have to fix it. The more she's here with my friends and teammates, the more I want her to be an actual part of my life. No fake dating, no friends with benefits, just a real, honest relationship. Yesterday, I would have sworn that's what she wanted too, but now I'm not so sure.

She's quiet as we grab a car to take us back to the condo. She changes into pajamas in the bathroom and I slide into bed. As she reenters the room, I wonder for a moment if she's going to run and try to sleep on the couch, but she slides under the covers and, surprisingly, rolls into my arms and rests her head on my chest.

"Leena, is everything alright?" I ask cautiously.

"Yeah, I'm just tired," she mumbles.

"Are you sure? You've seemed off tonight." I take a breath before continuing, "I hope I didn't do anything to make you uncomfortable."

"You didn't! I'm sorry, I'm just a little in my head tonight." She looks up at me and studies my face. "I did meet a friend of yours today, though."

"Oh yeah? Who was it?" I ask, glad to see her perking up a bit.

"She said her name was Sabrina. Apparently, you know her really well." She says with raised eyebrows. I sit up like a shot.

"What did she say?! I swear I haven't talked to her since last summer!" I babble in a panic. "Leena, you have to believe I would never get with a Floozy now that we're together." I run my hands through my hair and gaze closer at Leena's face. I thought at first that she was upset, but I can see now that she's trying not to laugh. As I narrow my eyes at her, she loses the battle and throws her head back, laughing.

"Oh, man. That was hilarious. You were freaking out!" she stammers through her giggles.

"I take it Sabrina didn't say anything bad then?" I ask in an annoyed tone. She's still chuckling a bit and wiping tears out of her eyes. "I'm glad my panic was entertaining for you."

"Don't be mad. I had an entire conversation with a girl you've slept with. I had to at least have some fun with it." I roll my eyes at her but can't help a small smile as she nudges me in the ribs. "She was actually really cool. I overheard her and a friend talking and she was super quick to clarify that you hadn't been together any time recently."

"Good. She's a nice girl, just not the relationship type." I say with a shrug. Leena nods and the mirth that she was so full of a minute ago fades from her eyes. I gather her back into my arms and lay us back down on the bed. My hand drifts from her stomach to the top of her shorts and she grabs my hand.

"Bailey. Um, is it okay if we don't have sex tonight? I'm just so tired and I've got a bit of a headache from being in the sun all day." She says timidly. I instantly bring my hand back up to her stomach and give her head a soft kiss.

"No problem. Do you need anything for your head? I have some ibuprofen and Aleve on the dresser."

"No, I'll be fine. I took Aleve earlier on the way to the bar. I just need to rest." She says as she closes her eyes. "I'm sorry. I know it's our last night before I head home, and I'm sure this isn't how you wanted to spend it."

The worry in her voice has the hairs on the back of my neck rising. Something's not right here. I lower her down to the surface of the bed so that I can hover over her and look directly into her eyes.

"Sunshine. I just want to be with you. Sex or no sex, I'm happy we're here together." She nods and her eyes fill with tears as she avoids my gaze.

"Leena. Look at me." Her eyes flick to mine and she worries her lower lip between her teeth. "Talk to me. What's going on in your head?"

"I'm sorry. This isn't even about you. I guess I'm just not used to no being taken for an answer." She closes her eyes again as a small tear slips down the side of her face into her hair. I go still and swallow hard to contain the rage I'm suddenly filled with. I clench my jaw and study her face.

"Who... did he...?" My unfinished questions stutter to a stop as I can't voice the horrible thoughts running through my head. I clench my eyes tight and fight for control. With my eyes still closed, I stammer, "Ignore me. You don't have to talk about any of this."

Leena's soft hand rests on my cheek and I open my eyes to look down at her. She studies my face for a bit.

"He never forced himself on me, if that's what you were trying not to ask." She says with a sad smile.

"Sunshine. You don't have to tell me." I say as I tuck her wild hair behind her ear and stare into her eyes. "You don't owe me any explanations"

She shakes her head. "I think I need to. Come, lay back down." She pulls me back down to the bed and rolls so that her upper body is draped across my torso. She rests her chin on my chest and looks up at me.

"I was with my ex, Adam, for almost five years. The beginning was good. We were both fresh out of college and having a great time living in Columbus. About three years into our relationship, he even proposed." She swallows hard and I can see that it's difficult for her to talk about that time, but I keep quiet. "Looking back there were red flags. He didn't care about my preferences or opinions, only looking out for what he wanted. Even simple things like ordering a pizza with toppings I liked or knowing what I would like to drink was too much work for him."

That explains her awestruck staring when I did those things after only knowing her for a few weeks. I'd like to wring Adam's neck for neglecting her and I'm certain this story is only going to get worse.

"We were both working to save for a house and planning the wedding when my Gram's health started declining. Once I moved back home to Ft. Starling, the problems really started. He complained I was gone all the time, that I was 'a bummer' to be around, that we didn't have enough sex. He stopped being okay with me not being in the mood." My body tenses and she pats my chest like I'm the one who needs comforting. Like she's reassuring me she's okay.

"Like I said, he never forced himself on me, but he was a master manipulator. He'd beg and guilt me into saying yes. If I gave him any hint of willingness, he went for it. He would tell me I was selfish for not wanting it enough." She pauses for a beat, and I run my hand through her silky hair.

"His gaslighting was constant. If I was upset about something he did, he'd talk me in circles until I was the one apologizing for being irrational. I should have known when Gram didn't want us to move the wedding up so she could attend that she didn't like him, but I turned a blind eye to everything until I couldn't anymore."

I clear my throat softly to ask. "What happened?" I wanted to stay quiet through her tale since this is the most she's ever opened up, but I couldn't help but ask.

She sighs. "He took it too far. He seemed irritated that Gram wasn't dying quicker. He was impatient to have me back in Columbus. My staying in Gram's house after her death annoyed him. The final straw was when he contacted a realtor to come look at her house to put it on the market." Her fists clench and I can sense the fury that still flows through at this memory.

"It had only been a month, and he wanted to sell her house. I was glad for every extra second I got with her, and being there helped me feel close to her once she was gone. When I asked him what he was thinking, he acted like he was trying to take care of me. He said he was just making sure we got the most inheritance that we could. He complained I should be 'over it' because 'it's not like I didn't know this was coming.' Like the fact that she was sick for a while should take away the grief that the one person who had been a constant for my entire life was gone."

"I really hate him. What an asshole." I can't hold back my anger on her behalf. She pats my chest again to soothe the tension in my body as she goes on with her story.

"It was like those words finally snapped me into reality. I slid my engagement ring off and told him that *my* inheritance was no longer his concern and that I'd be happy if I never saw him again."

"Wow. Good for you, Sunshine. I'd still like to punch him though... or hit him with my car." I say, wrapping my arms around her back. She chuckles softly.

"Maybe I shouldn't tell you the rest if it's going to push you to assault."

"There's fucking more?! Jesus fucking Christ!" I almost yell. Leena barks out a laugh.

"Just a bit. He sent me hateful messages constantly for a few weeks. Called me every name under the sun, insulted my Gram, and even admitted to cheating on me on multiple occasions. He blamed me for the cheating since I didn't put out enough. Eventually, I blocked him on everything and I didn't hear from him again." She blows out a breath.

"But years of that kind of emotional abuse took its toll, which is why it threw me for a loop when you were so fine with not having sex. Even now, I'm not used to 'I'm not in the mood' being the end of the conversation. I was mentally preparing myself to be guilted and pressured even though, intellectually, I know that's not something you'd do."

"Never in a million years, Sunshine." I assure her with a kiss to her forehead. She lets out a deep sigh as even more tension leaves her body.

"After everything ended, I spent about a year where I shut down on just about everyone. It's part of why Jessie has been so up my ass. Eventually, when I couldn't take the memories anymore, I sold Gram's house and bought the building to open Songbird."

"Fuck, Leena. I'm so sorry you had to go through all of that." I wrap my arms around her and hold her close. "And if I ever meet your ex, I will absolutely kick his ass. I don't even care. I have plenty of money for bail."

She laughs and snuggles into me. I pull the blankets up around us as we settle in.

"Thank you for sharing all that with me," I murmur, just as her eyes are drifting closed.

"Thank you for listening." She whispers back.

Her soft breaths even out as she falls asleep, but I can't sleep just yet. I'm still processing everything she laid out for me. It explains so much about her and why she was so against getting involved with anyone. Deep down, I know I want to be the one to make sure she never goes through anything like that again.

But will she let me? Tonight was a huge step forward, but I'm afraid of her retreating now that she's opened up so much. One thing's for sure. If she retreats, I'll sure as fuck be the one to chase her.

LEENA WAS STILL PRETTY subdued when she left this morning and now I have to wait fucking weeks until I get to see her again. I throw myself into training over the next few days to keep myself busy and try not to freak out too much.

She shared some huge revelations and I wish she hadn't had to leave so soon after. We've texted and FaceTimed, but things are still stilted.

Three days after she went home, I walk into the gym for my second workout of the day and grab the treadmill next to Dan, who nods his head at me. After a minute of walking, he pops an earbud out.

"Is this your second workout today? Something happen between you and Leena?" He asks, and I raise my eyebrows at him.

"Isn't this your second workout, too?" I point out.

He scoffs. "Yep. Had a fight with the wife over the weekend. I wondered if you were in the same boat." He grumbles.

"I didn't know that! Everything okay, man?" I ask. He gives me a shrug as he furrows his brow.

"Same fight we always have. I think it's time to start a family, but she wants me to retire first, so I'm not on the road when there's a baby in the mix." He says grumpily. I nod and shrug my shoulders.

"It makes sense that she wants you there for it. I take it you don't want to retire?" I ask with a smirk. None of us wants to retire. We'd all play into old age if management, or our bodies, would let us. But it's a foregone conclusion that retirement will happen for all of us, eventually.

"I'm not ready, man. I still have more in me, even if my shoulder hurts like a bitch most of the time. So we just keep circling the problem with neither one of us willing to give in." He shrugs and lets out a gigantic sigh. We walk in silence for a bit.

I get where he's coming from, not ready to give up the game that's been his whole life, but I think it also makes total sense Jessie doesn't want to have a baby while he's still traveling half the year. Hell, until Leena, I didn't want to even attempt a relationship while I was still playing ball. I can't even imagine leaving behind a kid all the time.

"What happened with you and Leena?" He asks, snapping me out of my thoughts.

"I don't know. Things are just weird. She opened up in a big way about her scumbag ex, but now I think she's retreating again."

"That asshole did a number on her, that's for sure. Although with you, I get peeks of her old self now and then." He picks up his treadmill's pace to an easy jog, and I match his speed.

"Why didn't anyone push her to get out of that nightmare sooner?"

He shrugs and shakes his head. "None of us knew how bad it was. We knew we didn't care for the guy, he always seemed kind of fake to me, but Leena kept most of the shit he pulled to herself until it all imploded. And then she shut down on everyone and turned into a shell of herself." We're quiet for a few minutes before he adds. "She's slowly been coming back to life over the last year or so, but I'll say I've seen the biggest difference in the weeks you've been together. She is the most herself when she's with you. You'll work it out."

With that, he pops his earbuds back in and picks up his pace, leaving me with my thoughts. He seems so sure that we'll work it out, but does Leena even want to? She was so adamant about being friends with benefits before spring training started, but since then, so much has happened between us.

Has that shifted her thinking, or does she now see us as just closer friends? Is she even more determined to keep me at arm's length after this weekend?

It's clear we need to have another defining the relationship talk, but part of me, the part that's already in love with her, is scared to find out what she's thinking. I sure as fuck am not going to ask the questions when we're two thousand miles apart.

When I'm home, after our season opener, we'll talk. Just a few weeks to get through. I pick up the speed on my treadmill as if I can make time move faster, too. It doesn't work, but at least when I fall into bed that night I'm too bone tired to stay up worrying.

THE MORNING OF THE season opener, I wake up in a fantastic mood. It's a bright sunny day even if late March in Ohio is still pretty chilly, it's perfect weather for baseball. I always love the start of a new season. Spring training is fun but the energy of the season opener is next level. Plus, I finally get to see Leena today after the game. We haven't seen each other in person since she left Arizona and I'm so ready.

I'm going through my morning game-day routine when I hear my phone buzz on the table. I open it to a text from Leena.

Leena:

> Break a leg today! (I know that's for theater and not
> sports but I think it still works!) I know you'll do
> great today but I have a little bad news. I'm super
> sick with a nasty cold and I'm not going to make it
> to the game. I'll be cheering you on from my couch
> as I dip in and out of consciousness though!

I stare at the text and read through it a good ten times. She's not coming to the game. Is she really sick? Her text seems normal, but is she actually avoiding me? It seems like too much of a coincidence considering how we left things in Arizona, but would she would straight-up lie?

Me:

> I'm sorry you're sick, Sunshine! I'll come over after
> the game. Do you want me to bring you anything?

Leena:

> Don't worry about me! You should go out with the
> team after you win today! Celebrate the new sea-
> son! Plus, I don't want to get you sick. Cass dropped
> off some soup and Gatorade yesterday so I'm set.

So she's not coming to the game and doesn't want me to come over. I set my phone down and stare at my kitchen wall, thinking of the best way to respond. Maybe she is sick and just wants me to have a good day with my team. She could really be worried about passing on whatever bug she has. Either way, I need to focus on the game today, so I type out a response.

Feel better, Sunshine! Let me know if you end up needing anything!

Leena loved a message

I set my phone down and go back to my late breakfast of Cheerios with banana slices and a side of bacon—the same breakfast my mom used to make me on game days. Thinking of my mom, I decide to FaceTime her.

"Happy season opener, Bailey Boy!" my mom says with a sing-song tone as her face fills my phone screen.

"Thanks, mama!" I respond with a smile at her decades-old nickname.

"Your dad's here too!" She says, swinging the camera around but still not landing it on my dad. I smile at the shot of her kitchen table and shake my head at her technology issues.

"Hey buddy, how's the arm feeling?" I hear my dad yell from off-camera. "Babe, you have the camera aimed at the table." He says softer to my mom. He helps her fix the camera and they both come into view.

"It's good! I think it's gonna be a good season." I answer.

"Of course it will!" My mom practically cheers. The thought crosses my mind of just how lucky I am to have my parents. Leena never really got to know hers and with her Gram gone, she doesn't have any blood relatives left. Not a second after the thought crosses my mind does my eagle-eyed mom catch my change in expression.

"What's wrong Bail?" She asks softly.

"I was just thinking about how lucky I am to have such great parents!" I say, trying to cover.

"And that thought made you sad because...?" I roll my eyes at my mother's ability to still read my mind at age 32.

"I was thinking that not everyone is as lucky." I clear my throat and look away.

"Are you thinking of someone in particular?" Her voice goes up in pitch. "Are you seeing someone?!"

I smile and shrug my shoulders. Leave it to my mom to turn a quick hello call into an investigation into my love life.

"I have been seeing someone. For a few months now, actually."

"Oh, my god!" she squeals. "Jim! He's finally got a girlfriend! Thank God!"

Do I have a girlfriend? We've never used the actual labels, and that hasn't bothered me before, but now it feels weird. The only label Leena's thrown out was friends with benefits, but that doesn't feel like it fits. It never really did.

"Tell me everything about her! Where did you meet? What is she like? When will you be getting married and giving me grandbabies? When can I meet her?!" She fires questions at me rapidly, not giving me a chance to answer any of them.

"Whoa, mom, slow way down. It's still new, and I need to head into the stadium for the game. I don't have time for a full inquisition right now." I tease.

"Ugh fine, I guess I'll let you go to do your job. At least tell me your girlfriend's name before you go?" She demands.

I smile and answer, "Leena, my girlfriend's name is Leena."

"Oh, I can't wait to meet her." She exclaims, putting a hand to her heart. "Tell her I said hello when you talk to her next! And good luck today! We'll be watching the streaming thing your brother set up for us when he was home for Christmas!"

"Thanks, mama, talk soon, love you!" I call, giving her a big smile.

"Love you too, baby!" She practically yells.

I hang up my phone and get my bag ready to head out to the stadium with our conversation ringing in my ears. Leena's been skittish about relationships, and I've tried to be respectful of that, but it's time we had an actual conversation about where we stand. Leena sure as fuck feels like my girlfriend. I want her to be and I can't keep doubting and guessing whether she's in this. Later tonight I'm going to find out the answer, but right now I have a ball game to win.

Chapter Sixteen

Leena

I'M PRETTY SURE I'M dying. Am I exaggerating? Absolutely, but I also can't remember a time that I've ever been this sick. My head is killing me. I can't breathe because my nose is all clogged and my lungs are tight in my chest. Plus, when I stand up too much, I get all dizzy and weak. I haven't left my apartment in days.

I'm huddled on my couch with the Flash game on the TV. The game I should fucking be at. Bailey looks so good, all handsome and focused. I do my best to stay awake, but I keep zoning out and the next time I'm able to focus, we're another couple of innings along. The Flash are dominating the team from Chicago and I'm fucking missing it thanks to this stupid plague.

I could tell Bailey was disappointed when I texted him earlier. I tried so hard to get up and moving this morning. I wanted to be at his game so fucking badly. I managed to get out of bed to shower, but then had to lie back down after and just couldn't find the energy to get the rest of the way ready. There was no way I'd make it to the stadium, let alone survive the entire game.

After about the fifth inning, I get a second wind so I decide to Face-Time with Annie.

"Whoa. What's wrong with you?" She asks as she sees my face. "You look like death."

"Gee, thanks. I appreciate that." I deadpan and she chuckles.

"Sorry babes. I call it like I see it. I take it you're not at the Flash game?" She asks sarcastically.

"Nope. I feel worse than I look. I've been half comatose ever since I attempted a shower this morning." I croak out in a whiney voice. "I'm pissed. Bailey is finally back in town and here I am with the fucking cold from hell."

"So it sounds like things are going well with him?" She smirks.

"Yes. Or they would be if I could see him. Also, if I can stop running my mouth about the past." I say as I press a hand to my forehead.

"What do you mean?" she asks, confused and I groan, embarrassed all over again for the emotional dump I took in Arizona.

"I told him all about Adam when I visited him at spring training. I spilled my guts about everything that went down. I'm half surprised he didn't make a run for it right there after I unloaded all of my baggage on him." I was so nervous after that weekend that he would realize I wasn't worth the effort of digging through all of that, but so far, he seems to be taking it in stride.

"Everyone has baggage babes," Annie says matter-of-factly. I huff out a laugh and she adds, "Some more than others..."

"That's an understatement. I have a whole freaking cargo hold's worth." I snark back at her.

"And the right person will help you carry it," she says softly. I shrug and roll my eyes even though her words make my heart clench, hoping she's right.

"So, what's new with you?" I ask, desperate to change the subject.

"Not much of anything. If I'm not working, I'm attempting to squeeze in a tiny amount of sleep, food, or exercise before I have to go back to working." She says with a deep sigh.

"Are you at least still liking the job?" I ask, worried about her again.

"I don't even know. I mean, I like the numbers and finance side of things, but there's so much pressure from the bosses to bring in more clients and bigger clients. There's always some drama or competition going around the office. I guess I miss being able to have a life."

"That's fair. Work-life balance is important. I'm worried you're going to burn out." I say. "Maybe you should take some time off? You could come home for a visit and I could freak out about my relationship in person." I whine as she laughs.

"I have no idea when I'll be able to take some time, but I'll try to pencil in more FaceTime bitch sessions."

"I'd appreciate that," I say sincerely.

I focus on the game for a second right as the camera zooms in on Bailey, jogging out to the mound. I let out a deep sigh. God, he's so hot. And sweet. And amazing in bed. What the fuck is he even doing with me?

"Something you want to share with the class?" Annie pipes up.

Shit. I low-key forgot we were still talking.

"I got distracted by the game," I say casually.

"Uh-huh. I turned the game on here when we started chatting. You got distracted by that hunk of man candy that you've been dating." She teases.

"I can neither confirm nor deny what distracted me." She laughs, knowing I'm full of shit. We watch the game together for the last couple of innings.

"Did the announcer just say the one guy wants to 'come inside' the other?" I ask Annie with a snicker.

She laughs. "Yeah, and then the other guy just 'went deep'!" Soon we're both cackling over the innuendos that the announcers can't seem to resist.

"How did I not notice how pornographic baseball is before?!" I laugh, trying to catch my breath. "Maybe it's the fuck ton of cold medicine I took."

"It's a possibility, but I don't know what my excuse would be?" Annie responds. "Exhaustion and an 80-hour work week?"

That only makes us laugh harder as the game's final inning wraps up. The Flash win 7-2 for a great start to their season.

"I miss you, Annie Lou. We should do this kind of thing more often." I murmur, officially losing steam now that the game is over.

"I miss you too, and I agree," she says, smiling. "Now you should probably go back to bed and get some rest. You look like you're about to fall over."

"You're not wrong, I'm fading fast over here," I confirm

"Night Night, Leena. Get better!" She says as she hangs up the call. I close out my phone and turn off the TV. I manage a quick bathroom break before collapsing back into my bed to pass out.

MY HEAD IS POUNDING. I open my eyes to glance around my dark apartment when the pounding starts again. Wait. That pounding is coming from the door. I turn on the lamp next to my bed and hobble over to the door. I open it to find a certain gorgeous man standing on the other side and I almost wonder if I'm still dreaming.

"Hey, Sunshine. How you feeling?" Bailey says with a soft smile. I poke him in the ribs to make sure he's there. The hard muscle under my finger confirms that he's real.

"You're really here!" I smile and shuffle forward, linking my arms around his waist. I try to breathe him in, but since my nose is still so stuffed up, all that does is start a coughing fit. I wave him inside while stumbling towards the fridge for the Gatorade Cass had brought me.

"Did you think I wasn't real there for a second?" He asks, chuckling.

"I thought I might be hallucinating from all the cold medicine in my system," I reply, collapsing back into my bed. "Plus, aren't you supposed to be out celebrating your win? I watched most of the game when I could keep my eyes open."

He ditches his shoes and jacket and strips out of his jeans before climbing into bed with me. He wraps me up in his enormous arms and snuggles in.

"I missed you too much. Plus, you weren't responding to texts, so I got a little worried."

"Ack, I'm sorry. I passed out hard once the game was over and there wasn't this sexy guy in baseball pants on my screen anymore." I say.

"Oh really? Which guy was that?" He asks with a grin.

I shrug. "I don't know. I'm pretty sure he plays for Chicago," I respond teasingly. Bailey huffs out a laugh and pinches my side to tickle me.

"Rude," he snaps playfully and I laugh, but that causes another coughing fit. After a long drink of Gatorade, I snuggle back into Bailey's chest.

"Hmm. I'm glad you came over." I murmur into his shirt. "I missed you."

He kisses the top of my head. "I missed you too. Wish you weren't sick, though. I don't like that I can't fix it."

"You're making it better just by being here," I tell him honestly. "Although I'm going to feel super guilty if you get sick now!"

"I'll take my chances." He murmurs into my hair. We're quiet for a few long moments before he speaks again.

"Leena?"

"Uh-hmm?" I say half asleep.

"Can I tell you something?" He asks with a very serious tone of voice that makes me instantly nervous.

"Yeah?"

"When you texted me this morning, I wondered if you were faking being sick to avoid me. I can see now that you weren't, but I was afraid you were using the time we spent apart to retreat from whatever this is we've been doing." He confesses.

It stings that he would doubt me like that, but I also don't blame him since I've been so skittish on the relationship front and things were admittedly weird after our visit.

"I know I was awkward after that last night in Arizona. I'm still kind of embarrassed that I unloaded all of my baggage on you." I shrug, unsure what else to say.

"You have no reason to be embarrassed. If anything, it made me feel closer to you. Like I could understand you better knowing some things you'd been through." He says sincerely. "Which leads me to my next topic."

I tense at his tone, going serious again. Is this where he says he's done? That he doesn't want to deal with my emotional cargo?

"I don't want us to be fake dating or friends with benefits or whatever other vague situationship we've been doing anymore." He says seriously.

My heart drops. I saw this coming, but fuck if it doesn't sting.

"Oh. Okay." Tears spring to my eyes. "Umm. So we'd what? Be friends? Tell everyone it didn't work out?"

He pulls back so that he can see my face better and a look of panic crosses his face.

"Shit. No. I'm sorry, I didn't say that right. I want us to be in a real relationship. I want you to be my girlfriend." He clarifies quickly. "I want us to be together for real."

"Oh! Really?" I ask, not quite believing what I'm hearing.

"Yes really. I ... care about you, Leena. I missed you constantly while I was at training camp. We should give this a real shot. I know you didn't want to be in a relationship, but I think we owe it to ourselves to at least try. And I think we already do all the relationship things, we'd only be changing the label. And just for us, everyone else already thinks we've been together for months because we kind of have when you think about it. So we just get rid of the rules that we haven't been following anyway and—"

"Bailey!" I interrupt his adorable babbling. I don't think I've seen him get nervous like this in the whole time we've known each other. "I care about you, too. We should try being officially together. You make me want to try being in a relationship again."

He lets out a huge breath, and his whole body relaxes with relief. I chuckle softly.

"Did you think I would say no?" I ask curiously.

"I wasn't sure where your head was at. The last time we talked about anything like this, you screamed 'friends with benefits' at me and ran." He says teasingly.

"Hey! That was a solid couple of months ago. And I freaked out!" I laugh and nudge him with my elbow. "Although, I'm going to be pissed tomorrow if I wake up and this was all a cold medicine fever dream."

He laughs and kisses my forehead. "I promise it's real, Sunshine. I'll remind you in the morning if I have to!" He flips the bedside lamp off and snuggles back into bed with me. "Now get some sleep so you can get better. I want to take my girlfriend out on a proper date soon."

Already half asleep, I murmur, "That would be nice." Then I pass out in my real boyfriend's arms and there's nowhere else I would rather be at this moment.

"I'm going to my first Flash home game tomorrow!" I say happily into the microphone, finally back to doing open mic after almost two months of being down for the count. The cold from hell turned into an upper respiratory infection and then into a lovely bout of pneumonia. It's taken forever for my voice and lung capacity to recover.

Of course, as soon as I was recovering, Cass managed to catch the same virus and was down for the count for weeks too. I stepped in to manage Songbird while she took time off to get well. Now, after almost two months of Bailey and I being in an official relationship, I'm finally getting to see him pitch a home game in person.

I spent most of April trying not to cough up a lung and not doing much more than lying in bed or on my couch. Bailey's been so busy with the travel of the season that we haven't seen much of each other, but when we are together, things are amazing. When we're apart, we text and FaceTime as often as we can.

I still can't quite shake the dread of waiting for the other shoe to drop, but I've never been in a relationship that's gone this well. Even in the early days with Adam, there were red flags I ignored. There were signs that should have clued me into what kind of man he was if I had cared to see them. So far Bailey and I are solid, which is why I've chosen another light and cheerful song to kick off open mic night.

"I don't know if everyone knows, but my boyfriend is the starting pitcher for the Flash, so I'm pretty excited to be going to the game." I smile and glance around the room. Most of the crowd is regulars, so there's not much surprise at my announcement. "Most of you know how much I love Sara Bareilles, so I thought I'd give you one of her rare happy songs!"

I launch into "The Light" and think about Bailey the whole time. Everything feels like it's back to normal in the best way. Cass is still sneaking videos of me when I sing happy songs like this. I've noticed that she doesn't bother when I sing one of my favorite sad songs. I still don't know what she's up to, but frankly, I've been too happy to be suspicious.

I finish my song and introduce Fred singing Shaboozey's "A Bar Song" decked out in his cowboy gear again. The crowd loves him and is singing along. I smile and shake my head at the old man before plopping myself onto a bar stool. Cass pours me a water and I smile up at her.

"You seem happy these days," she says, assessing me. "I noticed you referred to Bailey as your boyfriend in front of everyone. Going public like that is a big step."

"I know, but I'm tired of keeping things secret," I say tentatively.

"Makes sense," she nods as she mixes a drink. "How's that going, by the way? I only have vague memories of you telling me about your relationship status while I was delirious from the plague you gave me."

I huff out a laugh and shake my head at her nonsense.

"I said I was sorry! Plus, Bailey spent multiple nights with me while I was sick and didn't catch it, so really it's your own immune system's fault that you picked it up during a grocery drop."

Cass rolls her eyes and goes on with our conversation as if we didn't take a detour.

"I was concerned when you were burying your feelings under fake labels and avoiding anything real, but an actual relationship seems like a good step. You deserve to find love."

"Whoa, slow down. We've only been dating for a couple of months. Love still seems like a pretty big jump." I say, my stomach clenching in knots.

"Leena. This isn't going to work out if you're not honest with yourself," Cass huffs. "Stop hiding from your feelings. Because if I didn't know better, I'd say you're already in love with Bailey. And if you can't be honest with yourself and him, you shouldn't be doing this. You'll just end up hurting both of you." She shrugs and walks away like she didn't just drop a bomb on me.

Agreeing to an actual relationship to see where it goes was one thing, but being in love? Love leads to talking about the future. It leads to the discussion of forever. I'm so not ready for anything like that. I like how things are right now. I don't need anything to change. Just having a boyfriend is change enough for me.

I swallow down my panic and focus back on the open mic performances, hoping to distract myself from the fear that I can feel breathing down my neck.

Chapter Seventeen

Leena

I'M GLUED TO MY seat at the game. No one in our section has moved in several innings. I'm gripping Jessie's hand as Bailey takes the mound in the bottom of the final inning of the game. The WAG suite at the game is tense with excitement and no one is speaking much. All the tension comes from the fact that Bailey is a half-inning away from pitching a perfect game.

Jessie explained it to me when our section started to get excited during the sixth inning and I did a quick Google search since Jessie didn't want to elaborate too much. Superstitions are strong with this crew, so none of us have so much as thought about running to the bathroom or grabbing food from the suite's buffet line while Bailey's pitching.

I've noticed no one is so much as mentioning what he's doing for fear of jinxing him. After doing the quick research and discovering just how rare throwing a perfect game is, my nerves are a mess. I want this for him so badly that I'm shaking. I've never been much of a sports fan, but I can certainly see the appeal from the sheer amount of adrenaline that is coursing through my body.

From my seat, Bailey looks so calm, so self-assured. There hasn't been a moment in this entire game that he's seemed anything other than at total ease. Any time the camera pans close to him, he's got a smile on his face like he's having the time of his life. Fuck if that's not incredibly sexy. I'm nervous for him and unbelievably turned on.

I suddenly understand the Flash Floozies on a deeper level. The high of cheering on your team of hot, muscled athletes is a powerful aphrodisiac. I can understand why they're ready to jump any of the player's bones. I'm just focused on the one gorgeous man in baseball pants that I'll be going home with tonight.

My body doesn't seem to know what the fuck is happening as a wave of nervous nausea hits me. Bailey's just managed his first strikeout. Only two more to go.

"Oh, my god. I might puke." I murmur to Jessie as I grip her hand.

"I might join you. I'm so fucking nervous and he isn't even my boyfriend." She whispers back.

"Strike three. You're out!" calls the umpire. One more strike out with no hits and the game will be over and Bailey's name will go in the record books. I'm already so fucking proud. Thank god I was here for this game. I'd never forgive myself if I had to watch this one on TV.

"Okay. This is it." Jessie whispers.

"I don't know if I can watch," I whine, wanting to put my head under a blanket or something, but I don't dare take my eyes off Bailey.

"Strike one." Sweat drips down my back.

"Strike two." I tense literally every muscle in my body and will the baseball gods to smile on Bailey.

"Strike three. You're out!"

The stadium erupts. Our suite of wives and girlfriends goes absolutely nuts. We've just witnessed baseball history, and it's our guys who will be in the spotlight. My guy. The rush of adrenaline and relief that hits me is so intense that I can't hold back the actual tears as Jessie and I hug and scream and jump up and down.

Other WAGs come to give me hugs and say how proud they are of Bailey. Some of these women have known him for years and I can see how happy they are for him. Down on the field, the guys are in a big huddle with Bailey at the center. The camera keeps zooming in on his face and he has the biggest smile. I'm so beyond happy I was here for this. No matter what happens between us, this day will live in my memory forever.

JESSIE AND I WAIT in the lounge outside of the locker room entrance with the other WAGs. Everyone is still so hyped up from the perfect game. We've had a little time to refresh our makeup and empty our bladders, so we're a cheerful group of chatty partners when the guys trickle out.

Finally, Bailey leaves the locker room and everyone gathered starts cheering. My breath catches in my throat as his eyes find mine and suddenly I'm crying again as I race towards him and leap into his arms.

"There's my good luck charm!" He murmurs into my ear. I pull back so that I can kiss the bejesus out of him. My body melts into his as his tongue teases mine.

"I'm so fucking proud of you!" I exclaim when we finally detach. "That was incredible to watch! I'm pretty sure I'm gonna be on an adrenaline high for the next month!"

He laughs and lowers his forehead to connect with mine. "I'm so glad you're here. I swear you're good luck." He smiles down at me. Our hands intertwine as we make our way out to his truck so we can head to the bar for the celebration.

When we arrive at the bar, it's complete madness again as the room is filled with Flash fans. Everyone is cheering for Bailey and offering congratulations. We settle in with drinks and enjoy an afternoon of laughing and chatting with his teammates and their partners. I have to admit that this is the happiest I've been in a very long time. Possibly ever.

I'm sitting next to a wonderful, kind, and talented man. His friends and teammates are great people and their partners have welcomed me so thoroughly to the WAG club. For the first time since I lost Gram, my life seems almost complete. My heart feels healed. It's like I'm taking full breaths again and I feel fucking alive.

It's kind of like that moment in the movie version of *The Wizard of Oz* when Dorothy steps out of her sepia-toned house into the colorful world of Oz. I'm seeing in color again.

All thanks to Bailey.

I watch him as he's talking to Jessie across the table and it hits me that Cass was totally right. I'm in love with him. I wasn't even sure it was possible for me to love someone again. I was so broken for such a long time that I thought I'd lost that ability, but here it is. It's exhilarating but also fucking terrifying. Loving him means he has the power to destroy me completely. More than Adam ever did. So now I just have to trust that he won't break me.

As he senses me staring at him, he finds my gaze and holds it. I suddenly want him so badly I don't know if I can stand to wait. My desire must show in my eyes because his eyes darken as they meet mine.

"You ready to head out?" He asks quietly.

"Yes. Let's go home." He holds my eyes for just another moment before we stand and say quick goodbyes.

WE HUSTLE TOWARDS HIS truck as we leave the bar, both of us hurrying with the same purpose in mind. He helps me up into my seat and gives me a hard and quick kiss before rushing to his side. The tension is thick as he drives us to his house. Neither of us speaks as we let the anticipation rise. Today's adrenaline is back in full force.

When he parks in his garage, I don't even wait for him to open my door. We're both out of the truck like a shot and heading inside. As soon as he closes the door, we're crashing together. Our pace is frantic as we yank at each other's clothing. There's no finesse, no slow stripping, just a frenzy as we race to uncover bare skin.

We make our way down the hall to his bedroom, where we break apart to remove the last pieces of our clothing. Bailey lifts me and tosses me onto the bed as if I weigh nothing. I bounce a bit, but Bailey follows quickly and ranges his body over mine. He takes my mouth in an all-consuming kiss. I can feel his hard, velvety erection pressing against my clit. I'm already soaking wet and ready for him.

"Bailey." I moan into his mouth.

"Fuck Leena. I can't wait. I need to be inside of you." I let out a moan at his words. "Sunshine, I don't think I can go slow."

"Bailey, fuck me. Now. I want you so bad." I say breathily. He growls into my ear as he reaches down to line himself up to my entrance. With one hard thrust, he seats himself fully. I arch into him as he waits just a beat to allow my inner walls to adjust to his size. "Bailey. Move."

He bursts into motion as he pulls back and thrusts again, hard. He pistons his hips, driving his deliciously hard cock into me over and over. My orgasm builds higher and higher with every stroke. Bailey slows, only to lift one of my legs onto his shoulder, deepening the angle.

"Oh god, I'm so close. Don't stop." I whimper as his pace turns frantic. My moans turn to screams as he pushes my other leg up, hitting a spot so incredibly deep that it shatters all thought. I feel my core spasm and clench as I come apart under his talented body.

My orgasm triggers his, and he goes over the edge with me and we come apart together. He stills and lets out a loud groan as pours his release into me. He collapses back onto the bed and pulls me with him. We stay connected for a long moment as our heart rates and breathing return to normal.

"Holy shit. I'm not sure I've ever come that hard." He murmurs, rubbing a gentle hand down my back. His other hand tunnels its way through my hair as he studies my face. I give him a big smile.

"I know I haven't. That was ... I don't even know how ... I'm pretty sure that orgasm scrambled my brain." I say dazedly. He chuckles and smiles down at me.

He opens his mouth like he's going to say something and then closes it. I consider asking what he was going to say, but before I can, he kisses me deep and long. He helps me up and out of bed so we can get cleaned up in the bathroom.

He turns the shower on to heat up as he grabs towels and pops them into the towel warmer he has next to the shower door. When steam is coming from the huge rain shower head, he grabs my hand and leads me into the massive tile shower.

Chapter Eighteen

Bailey

THIS IS THE BEST day of my life so far. I started the day already pumped that my girl was finally going to be in the stands for a home game. Then I pitched the game of my fucking career. It still feels a bit like I'm dreaming. Perfect games are so rare, I would have never even dreamed of setting it as a goal for myself and now that game will be on my record forever. My name will go in the baseball history books as one of the few pitchers to throw a perfect game.

And now here I am with the perfect girl, the woman of my dreams. Leena is so gorgeous as she follows me into the shower. Her cheeks are still pink from the first round. Somehow, the sex just keeps getting better. I don't think I could ever get enough of her, but I'm sure as fuck going test that theory.

I pull her under the rain shower head and run my hands through her fiery hair. I pull her hair back to tilt her face to mine so that I can slant my lips over hers. Our kiss is slow and exploratory, the opposite of the frantic pace our earlier round took. I follow the trail of water down her jaw and along her neck.

She scrapes her nails down the front of my abs, exploring each divot. Her attention makes my muscles clench and my cock quickly hardens again as she takes it in her small hand. She pumps me a few times before she drops to her knees in front of me. We've been together for months, but this is the first time she's knelt in front of me like this. It will not take me long to come with her looking so gorgeous on her knees for me.

I sweep the wet hair out of her face as she makes eye contact and slowly circles her perfect pink tongue around the head of my dick before sucking it into her warm mouth. She runs her tongue around the tip again and then flattens it as she takes as much of me into her mouth as she can fit. She swallows as I feel my dick hit the soft flesh at the back of her throat and then pulls back, only to do it all over again.

"Oh fuck, Leena." I groan and grip her hair. I turn her head to get a better angle as I thrust gently into her mouth. She moans and reaches up to tug at my balls, and I can already feel the tingles shooting up the base of my spine. "Sunshine, I'm gonna come."

I start to pull away, but she grips my hips hard and sucks harder until I can't control it and I'm pouring my orgasm into her waiting mouth. She swallows again and licks every drop of my release off of my still-hard cock before she gets to her feet. I lower my head and rest my forehead against hers while attempting to slow my pounding heart and catch my breath.

"Jesus Christ, Leena. I wasn't expecting that." I pant. She smirks at me.

"That makes it more fun." She says with a devious smile.

"You're incredible." I smile down at her. "I...I'm so glad you were there today." *Fuck*, that's the second time tonight that I almost told her I loved her. I do, but I'm pretty sure that it's not something she's ready to hear. Things have been going so well between us these last couple of months. I don't want to freak her out now.

We stay in the shower, soaping each other up and making out until the water runs cold. We dry off quickly as the exhaustion of the day hits us both. All the adrenaline is fading from my body, leaving me bone-tired. I collapse into my bed as Leena finishes getting ready.

Leena puts her hair in a long copper braid and finally joins me in bed wearing one of my Flash tee shirts. I wrap her in my arms and inhale the soft coconut scent of her shampoo that now lives in my shower. Someday soon, I'll tell her how I feel. Maybe I'll be able to convince her to move in so we can fall asleep like this every night. I drift off, thinking about how great it would be to fall asleep with her in my arms forever.

A FEW DAYS LATER we have a day off, so I go to get a quick workout in before I meet Leena for a late lunch. We're supposed to hang out before open mic night at Songbird tonight. After my workout, as I'm getting dressed post-shower, Coach Murphy sticks his head into the locker room.

"Turner! Harrison wants to see you in his office." He barks out and walks away. Usually, it's not a good thing to be summoned to the team owner's office, but I'm guessing it has to do with the perfect game on Saturday. I finish getting dressed and grab my stuff before making my way through the stadium to Zack Harrison's office.

Zack's only about ten years older than me and we've known each other for a long time. I give his door a couple of quick knocks and crack it open. Coach is sitting in one chair in front of the desk while Zack sits behind the desk. I walk over and shake Zack's hand before taking a seat in the second chair.

"Coach said you wanted to see me?" I ask getting this meeting going.

"Yeah, Bailey. First, congratulations on Saturday's game. It was fucking incredible to watch." He says sincerely with a kind smile.

"Thank you. It was pretty incredible." I say, still riding the high of the game. He nods and sits back down behind his huge executive desk.

"Thanks to that perfect game, you're something of a hot commodity now," he says, furrowing his brow.

"What do you mean?"

"In the off-season, your agent had been seeking trade options. Is that right?" He asks.

"Yeah. I wanted to be closer to my family out west. But nothing came of it and I'm happy I stayed here in Ft. Starling." I explain.

Zack studies my face for a moment. "Well, it looks like those teams that your agent reached out to before are falling all over themselves to offer trade deals now." He shakes his head. "We have several high-dollar deals that are on the table."

My stomach drops. Fuck. Throwing a perfect game was supposed to be a good thing and now I'm going to be traded?

"Oh. Are you trading me?" I ask, swallowing hard. Zack leans back in his seat and crosses his arms.

"Some deals are pretty good, but I'll be honest, I'm not too keen on letting a pitcher like you go, so we're also offering you an extension contract." He raises his eyebrows and pauses before adding, "But I don't want to stand in your way if you want to move to one of these teams. I'm leaving the choice up to you. There's big money—we're talking millions in the triple digits—on the table for both of us if you go, but I really think we could be World Series-bound with the team we've got going now."

"I see. Can I have some time to think about it?"

"I can give you 72 hours. Just pop in before the game on Friday." He says tightly.

"Okay, thank you." I stand to leave, and both Coach and Zack stand as well. Zack reaches to shake my hand.

"We'd hate to lose you, but I understand wanting to see your family more. I moved home after college for that exact reason. Let me know what you decide." He gives me a smile and sits back down in his chair.

"I will. Thanks again." I say, stunned.

My head is swimming with indecision as I make my way out to my truck. Six months ago, this would have been a straightforward decision. I could move home and see my parents more than a couple of times a year. But six months ago, Leena wasn't in the picture.

Could I really move away from her when we're finally in such a good place? What if I asked her to go with me? Would she want to? Talking to Leena has to be my first step. She'll help me talk it through and we can decide together what our next steps should be.

I WALK INTO SONGBIRD to find Leena sitting at the keyboard playing a slow song. She's focusing on the piano part and not singing anything, so it must be a new one she's learning. She sees me heading towards her and a huge smile breaks across her beautiful face.

"Hey, Sunshine," I say, smiling at her as I grab a chair and move it near the keyboard. "Whatcha playing?"

"Oh, I'm just messing around with some new songs." She smiles at me. "How was your workout?"

"It was good. And then I had a meeting with the team owner." I say, working up to tell her my news.

"Is that a good thing or a bad thing?" She asks. "Is it like going to the principal's office?"

I bark out a laugh. "Sometimes it's a bad thing, but not this time. Or not all bad, I guess." I say carefully.

"Oh yeah? What did he want? To sing your praises and bow down at your feet?" She teases and smirks as I shake my head.

"Not exactly. It turns out he's been offered some trade deals for me after Saturday's game. Apparently, the teams that my agent was talking to at the beginning of the season are interested now." I say quietly.

Leena goes still with tension. She swallows hard. "Oh. That's great! That's exactly what you wanted, right?" She asks in a small voice. I can see the wheels in her head turn as she tries to figure out what this means for us.

"It was. He left it up to me whether I go or stay here. There's a lot of money on the table, but he doesn't want to lose me to another team." I say cautiously.

"But you want to move, right? That's what you said when we first met." She says slowly.

"I did. But that was before we started dating. Things have changed for me." She stands quickly from her chair to move behind the bar. She fiddles with glasses and garnishes. She's purposely avoiding my eye and I start to get a sick sensation in the pit of my stomach. "What's going on in your head, Sunshine?"

She closes her eyes and stills for a moment. When she opens her eyes, she's giving me the blank expression that I've learned means she's shutting down her feelings.

"We haven't been dating all that long. You can't make a decision this big based on us—on me." She says flatly. The turmoil in my stomach intensifies.

"No, we haven't, but what we have is special enough to be a factor," I say carefully. "Don't you think?"

"I don't know. That's a lot of pressure to put on a relationship that's still pretty new." She practically whispers. "This is everything you've been working for. You can't just give that up because we're together."

"We've been together for months. I'm in this." I'm afraid of going down this line of questioning but knowing that I need to. "Are you saying you're not? Do you see a future for us?"

"I'm saying it just seems too early to be answering that!" She answers, exasperatedly. "I mean, what if you stay for me and then this fizzles out in a month or two? Then you'll be stuck here for no reason."

I brace my hands on the bar in front of me, trying to keep hold of my temper, but it's not working. After everything we've been through, she still isn't all in. I'm still more invested than her, and that stings. I don't say anything, so she continues on.

"I don't want to hold you back. I-I can't, it's too much pressure. So maybe ... we should just let it go now." She swallows hard once and then, as if I'm watching a robot take her place, she shuts down. Her shoulders stiffen and the emotion leaves her face. She's shutting me out. I've lost her and it pisses me off.

"You were always going to have one foot out the door, weren't you?" I say in a sharp but quiet tone. She stares at the bar, not moving. "There was always going to be something, wasn't there? Some reason for you to bail? If it wasn't this trade deal, it would have been something else. Anything to keep you from experiencing emotions, correct?"

She continues to stare blankly, and it's pretty clear that she's done talking. My heart sinks realizing she was always going to find a way to back out of this relationship. It was only a matter of time and instead of seeing that from the beginning; I let myself get caught up in her. She told me she didn't believe in happily ever after and I chose not to believe her.

"Are you not going to say anything?" She slowly looks up at me. There's nothing on her face. No expression, no feeling.

"I'm sorry." She whispers.

"Me too," I say as I turn and walk out of the Songbird Cafe, leaving my heart behind shattered on the bar.

WHEN I GET BACK to my house, I don't even bother turning on the lights. I sink onto my couch and stare at the ceiling, trying to figure out what to do next. I still have to decide on the trade deal. A big part of me wants to take it just to get away from here, but that seems like a shitty way to decide something that will affect the rest of my career.

After about a few hours of sulking and sitting in my now dark living room, I hear a knock at my front door and my heart leaps into my throat. Hoping Leena's changed her mind and she's ready to fight for us, I race to the door flipping on lights as I go. When I get to the door, I deflate as I find Dan standing on the other side with a case of beer.

"Hey, man." He says as I let him in. "Thought you could use some company."

"I take it you heard Leena, and I broke up," I grumble as I flip on a light in the living room and grab the beer from him.

"Something like that." He says. "Jessie's at the bar now with her."

"I'm surprised she even cared enough to call Jessie over. When I left, she was like a robot. Completely shut down." I press my hands to my eyes to erase the last image I have of her blank face.

"You know that's not Leena, though, right?" He asks. "She's freaked out and was protecting herself from it."

I just grunt a response and crack open a beer. Dan grabs one for himself and settles into the other end of my couch.

"So what am I supposed to do? Just wait around forever until she's ready to be in a relationship?" I ask, exasperatedly.

"Nah, dude. You did the right thing walking away. If she's gonna decide to be in this, she's the one who has to make the leap." He says. "You put yourself out there, but she's got to meet you halfway."

I think about that for a minute. Did I put myself out there? I didn't tell her I love her. I implied I saw a future for us, but I didn't elaborate on what that future looked like in my mind.

"Ugh, I'm so fucking pathetic," I grumble.

"Eh, you're just in love. Either she'll pull her head out of her ass or you'll both move on." He says matter-of-factly. Like it's all so simple. "Now, should we talk about this trade situation?"

"I still don't know what I want to do. I don't want to take the trade just to escape the awkwardness with Leena, though. If I take it, it has to be for me." I say.

"That's a good point. What made you want to be traded in the first place?" He asks carefully. I hadn't told any of my teammates that I had been thinking about moving. Dan has been my closest friend for years and I feel a pang of guilt for not letting him in on my plans.

"I was thinking it would be nice to live closer to my parents. I hate only seeing them a couple of times a year. My brother and his family are on the East Coast, so my parents are kind of on their own and I'd like to be able to help out more." I explain. "Plus, I'm just tired of being on my own. I want family around."

"I get it, man. That's part of why I'm getting anxious to start our own family. Neither of us has many relatives, so I'm ready to put down some real roots." He says quietly. "Of course, I like to think of the Flash and all their wives and girlfriends as a big extended family. You're a part of that, you know?"

"I know. And I'm grateful for it, but I don't know... I don't know if it's enough." I swipe a hand down my face. "I think I'm gonna go to bed now. I'm ready to be done with this whole day."

"Okay, I'll head out." He shakes my hand and gives me the obligatory bro hug before heading towards the door. Before leaving, he adds, "For what it's worth, I'd be bummed to see you leave. But I know you gotta make this call based on what's best for you in the long run."

"Thanks, Dan," I say with a sad smile. He gives a quick wave and heads out the door to his car. I'd miss Dan if I moved teams. And all the Flash players that I've become close with over the last eight years. I add that thought to the mental tally I've started to keep and head to my room to get ready for bed.

I turn out all the lights and crawl into my bed, which seems giant and empty without Leena in it. I wait and hope for sleep to come, but I toss and turn as I keep replaying everything from the day. This fucking day. It started so amazing with a gorgeous sleepy Leena in my bed. I can still smell her coconut vanilla scent on my sheets. My workout was great. The pitching practice I did went awesome. Then everything went downhill from the moment Zack and Coach told me about the trades.

Right around midnight, I hear my phone buzz on the nightstand and for the second time tonight, my heart leaps at the thought of Leena reaching out. Instead, I find a message from an unknown number.

Unknown:

> Please don't give up on Leena. I know she was shitty today and that she's been holding back from you. But that doesn't mean she doesn't feel the way you do.

Me:

> Who is this?

Unknown:

> It's Cass. I know it's probably not my business, but as the person who knows exactly how everything started, I can't just let it go without asking you to not give up on her.

Me:

> She's the one that gave up. I can't force her to reciprocate my feelings.

Cass:

> You don't need to. Here. Watch these in order. Listen to the words, but make sure you also see just how much happier she gets as time goes on. That's because of you. Then watch the last one from tonight. I think you'll see her feelings are strong. She's just afraid of them.

She sends a link to a Google Drive folder. It's filled with videos and from the thumbnails, I can tell they're videos of Leena from open mic. The dates go all the way back to when we started fake dating, with the most recent one being tonight.

I get what Cass is trying to do but I'm way too drained to watch the videos now, so I click my phone screen off and go back to trying to sleep.

I'll watch them when I've got a little more clarity about what I'm doing and a little less heartache.

Chapter Nineteen

Leena

IT'S BEEN A LITTLE over 24 hours since I fucked everything up and I'm sitting at the bar watching Cass clean glasses. She said she needed my help in the bar, but considering there's only a handful of people here on a Wednesday afternoon, she was lying. I'm sure she just wants to keep an eye on me instead of letting me sulk and cry alone in my apartment. I hear the door open and a very familiar voice calls out.

"Excuse me, but can I get an extremely stiff drink please?" I whip my head around to find Annie standing in the doorway. I'm off my stool like a shot as I practically tackle her in a hug. I burst into tears all over again, so happy to see my best friend.

"Hey, babes. Jessie told me the cliff notes version of what happened. It'll be okay." She pats my back reassuringly.

"What are you doing here?" I ask through my tears.

"I told you I need a drink. I've had *a day*." She rolls her eyes and plops onto a bar stool. I stare at her until she continues, "Oh, you mean in Ft. Starling. My mom fell and wrenched her knee so badly that they decided to go ahead and do the knee replacement that they had planned to do next year. They released her yesterday, so I drove down to help get her home."

"What!? Why didn't you call me? I could have been at the hospital for you!" I exclaim and sink onto the bar stool next to her.

"It's alright. As soon as she called me after her fall and told me the plan for surgery, I started moving things around so I could take some time off work." Her expression darkens at the mention of work. "I needed some time off, anyway. Jessie filled me in on what's been going on around here and it felt like fate."

"I'm so glad to see you," I say with a watery smile.

"So. What the fuck happened?" She asks. "Last I checked, things were good with Bailey?"

"They were. They so were. I fucked it all up, Annie." I whimper as the tears start back up. You would think a full day of near-constant tears would cause me to run out, but so far, that is not the case.

"Jessie told me what happened. But I want to know why?" she asks gently.

"I don't even know. I panicked. All this time he hasn't mentioned moving away again and then he brought it up like he wanted me to tell him what he should do and I choked." I exclaim.

"It sounds like he wanted your input. He wasn't breaking things off, was he?" she asks.

"No. He was talking about a future." I practically wail. All the emotions I've been keeping to myself are letting loose now that Annie's here. It's like a dam has broken and all of my true feelings are rushing out. "I got overwhelmed and freaked out and I shut down. I acted like I didn't care at all. Oh god, Annie. He looked so hurt."

"Obviously, you care. Do you want to be with him?" She asks as she stands and wraps her arms around me.

"Yes. I think I love him." I choke out through the tears. "But it's too late. I messed up."

"Have you talked to him at all?" She questions delicately, pushing my hair out of my face. Cass hands a tissue to me across the bar and I attempt to mop the tears flowing down my face.

"No. What would I even say? I'm sorry I was chicken shit? Please love me?" I exclaim, exasperated.

"I mean, it couldn't hurt!" She reaches across the bar and hands me another tissue. I huff out a laugh. Because it absolutely could hurt. It could break me apart. "Leena, how many romance novels have you read?"

"You mean like this year or in general?" I ask, confused by her change in topic.

"I wasn't looking for a literal number. More to point out that you read a shit ton of romances and what does one character do when they've totally fucked up but want to win the other character back?" She asks slowly, waiting for me to get what she's saying.

"Umm, a grand gesture?" I ask tentatively, seeing where she's going with this.

"You bet your sweet ass a grand gesture. So the question is, do you want to fight for Bailey?"

I stare at the bar top for a long moment. Fighting for him means putting myself out there in a way I never would before. But if the last day is anything like how it will feel to not have Bailey in my life, I know what I need to do. I can't just let him go.

"Did you have something in mind?" I ask, and Annie gives me a huge smile.

"I've called in reinforcements. We'll figure it out!"

AN HOUR LATER, I'M sitting at the bar with Cass, Jessie, Annie, and Fred. Fred came by to give me some cookies from Gail and to check in since he was here for my spectacular meltdown at open mic last night. He stayed to help us figure out my grand gesture to win Bailey back, even making a few phone calls to help arrange some of the logistics.

Fred hangs up his phone. "Okay, everything's all set. Zack's tech guy will email me specs for the video." He says as he takes a bite out of the pizza we ordered.

"Thanks, Fred. Thanks to all of you. I couldn't do this without you and I'll really need all of you if this blows up in my face." I say with a sad smile. It's a good plan but I'm still scared that it won't be enough.

"It's not going to blow up in your face!" Cass says. "Besides... I... laid some groundwork before I knew you were going to grand gesture him." She shrugs and takes a drink of her beer.

"What do you mean you laid some groundwork?!" I ask, suddenly on alert since she's not making eye contact.

"Well... I've been taking a few videos of you doing open mic. Particularly on nights when you would sing happy love songs." She says, tentatively.

"Yeah...?"

"Um, I sent him the videos. All of them. Plus the one I took from last night." She gives me a guilty smile.

"YOU WHAT?!" I practically yell. "Cass!! Why would you do that?!"

"You were devastated. I just thought I'd suggest that he shouldn't give up on you." She shrugs.

"So…he's seen those videos…but he didn't reach out or anything." I close my eyes and I swallow hard. "Which means… he's probably done with me for good."

"You don't know that!" Annie pipes up.

"Yeah, for one, he might not have watched the videos! He just has access to them. Or he might need to process them a bit," Jessie adds.

"Oh god, maybe this grand gesture is a mistake," I say on the verge of tears.

"It's never a mistake to tell someone your true feelings. Especially if you love them." Fred says quietly. He clears his throat softly before adding, "Leena, you've lost more loved ones than most people your age. You know better than most that life is short. This may not work out the way you want, but you won't regret making sure Bailey knows you love him. Your Gram would tell you the same thing."

Tears spring to my eyes as I think about what Gram would say about all of this. She never particularly liked Adam, but I can almost imagine what she would have said about Bailey. She would have told me to "lock that man down" a long time ago. I take a deep breath and nod my head as I get my emotions under control.

"You're right, Fred. She would hate that I shut him out like I did. She would tell me I need to make it right." I say with a sad smile.

"Lizzie always wanted to make sure you were happy and taken care of. Having seen you with the boy these last few months, I think she would have loved him." Fred smiles. "She probably would have said something inappropriate about his ass and told you to marry him."

That makes me laugh out loud because Fred is not wrong. My Gram loved pointing out handsome men and ogling celebrities and athletes. She was a huge flirt and would have been obsessed with Bailey. This is the right thing to do. I will tell Bailey exactly how I feel about him and the rest will be up to him.

"Alright. We're doing this. Now someone take my mind off of it before I stress myself out even more!" I say through a watery smile.

"Would you like to hear about how a man I've despised for 12 years saw me in just a tee shirt and underwear this morning?" Annie says with a snarky tone.

"WHAT?!" Jessie and I yell at the same time before I add, "Why didn't you start with this information when you first got here?!"

Annie shrugs. "We were in crisis mode. I wasn't gonna bring up my mortifying morning."

"Girl, spill!" Jessie demands.

"Ugh, do you remember Eric Reynolds? Scott's freshman roommate?" She asks.

Do we remember? Oh man, do we remember. Jessie and I share a look and I can tell we're both thinking the same thing. Annie's constant battling with her college boyfriend's roommate was a huge topic of discussion between the two of us for that entire year.

"Uh yeah, we remember him," I confirm with a smirk.

"Well, it turns out he's a physical therapist."

"Oh yeah! He works with the guys on the team sometimes." Jessie adds.

"He also does some in-home PT for people who have had surgeries. And my mother neglected to tell me he would be in our house this morning." She covers her face with her hands. "So I went in to check on her in just my sleep shirt and undies, and there he was."

"Oh, my god! What did you do? What did he say?" I ask doing my best not to laugh at her predicament.

"Well, my mom freaked when she saw me and was like, 'Annie put on some pants we have company' but then Eric said, 'it's nothing I haven't seen before. Annie here used to spend plenty of time in my dorm room in less clothing than that.'" She sighs before adding, "Which, of course, led to my mother demanding an explanation."

"Oh my," Jessie murmurs.

"Yeah." Annie deadpans. "So then I had to stumble through an explanation that Scott was his old roommate and that I would hang out in their dorm a lot. Eric couldn't resist insulting me before I stormed out."

Annie rolls her eyes with a huff, and Jessie and I share another knowing glance.

"What? What was that look?!" Annie demands.

"Um, well, back in college we thought that you and Eric would get together..." Jessie explains.

Annie lets out a horrified gasp. "Are you fucking joking?!" she snaps.

"It's just you were always sniping at each other and complaining about him," I explain.

"Plus, the sexual tension between you too could be cut with a knife," Jessie adds.

"WHAT?!" Annie practically yells, and Jessie and I both snicker at her horrified tone.

"We always thought that the fighting would eventually turn into you jumping each other's bones," I say with a shrug and a laugh.

"Oh, my god. Well, that would never happen. I can't stand him and he hates me."

Jessie and I share another smirking look. I shrug and raise my eyebrows at her.

"Never say never!" I say. "After all, I swore I'd never put my heart on the line again and I'm about to spill my guts in front of thousands of people."

And just like that, I'm back to being nervous about what I'm about to do tomorrow afternoon. But it's a good nervous. A hopeful nervous. I'll just have to cling to the hope that Bailey will forgive me for the next 48 hours, and then after that I'll know for sure what my future holds.

Chapter Twenty

Bailey

FRIDAY MORNING I HAVE no more clarity or less heartache than I did three days ago. I pitched yesterday but my heart wasn't in it and Coach put in a relief pitcher in the fifth inning. I probably won't pitch today since I'm later in the rotation but I get up to start my game day routine, anyway. I do my quick warm-up workout, make my breakfast, and decide it's time to loop in my parents on the decision I have to make. The FaceTime rings through and my dad's face fills the screen.

"Hey there, son. Getting ready for game day? Think you can throw another perfect one?!" He asks with his chipper teasing tone. He glances more closely at my face on the screen. "Jesus, Bail, you look like shit. Everything okay?"

My mom's voice starts up in the background. "What's wrong? Is he sick? Did something happen?" The screen wobbles as she comes to sit next to my dad. Once she's in the frame, she gasps. "You do look terrible, sweetie. Are you sick? What's going on?!"

"Umm, well, I have some news. I might take a trade deal that would let me move closer to you guys." They both stay quiet for a bit. They share a glance before my dad clears his throat.

"Is that what you want to do?" He asks.

"Yeah. Or at least it was before this season started," I respond quietly.

"Uh-huh. What about Leena?" My mom asks simply. I let out an enormous sigh. I press my fingers to my temple to ward off the headache I already feel approaching.

"What about her, Mom? She's not... a factor anymore." Just saying those words is like a stab in my gut.

"Does she not want you to go? Did she give you an ultimatum?" Mom digs. I knew she would, but it still stings to talk about.

"No, pretty much the opposite. She said it was too much pressure to have our relationship be a factor in my decision, so she took herself out of the equation and broke things off. It's obvious that I cared more than she did." I choke out bitterly. My parents share a long glance but stay silent. When neither of them speaks up, I lose patience.

"Guys what? I can see you doing that mind-reading thing. Just say it." My mom clears her throat and comes back with something I never expected.

"Bailey, did you know that in college, I broke up with your father for one summer?" Mom asks.

"What?! No! You guys have never mentioned it." I exclaim. My mom presses her lips into a tight line.

"Well, it's not something I was very proud of. Your dad started to talk about getting married after school was done and, for some reason, I panicked. I thought I needed time on my own to experience life. Instead, I experienced three miserable months traveling alone through Europe and missing him. All the places I wanted to visit and things I wanted to do that summer, I realized I would have enjoyed them more if he were there with me." She takes a sip of her coffee.

"When we came back for our senior year in the fall, I begged him to forgive me. I told him I realized what an idiot I had been, and that I had just freaked out about the future. He was kind enough to give me another chance and we've been together for thirty-seven years since then."

"Mom, what does this have to do with me and Leena?" I ask, pinching the bridge of my nose.

"Do you think maybe she just panicked? You came to her with a huge career decision and that could seem similar to bringing up marriage. You wanted to factor her into the next several years of your life. That could freak out someone who's in a relatively new relationship." She suggests gently.

I'm quiet for a few moments as I take in what my mom is saying. Was Leena just scared that I was asking her to make a big decision about the future?

Shit.

I didn't tell her I love her because I was afraid of spooking her. Did I do exactly that by wanting her input on the trade deal? Did I dump a ton of pressure on our relationship and then get pissed when she panicked?

"Fuck. I might have messed this up." I groan into my hands. Mom chuckles.

"It sounds like you kids need to have a real, honest conversation." She says smugly.

"Yeah, I think you're right. I'm gonna go over to her place after the game today and see her."

"I think that's probably a good plan, bud. Tell her the whole truth if you want her to do the same," my dad encourages with a soft smile. "If you wait for her to say it first, you may never hear what she's thinking. Especially since she seems skittish. Sometimes you have to take the risk."

"Ugh, I know. I ... I thought about telling her I love her several times, but I always held it back because I was afraid." I admit, sheepishly.

"Yeah, that lack of communication will get you every time," he chuckles. "So, what are you going to do about the trade?"

"I don't know. The offers are big. They'd set me up for a long time even when baseball is done, but I'm just not sure I'm done playing for the Flash. We've all gotten really cohesive playing together this year and I like the culture of the team," I explain. "On the other hand, I don't love living so far away from you guys. I want to be around to help you out as you get older."

"Jim, I'm pretty sure he's implying that we're elderly," my mom scoffs. Dad laughs too and shakes his head.

"Whatever you do, decide based on what you want and where you see your career going. We're still quite young and mobile. Besides, we've been toying with the idea of moving towards you and Griffin. You're only one state away from each other, so we might just move there. Don't factor us into your decision!" My dad smiles. "We'll cheer for whatever team you play for."

"You guys are really thinking of moving here?" I say, surprised. I didn't know that was an option. They both nod and shrug.

"Just an idea we've been toying with," my dad says.

"We miss our boys and our grandbabies," Mom interjects. "And if we had even more grandbabies on the way, that would be a done deal..."

I shake my head and her shameless grandbaby fever. We're a long way from that since Leena shut down at the mention of a vague future together. I'm pretty sure we'd find a Leena-shaped hole in the wall if I brought up the idea of giving my mom more grandkids.

"Mom, you don't even know if we're going to get back together!" I say, shaking my head at her.

"You'll work it out. I have a good feeling about her," she says, smiling.

We say our goodbyes and disconnect the call. Before I finish getting ready for the game, I know there's one more thing I need to do.

It's time to watch the videos Cass sent me.

I SET UP MY iPad on the coffee table and queue up the first video. This one is dated back in early February before training camp. We were still doing the friends-with-benefits nonsense, but here's Leena singing a Taylor Swift song about love beginning again. Each video has similar vibes. Happy songs I've never heard her sing.

They're all originally by her favorite artists. Sara Bareilles, Christina Perri, Anna Nalick, Taylor Swift, Demi Lovato, and of course, several Broadway tunes make appearances. Why did she never sing these songs when I was there? I attended a ton of open mic nights and she always chose her infamous sad songs. Did she save the happy and hopeful songs for nights I was absent to avoid getting my hopes up? Or was it because she was afraid to show me how she really felt?

The sentiment in the songs progresses from being afraid of falling in love and trying to avoid it to straight-up love songs. The second to last video is "The Light" by Sara Bareilles and it's a declaration of wanting to be together forever. She performed that one the night before my perfect game. Is that what she was thinking that night we were together before everything went wrong?

Finally, I come to the last video. This one's date is the day shit hit the fan. I can see the second she pops onto the screen that she's miserable. Her face is red and puffy like she'd been crying. She croaks out the name of the song, another Sara Bareilles song called "Breathe Again" and clears her throat before she starts playing.

Fuck. This one's a breakup song. It's haunting, and she looks like she's in so much pain singing it. When she gets to the bridge where the lyric is literally "it hurts to be here" the tears start but she doesn't stop singing. She has her eyes closed and there's not a doubt in my mind that she means every one of these words.

I understand why Cass sent me these videos. Any doubts that Leena shares my feelings are gone. I take a deep breath and check my phone. Fuck, if I had time I'd go and find her right now, but it's already time for me to head to the stadium. As soon as this game is over, I'm going to find her, though. I'm going to win back my girl. But first, I have to go see Zack and give him my decision.

I'M ANXIOUSLY WARMING UP at the side of the dugout as I hear the pre-game entertainment get started. I don't even need to be warming up yet since I'm not first up in the pitching rotation today, but I can't sit still. If I could bail on the game altogether and go straight to Leena's, I would. After we stand in a lineup for the national anthem, I go back to sit in the dugout to wait out all the other ceremonial shit. Dan comes over and gets my attention.

"Hey man, you may want to come watch this video." I give him a confused look since there's not usually a video before the game starts, but follow him anyway to where I can see the huge jumbo screen. Suddenly, Leena's beautiful face fills the screen. My heart trips in my chest at the sight of her. What the fuck is happening?

"Hi there Flash fans! My name is Leena and I'm the owner of the Songbird Cafe here in Ft. Starling. Mr. Zack Harrison was nice enough to let me share this little video so that I could make sure everyone's favorite pitcher knows exactly how I feel about him. This song was originally by Christina Perri and it's called 'The Words' and it sums up most of what I want to say."

She plays a beautiful song that flat-out says she's in love. She loves me. My heart pounds like it's going to burst out of my chest. God, I don't want to wait out this game. I want to race over to Songbird to make sure that she knows I love her, too. I'm coming out of my skin with the urge to find her.

I don't move though. I can't take my eyes off the video on the screen. When the song is done, the stadium goes crazy. My chest swells with pride at the thousands of people cheering for my girl. The crowd volume ramps up and at first, I think they just enjoyed the song, but then I see her.

Leena, my Sunshine, is standing on the pitcher's mound holding a baseball. She's wearing jean shorts and her Flash WAGs shirt I know has my last name written across her shoulders. Her eyes are wide as she takes in the crowd and tugs on her shirt. She is so far out of her element and she's never looked more beautiful.

I'm frozen in place until I hear the announcer asking me to meet her on the mound. Dan's firm clap on my shoulder snaps me out of my daze and sends me racing across the field to get my girl.

Chapter Twenty-One

Leena

THIS PLAN IS INSANE. Not for the first time today, I feel like I might throw up. I'm standing on the pitcher's mound and staring at thousands of screaming baseball fans. The crowd loved the video, but I only care about one man's reaction.

My gaze scans the dugout, but I don't immediately see Bailey. Did he see the video? Oh shit. What if he didn't even see it and I'm standing out here for no reason?

The announcer comes on over the loudspeaker. "Ladies and gentlemen, help me welcome local business owner Leena Mitchell to throw out the first pitch. Ms. Mitchell has let me know she may need some guidance on how to throw the ball and is requesting our own Bailey Turner join her on the mound."

I stand frozen on the mound and grip the baseball tightly. I wait, every muscle clenched in panic, to find out how Bailey reacts to my grand gesture. Finally, after what feels like hours but was probably just a few seconds, my breath catches in my chest and my eyes fill with tears as I see Bailey run out from the dugout with a big grin on his face.

He barely even slows down as he grabs me off the pitcher's mound and crashes his lips into mine. A sob of relief escapes from my chest and I cling to him. I don't care if thousands of people are watching us. It's such a relief to be held in his arms. I can't believe I almost lost him. I pull away, needing to look into his eyes.

"I'm so sorry. I panicked and, instead of talking to you, I shut down. I love you. I think I've loved you for a long time." I say, searching his eyes for proof that he's going to forgive me. He presses a hard and quick kiss to my lips.

"I think I've loved you since the moment I followed your voice into your bar. And I'm sorry too. I put all this pressure on you and then got mad when you understandably freaked out." He lowers his forehead to mine as he holds onto me.

"I don't care where you get traded, I'll go with you. If I have to follow you all over the country opening new Songbird locations, I will, as long as we're together." I say, and I mean it. I am all in and I refuse to let my fear and baggage get in the way of us again. He grins down at me.

"That's good to know, but I'm not going anywhere. I turned down the trade deals. I'm happy here in Ft. Starling." He explains.

"You didn't have to do that for me."

"I did it for me," he says sincerely. "This team is my family and Ft. Starling feels like home. You being here is just the icing on the cake."

"I love you so much."

"I love you too, Sunshine," he replies with a huge smile on his face and just the slightest sheen of tears in his eyes.

Realizing that we're still standing on the pitcher's mound in front of thousands of baseball fans, I step back and clear my throat.

"Now, do you think you could teach me how to throw a ball so we can get this game going? The sooner it starts, the sooner we can get out of here." I wink, giving him a seductive look and biting down on my lower lip. His gaze darkens as he focuses his gaze on my lips.

"Just toss it. It'll be faster." He says, laughing.

I laugh and follow his directions. It doesn't go very far, but it gets things started. The start of this game and the start of forever with Bailey.

SONGBIRD ERUPTS WITH CHEERS as we enter the front doors. After the Flash won their game 6-2 we decided to celebrate at open mic night. The bar is packed, and I recognize almost everyone there. There are a few open mic regulars, but most of the crowd is made up of Flash players and their spouses.

To my surprise and delight, there is even a group of Floozies sitting at a table next to some WAGs. Sabrina, who it turns out is actually the unofficial leader of the Floozies, is chatting amicably with Jessie and Leslie. It gives me hope that we'll be able to make our charity softball game idea a reality here soon.

Annie is at the bar with Fred and Cass laughing over a story Fred is telling. Fred's wearing his cowboy getup again and his wife Gail joined him tonight, so we're probably in for another rowdy country tune.

As I gaze around the room, I'm struck by how much my life has changed in the last six months. Songbird was always my safe space where I could hide away from feeling the pain of my losses. It's still my safe space, but now here it's filled with this new family of sorts, and I know Gram would be so proud. She'd love to see me opening my heart, not just to Bailey, but to this entire room full of friends.

"You good, Sunshine?" Bailey asks, noticing the tears in my eyes.

"Yes. I'm wonderful." I smile up at him and squeeze his hand before heading to the stage to get the open mic started. I sit at the piano and lower the mic. Taking a deep breath, I survey the room full of people I love.

"I love to sing sad songs." The entire crowd chuckles, and I find Bailey's eye to give him a wink. "But thanks to all you wonderful folks here tonight, I don't particularly want to sing anything sad tonight. So this one is for all of you."

I launch into the bouncy beat of "Be My Forever" by Christina Perri and sing the cheery tune for this group of people who have become my family and the gorgeous man grinning at me from the bar. As I sing, the crowd claps along, and the song ends with cheers and applause.

I introduce Fred to the crowd and make my way over to Bailey at the bar. He wraps his arms around me as I lean against him and drop a kiss into my hair.

"Forever sounds good to me, Sunshine," he murmurs into my ear. I turn in his arms and smile up at him.

"It's a good start. Now let's go home."

"Is home my house?" he teases with a grin. I study him for a moment, getting a little lost in the dark chocolate color of his eyes. He lowers his forehead to mine, making it easier for him to hear me when I respond.

"Home is wherever you are."

Leena

Epilogue

Leena

8 Months Later

"WHY ARE WE HERE? I thought we were going out for girls' night?!" I ask Jessie and Annie. The guys had some sort of training tonight, so we made a night out of it. "I wouldn't have gotten dressed up if I knew we were just going to the bar I own!"

Annie rolls her eyes at me and Jessie shakes her head as they each hold one of my arms, dragging me through the doors of the Songbird Cafe. Since moving into Bailey's house across town almost six months ago, I haven't spent as much time here. I come for the occasional open mic night, but Cass has everything under control.

"Cass said there's an open mic act she thinks you'll like. We can still go out after," Jessie says.

"Oh, alright." I shrug. "At least we drink free here!"

"Says who?" Cass deadpans at me as I plop onto a bar stool near the stage.

"Says me? The owner? I may not be here as often, but I do still own the place!" I snark back at her. She rolls her eyes, but she smirks as she grabs me a gin and Sprite. I glance around the room. "So where's the mystery open mic act you summoned us here for?"

"I think they went to the bathroom." She says as shrugs, "I'll get it going in a few minutes."

I smile to myself as I look around the room. I may not spend every waking minute in this room anymore, but I still love this place that helped me to heal and brought me Bailey.

We've been pretty much inseparable ever since my baseball game grand gesture. And after spending some time in therapy, both separately and together, we do a much better job of communicating. Therapy has been a revelation for me in working through the traumas of losing my parents and Gram and dealing with any residual effects of Adam's abuse. I still have bad days because, as my therapist likes to say, "healing isn't linear," but I'm able to live my life with actual hope for the future.

Cass pops onto the stage to announce the start of open mic just as Annie elbows me, trying to get her phone out of her pocket. She rolls her eyes and declines the call.

"What was that?" I ask with my eyebrows raised.

"Just Eric. It's like he doesn't realize it's a Friday night and that his employees are out having lives." She complains. I nudge her and waggle my eyebrows suggestively.

"Maybe he wasn't calling as your boss?" I ask. "Maybe it was a booty call."

"I told you that is not happening. I learned my lesson in Chicago. I'm never sleeping with my boss again." Annie says emphatically.

"I mean, is he technically even your boss? You're helping him out more as a favor than as an actual employee, right?" I ask, knowing exactly how quickly she'll shoot holes in that theory.

"He's paying me to clean up the mess he and his old assistant made of the books. That makes him my boss. Bosses are off-limits."

I bite my tongue to avoid telling her to 'never say never' since there's an insane amount of chemistry between her and Eric. I smirk into my drink as an extremely familiar voice catches my attention over the microphone. I whip my head around to face the stage where my gorgeous boyfriend is standing at the microphone.

"Hi everyone! My name is Bailey Turner and I just want to dedicate this song to the love of my life, my Sunshine." Bailey meets my eyes and winks as my jaw drops.

An instrumental version of John Legend's "All of Me" plays over the speaker and Bailey starts to sing. I am utterly shocked at the incredible voice coming out of my man's mouth. What the fuck!? Why has he never told me he can sing? What on earth is going on here?

When he finishes the song, he puts the microphone back on the stand but summons me up to the stage. I gaze up at him and shake my head as I poke him in his hard, muscular chest.

"Where has this been for the last year and a half? You know you're going to have to do duets with me now, right?" I say teasingly.

"I'll sing duets with you for the rest of my life if you just say yes."

With that, he sinks to one knee and produces a small velvet box from his pocket. I gasp as the crowd cheers and whistles around us.

"I love you more than anything in the world, Leena. I want to spend every day of the rest of my life showing you just how much. Will you marry me?" He cracks open the box, revealing the most gorgeous rose gold ring. A large round diamond sits in the center with a halo of sparkling emeralds and soft pink stones circling it. An intricate vine design is carved into the band. I couldn't have designed a more perfect ring if I had done it myself. I couldn't have designed a more perfect life than the one Bailey is giving me.

"Yes! Of course yes! I love you so much!" The happy tears roll down my cheeks as Bailey slides the ring on my finger and crashes his lips into mine. The bar crowd transitions into an impromptu engagement party as Cass busts out bottles of champagne from behind the bar.

The guys from the team materialize from the kitchen area where they were waiting, so they didn't tip me off to the surprise, including a certain physical therapist that Annie won't be too happy to see. Eric has blended right into hanging out with the Flash now that he's spending more time working with them. I see him and Annie spot each other from across the bar and I swear to god I can see the sparks flying between them. She can be in denial all she wants, but I see what's happening. It's only a matter of time.

Jessie comes over to give us a big hug. Dan hovers behind her with a big grin on his face. He shakes Bailey's hand as they offer their congratulations. Jessie's expression turns mischievous as she smirks at us.

"I guess it's good I set you up, huh? And you guys gave me so much shit about it! Look at you now!"

Bailey and I smile at each other. We never told Jessie that we actually started dating to thwart her plans. We found the loves of our lives. I guess we can give her credit for the setup, her and the Songbird Cafe.

The End

Thank you for reading my debut novel! Visit me at mag gielinnsharpe.com to join my mailing list and receive a free bonus epilogue all about Leena and Bailey's steamy engagement night.

Curious about any of the music found in The Songbird Setup? Checkout this playlistto find all of the songs mentioned as well as a few extras!

Want More?

Turn the page for a sneak peek of Annie and Eric's story, The Boss Boycott.

The Boss Boycott

Annie

I WAKE UP TO the sound of voices and covered in a light sheen of sweat. Even in just a baggy t-shirt, my childhood room gets too warm at night for comfort during the hot summer months. It's only late May now, so it's only going to get worse. Maybe I'll invest in a window air conditioner if I end up staying longer than a couple of weeks.

Mom swears she won't need my help longer than that, but I'm not so sure. A knee replacement is no joke, and she's struggling hard now that she's back home. Thank God her bedroom is at least on the first floor of her small house. Her home office is across the hall from my room, but she can work from the dining room table until she gets more comfortable with the stairs.

I sit up and check the time on my phone. It's only nine in the morning, so why is mom's TV so loud? I drag myself out of bed and head down to check on her. I don't bother changing out of my ratty Ohio State tee before groggily stomping my way down the stairs. Once I make sure she's good, I'll collapse back into bed for a couple more hours. I stayed up way too late last night trying to play catch up on the work that's been piling up while I'm home.

I'm technically using vacation time, but since the financial planning and investment firm I work for is one of the most high-profile firms in Chicago, there's no such thing as time off. I had to fight with Kevin, my jackass of a supervisor, just to take these couple of weeks to help my mom. He couldn't seem to get it through his head that my mom having emergency surgery was something I needed to come home for.

After taking a nasty fall at her dance exercise class that violently wrenched her knee, her doctor moved up the knee replacement she had been planning for next year. Since my mom and I only have each other—my deadbeat dad walked out on us when I was seven—I loaded up my mermaid blue Honda Fit and hit the road back home to Ft. Starling, Ohio.

I stumble into mom's room where the voices seem to have quieted down for now. I glance over to where she's reclining in bed. She opens her eyes and takes one glance at my bare legs and her eyes go wide.

"Annie Louise Martin, where are your pants?! Or your bra? We have company!" she hisses through clenched teeth. I start to ask what she's talking about when I hear a deep and familiar chuckle from behind me.

"Oh, don't worry Ms. Martin, it's nothing I haven't seen before. Right, Annie?"

I clench my eyes shut and ball my hands into fists for a second before turning to see Eric Reynolds staring down at me with a cocky smirk on his handsome face. He's barely changed in the almost 12 years since I've seen him.

He styles his dark blonde hair to be slightly messy on top, and his eyes remain the same piercing blue I remember from college. His only sign of aging are a few small lines framing his eyes that only make him seem distinguished, the prick. He's bigger than I remember. He was always tall, but his lanky body has filled out with muscle that was definitely not there when he was 18.

"Excuse me?!" my mother exclaims, snapping me out of my perusal of grown-up Eric.

"Eric's being an ass, as usual." I explain. "You remember my boyfriend Scott from freshman year?"

I can see from the look on her face that she doesn't. Honestly, I barely remember Scott despite our months long relationship. If it weren't for my unending war with his hot but dickish roommate, I might have forgotten him altogether.

"Uh, vaguely," she finally answers.

"Scott was my roommate freshman year, and Annie here was practically the unofficial extra roommate that I never asked for. She was in our room all the time eating our food, making a mess, and running around without enough clothing." Eric interjects.

"I did not!" I seethe back at him. "You're just making shit up now!"

"Whatever you say, sweetheart." He says with a shrug. "I just know I found you in my room way more often than I would have liked."

"What the fuck are you even doing here?!" I practically yell. He has a way of getting directly underneath my skin. I've had enough of his smug, handsome face and his asshole attitude—all made more awkward by the fact that I'm not wearing pants or a bra.

"Annie!" my mom scolds. "Dr. Reynolds is my physical therapist. He owns the practice and was here getting me set up for the first couple of weeks of at home care."

"It would have been nice if you had told me you had PT coming this morning." I say through clenched teeth. "I would have gotten dressed before I came down if I was expecting someone to be here."

Eric scoffs and gives me a slow, up and down perusal that I can feel in the pit of my stomach. He lingers on my bare legs before finishing his appraisal. The tension between us is thick, and it's hard to tell whether I'd like to kill him or drag him to a room my mother is not in and beg him to fuck me senseless. I shake my head to remove that disturbing thought and his mouth turns up into a wolf like grin as if he could read my mind.

"Not a big deal," Eric shrugs, like he wasn't just checking me out a moment before. "Like I said, it's nothing I haven't seen before. Besides, that was over a decade ago, and I guess some of us didn't age all that well, huh?"

I gasp loudly and ball my hands into fists, fighting the urge to throat-punch him. I give him one last scathing glance, turn on my heel, and march out of the room. What an ass, but I guess I shouldn't be surprised. From the moment he found me in his room after I started dating Scott, he's been a total dick to me. We used to fight any time we were in the same room. He always made it clear that I wasn't welcome in his room, which only made me want to hang out there more, just to piss him off.

I stomp my way up to my room and slam the door for good measure. I flop back onto the bed and close my eyes. I am not running on enough sleep to be dealing with assholes like Eric Reynolds. Before I know it, I'm drifting off with Eric's stunning blue eyes as the last thing I think about.

Eric

ANNIE FUCKING MARTIN. I should have known when I read the last name on Sherrie Martin's intake paperwork, but it's a pretty common last name, so I didn't think anything of it. It was a shock seeing her—especially seeing so much of her—that I almost lost track of finishing out my patient's appointment.

Get it together.

I get all kinds of people in my line of work, but no one in my 30 years has ever gotten under my skin like Annie Martin. The first time we met, I thought I'd found my dream girl, but it turns out she was more like my nightmare. In college, we fought constantly, always doing our level best to piss off the other. After a while, it became like a game to find out how much I could push her.

In twelve years, not much has changed. I still got that same rush of adrenaline from fighting with her. If I'm being honest, that adrenaline was paired with a decent dose of lust and I had to drop my messenger bag over the front of my body to hide the proof.

It didn't help that Annie's only gotten hotter with age. She was pretty at 18, but now she's drop-dead gorgeous. Even with her light brown hair piled into a messy bun and not a stitch of make-up, she's the most beautiful girl I've ever known. I even got a whiff of her familiar orange blossom and cinnamon scent as she stormed out that took me right back to college.

And just like back in college, now that she's left the room, I'm being hit with the familiar wave of regret and guilt. When we're in the heat of the fight, it's easy to say shitty things to her, but the aftermath never feels good. I clench my fists, pissed at myself for the things I said.

Dammit. Was it really necessary for me to do this same juvenile shit? We weren't in college anymore and she's not blowing me off for my douchebag roommate. There is no excuse for being such a jackass. Luckily Sherrie mentioned that Annie's only in town for a couple of weeks to help while she recovers. Then she'll be back to her big city life and I won't have to worry about running into her.

"Well Sherrie, it was lovely to meet you. One of the PTs on my staff will be here two more times this week and then three next week. After that, you'll come to appointments in our office." I gather my things and help Sherrie rearrange her knee with ice packs. "You take care. I'll check in with you in a couple of weeks in the office."

"Thanks, Dr. Reynolds," she replies, smiling up at me. She looks so much like an older version of Annie that it catches me off guard.

"Um... will you tell Annie...uh just tell her I'm sorry for what I said?" I murmur. I rake my hands through my hair, embarrassed.

Sherrie studies me for a long moment with a calculating look on her face. She's clearly trying to figure out what kind of history I have with her daughter. I swallow hard and clench my jaw as she stares me down.

"Wouldn't you like to tell her that yourself? I can call her back down here?" she offers. I shake my head quickly.

"No, it's probably best if you just pass along the message. We're likely just to start fighting again if we're in the same room."

"Mmhmm," she replies, still staring me down. Sherrie Martin must be one hell of an attorney because she's intimidating as hell. I can understand where Annie gets it. Finally, she nods as if she's decided, "Alright, Eric. I'll pass the message along."

"Thanks. Have a good one," I say quickly and I get the fuck out of there.

As I'm driving back to the office, I'm still kicking myself for being such a dick to Annie. I spent so much of freshman year both pissed at her and pining for her and now here I had a second chance to give her a new impression of me and I stuck with the same old one. I blew it with her. Again.

Parked in the lot outside of my physical therapy office, I lean my head back against the seat and close my eyes, taking a moment to picture Annie as she looked this morning. I resolve right there, if I'm around her again, if I get another chance, I'm not going to mess it up.

Third time's the charm, right?

Will Annie give into the sparks flying between her and Eric or will she keep him in the enemy-turned-forbidden-boss zone forever? Find out in The Boss Boycott.

Acknowledgements

Writing my debut novel was a huge undertaking and I couldn't have done it without some amazing people in my life.

My husband, Blair, for always being on board with whatever I want to pursue. For always supporting me and never complaining when I'm spending time in my own fictional world. Also, for his unending sports knowledge. I'm pretty sure it's his fault my debut novel was a sports romance. He also gets credit for naming the Ft. Starling Flash.

My boys who I hope never read this. Thank you for letting Mommy write while you watch endless amounts of Bluey and YouTube Kids.

To my mom who has always been my biggest cheerleader and has become one of my best friends. Thank you for being my sounding board, my shopping buddy, my confidant, and my live-in babysitter. I'm sorry for all the spicy scenes and F-bombs, but I did warn you!

To Rachel for being my ride or die for the last 17 years. You're the best friend and un-biological sister a girl could have. And to Kaitlynne for always being able to pick back up right where we left off regardless of the time we've spent apart. You're the Glindas to my Elphaba forever.

My beta readers Katie P., Kaitlin, Jami, Abby, and Casey. Thank you for taking the time to read my book and give me feedback. Thank you for your honesty and support to make this book the best it could be.

My editor Karoline at StarCrossed Passions for being the first person to read my work and not ripping me to shreds. Thank you for your guidance and ideas in forming this book.

A huge shoutout to Storyline Bookshop in Upper Arlington, OH for being the ideal bookstore for both enjoying books and writing this one. I'll be back on your comfy couch very soon.

To the ladies of Fit4Mom Columbus North for your constant support in life and motherhood. I love our village and I couldn't have done this without you. Thank you for showing up for me always and for your excitement about this book. You make me feel brave.

The All Write Well, Book Boss GSD/Success Alliance, and Romance Writer Support League online communities. I would be lost in the world of indie publishing without your infinite wisdom and kindness.

To Taco Bell for bringing back Nacho Fries and BIGGBY Coffee for providing copious amounts of caffeine. You guys keep me going on days when I stayed up way too late reading and/or writing.

Finally, to you the reader. None of this is possible without readers and I love you for taking the time to read my book baby. Let's be book besties!

About the Author

MAGGIE LINN SHARPE HAS been creating worlds and characters in her mind for as long as she can remember. Because no career path felt quite right, despite her efforts, and motherhood limited her social time, she decided to try writing a romance novel. Now she's pretty sure she won't be able to stop.

Maggie lives outside of Columbus, Ohio with her husband, her two boys, and her mother. When she's not writing, she's usually reading romance, obsessing about musicals, or spending time with her kiddos, which usually involves learning more than she wanted to know about Minecraft and watching the Bluey on repeat.

Also by Maggie

The Songbird Cafe Series

The Songbird Setup (Leena & Bailey)

The Boss Boycott (Annie & Eric)

Connect with Maggie

www.ingramcontent.com/pod-product-compliance
Lightning Source LLC
Chambersburg PA
CBHW020138120726
47903CB00007B/2317

THE WEIGHT OF ALMOST KNOWING

A curious
anthology

P◑P | PHX OASIS PRESS

Title: The Weight of Almost Knowing
ISBN: 979-8-9937406-0-7

Cover + Book design: Felicia Penza

PHX Oasis Press gratefully acknowledges the support of the Community of Literary Magazines and Presses for their wonderful resources and community.

Printed in the United States of America.

Introduction

At a time when all knowledge is accessible at our fingertips, curiosity remains the systolic force of the human experience. Coursing through our bodies is a ceaseless desire to explore the world around us and reach an understanding of our shared existence.

Acts of curiosity don't have to result in grand inventions. In fact, curiosity often comes to us quietly. It builds on itself in small moments before entering our consciousness, filling us with new questions. The very act of picking up this anthology and reading these words stemmed from an act of curiosity. Good for you. Stay curious, reader.

While we often think of curiosity alongside the faces of famed scientists and innovations, it is actually laced throughout everything we do. Curiosity is the ingredients we mix together for a cake, the way we arrange letters, words, and blank spaces on a page, the million ways we can hold another's hand.

Curiosity is an ever-present song of wonder that marches us forward. This repetitive, deeply personal drive for discovery and connection has prevailed for the entirety of human existence. In our shared second in the forever of this universe, we have used this singular moment to explore unknowns together. Gloriously, our search is never over, perpetually reaching for more, and forever almost knowing.

Contents

Fiction

READER ADVISORY: This book explores themes that may be difficult for some readers. To avoid spoilers while still giving readers the information they need to make informed choices, detailed content warnings are provided on page 159.

"Alice: How long is forever?
White Rabbit: Sometimes, just one second."

— Author unknown

Fiction

The Sale

TRACY HOLOHAN

I was done. Not just a little bit, mind you. I was so completely done that I couldn't have started up again for all the tea in China. I sat pondering if China actually had any more tea than any other country while I watched the stranger approach.

"You sittin' on the side of the road like you just gonna die here."

"Might," I said bitterly.

I expected him to walk on by. Most people would have, and fast too, judging that the tall, lanky youngin' in tattered clothes with blood running freely out his nose might be angry or even downright dangerous. I was just that; definitely mad as a hornet, and right at that moment I felt pretty dangerous, too.

He didn't, though. He eased his bulk down to the curb with a sigh, near enough to talk to me, but not close enough to get hit if I lashed out with a fist or a knife. I didn't though. My fists were done in, bloody and bruised, and I didn't have a knife, or a pot to piss in, come to that. I stared at the stretch of weeds growing through the cracks in the space between us.

He made himself comfortable, stretching his boot-clad feet over the gutter between the hunk of broken concrete calling itself a sidewalk and the stretch of ragged asphalt masquerading as a road. He pulled aside his plaid jacket and drew a watch bob out of his waist coat. I watched him furtively through my too long fringe of greasy hair, curious to spite myself.

1

Without sayin' a word or lookin' at me, he handed me a handkerchief. Gray with age, but clean and folded neat. I glanced at him, and he pantomimed wiping his nose while still starin' at his watch. I took the hint and wiped the square of cloth over the worst of the blood, careful to go easy on the still painful parts. I worked at wiping my hands clean, but between the dirt and the blood I didn't make much progress. I shrugged and tried to hand the bloodied square of cloth back to him.

"Put it in your pocket, boy," he said. "It's lookin' like you need it more'n me."

I couldn't argue with that. I put the square of linen in my shirt pocket and looked at him, wondering what might be comin' next.

Nothin' as far as I could tell. The man didn't look at me or even move much, focused as he was on the pocket watch in his hand. I took the time to study him and found I was lookin' at an odd creature indeed. There weren't but maybe three hairs on the top of his head, slicked down across his pate. His fringe, though, was thick and long, dark as sin and pulled tight to a ponytail in the back of his head, then braided down his back near to the bottom of his jacket. Weren't what I was used to seein', being as I just got kicked out of school for the day due to my too long hair. Well, that and fightin'. He weren't a big man, but he had extra meat across his middle, also rare in these parts. Most of us in this neck of the woods aren't much more than walkin' skeletons. He dressed in peculiar old-fashioned clothes; I'd seen some in picture books of fancy people. His clothes nearly wore out, but clean and cared for some.

My attention wavered as a group of people turned the corner and shambled toward us. A tall, stooped man had one of his giant ham hands on the neck of a broke-down woman, pushing her along. Trailing behind them were four ragged girl youngins, up to maybe ten years and down to no more than three. My family, as it were.

I started to rise, seein' as it was time to take my punishment, but the man on the curb cleared his throat in what seemed a meaningful way. I stopped and looked at him and he made a gesture with his hand that I should sit back down, all the while focused at that darned watch. I didn't see why not, seein' as how I was gonna get whooped sitting or standing so I plunked myself back down on the sidewalk and stared defiantly at the man holding my ma by her neck.

It surprised me he didn't seem to see me, goggling as he was at the plaid-coated man sittin' next to me. "This him?" he asked Ma, shaking her roughly.

Ma whimpered a bit as my four half-siblings huddled around her skirts, trying to stay out of his reach. She managed a nod.

"She sold the boy out too light," my step-pa stated bluntly, starin' at the watch bob man. "The youngins' and the woman haven't ate in two suns."

I startled at the word sold, but I guess I weren't surprised. I'd heard of it happening all over these parts, selling the strongest in hopes of buying more time to see if things changed. They never did, mind you. At least the watch bob man seemed to care that I was bleedin'. Goin' with him couldn't be any worse than what I got at home.

The watch bob man snapped his watch closed and tucked it carefully into his waist coat. He looked up for the first time, but not at me. He settled a look of mild curiosity on my step-pa. "I assume you have," he said.

The local accent I'd heard the few times he spoke to me had disappeared completely. In its place I heard the cultured lilt of the leaders we listened to dutifully through massive speakers when we gathered in the town square every rest day.

My step-pa took a half-step back, surprised as I was by the sound of the watch bob man's voice.

"Um, course I have. Can't work unless I eat. Can't take care of the family unless I work." He finished that bit of logic in a proud tone.

"And yet you don't."

Step-pa cocked his head at the man, reminding me of the pup I had when Pa had been alive. The pup step-pa put an arrow through and made Ma cook up for dinner. "Don't what?" he asked dully.

The watch bob man used a cane I hadn't noticed before to lever himself off the sidewalk. He stood stretchin' his back a moment, then walked himself over to Step-Pa. Standin' toe-to-toe, Step-Pa seemed to shrink, though watch bob man weren't sized so as to be scary. He took his hand off Ma and crossed his arms over his self.

"Don't," continued the watch bob man in a conversational tone, his expression mild. "Work. Or take care of your family, for that matter."

My step-pa sputtered and took another step back. "Course I take care of 'em," he blustered.

Watch bob man took a leather purse out of his waist coat and handed it to my ma. "Step out of the way, ma'am," he said quietly as he took out his watch. Ma stepped lively and backed away from my step-pa, pushing the youngins' behind her like frightened goslings toward where I sat on the sidewalk. I grabbed the littlest and put her on my lap so she wouldn't fix to run away.

He snapped the watch open. "Look here, please," he said in that oddly mild tone of voice, shoving the watch right up to my step-pa's face. Step-Pa gave the watch bob man a startled look and glanced down at the watch.

I can't rightly wrap my head around what happened next. There were a rush of air like a cyclone and then Step-Pa just weren't there anymore. Some dry leaves swirled for a few seconds longer, then settled gently on the sidewalk. Watch bob man snapped the watch closed and put it carefully back into his waist coat, handling it as though it were suddenly heavy as lead. I scrambled to my feet holding my squirming stepsister in a tight grip, breathin' heavier than I needed to.

Into the silence that followed, the watch bob man heaved a sigh. "The son will save us all someday," he muttered softly in a musing tone, staring into the distance. He shook himself a bit and turned to my ma. "There's money enough in the purse to feed you and your brood for a few weeks and put some meat onto their bones. The paper it is wrapped in contains an address in the next town over. Go with your girls and the people there will give you honest work cleaning rooms. You'll work hard, but you and yours will be fed and safe."

Ma had tears in her eyes. "My son?" she asked.

The watch bob man's eyes softened just a bit. "You sold him. He goes with me."

4

TRACY HOLOHAN

Bessie Rose

LORI APPLEBY HOKE

I'm looking at a photo of my mom's family taken in 1940. She and seven of her siblings, ranging from eighteen months to seventeen years, pose around the family's late 1930s Chevy. My grandfather is perched against the running board with the youngest child in his lap, while my grandmother sits inside the car, attempting a smile as she awaits a ride to the hospital to deliver her tenth baby. You'd never know that this woman, the center of her family's universe, was abandoned as an infant outside an orphanage and raised as a commodity.

My grandmother was an indentured child.

It says so in bold, all caps, 60-point font on her indenture contract. Across the center of the page are the words INDENTURE/FEMALE CHILD, and on the line below in flowing cursive is her name: Bessie Kahn. Grandma knew from an early age that she'd been left in a cradle outside the New York Foundling Hospital, a note pinned to her blanket stating her birth date of April 3, 1899. The Sisters of Charity started the Foundling thirty years prior during a wave of infant abandonment in the streets. To protect as many babies as possible, they placed a cradle outside the hospital so that anyone could leave a baby with no questions asked.

Over 250,000 homeless, impoverished, and orphaned children were abandoned on the streets of New York between 1854 and 1929. They resorted to selling matches and newspapers to get money for food and squeezed themselves into dark spaces in alleys to sleep. Some created gangs to protect themselves from danger on the streets, and some, as young as five years old, were arrested and locked up with criminals.

Charles Loring Brace, a child welfare advocate, philanthropist, and Methodist minister, founded the Children's Aid Society in 1854. He believed the solution to this problem was to transfer children from the poverty and destitution of New York to farm families who lived in the Midwest. He founded the Orphan Train movement the same year to start delivering these orphans to their new homes. The New York Foundling Hospital participated in the movement because they believed their orphans would thrive when placed with loving, caring families. And when the parishioners at Maria Hilf Catholic Church in Frankenstein, Missouri, heard about the plight of these orphans, seven local families offered to welcome children into their homes.

Within a couple of months of taking in my grandmother, a Jewish baby, the Sisters of Charity had Bessie Kahn baptized Catholic. Bessie lived at the Foundling until just after her second birthday, when she rode the Orphan Train to meet her destiny. I'm met with reactions ranging from interest to surprise to horror whenever I've shared my grandmother's story. Most people I've spoken with have never heard of the Orphan Train.

Because Bessie and her fellow Foundlings were requested by the Frankenstein families, fate was kinder to them than to many other Orphan Train riders. Some farm families weren't prepared for the children, nor capable of caring for them. Some of the orphans were treated like hired help and never accepted into the family fold. Some were bullied and excluded by their peers. Some never found homes. There were counts of exploitation, abuse, and rape. There were widowed farmers looking for teenage wives. Most orphans were paraded from the train depot to the auction block, where their bones and teeth were poked and prodded by potential foster parents to check for their suitability as farm hands. Brothers and sisters were often separated. After being placed with their families, some children ran away. Some ended their lives because of deplorable conditions.

Dressed in a blue-and-white striped cotton dress with a ruffled collar, hand stitched by one of the Sisters of Charity, Bessie boarded the Orphan Train at Grand Central Station for a two-day journey to Frankenstein where she would meet her parents, Paul and Gertrude Gentges, and their adult sons Henry and Alex. Within a month of Bessie's arrival, the Gentges adopted her and changed her name to Rose.

I get choked up to imagine my grandmother as an orphaned toddler. What was it like for this tiny girl to leave the familiarity of the only life she'd ever known and move in with strangers who spoke only German and were old enough to be her grandparents? What went through her mind as she rode the iron horse from overcrowded, soot-covered New York into fresh air and sweeping green fields dotted with horses and cows? Without raising Bessie from birth, how did Gertrude figure out what she needed, and how did Bessie come to understand she had a new name?

My grandmother's indenture contract clearly states Paul and Gertrude's responsibility was to "treat her with care and tenderness as if she were in fact their own child." Throughout her life, my grandmother believed that if her birth mother had truly loved her, she would not have given her up. Feeling abandoned by your birth mother is one thing, but learning that your new family was contractually obligated to care for you had to do a number on your sense of belonging as a child.

Another photo of young Rose always haunts me. She's standing in front of the Frankenstein Catholic School with her classmates, four nuns, and a priest. She is the only child looking down instead of at the camera. Maybe she wasn't feeling well that day, but to me she looks like a little girl who felt she didn't belong.

When Rose was in seventh grade, she was pressured into dropping out of school and moving thirty miles away to Jefferson City to find a job. The Foundling Hospital made her indenture contract around the same time, proclaiming that she "has arrived at a suitable age to be indentured" and that Rose could now go to work to provide financial support to the family. But the contract also states her parents' responsibility to ensure that she was "taught all branches of education as required by law, including reading, writing, and arithmetic through the eighth grade." In addition to the contract's conflicting direction to put her to work despite not finishing her formal education, Rose's father died, her mother's health was declining, and a manipulative sister-in-law continuously made her feel unwelcome in the family. In essence, the indenture contract gave her family permission to make this cruel decision to send her away. I wonder if Rose ever fully understood the implications of her contract.

Rose lived with extended family while working various jobs in Jefferson City over the next five years. On the holidays or rare weekends when she went home to Frankenstein, she stayed with friends instead of her family. Rose had friends in Denver who repeatedly asked her to join them. When she turned eighteen, she headed for the mile-high city. She landed a coveted job at a book bindery, but what seemed to matter most to her was being with friends who loved and appreciated her for who she was. As her circle grew, so did her social life. I look at photos of her lounging with her pals on a picnic blanket, laughing and hamming it up for the camera. There's a photo of her and her girlfriends decked out in their Sunday best, dipping their toes in an icy creek, and another one of the group posing in an automobile, likely taken before a ride in the country. Her smiling face in those photos tells me that she found a place of belonging. I hope she was having the time of her life.

After living in Denver for three years, Rose started corresponding with her future husband, Frank Mulville, through the suggestion of a mutual friend. The two became acquainted through a year of letter writing — Rose in Colorado and Frank in Montana. After meeting in person, within a couple of weeks Rose and Frank set a wedding date. They married in January of 1922. Frank's work as a blacksmith took them from Montana to California during the early years of their marriage. When the Roosevelt Irrigation District in Arizona opened up the Buckeye Valley to farming, the farmers recruited Frank to open a blacksmithing shop, which became a thriving business that supported his family for decades.

When Frank sold his blacksmithing business, he and Rose moved to Manitou Springs, Colorado, and bought the Rockwood Lodge. Although Frank was officially retired, Rose's work did not end. She cleaned guest rooms and bathrooms. She cooked for guests, boarders, and cherished family visitors. There could not have been a more idyllic place for us grandkids to visit than this two-story flagstone lodge that was nestled into the base of a foliage-covered hill. The best part about spending time with Grandma was enjoying her cooking. She wasn't one of those warm-and-fuzzy grandmothers who showered us with hugs and kisses, but she clearly showed her love through the food she made. You could taste it in her turkey dinners, in her homemade bread, in her sugar cookies. We were the beneficiaries of all those years she spent honing her skills nourishing the ones she cared about.

Eventually my grandparents sold the lodge and returned to Arizona. When Frank died after suffering a few debilitating strokes, Rose alternated living with my mother and two of my aunts a few months at a time. She asked her daughters to not place her in a nursing home; she told them she would feel abandoned all over again. Her daughters cared for her as long as they could, but eventually their own health challenges necessitated placing their beloved mother in an assisted living home. I remember Grandma being agreeable to this arrangement, but I wonder if on some level her fear of being abandoned was realized. She died peacefully in her sleep just six weeks into her time at the home with family at her bedside.

I contemplate possible outcomes of my grandmother's life had she not been abandoned at the Foundling. She could have been left to die in a dark alley, in which case I would not be here. Even though there is no evidence to support this, family lore has it her parents were a teenage, Jewish couple who came from Germany to America for a better life, but because they were not married, they gave her up.

While she never found her birth mother, Rose found love and a sense of belonging within her own family. A true matriarch, her legacy includes ten children, thirty-nine grandchildren, seventy-eight great grandchildren, and countless great greats. Her job as a mother and wife was nonstop. Rose cooked meals from morning until evening for her family, she grew most of their vegetables, she killed chickens in the backyard for that night's supper, and she sewed all of her children's clothes. She nursed illnesses when she didn't feel well herself and while she was pregnant with the next child. Did she ever have five minutes to herself, or give any thought to what she would do with free time? Was she truly fulfilled by constantly serving her husband and children, or did she willingly accept this as her destiny? When I look at photos taken of my grandmother smiling over the years, I wonder if she was truly enjoying the moment or if she was thinking about her next household task.

Rose always kept an eye out for others, perhaps because she knew what it felt like to be on the outside looking in. She never turned away anyone who was hungry. During the Great Depression, her home was constantly filled with neighborhood kids who often found their only meal of the day at her table. When vagrant men traveling through town came knocking on Rose's door asking for food, she asked them to do a bit of work as a way to respect their dignity, then gave them a hot meal and a sandwich or two for the road. She didn't want her neighbors in need to feel like they were accepting charity, so she had her children deliver hot meals that included a note telling them to enjoy these leftovers.

Grandma was the most devout Catholic I've ever known, but I don't think that was due to the stipulation in the contract for her parents to "bring her up in a moral and correct manner in the Catholic faith." I believe that had she been raised according to Judaism, she would have approached her life with the same level of conviction and devotion as she did with the Catholic faith. That was the essence of who she was. I can see her in her final years sitting in her blue recliner in my mom's family room, fingers gliding from one olive wood Rosary bead to the next, lips moving in silent prayer. If she wasn't reading or eating, she was praying for all of us.

Even though Grandma's budget was limited, she always acknowledged the special occasions of her grandchildren. She taped five dimes inside our birthday cards with the message "go get yourself a little treat." For high school graduations she gave the grandsons a shaving kit, and the granddaughters got a brush, comb, and mirror set. I treasure the embroidered pillowcases she made me as a wedding gift when she was ninety-two. Rose was a prolific letter writer whose penmanship and prose did not belie the fact that her formal education ended at seventh grade. When I look at her scrawling cursive on the cards she sent me, I hear her telling me to say my prayers every day.

Whenever Grandma and I talked about her riding the Orphan Train, without fail she mentioned wearing that little blue-and-white striped dress and being carried from the train to her parents by the parish priest. This was a woman who lived through the sinking of the Titanic, the completion of the Panama Canal, and the first moon walk, yet the memory that withstood the test of time was coming to live with her new family when she was just two years old.

I realize that I'll probably never have the answers to my questions about Rose's story. Some of my cousins have done in-depth research via ancestry. com and 23andMe, and while they've confirmed Grandma's Jewish ethnicity, they've had no luck locating relatives. All the New York Foundling Hospital could offer me was a duplicate copy of her indenture contract. I feel like I'm missing part of my heritage, but then I think about what it was like for Grandma to live until almost 102 and never know who her mother was. If the stars had aligned for the two of them to meet at some point, would it have been affirming, or would she have regretted it?

As one of those thirty-nine grandchildren who was baptized and raised Catholic, I've not been a believer since high school. While I don't participate in organized religion of any kind, I've found that certain rituals bring me comfort and connection. So at Hanukkah I light the menorah. I don't know the prayers, but I tune into Grandma. I thank her for the rich heritage she left us. I tell her that I admire her resilience, her tenacity, her strength. I thank her for my prominent cheekbones and my unenviable frizzy hair. And I tell her that I am so grateful that she, Bessie Rose, is my grandmother.

Poetry

Angiosperms and Other Fruit-Bearing Plants

TINAMARIE COX

Sometimes I wonder if I had to find the sun to bloom and if I should have let the bright warmth coax my soft petals open, spread wide, and become welcoming.

I think about the curious bees who looked to dip their tongues into my center, lick and lap in ecstasy, please their bellies, and bathe in my pollen so carelessly.

I remember all the honey bees and how they buzzed inside me, how they left my cup less full for the promises of richer blossoms, more vivid colors, and temptresses with fresher offers.

And the lonely bee that returned, still coated in my dust, body humming, legs rubbing, tongue flicking like a nervous finger tapping, and asking after my ovaries.

With my beauty fleeting, petals wasting, and prospects depleted, I turn inward, feeding back into my nature, the purpose of my body, and watch as my future grows and shrinks simultaneously.

I shed all that could attract to become a memory and a glimpse into everything that will never change.

Fiction

A Slip of Paper

ERIC THURSTON

The idea came to Andrew while he was soaking in the bath. A bulb and socket dangling over the tub were more than a cartoon symbol of his desperate idea of escape. They were an electrified Sword of Damocles. Likely, some former renter complained that the bathroom was dark, so the landlord took five minutes out of his busy day being an asshole to staple a light to the bathroom ceiling.

Andrew wondered when the humidity would soften the paper and chalk of the drywall enough for the staples to pop out one by one, letting the socket swing into the water, rerouting the current through the drain and anything in the way. While electrocution was horrific, with clenched muscles, painful vibration, and cardiac arrest, Andrew was thrilled with the idea he'd be warm for an instant before death.

Fucking cold. Fucking Northern Indiana and its endless gray winters.

He reached for a towel, but of course, there wasn't one. Andrew didn't plan for the simplest of things, hoping the universe or God would take care of him. But it, or He, never did. Making a mad dash for the bedroom, he grabbed a sweatshirt to dry himself, then jumped into bed and burrowed under old quilts and laundry, shivering until his body heat filled the cocoon.

Every time he lay down for the night, he thought of the Elephant Man. That poor soul just wanted to sleep on a pillow like everyone else, and when he did, the weight of his deformed head killed him. Sunday afternoons,

Andrew's girlfriend Bethany read books out loud while he watched a game with the sound off, pretending he wasn't listening to her. But he absorbed every word she read. When she finished *The Elephant Man*, Andrew lied to explain his tears, saying he had allergies.

Bethany worked on her MA in English while Andrew dreamed of driving a bigger forklift. One day he made the mistake of asking her if she could spend forever with a guy who thought poetry was stupid. She paused for what seemed like years, caressed his cheek, then said *goodbye*. He wasn't sure if it was, *see you tomorrow* goodbye or, *have a good life* goodbye.

On the way out of his apartment, Bethany stopped at the bathroom to collect her mysterious woman stuff. It was the, *have a good life* goodbye. The only signs she ever existed were a large number of hair ties and a hundred books she left behind. The books, her partially futile attempt to awaken him.

At least with her leaving, the universe had made his life easier.

Andrew rolled onto his side within his cocoon and gazed at the soft orange glow of the night light his grandpop had given him when he was little. A covered wagon made from a cholla cactus. He said *choy yuh* out loud. Had to say it right. A southwestern scene was printed on its plastic cover. Red and orange sunset, distant mountains and *sa waar rowz* in the foreground. While the glow from the seven-watt candelabra bulb didn't warm the room, it warmed his soul.

He imagined one day springing from his cocoon to emerge as a butterfly and migrate to a warmer home. Once when he was drunk, he told Bethany about his escape fantasy. After she corrected him—apparently butterflies come from chrysalises not cocoons—she tried getting him to tell her more, but he shut down.

The following week, on a morning mired in gray, Andrew was submerged in the bath, hoping to get heat deep enough into his body to reach his soul so he could face another day at the warehouse. Another day of driving a forklift, jamming rolls of carpet into trucks, the overhead doors always open.

He looked up at the veiny cracks in the paint that sketched a fantasy map of highways across the ceiling. The bulb of enlightenment hung a little closer to the tub, the first staple missing. He reached up to the heavens, hoping his plea of escape would be heard. On that Monday, it finally did. The buzz of excitement, a flash of light, and the realization hit him like a punch in the gut.

Today was the day fantasy became reality.

He leapt from the tub, trying not to drip on Bethany's books that were still strewn everywhere even though she was gone, got dressed without drying himself, and pulled a box from the closet. His one attempt to plan ahead, the box held T-shirts, shorts, and a pair of flip flops still linked together by the price tag string. He carefully wrapped the covered wagon light in a towel like the sacred relic it was. That meant he'd have the towel too which, according to *The Hitchhiker's Guide*, is a massively useful thing. Damn, he couldn't get Bethany and her books out of his head.

That morning Andrew stepped into a new world. The sun was out for the first time in weeks, and it was a mild day which was cruel because of the false hope that winter would eventually end. The next day, all hope would be crushed by freezing, screaming wind with its icy fingers searching through his clothes, and more snow. But Andrew wouldn't be there to see that beautiful blanket turn into a gritty mess.

South for warmth, west for saguaros. He had the highways memorized, starting with the 69 south from Fort Wayne, ending on 17 south into Phoenix. The trip was a blur of white line fever, that highway hypnosis where drivers cover long distances with little recall, which was fine with him since it was the destination, not the journey, that mattered to Andrew.

Welcome to Arizona, The Grand Canyon State greeted him. He saw the sign as *Welcome Home, Andrew*. To a guy who'd never been west of the Mississippi, Arizona was another planet, the azure sky and the distant mountains appearing like sleeping dragons. He stopped during the day, rejoiced in the dry, warm air scented with creosote, and watched skittering lizards and galloping javelina. No, it was *have a leen ah*. When Andrew stopped at night, he gazed in wonder at the Milky Way splashed across the cloudless sky. He saw meteors, and dots of light that were other worlds, all to the crazed yipping and howling of coyotes in the distance.

Driving through the desert, he came upon the scene from his night light. A setting sun and saguaros. But in this scene, someone stood on the shoulder of the highway. As Andrew drove close, an old man pointed at him ominously in a *Ghost of Christmas* sort of way, then he changed forefinger to thumb. Andrew sure as hell wasn't planning to pick him up. Old guys knew every damn thing, and were always boring. But he shocked himself and pulled off the interstate.

The old man groaned as he got in, then farted when he twisted around searching for the seatbelt.

Finally giving up, the old man said, "Hell, I'm not long for this world, anyhoo." Then he added, "Thanks for the ride. I'm going to Flag."

"Flag?"

"Flagstaff."

"Ah."

"Name's Thomas," he said and held out a hand that looked like a latex glove stretched over bones.

Andrew hesitantly shook it.

"I'm Andrew. I'm going to Phoenix." He pulled them onto the deserted highway.

"You on vacation?" Old Thomas asked.

"Moving there."

"Job?"

"I don't have one yet."

"A new adventure, eh?"

"I suppose so. I mostly just want to get warm."

"You're not going to write a book or join a band or start a business?"

"No. Like I said, I just want to get warm. I'm from Indiana. Fort Wayne," Andrew said as if that explained everything.

"Oh, sorry. Spent some time in Fort Wayne myself. Did you know Johnny Appleseed's buried there?"

"Yes, near the Coliseum."

Thomas laughed. "Wasn't sick a day in his life. Then he went to Fort Wayne, got sick, and died."

"Yeah, I heard that."

They drove on. He could feel the old guy watching him like he was some sort of prey.

"Well, I do have a plan," Andrew said to break the silence.

"There you go."

"When I get to Phoenix, I'll get my class seven certification."

"What's that?"

"Forklifts. I have my class one through five certs. Seven is rough terrain. Construction's where the money is."

"Well, shoot for the stars."

"You're probably wondering why I don't have a class six cert. It's not . . ."

"Not long until the election," Old Thomas interrupted. "This one's important. *Course* they all are. You'll have to register here in Arizona."

"Oh, I don't bother with that stuff. Doesn't affect me. I like to keep my life simple. Focus on my career."

"Career?" Thomas asked.

"Driving forklift."

"That a career, is it?"

"Well, it's all I've known since high school."

The old man looked out the window and said, "This kid's as shallow as the Platte River."

"What?" Andrew asked.

"Mile wide and an inch deep."

"Damn, I give you a ride and it turns out you're an asshole."

"I was an asshole before you picked me up," Thomas said with a laugh. "But did you ever think there's a world beyond forklifts and getting warm?"

21

Andrew spoke slowly so the old guy could grasp it, "Like I said, I keep my life simple."

"Well son, nothing personal, but you're living in a mighty small world."

"Sounds personal. At least I have a car," Andrew shot back.

"True. She's a classic." Thomas patted the cracked dash. "You're pretty happy then?"

"Uh, yeah. I will be when I get warm."

The old man didn't say anything more, but Andrew felt the need to justify his existence and said with a shrug, "I'm living life the best I know."

Thomas said, "Maya Angelou wrote it beautifully. *I did then . . .*"

Andrew spoke over him. "*I did then what I knew how to do. Now that I know better, I do better.*"

"Damn son. Look at you."

"My girlfriend, my ex-girlfriend, was always trying to broaden my horizons with poetry and such. I don't like poetry," he added quickly so the old guy wouldn't think he was weird. Truth was, he loved the poetry Bethany read to him. William Blake's line, *The imagination is not a state: it is the human existence itself,* often wandered through Andrew's brain.

Old Thomas rapped his knuckle on the window and said, "We don't have much time. How would you like to have the universe opened to you?"

"No, I'm good. Thanks."

"What if you could experience the ecstasy of creation, aching loneliness, and love fueled connections to humanity? What if you could travel back in time? Be there when a prince becomes Buddah or be transformed from the genius of a sermon? See a planet turned into a sun? Discover that a respected doctor and a murderer are the same man? Find out what a waiter's fart is?"

"Actually, I just want to get warm and . . ."

"Get your class seven certification." Thomas waved his hand dismissively. "Look, I know I'm making you uncomfortable. You can let me out here."

Pulling off the highway, Andrew wondered, could the old guy actually reveal the universe? What the hell was a waiter's fart? He looked like some homeless guy. Of course, so did Gandalf.

Stopping the car, Andrew said, "We're in the middle of nowhere. You sure you want out here?"

"I'll be fine. I like to wander and remember, all . . ."

"*All who wander aren't lost*," Andrew said then added, "My ex-girlfriend gave me a mug with that on it."

Old Thomas rooted around in his pockets.

"Here's something for your troubles."

Andrew shook his head, "That's okay."

Thomas held up a slip of paper about the size of a business card.

"Isn't money. Something more valuable." He placed the paper on the dash. "Got to warn you, there's no going back."

"Oh, I'm never going back to Indiana."

The old man opened the door and a warm breeze filled the car. Andrew caught the paper before it blew away and trapped it in the ashtray. He turned back, but old Thomas had disappeared into the desert. Andrew touched the little paper to make sure at least that was real.

He pulled into Phoenix on a blessedly hot Friday morning, carried along in the rapids of rush hour traffic flowing south on the 17. Andrew had driven into an exotic world of tiled roofs, stucco, and arches. Signs with Spanish were everywhere. *Vote Here/Vote Aquí*. To the east was Camelback Mountain making it possible to imagine the Great Pyramid of Giza.

He stayed in a house deep in Phoenix. A date palm towered in the backyard, making Andrew feel like Wart when he crawled under plants as an ant in the *Book of Merlyn*. Sitting under the tree, he thought of Bethany and her books. He let the warmth soak into his soul as he munched on fallen dates. One day it rained and all the dry vegetation rejoiced in a riotous explosion of life. Even the cockroaches were amazing. Three inches long and they could fly, like something out of *Jurassic Park*. There was a saguaro with its elephant corduroy hide. The spines scaring away touch. Andrew realized he used to be a cactus but didn't need his spines anymore.

He also didn't need his covered wagon night light to sleep, feeling as if he was safe and warm within it. Safe to start a new adventure. The scary leap for another forklift certification. He drove to the main library intending to study for the class seven test but sat in the parking lot feeling lost. He could no longer see himself driving a construction—or *any*—forklift. When a dusty wind blew through his car, the little paper stuck in the ashtray fluttered like a trapped bird. Andrew freed it, then read it. It was a list of book titles and authors, handwritten in tiny cursive on both sides that seemed to fluoresce in the sun.

Strange names. Camus, Cervantes, Kafka, Tolstoy, Vonnegut.

He stuck the little paper in his pocket and entered the library in T-shirt and shorts, legs blinding white. Trying to walk in flip flops without slapping the floor, he said *sa waar rowz* under his breath. Practicing. In case a cactus conversation came up, people would think him a local.

An old woman with a knowing look gazed at him from the information desk.

"I uh," he started, intending to ask where he could find OSHA resources, but hesitated, embarrassed. Old Thomas was right, his world was small.

Instead, he pulled out the slip of paper and showed it to her, saying, "An old man gave me this."

She studied the list with a smile. "Very nice. Of course we have all of them." Then, pointing to the back of the library, she said, "It's all fiction."

As he walked away he heard the old woman say, "Take care. There is no going back."

Andrew paused, shrugged, then walked deep into the library. In the maze of aisles, he expected a minotaur to come charging around the next corner. Running his finger along the spines of books, one stuck out from the rest. *The Canterbury Tales*. Yes, it was on the list. He took it to a little carrel fort, fearing disappointment. The classics were deadly boring. The library, freezing like all public buildings in The Valley. He had to get outside in the heat.

Driving west, he came upon Encanto Park with its bandshell, lagoon, and Enchanted Island. Strangely compelling was a group of people sitting on blankets in a circle, books all around. They argued and laughed, getting mad, and having fun. Andrew sat in the shade of a palm tree and began reading. He was on a pilgrimage with garrulous characters including a valiant knight, a corrupt pardoner, and there's a naked ass in a window. Okay, maybe classics aren't boring.

A hundred trips to the library. Countless hours reading under his palm tree at Encanto. Nourished by words, he fell into books like a man plunging into an oasis. *War and Peace* was a gossipy soap opera with the epic backdrop of war. St. Augustine explained to him why Rome fell. He read the Bible and preachers could no longer tell him what to believe. He was seized with 1984's paranoia but somehow felt more human. Andrew travelled the cosmos discovering he was made of starstuff. In fantastically named *Gargantua and Pantagruel* he learned about Northern Renaissance ideals from giants. Oh, so a waiter's fart is when the stew follows. Andrew thought that was wonderfully ribald.

One evening, he closed the last book on the list having read all fifty and fifty more that caught his eye. Surely, he had to read everything by Steinbeck. Mice and a dust bowl and traveling with Charley. He fell asleep in the grass with the weight of a hundred books in his head. When Andrew woke, the park was deserted except for the circle of people, their passions and books. He walked close, with an idea of joining them. But he was just a forklift driver. They were intellectuals. No. He *used* to be a forklift driver. Then he saw little papers in the grass and sticking out of books. Pulling out his own well-worn slip with a smile, Andrew sat in the empty space waiting for him.

Two burly Fort Wayne cops loomed over the nervous landlord in the cold bathroom.

"I've never seen that socket," he said, unable to meet their eyes.

One cop shook his head. "Sure as fuck isn't up to code."

They looked down on the scene. Books scattered all over the floor, a couple floated in the soapy bathwater along with curved fragments of glass, and there was Andrew with a smile, the light socket clenched in his fist.

26

Nonfiction

That Sunday Dinner

JERALD RIIBE

There once was a boy anxious to save the world.

Baby Boomers in the twenty-first century have acquired a reputation for goal-driven competitiveness, loyalty, and a strong belief their work identifies their values. Growing up in a world dominated by the United States post-World War II, it was natural to see America as exceptional. The never-say-die attitude of Americans, the enduring belief in free enterprise, and the knowledge the United States was the best country ever created. Our country stood for justice, freedom, and hope, at least for people like me. Our threat was the Communists working through guile and treachery to destroy the American Way.

As an eight-year-old in 1964, I was fascinated with the world of espionage. Spies were the soldiers fighting our enemies during the Cold War. The sentries on the wall protecting our precious way of life. The grace and coolness of secret agents, practicing their spy craft, replaced the sheriffs of the Old West as the new American hero. Thanks to television there was no shortage of role models for the spy life. Judo and karate, mixed with gadgetry, was the perfect shaken-not-stirred cocktail for this third grader.

A young introvert with an active imagination already has important spy qualities: the ability to work in isolation and find satisfaction in the process. Being alone for some is a precursor to loneliness, but for me it was the time to plan, plot, and play without the fear of judgment or ridicule.

When I read of heroes from the past, I felt a calling to prepare myself to be a soldier in the shadows. A man, at some time in the future, who would demonstrate patriotic bravery with a humbleness of spirit. I had a calling.

Seeing myself as spy material, I decided to practice the skills I would need to defeat the dark side. It is not easy to learn the martial arts of the Far East alone in rural Nebraska. But a spy must be able to improvise and work with the materials at hand. I was ready for the challenge.

I started by practicing air karate chops upon unsuspecting imaginary foes. My ability to body throw a bed pillow over my shoulder and then quickly subdue the feather-filled villain put me at the top of my one-person, self-taught class. I felt my hand-to-hand combat skills were on par with an agent in the field. Eight-year-olds are very adept at critically assessing and measuring competence.

In hindsight, my training with evil pillows and ghostlike attackers would have served me better in seclusion. It was beyond the pale to consider my hard work in developing fighting skills might be seen by others as a seizure-like episode of the body, mind, or both. There is a reason the secret precedes the agent. I digress.

Hidden weapons are critical for a spy to complete a mission. The fact I had none did not deter my preparations to become a world-saving super spy. Unfortunately, my dad did not bring home his anti-aircraft machine gun or .45 Colt pistol from the war. If only Dad had known his son would be part of an international force for justice and the American Way. Spilled milk.

I gazed upon my treasured collections kept in a King Edward cigar box and let my imagination run wild. I had a ball point pen, several rubber bands, a paper clip, and a flattened penny found near the railroad tracks. Some may see a motley gathering of the useless. Nothing is without value when a spy is in the field. I was a third grader and had seen the power of the rubber band in my wind-up balsa airplane glider. I had felt the sting of a spit wad in the back of my head in school. Finally, I had in my grasp a secret weapon.

I unscrewed the ballpoint pen and removed the ink stem. Ball point pens, the frequent gift to customers from gas stations to banks, were similar. The top part had a pocket clip. For civilians, this was simply a convenience; for a budding spy it was a projectile launcher. Securing a rubber band to the clip allowed a thin steel wire fashioned from the paper clip to take flight, and, in the hand of a professional, to neutralize the enemy. I only had one paper clip, so my first shot had to count.

I put the pen back together, but instead of an ink stem, the bottom section contained a rubber band and the straightened paper clip. I practiced assembling my weapon and shooting the paper clip at a target on my bedroom wall at a rapid pace. I became confident in my ability to stop an attacker with this innocent-appearing ball point pen / lethal projectile launcher. Unfounded confidence in one's capacity is always highest when untested.

Espionage is more than judo and hidden weapons. It also requires the skill of lurking about and listening to private conversations to find the location of the stolen nuclear missile and the army of henchmen waiting to take over the world. That is the easy part. Discovering the secret headquarters of the evildoers is all fine and dandy. A spy needs to get that information to the person known only as "the Chief" as quickly as possible.

Codes are the lifeblood of secretly transmitting information. A spy needs a system to hide a message within a message. My problem was solved while browsing the local five and dime store one afternoon. On the shelf was a coding and decoding machine endorsed by none other than Agent 007. Hidden in plain sight, I had been given the power to send secret messages. Twenty-nine cents later, I left the store with my authentic coding machine. I kept the device in the brown paper bag and took a different route home. You cannot be too careful.

Naturally, I decided that if eavesdropping was an important part of any secret agent's daily routine, I needed to practice. I began to listen in on others' conversations with intent. This could seem to some as impolite at best, and probably creepy by most. That would be the case if not for the fact I was in training to protect America and the free world. A secret agent often must get their hands dirty to complete a mission. An eight-year-old boy, I understood dirty hands.

I followed a strict protocol for my invasion of others' privacy. I listened and took notes in my pocket-sized spiral-bound book. After the training mission was complete, I retreated to my bedroom to code the notes using my official 007 device. The coded notes were secreted in my most secure location, the King Edward cigar box hidden under my bed.

Spy training is intense, physically and mentally. A person seeking the status of secret agent cannot let their guard down. And sometimes, training missions need to take a different course. A break in the routine of our family was Sunday dinner with extended relatives. Aunts and uncles would come to our house, or we would go to theirs. The dinner was secondary to the conversations of family gossip, health problems, and others' misfortune. On one particular Sunday, I didn't realize I would be at the table as well as on the menu.

In keeping with the summer custom for family soirées, the adults convened to the front porch. A spy knows loose lips sink ships, so this family conversation was a perfect opportunity to gather intel. Never the slacker, I grabbed my notebook and, with great stealth, positioned myself near the window to clearly hear every word.

I wish I had not.

I suppose even veteran secret agents hear things that cause them pain. I was not that hardened. My stomach must have heard the words at the same time they hit my brain, because I felt like I was going to throw up. That day, I did not take notes. I did not create a coded file. I went to my room and flopped on the bed. I lay there, abject loneliness washing over me. At eight years old, I realized I was a part of the family, but also very *apart* from them.

The world which occupied my imagination was important to me. It was a place where I felt hopeful and safe. It was a world free of poverty, religion, and bigotry. It did not include empty milk bottles, shoes with holes, arguments about money, or a trailer house. Imagination is the grist for solving problems in the world, but it can also be the salve that protects you from the world's problems. I knew my play was not real. It was a respite.

I had overheard my parents trying to explain to my aunt and uncle their worry that something was not right about me. The phrases hung in my head and rented space in my mind: *All he wants to do is read, go to the library, and watch TV. When I was his age, I learned to work. Books won't feed you. Sometimes I wonder if he's touched in the head. At this rate, he will be as useful as tits on a boar. There must be something wrong with him to be so odd.*

The words from my parents' mouths hurt deeply. The responses given by my godparents, my favorite aunt and uncle, stung as sharply.

A shy boy can find comfort and solace in books, movies, and play. A shy boy also finds acceptance from adults through conversations which seem to show respect for his interests and thoughts. When you find that acceptance was not deep or genuine, an introvert will find loneliness.

A person seeking the truth should remember to be prepared for what they find. I never shared with my parents that I had overheard their conversation. I never forgot the power of their words. While a painful experience is difficult, it can also be the fiber for resolve. I never quit believing I could have a future unlike my family's present.

A few hours later my mom called that it was dinner time. I would have to leave my sanctuary and have a meal with my parents and my aunt and uncle. I thought I was going to cry with embarrassment. At that moment it came to me. This was a true test of my espionage mettle. Would I give up important information to a super villain just because she was torturing me? I would never reveal my secrets and today I had a big one.

I walked out of my room and casually took my seat at the table. I smiled and quietly ate my meal. The adults visited the familiar themes. Complaints about farm prices. Government spending on rockets and space. Wondering if our boys would be sent to fight in Vietnam. Angry the coloreds thought they were like us.

I listened without speaking, filling their expectations of the seen, but unheard, child. I felt connected to my family through the familiar ways stories were shared, the comfort of favorite meals and being at the table together. I also felt a disconnect from their values, hopes, and lives. I knew I loved them. And I knew I never wanted to become them.

My work at this mealtime was clear. I retreated to the shadows where secret agents live. I listened while taking mental notes of the conversations of the adults. I would be busy later, with so much to code, file, and store in my King Edward cigar box. The day had been hard and difficult, but I persevered. If learning, reading, pondering new ideas, and dreaming of a better world were odd, I hoped I would never quit being weird.

There once was an anxious boy who wanted to save the world.

JERALD RIIBE

The Launch

HOPE SPEAR

I round the corner of the room
I spy my small daughter standing
On the back of the couch
Inspecting the ceiling fan
I realize rapidly she is up to something
"Stopppp!"
I cry as her feet leave the couch
Her arms outstretched
As she propels toward the ceiling fan
I move in slow motion
To catch her
She misses the fan
Lands on her feet
"What were you doing?!"
"Checking if I could fly.
I can't."
She shrugs
Moving on with her day

Arman is Not Well

JORDAN BECKETT

A rman is not well.

It's been ten days since he and Galina ventured into the tundra near the Laptev Sea to take methane readings from the *Thermokarst* lakes, the lace-like bodies of water formed from the thawing and re-freezing of the permafrost. Dr. Galina Antonova was the leader of this climate science outpost, and she didn't typically take graduate students into the field, particularly students studying ocean circulation patterns. Still, there was a smaller crew at the hub than usual, so she'd made an exception. He'd felt both honored and intimidated.

"Will the ice break?" he'd asked.

"Not if we're careful," she'd replied. "You know, the impact of methane on ocean acidification might be an interesting subject for you to explore for your graduate thesis."

"Carbon has more impact."

She'd pointed to an area of ice with seemingly thousands of air bubbles trapped beneath. "Methane. Eighty times more damaging to our atmosphere than carbon dioxide. What happens when methane mixes with oxygen?"

"I see your point," he'd responded.

They'd walked on for a bit, and then she said, "This section is weakening. We'll set up the traps here. Stay close to the edge…it's safer."

Following her instructions, he'd spread heavy sheets of plastic over the gas sensor placed on the surface, weighted them down, and walked off the brittle ice to solid ground.

"What causes the methane to bubble like that?" he'd asked.

She'd stared at the sky and said, "Snow."

"Snow?"

"Among other things. The average temperature here has risen three degrees Celsius in the last fifty years. That warming brings more precipitation to the Arctic. In just the last decade, we've seen an average of twenty centimeters more snow each year. It's like a cozy blanket covering the earth, keeping out the winter chill."

"Warming the methane?"

"Thawing the ground," she'd corrected. "By another two to three degrees." She'd turned suddenly, grabbing him by the hand. "Do you know we have dated the methane released from these fields as between 30,000 and 40,000 years old? That is the Pleistocene era. Ancient. Mysterious."

Arman had felt a shiver that had nothing to do with the numbing cold.

"Watch for the bubbles," she'd said before striding ahead of him.

He'd stood, for a moment, thinking about the implications of all that excess methane mixing with the oxygen in the oceans. Lost in thought, he'd looked up to find her far ahead. In his haste to catch up, he forgot her warning. He'd felt the ice crack, his foot plunging into the muck beneath. A sharp, slicing pain almost caused him to cry out, but he'd held it back, too embarrassed to admit he'd been so careless.

He'd pulled his foot free of the crack in the ice and trudged on, being more careful to watch the ice for weakness. They'd finished setting their traps and sat in the truck as she used the satellite remote to bring the sensors online. They would measure the escaping gas when the pressure finally broke the ice.

"Thanks for the climate lesson," he'd said when they arrived at the research outpost. Reaching his quarters, he'd removed his boot to find a deep cut on his leg. He'd washed the blood from his sock in the bathroom sink and dug a bandage from his pack. It would do.

. . . .

But Arman is not well.

"Cranky," Galina said, the first time he'd snapped at her over something minor.

When he flew into a rage at a post-doc about scheduling the lab, she'd been sterner. "Your behavior is inappropriate, Arman. Control yourself."

Who was she to lecture him? he'd thought, scratching the wound on his leg. It had been five days since his fall on the tundra, and since that day, a sense of urgency had grown within him, such as he'd never felt. Like he'd awakened from a dream of life into the real thing.

He'd written obsessively, often through the night, pages numbering into the hundreds. He was eager to share his revelations with Galina so that she would understand how important his work was:

- Ocean acidification was inevitable, as was global climate change.
- We've been looking at the problem wrong.
- It cannot be stopped.
- We must prepare to conquer this new world as we conquered the old.

His words had jumbled together in his mind, spilling furiously from his pen into a new manifesto.

. . . .

"What is this?" she'd asked when he'd handed her his handwritten notebooks.

"They're numbered. You have to read them in order," he'd replied. "This is the answer to all the questions."

"Shouldn't you give these to Dr. Kulik?" she'd responded, trying to hand them back. "He's your advisor."

"He won't understand it. It has to be you. Just read it. Please?"

. . . .

It has now been ten days since the incident on the tundra, and this afternoon, Arman is hyper-restless. His skin feels like tissue and his veins like rivers of fire. He looks around the cafeteria and imagines the shock on their faces were he to self-immolate over his meal of stewed beef and cabbage.

He sees Galina Antonova at a table across the room, laughing with her luncheon companions. Did he hear someone say his name? One of the others, a post-doc named Andreev, is looking his way. He locks eyes with Arman, and a ghost of a smile crosses his face. Is she telling them of his research? Why are they laughing? Are they laughing at him?

He can hear his heart beating in his head, a muffled thrum, like the echo of earthquakes beneath the sea. His vision blurs and clears as he stares at the food on his plate. His breathing quickens as the joint of beef throbs and expands, until at last it bursts open and a writhing mass of worms covers his plate.

Jumping to his feet, Arman sweeps the tray from the table, then flips the table itself. A shocked silence greets him from the others in the dining room.

"The food has worms!" he yells.

Galina looks at her plate and then at Arman, who stands warily as she slowly rises and walks toward him.

"Arman, calm down. There are no worms."

"There are worms! I saw them!" He gestures toward the floor, his dinner knife firmly in hand as she approaches him, her hands extended.

"It's ok, Arman. You're just tired. You need resssssst." Her tongue darts out, catching the edge of her mouth. "Ssssit down," she hisses. Hisses!

Snake woman, he thinks.

"You're not well…"

With a shout, Arman raises the dinner knife in his hand and slashes at the creature coming towards him. His knife makes contact with a tentacle, and she roars, retreating as he advances toward the Snake Queen and her court. The Queen's men drag her away as a high-pitched keen screams through Arman's head, dropping him to his knees, his hands pressing tightly to either side of his skull.

When the noise ceases, he looks around the room and realizes they have all escaped. He tries to follow, but the door is locked. Trapped! Backing away, he sees her through the small glass in the door, taunting him. His vision darkens as he rages in his makeshift cage. And always, the sibilant echo in his head. Her all along, he thinks, picking up the steak knife from the floor.

Galina watches through the window in horror as he sinks the blade through his left eye socket.

Arman's blood is everywhere. After his collapse, the men moved him to the infirmary, tying him tightly to the bed in case he woke. The rest of the crew, including Galina, remains in the dining room, cleaning in shocked silence. She picks up the knife that Arman had flung to the side, red-tinged sclera shining in the harsh fluorescent light.

"How's your arm?" The question comes from Dr. Boris Kulik, her colleague and Arman's advisor.

"Just a scratch," she says, showing him.

"It's bleeding, Galina. You should have that looked at in the infirmary."

"I will. I just wanted to give them time to deal with Arman." She gestures to her arm. "Most of this blood is his, anyway."

"Shocking," he says, shaking his head.

"He's not been himself, Boris."

"How so?"

"Angry outbursts. Closeting himself in his room. Yesterday he gave me six notebooks of nonsensical writing."

"What do you think is going on with him?"

"I don't know. Stress? Lack of sleep?" She sighs. "All I know is that Arman is not well."

Galina makes her way to the infirmary, the wound on her arm wrapped in a kitchen towel that Boris has improvised. She needs to make a call to Yakutsk to arrange a med-evac. That's the protocol for serious events. The consequences of working at the edge of the world, she thinks.

"How is he?" she asks the medic, Ivan.

"Calmer now. I administered a sedative," he replies. "Galina...there is something you should see."

Galina approaches the bed where Arman lies, still tied to the frame. Both eyes are tightly bandaged.

"Over here."

Ivan steps aside to let her peer into his microscope.

She shudders as she looks at the squiggling subject. "What is this?"

"I pulled it from his eye socket. It's some sort of nematode. A worm. I can't identify it specifically. It doesn't seem to conform to any known species, but an entomologist would know better. There are more in his right eye. They wouldn't flush out, so I bandaged both." He shrugs his shoulders. "We are just a glorified first aid station here. I'm not equipped for this. I noted it in his chart for the med-evac team, whenever they get here."

Galina turned back to Arman, noting the bandage on his leg.

"Yeah," said Ivan, catching her look. "Nasty wound. Definitely not from today. Now, let's look at your arm."

Human blood is a warm bath for a creature suspended in cryptobiosis for thousands of years. It has been ten days since it felt life returning. It found the flow and rode it through the body, feeding on the heme, growing strong enough to reproduce.

Come, children. There are tastier treats ahead.

The soft grey tissue of the pre-frontal cortex was a particular delight.

Their world grew crowded. And then their host offered a way out. A silver road was introduced, covered in blood and viscera. They clambered aboard and entered a new world. So many hosts, welcoming their tiny blood-coated bodies.

The med-evac arrives in the morning to take two patients to the region's medical center.

Galina is not well.

JORDAN BECKETT

Nonfiction

The Desert Canvas: Keith Haring's Phoenix Intervention

GLEN LOVELAND

The Sonoran Desert light possesses a paradox that has vexed artists for centuries—a luminous austerity that both annihilates and sanctifies. It is a light that strips pretense, revealing form in its most elemental state. Into this crucible of sun and shadow stepped Keith Haring in March of 1986, his New York-bred iconography poised to collide with the ancient contours of Arizona. What emerged was not merely a mural but a fleeting manifesto on the universality of art, a testament to curiosity's power to transcend geography and mortality.

Haring's arrival in Phoenix marked a curious juncture in his meteoric career. By then, his radiant babies and barking dogs had vaulted from subway tunnels to global acclaim, their kinetic energy emblematic of 1980s New York's gritty vitality. Yet beneath the surface, a darker narrative loomed. The AIDS crisis, then a spectral force ravaging Haring's community, lent urgency to his work—an urgency that would crescendo in his final years. Though undiagnosed at the time of the Phoenix mural, Haring carried with him the weight of impending loss, a subtext that sharpened his creative fervor.

The invitation from the Phoenix Art Museum was itself an act of cultural daring. Arizona in the mid-1980s stood at a crossroads, its artistic identity shaped by competing traditions: the ancestral petroglyphs of the Hohokam, the bold Chicano murals of Tucson's Barrio Viejo, and the stark modernism of nascent desert architecture. Into this milieu, Haring brought a distinctly urban lexicon—a visual patois born of subway chalk and nightclub walls. The collision was deliberate. "I want to make art that's as public as possible," Haring had declared years earlier, "art that's *for* people, not about ownership." Phoenix, with its sprawling highways and sunbaked plazas, offered a new frontier for this democratizing mission.

The mural's creation was a spectacle of endurance. Witnesses recount Haring arriving at dawn, a slight figure dwarfed by the museum's concrete expanse. Temperatures soared past 90 degrees by midmorning, yet he worked without pause, his movements a fusion of choreography and compulsion. Local artist Rafael Soto, then a student, recalls the scene: "He didn't sketch, didn't measure—just attacked the wall like it was a living thing. It was jazz in visual form." Haring's process, often mischaracterized as naïve, was in fact deeply disciplined. Each undulating line, each interlocking figure, betrayed an intuitive grasp of balance and rhythm honed through years of graffiti's guerrilla improvisations.

What distinguished the Phoenix mural was its subtle dialogue with place. Amidst the familiar DNA of dancing silhouettes and radiant hearts, Haring wove motifs that whispered of the desert. Serpentine forms echoed the sinuous curves of the Salt River's ancient canals, while a palette of terracotta and ochre—softer than his usual electric hues—paid homage to the surrounding landscape. Art historian Dr. Elena Marquez notes, "He wasn't appropriating, but *responding*. The mural became a membrane between cultures, absorbing Arizona's essence while imprinting his own."

This exchange extended to the human sphere. As the day wore on, a crowd gathered—schoolchildren, retirees, off-duty waiters. Haring, ever the populist, handed brushes to onlookers, transforming spectators into collaborators. Maria Gutierrez, then a twelve-year-old witness, describes etching a small bird beside Haring's figures: "He told me, 'Art's not precious. It's a conversation.'" Such gestures epitomized Haring's ethos, challenging the art world's hierarchies long before "participatory art" entered the lexicon.

The mural's impermanence—a hallmark of Haring's public works—lent it a poignant resonance. Unlike the bronze monuments dotting Eastern cities, this was art that embraced its own mortality. Within months, the wall was whitewashed, its vibrant forms surrendered to Arizona's relentless light. Yet in its erasure lay a quiet defiance. As Haring himself mused, "The beauty of temporary art is that it exists *in* people, not just on walls."

The aftershocks of this ephemeral act rippled through Arizona's art scene. For Chicano muralist Carlos Ortega, Haring's visit was catalytic: "He showed us that our stories could hold global resonance without losing their roots." Younger artists, like installationist Leah Kim, cite the mural as a touchstone: "It taught me that place isn't a backdrop—it's a collaborator." Even the museum's architecture evolved; its once-sterile south wall became a rotating canvas for site-specific works, a legacy of Haring's intervention.

Haring's Phoenix sojourn also illuminates a broader tension in art history—the dance between regional identity and global vision. In an era before social media's flattening effect, Haring pursued a tactile cosmopolitanism, seeking kinship across borders. His desert mural, though vanished, prefigured today's street art movement, where Banksy's stencils and Kobra's kaleidoscopes migrate from São Paulo to Shoreditch, adapting yet retaining their core syntax.

Curiosity, the anthology's thematic lodestar, pulses through this narrative. Haring's was not the idle curiosity of a tourist, but a profound inquiry into how art might bridge disparate worlds. His Phoenix mural asked: Can urban hieroglyphs speak in the desert? Can transience convey permanence? The answers, etched in sweat and acrylic, affirmed art's capacity to transform alienation into communion.

In our present age of digital saturation, Haring's Phoenix intervention feels both archaic and urgently relevant. It reminds us that art's power lies not in its persistence, but in its ability to ignite collective imagination—if only for a sun-drenched afternoon. As the Sonoran light continues its eternal work, bleaching walls and blurring memories, Haring's true legacy endures: a clarion call to create boldly, connect deeply, and let curiosity be our compass.

her untold story

JUNE POWERS

pain was the color of her untold story,
curious   even to herself to admit
there was a story - she collected phrases
in a notebook for later review and small broken
objects from outside   for inspiration. the brokenness
of the objects gave her hope in a strange way.
in a curious way   she was confident
she could fix them   and show them how
to inspire others - in a window or on a bookshelf.
besides a bookshelf   she needed something
to cling to and worship each morning
for the day to go even halfway right,
so she danced   in the kitchen before coffee and tried
to visualize pleasant friends laughing – floating
mid-air, and visitors knocking at the door.
she struggled with inappropriate questions
being shunted her way sometimes   it happened
when meeting new people – projection she thought
before finishing her sentences.
her sentences became soliloquies spoken to the puddles

created by blue rain and culture robbers while waiting
for busses   she wondered why she was always alone
if she talked so much. she drifted out of and into dreams
and a certain patchworked chaos – uncomfortable enough
to make a suitable life.
when she remembered,   she liked to stare at suitable sunsets
count the colors and question the quality of their existence
so beautiful   so distanced   so different from her life yesterday.
yesterday shadowed today   with the heaviness
of unsaid things in her handbag   she ached on that side
in particular   leaning from the hurt   the questions   the memories
and the phrases in her notebook,   now in her bag.
she proceeded   even though unsure   which way to go.

JUNE POWERS

Fiction

Lil' Gecko

MIKE WILLIAMS

I've been crawling all day, my suction cups are throbbing. Wet grass soothes my webbed feet, the green blades as high as my back. My skin soaks in the moisture. *It's the best.* Rain sprinkles on me in pitter-patters, odd since the sky is sunny and blue. I quickly realize the 'rain' sprays from rotating pistons in the ground. *What magic!*

They say this place is dangerous. The elder geckos have told the stories a thousand times. But I was so hot and tired the wet lawn won me over. Maybe I'm foolish, but I have come to doubt whether the terrible monster they speak of is real. True, those who come here don't come back. Yet, it seems a leap to assume some beast ate them. What's the point in skipping the refreshing grass if the monster doesn't even exist? I guess I'll either enjoy my time or die finding out.

Through the greenery, I see a stone platform with wood structures designed to support the weight of giants. The platform connects to a building with brush-painted walls, hanging plants, and windows with blue curtains.

So, it's the home of a giant? That's the monster? Big deal. They're so tall they rarely notice us.

I crawl onto the stone platform and stand beside a wood post with ledges reaching out like tree branches. *Skrtch, skrtch.* A rough scraping shudders from above. My gut churns into a knot. Claw marks on the post catch my eye. Deep and smooth, they run in groups of four.

53

That's alarming. Maybe I should…
But the thought goes unfinished because I spot…

Crickets! A full orchestra cluster together under one of the structures. My mouth waters—I am helplessly drawn to them. I snag a few, but the rest hop away and crawl through a small crack in the door frame of the home. Maybe they think it's too narrow for me, but I wiggle inside, no problem.

My toes pitter-patter on the tile. It's slippery at first, but I find my footing. The air is perfect—calm and cool. Structures where giants eat, drink, and laugh together tower over me. Maybe a youngling like me should be nervous, but I'm not. I'm enthralled.

I spot the trove of crickets, and my mouth waters again. Food, shelter, and cool air all in one place. What's more to ask? Belly full, I lie on my back to nap on the chilled tile, sprawled out in the open. Life is good. So good, I forget.

Until.

A clawed paw scoops me up. Orange and yellow fur surrounds me and pokes my eyes. The beast holds me inches from its face, its fangs a sneer. Sadistic visions flicker behind green snake eyes.

"Wrong place, wrong time." The croon, a hideous rasp. "Now, you're my treat." It slams me on the ground. A claw jabs into my chest. "And I play with my food."

The claw slashes my torso. Excruciating pain jolts through me. Blood trickles down my body, across my legs and tail. I'm not ripped open, but I *will* have a scar for the rest of my life—if I make it.

Holding me down, the monster clenches my head between its teeth. It squeezes tighter and tighter, a little at a time. Pressure builds behind my eyeballs. Just before my head pops like a grape, I'm flung in the air. I flip, a leaf in the wind, only to land back on its paw. Fling, catch. Fling, catch. Fling, catch. After a while, it must get bored, blood lust eager. It pins me down, scratches my face over and over. Splotches of blood cover me head to toe by the time the monster is done.

Time for another game of catch. It tosses me up high and waits with a ready claw. Eventually, it will get bored. And when it does…

I flail frantically on my way down. The motion of my body makes me bounce off its paw and fall to the ground. I'm free—but not for long.

Luck has my back! I spot a small crack between the wall and the floor. I scurry, the monster hot on my trail. By mere inches, I avoid its swipe and slide through the crack, crawl deep into the crevice, out of reach. But boy, does this thing want to get me. It scratches at my hiding place so hard, pieces of wall flake off. The dust makes me cough. Small price to pay to stay alive.

Finally, it concedes. The monster crouches, face up close, and spots me with one eye. It hisses, "You're not getting out of here in one piece." The stench of rotten tuna barrels out of its mouth. Then, it moves along. Out of sight, but I know not gone. For the moment, I'm safe.

I'm also trapped.

Trembles rivet through my body. My wounds burn. I can feel the monster just waiting for an opportunity to strike. The dark crevice I'm in tunnels left and right. I follow it left until I find myself in a box where pipes weave through the top. One drips water. Drip. Drip. Drip. Enough for a shower, but not enough to quench my thirst. It's fine; I can't stand another moment covered in blood. I rinse it away, revealing my emerald skin. The maroon gash down my midsection stings as I flush blood and dirt out of it.

Now that I'm clean and the wound is clotted, it's time to go. I climb the largest pipe and reach the top. At first, I feel hopeless. The roof of the box seems rock solid. Then I spot a thin ray of light: an opening! The space is narrow, but I suck it in and wiggle through.

I'm on a counter, a windowsill overhead. A large spout with a handle hangs over a deep metal bowl with a drain in the middle. Small puddles of water speckle the bottom of the bowl. It's exactly what I need.

The fur-coated monster perches on one of the giant's sitting structures. Its attention is locked on the spot I was in, tail wagging in short jitters. The hunger in its eyes reminds me of my appetite for crickets.

I quietly slide down the side of the bowl and reach the bottom. The water feels so good going down my throat.

Suddenly, the screech of the monster's claws on metal cuts in. I turn around and barely dodge its swipe. I scurry up behind the water spout. It lunges, accidentally hitting the lever of the spout. Water drenches the beast. It scrambles to get out of the bowl but slips on the counter and falls.

I run to the other end of the counter and climb a giant white box that's cold to the touch. I catch sight of the monster shaking water off its coat. We lock eyes. It snarls. Above me is a vent in the wall, so I crawl in. The beast can't get me here.

"You think you're clever, huh?" It shouts. "Just wait until the air kicks on. You'll be blown away, and I'll be ready. Count on it!"

A demented glare etched on its face, it sprints *everywhere*. I can tell it's visiting every vent in the house, over and over, to thwart any escape attempt. Even so, I wonder if the beast is bluffing. *What air is it even talking about?*

As if on cue, a cold draft flows through the metal tunnels. It starts as a breeze and then storms. My suction cup fingers hold on for dear life. They're about to give when the wind ... stops.

I struggle to catch my breath. My heart pounds.

"That was a light one." The beast's voice resonates through the house. "Just wait until the next one."

It's *not* bluffing.

I travel vent to vent through the maze of tunnels, peering out each one to survey the rooms. The best exit is the front door, which is open but covered by a screen. Beneath the screen door is an opening just big enough for me, but too small for the beast. It's perfect. But the beast has to know this, too.

I need to debilitate the thing long enough to escape.

I look over every room again, one at a time. Search for anything to help in my battle. Exhausted, panic brews in me. *Will I be trapped in these tunnels forever, doomed to call this my home? Cling for dear life through every wind storm, wondering if it will be my last?*

From out of the blue, an idea strikes. A structure hangs from the ceiling in a room with plush giant seats set in a circle. The structure's wood blades are lodged into a metal sphere that spins around a bright light. My older brothers and sisters told me stories about mini-suns in the houses of giants. Suns controlled by a switch on the wall.

Is this contraption the same? Can I use it to distract the monster?

It's not the best idea, but it's all I can come up with.

I wiggle through the vent, leap from the wall, and land on one of the blades. My fingers stick to the wood, strong enough I won't fall off. The spinning makes me dizzy, but I must hold on.

The monster barrels out of the hall. It spots me immediately. Fangs gleam through its hungry grin. *Maybe it's too dangerous up here for it to get me.*

Nope. It's intent on the hunt. The giant's sitting structures and bookshelves serve as a climbing wall for the beast. It readies itself atop the bookshelves, then leaps. It shoots for the blade I'm on, but lands on the one next to me. To my surprise, its claws keep it in place.

"I got you now!" Its hiss sends a shiver through my bones.

It's now or never. If there's a switch, I need to find it. I peer over my shoulder where at any moment, the beast will pounce.

I'm trying to find the spot on the wall, but... THERE IT IS! A white panel. A rectangle with a small lever above a switch. *My siblings told me about a switch, but a lever?* Doesn't matter. I have to take the shot.

Just as the beast leaps, I do, too. I grab the lever, slide it down with two clicks. I hold on, the beast eyeing me with its now familiar murder glare. But the blades are doing the opposite of what I wanted; they're slowing down. Drool falls from the beast's grin.

I'm freaking out. In my panic I hit the switch below my feet. Everything goes dark. *Oops!* I flip the light back on in time to see the beast about to pounce. Scared witless, I fall. My flailing hands ratchet the lever up by six clicks. The blades spin faster. The beast hangs on tight, but the blades whirl the monster in an orange blur. It can't hold on, launches off its perch with a scream, sails, then lands on a cushioned seat with a thump. The cushion bursts open in a cloud of feathers.

I scurry toward the front door while the beast is lost in the blizzard. It leaps out of the cushion, sprints, and stands between me and the door.

"Where do you think you're going?!"

It towers over me and I gulp. Once again, I have one option: RUN!

I haul my tail back to the room where we met and jump to the counter's edge, but my hand sticks to a paper bag. The beast sees me, must think it's got me, and leaps. My grip fails, dragging the bag over the beast's head. It lands on the floor, helplessly scrambling to claw the bag off.

I can't lie; it's fun to watch.

I notice a stack of plastic bottles against the wall, balanced like a six-level pyramid. Filled with red liquid, a picture of a tomato decorates the front. A devilish idea occurs to me. I lunge and kick the monster in the side—my small size be damned. It falls, summersaults across the room, and slams into the pyramid. Bottles topple over the monster and pop open. Tomato sauce splatters everywhere. It looks like a murder scene.

The beast bursts out of the pile with a roar. Fur covered in sauce, ripped bag on its head, it tears the paper to red-drenched ribbons. Bloodshot eyes lock on me, burning with rage. It's had *enough*.

I book it down the hall. I don't know why. It's a stupid move. But it's too late. The beast is hot on my tail. Something made of soft gray fabric lays on the floor. *Giant clothes?* I dive into one of the sleeves and squirm through the fabric. In the middle are three exits: two large ones on the sides and a sleeve in front of me. I have only a moment to think before the beast bursts in on the right.

Time to GO!

The opening on the left seems obvious, but my gut tells me to take the sleeve. I dart just in time to avoid the beast's paw and scurry through the sleeve. The beast crawls after me, then ... stops.

Did I outrun it?

58

I emerge and look back. The sleeve is too small for the beast. It's trapped, like a rat inside a snake. Only a matter of time until it tears through. I scurry away, the beast's shredding screech ringing in my ears. I reach the front door and slip under the screen.

I'm finally free!

Never have I been so happy to feel the heat. I take a moment to catch my breath. Once my heart settles, something stabs my tail. I yelp and look back—the beast! *How did it get here so fast?* A flap in the wall next to the front door waves back and forth, then stops with a click. *There's a secret door. Of course.*

Bloodshot eyes glare down on me through tomato-tinged fur. The claw digs deeper, pierces through my tail.

"I am so ready to end this!" The beast yells.

I beat my legs against the ground as hard as possible, pulling against the beast's claw. Little fissures form at the base of my tail.

The beast raises its paw. "It's been fun…" Its claws protract.

I pull at my tail. Pull, pull, pull! The tears deepen. Wind breezes through a growing space between my tail and body.

"But now I'm done, and it's time for slaughter."

As the claw comes down, I make one final tug. My tail rips off. I fling away like a rubber band, barely dodging the claw. The beast is confused, which gives me a chance to book it. It quickly pursues. It lunges. Time seems to stop as I realize I'm done for. It has me in reach. It's going to get me. Then, a miracle intercepts.

A blonde giant rounds the corner, scoops up the beast mid-air, cradles it like a baby.

She gives it an *adoring scorn*. "Sunshine! Leave the poor lil' gecko alone."

The beast looks up at her with dough eyes. "Mmrrrooowwww."

The giant laughs, scratches the purring menace behind the ear, and carries it inside.

There's a brief silence, then I hear the giant shout, "Are you kidding me? What a mess! Is this my homemade tomato sauce in your fur? Gross!"

At long last, I'm free. For real, this time. I'm lucky to leave with my hide intact—I *really* am. And the next time I want to beat the heat by exploring the unknown, I will look at my scars and find some shade instead. As I look back at the spot where my tail used to be, I realize the beast was right. I didn't get out in one piece. But I got out alive.

MIKE WILLIAMS

Who's to Blame?

JULIE ERFLE

In my mind's eye she is short—five feet, maybe a smidge more—with a face weathered by an unkind sun and the twisty knuckles and arthritic knees that accompany a life of manual labor. Perhaps she cleans homes for the millionaires of Paradise Valley or works at the chicken farms on the west side of the valley. I do not know. I do not care. She is the mother of my husband's killer. And though I have never met her, I hate her all the same.

The morning of September 18 was beautiful. The kind of day when the slightest of chills—one perceptible only to long-time desert dwellers—swept the air, and the anticipation of fall awakened senses deadened by the monotony of sweltering summer days. I drove the morning carpool, dropped off my first-grade son and his friend in their classroom, then headed home with my toddler in tow. But the beauty of that morning darkened seconds after I pulled out of the school parking lot and heard a traffic report on the radio.

There's still some slowing along the 51 near Northern as well as the Broadway Curve. But watch out for emergency vehicles at 24th Street and Thomas, where a serious officer-involved shooting has occurred.

"Fuck," I whispered. *That's Nick.*

It was the first thought that popped into my head, but I quickly dismissed it, then scolded myself for even thinking such a thing. My husband was a highly decorated police officer, too adept to be in that position. And he had just recovered from a two-year battle with testicular cancer, one that required three surgeries, chemotherapy, out-of-state travel, and months of hospital stays for a surgical complication that nearly took his life. There was no way the universe or God or whatever it was that controlled our destinies could be that cruel. Still, I dialed his cell and left a message, then held my breath when I turned into my neighborhood, afraid I'd see a patrol car idling in my driveway.

I spent the next thirty minutes folding laundry, downing a cup of coffee, scrubbing my kitchen counters, cleaning up the toys around my toddler, and downing yet another cup of coffee, until the caffeine and adrenaline crested. Then I grabbed my cordless telephone and shut myself in my bedroom.

"Mountain View precinct, this is Stephanie."

"Hi Stephanie, this is Julie Erfle. I heard about the shooting, and…and I just need to know it wasn't Nick."

A long pause.

"Um, Julie?"

"Yeah?"

"There's a lot going on right now. Can I put you on hold for a minute?"

"Sure."

I resumed my pacing, this time creating a figure-eight across my bedroom floor. I paused at the window, searching for a patrol car. I paced. I paused. I paced.

"Julie, you still there?"

I paused. "Yes, yes, I'm here."

"Yeah, um, so we don't have that information yet, but I can let you know when we do. Are you at home right now?"

"Yeah. Yeah, I'm at home."

I hung up the phone, knowing Stephanie's last question was a harbinger to the thing all police spouses feared, but tried to convince myself otherwise.

My pacing expanded into the kitchen. Minutes later, officers were at my door. They rushed me to the hospital, then herded me into a small room with a priest and two detectives. The doctor walked in, met my eyes, then lowered his head with a gentle shake.

. . . .

I had worked in television, so I already knew how the next few days would play out, with reporters clamoring for an interview, a candlelight vigil at the site of the murder, a televised funeral with a miles-long procession of police cars and motorcycles and strangers lining the route, waving American flags or blue ribbons.

What I was not prepared for was the politicizing of my husband's murder: the politician who fundraised off his death, the police union president who pressured me to take a side in his feud with the police chief, the radio host who said I was partially responsible for the future deaths of police officers.

You see, my husband's killer was undocumented. Brought across the border as a toddler. Educated in Arizona schools. A member of a local gang with a rap sheet and a previous deportation. And this was Phoenix, circa 2007, where fear and hate—fueled by misinformation and right-wing media—were spreading like wildfire across the Mogollon Rim.

Nobody questioned my anger toward my husband's killer. They assumed it was because he was "illegal" and if I spoke out, I would endorse calls for mass deportations.

But they were wrong.

I didn't hate Nick's killer because he was born in Mexico. I hated him for stealing my family's future. For the memories our sons would never have the chance to make. For the violence he committed against my husband's body. For the void that could never be filled.

I was able to separate the evil perpetrated by this man from the collective anger leveled against all undocumented immigrants, and months after Nick's murder, I rejected enforcement-only immigration solutions and publicly embraced humane reforms, hence the vitriol lobbed at me by the same people who initially elevated me as a sympathetic victim.

But for some reason, I could not separate the actions of this individual from the perceived sins of his mother. This woman—whom I never met, whose name I did not know—became my obsession.

She must have been an abusive parent, I reasoned. Someone who modeled violence. That would explain the actions of her son. Or maybe she spoiled him, made him into a kind of king who could do no wrong, a coddled child who turned into an unruly teenager and a murderous adult. I refused to find empathy for her, never considering she might be a victim of violence as well. Instead, I fantasized about confronting her in a courtroom, screaming obscenities in her face, demanding an apology for raising a killer, and refusing forgiveness even as she pleaded on bent knees.

The cruelty inherent in those daydreams surprised me, though for years I shrugged it off, believing my reaction was one of traumatic necessity. I never had the opportunity to confront my husband's killer. After he mortally wounded Nick, he hijacked a car and took a hostage, then was gunned down during a standoff with police. Perhaps I needed someone to fault, someone who was still breathing. But why did I choose to condemn her and only her? Why did I never once consider the killer's father?

There's a term for this line of thinking: mother-blame. It's when we place responsibility for a child's behaviors or outcomes squarely on the shoulders of the mother, ignoring the role of a father or other factors that can influence a child's actions, such as environmental stressors like poverty or underlying psychological or developmental issues. Mother-blame is a societal problem, one rooted in patriarchal norms that assign women as the sole caretakers in their children's lives.

Our country has a long and scarred history of holding mothers responsible for everything from a child's lack of self-discipline to schizophrenia. Psychologists originally blamed autism on "refrigerator moms"—moms considered too distant. Sigmund Freud, the psychologist who obsessed over psychosexual development (and whose incorrect theories, I would argue, have had a lasting, negative impact on mothers), claimed punitive toilet training caused obsessive compulsive disorder. Addiction, as well, was blamed on poor breastfeeding habits. Every conceivable deficit led back to moms, and they were cautioned against being too domineering, too passive, too cuddly, too cold.

That I fell prey to mother-blame is a deeply embarrassing admission since I consider myself a feminist. Have been since my junior year of college when I enrolled in a women's studies class and morphed from a conservative, devout Catholic into a progressive Unitarian Universalist. As a feminist, I was supposed to smash the patriarchy, not uphold it. But as I look back now, I realize my reproach of a nameless woman's child-rearing was not a one-off situation based on grief, and despite my education and awareness, I had internalized this norm.

Years after Nick's murder, I was paging through one of my journals and noticed an entry that detailed an imaginary encounter between myself and the killer's mother. I described how this woman looked and talked and intimated about her beliefs, painting a picture of someone I was already familiar with: my mother.

My parents had a traditional, mid-century marriage, one where Mom did all the cleaning and cooking and child-rearing, while Dad focused on his occupation. Because Mom was the parent responsible for a litter of children and the one who doled out discipline—often with the metal ends of belts or wire hangers or two-by-fours—she was also the one I held responsible for the physical and emotional scars of my childhood. My father, on the other hand, was held in esteem. He was the respected business owner. The church board and community volunteer. The pious husband and father who worked to keep his family fed while being met with constant criticism from my mother.

It wasn't until after my thirty-first birthday, when Nick was recovering from a complicated lymph node dissection, that I viewed my childhood through a sharper lens. My husband spent three months in and out of various hospitals that summer. He was shedding fat and muscle, wasting away from an undiscovered hole in his intestine. During the day, I tracked down doctors and demanded tests and fought with our insurance company as I shuttled our toddler and preschooler back and forth to the hospital and swim lessons and playdates. At night, I washed stacks of dishes and paid the bills and cut the grass and tossed more laundry into the wash and spent hours hunched over my computer, scouring the web for answers to various abnormal lab results, or the pros and cons of alternative treatments. Neither of our families lived in Arizona, but almost all of them traveled to Phoenix at some point to lend a hand.

My dad was the exception.

"Anything around the house you need help with?" my Uncle Matt asked after calling to let me know he was in town that week. "Or has your dad already taken care of everything?"

"Dad?" I shook my head. "No, Dad's never even been to Arizona."

"But doesn't he know what's happening with Nick?"

And that's when the story of my past required a revision, when the excuses I made for my father's absences rang hollow. Dad had placed himself at arms-length, blending into the background of my life like a spectator at a ball game, while my mother—even when playing the role of an opponent—kept herself in the game. Mom flew into Phoenix to care for her grandkids when Nick and I traveled out of state for his surgery. She did not think twice about dropping what she was doing in order to help, and for the first time in my life, I recognized myself in her. Not the pointy chin or the fair skin we shared, but the heaviness of our responsibilities. I was submerged in chaos much the same way she had been drowning under the weight of cloth diapers and homemade casseroles and brawling children and handsewn outfits and sticky countertops and empty refrigerator shelves.

This new understanding should have helped me find empathy for other mothers, including myself. But after Nick's murder, not only did I spend months blaming the killer's mother for his actions, I then spent years blaming myself for my children's outbursts and academic struggles and emotional setbacks.

It was easy for me to bear that cross, as I had long believed I was the lesser parent. The one who knew what not to do but required books and parenting groups to figure out what came naturally for my husband. Since I wasn't good at distraction or play, I believed it was my fault the kids squabbled so much. If I had been more attentive to my youngest, perhaps I could have prevented his learning disability. If I were a better model of patience, my oldest wouldn't have been so angry.

My fears were reinforced when one of my sons was a fifth grader, and I was called to his principal's office for the third time that year. He was struggling to make friends and had executive functioning issues, misplacing his textbooks, losing track of water bottles, forgetting to turn in homework assignments. This time, he was in trouble for play fighting with another student in the lunch line, which was considered an act of aggression.

The principal was aware my son's father had been murdered a few years earlier, not long after a prolonged battle with cancer. She also knew my son was working with a therapist to address his anxiety. But she questioned whether there was "something else" going on at home.

"Are you sure you're doing everything you can?" she asked.

It was the same question I asked myself every day, multiple times throughout the day. Was I doing enough for my kids? Was *I* enough?

The Not Good Enough Mom is today's version of mother-blame. For the most part, our society no longer points the finger at so-called refrigerator moms or smothering moms as the cause of their child's mental health diagnosis or addiction because we better understand the role of biology. Nature is a more powerful determinate than nurture. However, although we may not consider mothers the source of their children's afflictions, we still hold them accountable for fixing them.

When my youngest was diagnosed with a learning disability, I felt alone in my efforts to help him. Though I had a name—and a reason—for why he struggled to rhyme or identify letters, that was all I had. There was no agreed upon roadmap. No "here's what you or your child's school should do next." No easy access to resources. I had to sift through conflicting advice, search out programs and pay for tutors, educate teachers about the myths of dyslexia, and press administrators for proper accommodations.

My son learned to read, and by middle school, he was in advanced classes and on the honor roll. Teachers and administrators offered kudos. I was now The Good Mom. The hero. But while I loved recognition of my efforts, I also understood part of my son's success was the result of luck and privilege. My husband had been dyslexic, so I knew the signs and insisted on early testing. I was also able to afford a comprehensive, private evaluation and intensive tutoring.

After I helped launch a nonprofit that supported parents whose children had learning and attention differences, I met numerous mothers who did not have those luxuries. Many of their children didn't receive a diagnosis or interventions until junior high or high school, and by that time, frustration and feelings of worthlessness had taken hold. These were often the kids who dropped out of school or ended up on the street. And these were the mothers we judged as bad. As insufficiently selfless.

These women were not lazy. Or indifferent. They went to battle for their children, becoming well-versed in medical terminology and legal jargon—some even overcoming language barriers—so they could advocate for their kids. But despite their best intentions, their children suffered setbacks, and like moms in similar situations, they blamed themselves, believing they could have done more, they should have done more, they just weren't good enough.

So many of us do the same. We find fault with the individual because it's easier than questioning the system. We blame the killer's mom because it's easier than acknowledging the structural deficiencies in our communities.

Today, I am likely around the same age the killer's mom was when her son took another man's life. I no longer ruminate about her parenting skills or dream of angry confrontations. I have no knowledge of the circumstances of her life or the struggles she faced. And in the end, none of it matters, as she was never responsible for my husband's murder, and I have no reason to hate her.

My sons now straddle the age of their father's killer. Their prefrontal cortex—the part of the brain responsible for reasoning and impulse control—is still developing, yet they are recognized as adults, with the same level of culpability as their fifty-year-old mother. Though I am more cognizant of the unique stressors and privileges that have created obstacles and advantages for them, I still have to remind myself that I am neither the reason nor the excuse for who they have become. I am neither the bad mom nor the hero. I am simply a mom who was and continues to do the best I can. And that is good enough.

72

A Woman on Stage

ILANA LYDIA

I am the spirit of each and every one of you.
I am the dreamtime self-aware.
I am the nagging suspicion that there is more to life than meets the eye.
I am empty of meaning, except for that which you give me. You give me everything, because I am you.

Here is the secret I can impart to you now:
Life is short.
Plays are shorter.
If you get caught playing in life, God help you, you're done.

Here is the offering I make to your divinity within:
I am no more a character than you are.
I am no less a character than you are.
Are we here, just meant to entertain the gods?

Shhh . . . don't go back to sleep.

Take this news and let it course through your veins.
Take this gift and let it give you life anew.
You are not real—What freedom! What joy!
You are the most real thing in this moment in time—What freedom!
What joy!

Quickly! The mind can only remain hyper-aware for so long.
The door is closing.
The opportunity is slipping away.
See the stage you stand on now, while you're able.
I see you no longer, as you no longer see yourself.

These words.
I do not write them.
I worry one day I may try to speak them aloud, and nothing—

> *But we'll never know what else she has to say, as
> her script has run out. A moment of panic as she scratches
> at her throat and tries to produce a sound. Then her
> manner calms as she adopts her opening pose.*

ILANA LYDIA

Fiction

Legacy

GAYLA WIGAL ROBINSON

"Grandma! We brought your favorite." Emma bounds into the house, past Willa who holds the door open. "Café mocha, extra whipped cream! Mother says it's your favorite."

Maybe ten years ago. I look beyond her to my empty-handed daughter. It shouldn't hurt, but it does. In all probability, this is my last Mother's Day. I wanted something more than a paper container of coffee.

For my granddaughter's sake, I put on a cheerful smile. "I'm glad you finally arrived." I take the cup from Emma before it spills through the lid.

My daughter wears a knife-pleated navy pantsuit, a perfectly tied bow at her neck. Coiffed hair lacquered like a helmet, sunglasses cover her eyes. Her lips are slightly pursed. So haughty. So rigid.

My throat tightens. I suspect today may be a repeat of the handful of visits we've had in the last year.

Removing her sunglasses, she bends down to give me a stiff hug. I tug the oxygen tubing from my nostrils and smell her breath. No evidence of late-night revelry or morning espresso. That's not proof, though.

It galls me that I'm reduced to making distasteful comparisons, yet I still ask Emma, "Did you do anything special for *your* mother today?"

Emma hopscotches across the tiled floor. "I made Mommy toast with sprinkles, and in school we made macaroni necklaces." Pride shines in her voice.

My daughter stands at the window, scrutinizes her manicure. No dried pasta hangs from her neck, that I can see.

I never received a handmade token for any holiday. Maybe Willa did—she spent more time with her. Sometimes I regret that. But my work was important. We all do what we must. *Surely, I can't be jealous of stringed noodles?*

Willa offers lemonade, but it's refused.

"Emma." I fiddle with my oxygen tubing. "Where are your manners? Say hello to Willa."

My companion bends down to meet her, eye to eye. "How are you, Emma?"

"For God's sake, give it up!" My daughter huffs. "We don't have to participate in your sick fantasy of a family."

She twirls her sunglasses. Perfect figure eights, over and over. Perfectly. The sign for infinity.

And that's when I know.

My breath catches. Today was supposed to be different. I wanted my daughter to be here. To accept my apology for all the ways she thinks I failed her. My contributions to Automation and Robotics demanded attention and time. And now, I don't have much time left. Despite all of mankind's advances in medicine, cancer always seems to find a way.

My hand trembles as I take a lukewarm sip. The cream and chocolate do nothing to temper the bitterness.

"It's good, Emma. Thank you." I set the coffee aside. Adjust the quilt on my lap. There's still time to connect with my granddaughter. "How is ballet class?"

"Grandma! I quit that *years* ago." She draws out the word as only a six-year-old can. "I'm into robots now."

My heart leaps. Maybe my DNA won't be wasted after all. Maybe Emma takes after me.

"Did I ever tell you I designed…"

"We're not here to listen to you again extol your great career and the sacrifices you made," my daughter snaps. "If you had made different choices, maybe there would have been different outcomes."

How long have those words been rehearsed, embedded, to be at the ready, waiting for just the right opportunity? My daughter must truly resent me.

She reaches for Emma's hand. "Time for us to go."

Frantic, I tug my granddaughter closer, run my fingers through her silky blonde hair. This may be my last chance.

"Can't you stay?" I despise the longing that's crept into my voice.

The door slams behind them.

"How can my daughter do this to me?" I scrape away angry tears. "You're more like family than she is, Willa. You've been with me for what, thirty-five years?" I push off the quilt. The heat is stifling.

"Since the day your daughter began walking. Thirty-two years, eight months, three days and …"

"No matter." I wave her off. "You witnessed her ingratitude just now, didn't you?"

"Yes, Mother."

"Mother?" The glitch is alarming. "Have you re-written your own code? I programmed you to always address me as Dr. Capek."

With the cadence of a metronome, Willa pats my shoulder. "The social convention is for women who have given birth to hear that word of endearment on the second Sunday of May."

I push her hand away, gesture at the closed door. "Tell me, what model is it?" I crank up the oxygen flow and breathe deep. "They've certainly progressed since I made you in the lab. That AI surrogate looks just like my Hanna."

"A KIMM 2034."

A wasp lands on the cup lid, antennae probing a droplet of whipped cream.

"Am I so wrong in asking my daughter to show up in person and bring my only grandchild?"

It's a rhetorical question, something Willa still struggles with.

"As an early language model, I cannot tell you who is wrong or right. However, I can say that acknowledging the harm one has caused…"

"Enough."

I'm exhausted. The wasp flies away. Is it satiated or disappointed?

A sudden thought jolts me. Emma used both words, *Mother* and *Mommy*. Hanna used to call Willa *Mother*. Is history repeating itself? Or are they both...

"Willa..." I try to swallow the doubt. "Is the child... Wait." It's hard to breathe. "Do I really want to know?"

I let the wisp of blonde hair fall to the floor.

"Another rhetorical question, Mother?"

GAYLA WIGAL ROBINSON

Embers

BONNIE DANOWSKI

The logs in the fireplace glow
Creating dreams with shadows
On the walls.

They sit together on the sofa
Both cautiously wondering.

What now, she says.
What do you think, he responds.
I only want to be here, be here with you.
Nothing more, that's all.

How quickly we trusted one another.
We've said things
Even secrets never before shared.
It's been so easy.

There is a spark
Between us, waiting
Waiting to be lit.
What do you think?

Well, maybe, but remember.
Remember her?
I remember him
I miss him, still.

What if they are watching?
What would you do?
What would I do?
But they aren't.

I think they would be happy
That we are here
Sitting in the fire's golden glow
As it lights the room and warms us.

Move closer then.
Let's see what happens.

BONNIE DANOWSKI

Just a Peek

ELLE LECARRE

Martha McCullum's chubby fingers poked at the black keyboard letters like an ivory-billed woodpecker on an elm tree during mating season. All elegance was lost in her flat jabs that hit between the keys more often than on them in her feeble attempt to spell the word "binoculars" correctly. She didn't need anything professional or state of the art. She just needed to see across the street, preferably into Mr. Clarence Owen's backyard.

She wondered if binoculars would sit well with her bifocals that perched low on her rosacea-flushed nose as she noted activity in the neighborhood from the comfort of her oversized chair. Covered in a toile of rose and green vine, the chair faced her large front window. She always scrunched a knitted pink throw behind her, next to her doily-designed pillow.

Some days, when the neighborhood was quiet, she read her true crime magazines and mystery novels or worked crossword puzzles. Other days she knit sweaters for newborns at the community hospital up the street. She was philanthropic like that, helping those less fortunate, she told her neighbors.

"You can never be too careful," she would tell her husband Jim about her surveillance.

Jim usually grunted and returned to the current sport on television. Whether that grunt indicated agreement or disapproval, she had no way of knowing. Jim had retired from the postal service after forty-one years and still spent most of his free time "resting" his legs on the couch. His only lifting these days included the remote in his left hand and a cold beer in his right. Jim's hair was a little whiter, a little thinner, but he hadn't changed much since retiring, barring the development of an eye roll executed whenever Martha's notebook appeared, her pages filled with scribbles and date stamps:

Tom Murphy, blue track suit, morning run, 3/04 Tues. 7:27 am

Stray black cat digging in John Newmeyer's roses, 3/05 Weds. 3:15 pm

Kay Simms - Cadillac? New? How do they afford it? Odd, 3/06 Thurs. 2:10 pm

The new neighbor, Mr. Owen, if that *was* his real name, was a busy man. Most days Martha spotted him wearing old sweaters and faded corduroy trousers, a well-used brown towel hung from his back pocket. He had moved in just a few weeks before, arriving in an older model Jeep, a woman Martha was certain must be his wife riding passenger.

Martha had already made an entry for the Owens in her notebook. The minute the previous owners sold the home, Martha had looked up the new owners through the county's assessor office. The more recent entry was more concerning:

Owen, Clarence & Darla 3/8 seen in backyard, 10:45 pm dark, v. suspicious.

So suspicious, she added:

Heavy gloves. Boots - mud, digging? Bright reflection - shovel?

Martha fumed, then chastised herself for not having gone over to meet the Owens after seeing them drive up. But that day she'd had a pie in the oven. By the time she pulled it out, they were inside and closing the garage door. The Owens had not noticed Martha's frenzied waving through the window.

Martha saw her neighbor Zoe Pinkett walking up the street with her Scottish Terrier, Scotty. "Absolutely ridiculous name," Martha muttered under her breath before grabbing her coat off the tree by the front door and marching out to meet them. Zoe saw Martha coming and side-stepped to cross the wide street, but it was too late.

Martha watched as Zoe's long angled bob, similar in color and texture to Scotty's, flew across her bare face as she whipped her head around at the sound of her voice.

"Hello, Zoe!" Martha cooed. "Lovely day, isn't it?"

Zoe's usual bright expression paled a little as Martha beelined toward her. She nodded to Martha. Scotty stopped, whined, and looked up at his owner with a pleading expression. Zoe leaned down to pet him.

"I know, Scotty, it's just for a moment," she whispered, loud enough for Martha to hear.

"Zoe!" Martha barked. "Are you aware of what is happening in this neighborhood?" Martha leaned in slowly, lowered her voice and continued. "That man," Martha jerked her dish-water brown, perm-fried head toward the Owen house, "was in his backyard well past eleven p.m. again last night." She jabbed a coral-colored fingertip in the direction of the Owen house and hissed, "What do you think he's up to?"

Martha wrung her hands. She caught and held Zoe's wary blue eyes, imploring Zoe to collude with her, or at least acknowledge the significance of her information. After all, this could very well be a matter of national security.

Zoe sighed, glancing momentarily to the heavens. She shifted her weight to the other foot, her voice calm.

"Maybe he was letting a dog out before bed?"

Martha's eyes shot open wide, her brows all but disappearing into her hairline in surprise.

"I didn't know he had a dog!" Her lids closed to mere slits. *How could Zoe have known that before I did?* "What kind of dog does a man like that have?" Martha shot the question out like a bird startled from its nest.

Zoe blinked. "Well, I think it's a Doberman Pinscher, but it was dark. It may have been a Weimaraner. Not sure."

Martha latched on to the thought like a baby to a bottle, refusing to let go. "So, he needs a guard dog, does he? Of course!" She jerked her head several more times in the direction of Mr. Owen's house, eyes wide with intrigue. "I knew he was hiding something back there!"

"It's a beautiful dog. I'm sure he just likes the breed. I'm also sure there's nothing nefarious going on, Martha." Zoe tugged at the leash. "I've got to get Scotty home." She turned abruptly, called over her shoulder, "See you later, Martha."

Martha watched her go; certain Zoe's hasty exit was related to her fear of talking about Mr. Owen. *Why else would she be in such a hurry to get away?* Martha turned and marched back to her home, eager to take notes in her little book.

Alarmed by a shadowy movement near her feet, she looked down to find the stray black cat she had noticed in Mr. Newmeyer's roses. The sinewy feline stopped mid-stride and turned to look at Martha. After a moment, he sat down on the edge of the lawn and stared at her with cool, yellow eyes. Martha recoiled, clutching the front of her blouse. She stepped around the unwanted beast, wrinkled her nose, and backed toward her house.

"Shoo! Shoo!" Martha waved her hands in her hasty retreat.

The right rear wheel of the Piggly-Wiggly grocery store shopping cart gave off a high-pitched whee-scrunch, whee-scrunch, whee-scrunch as Martha pushed it down the aisle. She needed batteries for her flashlight, the big black 5400 lumens tactical Phantom 5-X model she had purchased *by accident* online when she was looking for a spotlight bulb for the den. After her conversation with Zoe, she decided to keep it.

Whee-scrunching around the corner, Martha scuffed into the home improvement aisle. Her eyes bulged as she spotted Mr. Owen at the far end. Whipping her head to the right, she pretended to scrutinize the paint thinner cans. With nothing less than bombastic side-eye, she observed Mr. Owen's cart. An axe, two boxes of lye, and some hemp twine along with a black tarp under which other items were hidden. Martha's eyes narrowed. *Oh, my goodness! What does he need those things for?* She couldn't resist the urge to whee-scrunch her cart over to him.

In his mid-to-late sixties, Clarence Owen's close-cut, battleship-gray hair lined a balding crown. Keen gray eyes belied the world-weary, impassive expression on his tanned face.

"Well, hello!" Martha cooed, her smile sweeter than honey from the hive. "You must be my new neighbor on Ravens Drive. I'm sure you know me, Martha. I live across the street. Somewhat of a neighborhood ambassador, I might add."

Mr. Owen stepped back, eyes on Martha, disinclination on display. But as he drew in a breath to speak, Martha cut in.

"So, where are you and your wife from? I understand you are renovating your backyard, I believe, and your project is…?" This time, Martha's eyebrows pushed even her forehead wrinkles up toward her hairline. Lips pursed, she leaned forward in heightened anticipation.

Mr. Owen had sufficient class to nod with decorum. His white-knuckled left hand gripped the cart handle, his body positioned between the cart and Martha.

"Nice to meet you, Mrs. er..Martha?"

"It's Mrs. McCullum. Mrs. Martha G. McCullum." She drew the G out. "Related, of course, to the McCullums of Aberdeenshire, Scotland." She jiggled like a bobble-head doll. "Oh, you must be familiar with the McCullums of Scotland, very, very important people, you know." She clicked her tongue and stood back with an air of secret knowledge. After furtive glances to ensure no one else was listening, she leaned forward and whispered, "They say we're related to royalty, you know." Martha tilted back and folded her hands across her ample bosom.

"Oh! Uh…I see, uhm…" Mr. Owen croaked, though Martha couldn't tell if it was from amusement or confusion. He tapped a right finger on his sucked-in lips, cupped his chin with his thumb and forefinger, an introspective frown on his face.

"That's very interesting, Mrs. McCullum." He regained his composure. "It's a pleasure to meet you."

An awkward silence ensued, Martha nodding, Mr. Owen tapping his fingers on the cart handle.

Martha pressed on. "Uhm, the house project? Lovely! What is it you're working on? I'm sure I could find you some help if you need it. I know everyone in the neighborhood, as I said." Martha purred.

"Yes." Mr. Owen stiffened. "I'm sure you can be very helpful. I'll keep that in mind. I'm certain we will have the opportunity to speak again, but I must excuse myself. I'm late. Good day." He nodded and pushed down the aisle.

Martha trotted a few steps behind him. "So soon? No need to hurry away. Well, perhaps next time. So much to discuss, you know." She waved at his retreating back, her brows knit over milky brown eyes. *How rude rushing off like that, and nervous, indeed! What on earth is he up to?*

The binoculars having arrived in the mail, the notebook entries increased over the next few days:
Mr. Owen, backyard 3/13 Thursday, digging in far corner, 11:05 pm
Zoe 3/14, walking dog 2:15 pm, chased stray cat away. Good riddance!
C. Owen, 3/14 9:20 pm, backyard, laying out tarp...midnight! Still out there.
Jin B. 3/15 bicycle had flat, pushed it home 3:37 pm
C. Owen, 1:50 am 3/16 backyard, unable to see...
Martha sought a better view from the upstairs bathroom's small window, but was unsuccessful, the toilet lid collapsing under her weight. The three-tiered plastic shelving unit toppled with her, creating a raucous clatter.

A startled shout bellowed from the bedroom. "What the..." This was followed by the flurry of ruffled bedding. "Dang it, Martha! I'm trying to sleep!"

Martha struggled to get up off the floor. The rug slid under her feet, and she grabbed onto the sink countertop to steady herself. "It's fine! I'm fine! Nothing to worry about," she called back to Jim, gingerly extracting the hairbrush poking into her bum.

"For Pete's sake, Martha!" He yelled. "Go to bed!"

Martha's notes continued, with increasing question marks and exclamations:
Darla Owen not seen since move in day, missing, Mon. 3/17 where is she??!

C. Owen 3/18 10:25 pm pushing dirt around yard with wheelbarrow!

By Wednesday, the inside of Martha's cheek was sore from unconscious chewing. She fretted about the house, patrolling back and forth between the front room and bedroom windows in search of a prime surveillance post for her binoculars.

Convinced as she was that no respectable neighbor would be traipsing about at such late hours, she now felt it her duty to act. After all, a *secure neighborhood was everyone's business, wasn't it?* She assured herself lives were at stake and time was running out. She settled on an audacious idea, planning her strategy while sitting in front of the big window in her favorite chair, pencil and paper in hand, once or twice perusing a true crime magazine for research purposes.

After a dinner of mashed potatoes, peas, and pork chops, and certain that Jim was settled in his den in front of the television for the night, Martha went upstairs. Donning her tennis shoes, an old black sweater, and gloves from Jim's closet, she finished by pulling a floppy, dark-colored garden hat over her head. With her large 5400 lumens tactical Phantom 5-X flashlight, she snuck out the side door.

The March night was cold but crisp, and quiet as death. Goosebumps rose upon her arms as Martha crept along the hedge at the side of her yard. She lingered, eyes wide, head swiveling in rapid succession from side to side. The street was deserted, the Owen house shut tight.

Martha sprinted as fast as her thick legs could carry her across the dark street. She ducked behind a bush in the Owens' yard. Waited, breathing in shallow gulps, eyes closed, listening with heightened focus for any sign of discovery. There was nothing but quiet in the inky black of the night.

Creeping to the Owen's solid wooden gate, her clammy hands struggled with the rusty latch. The wrought iron bar scraped over the metal catch, so loud, Martha's heart leapt in her chest. In agonizingly tiny increments she pushed the gate open. Jaw clenched, she prayed the hinges wouldn't squeak. Wiping the sweat from her forehead she rested a moment to catch her breath.

Okay, ok, ok.

On tiptoes along the concrete pavers, she smashed herself up against the house as she neared the backyard. A faint light shone, casting dim, sinister shadows across the darkened lawn. Martha was so close now. She crouched low, the roughness of the house against her outstretched palm. She just needed to look around the corner.

Just a peek.

Trembling, she switched on the flashlight and was blinded by the deluge of coruscating brightness. Hands shaking, her vision obscured, she stepped around the corner.

First, she heard a low, menacing growl. Then a shout as a dog lunged toward her. A towering figure rose from the shadows, a knife glinting in its hand. Martha froze; her breath sucked away like a decompressed plastic bottle. The pounding of her heart spiked beyond measure. With a silent scream, mouth stretched wide, fear crept up her neck. Her eyes popped out of her scarlet-inflamed face, shiny and beaded with sweat. The figure moved toward her.

He's going to murder me!

Martha dropped the flashlight, whirled, and ran in panicked terror toward her house.

Martha didn't see the black Tahoe until it was upon her. She flipped up into the air, over the hood, and landed in a glass-shattering crash on the windshield. An ear-splitting screech from brakes skidding reverberated through the neighborhood. Martha's body rolled violently down the hood and fell headfirst, with a skull-crunching thud to the asphalt.

The last thing she ever saw, before death's darkness took her, was the cat sitting still as a statue on the edge of the sidewalk, save for the black tail twitching right and left, left and right, its yellow, blinkless eyes glowering at her crumpled body.

According to Zoe, who spoke with the local police, Mr. Owen was gardening that night when it all happened, spade in hand, shovels, a tarp, and handy bags of fertilizer nearby. Suffering from insomnia for many years, Mr. Owen had taken up the growing of night-time blooming flowers: The Chocolate Daisy, named for its luscious chocolate aroma, and the Moonflower whose poisonous, white, trumpet-shaped flowers unfurl under the illumination of the moon's light. His specialty was the elusive Queen of the Night, whose large showy flowers occurred as a singular bloom each year. Calculating to the day, Mr. Owen would send out annual invitations to his neighbors to show off his exceptional and rare garden. Martha would have been thrilled for a peek at that!

Poetry

Quiet Observations

NOUR KANDALAFT

I sit by the window and outside I can see
The world moving forward without me
People walking past and cars that stop by
And in the distance, two squirrels climbing a tree
It's hard for me to believe
Each one of these people has a life like me
I wonder how many have tear-stained cheeks
And are carrying a heart filled with grief
I wonder how many had life be kind to them
And made them believe
In themselves, but also in its beauty
I wonder if the little girl will change the world someday as she dreams
Or if life will leave her broken and empty
I wonder about the little boy with a basketball in his hands
What will life make of him and his paths
And I sit by the window and let my imagination dance
About the life of all those walking past
As if I am watching from behind the scenes
My life on hold while theirs is made complete

And it doesn't take me long
Until I start seeing pieces of me in all those passing along
Each leading a different life
But the same one, simultaneously
A realization that our lives are intertwined
And bound by humanity

Fiction

No Farewell

DEREK BARTON

The four-foot, dull silver-plated coffin loomed at the front of the chapel. It was smaller than Jassam expected, yet intimidating. It sat upon a cloth-covered wooden platform, six miniature wheels peeking out underneath. A wreath of delicate white and orange flowers brought a brief smile to his lips. Tears welled. Her favorites. Seven short rows of empty wood benches stood between him and the casket. Radiant, Cassia's eyes shone from her class photo on a nearby easel. Jassam trembled.

How can one prepare for such a day? Someone, probably one of the chapel staff, had placed a tiny silver gem-crusted toy owl at the head of his daughter's coffin. The last thing Jassam had ever given her.

His heart ached within his chest, the pain alien to him. In all his fifty-six years, he had never felt such raw emotion. His breath labored and wheezed, fought to escape his frail lungs. This was beyond his limits. Legs unwilling to carry him further into the chapel, Jassam sank to his knees. Fat tears slid down his stubbled cheeks.

A hand landed gingerly on his shoulder. He slowly raised his face to find Beyani, Cassia's caregiver for the last two years. During his wife's drawn-out battle with cancer, Jassam had had to work deep in the belly of the coal mines, forced to complete his Control Pacific Core contract.

"Jassam, here… let me help you," Beyani's dark hair was slicked down in front, as somber as her blue blouse and black skirt.

101

He nodded, powerless to get to his feet. "She's really gone?" he moaned. "Oh, what did I do?"

"Stop that. You couldn't have known," her voice soft and sincere.

Jassam shook his head, refuting her words. *All alone. Terrified. I should have been with her!* He berated himself, but said no more as she pulled him up.

Today, he was not garbed in his customary miner's overalls. Today, he wore his finest suit: a dark gray jacket, polished black boots. A felt fedora of matching dark gray hid his limited salt-and-pepper hair. Control Pacific had excused him for the funeral, given him a week to put his affairs in order, mourn, and bury his only child. *A week.*

People milled about in the hallway behind him. He didn't recognize any of them.

"Come, come. Jassam, please," Beyani's warm hand held his, guiding him to a bench near the front. They sat for a few minutes in the quiet together. "I think most of the others attended Mayor Dae Avonne's funeral yesterday. Couldn't afford to take today off, too."

An awkward silence fell upon them. Rows of light purple candles lined the walls, broken up by orange clay pots and marble statues. He stared at the fine tapestries, at a massive mural of a mountain amid a stormy seafront. Part of him, outraged no one would show for Cassia. Her life had been as important as any of the others. Yet, another part of him, relieved to be alone in his grief. *Make this horrible day be over.*

"I gave her the owl at the airport. How someone found it in the wreckage, knew it was hers; I can't fathom." His voice trembled. Jassam squeezed his eyes shut, worked to gather control.

I missed you, Daddy. I am so happy to see you both!

The words shot through him, distant, barely louder than a whisper. The voice feminine, cheerful, young. He opened his eyes, snapped a look over his shoulder. No one was behind him. None of the people from the lobby had come inside.

"What's wrong? Are you okay?" Beyani studied him.

Jassam nodded. "I... yes, I –"

You both look so nice, but sad... I wish I could hug you, Cassia whispered.

He jumped to his feet. "I've got to smoke. I'll be back. Just need some air."

Outside on the temple grounds, Jassam leaned against the property fencing. Head pounding, his heart drummed like a steel hammer inside his chest. His hands shook as he pulled out his black cigarette case and box of wooden matchsticks from a hidden jacket pocket.

Just my imagination. I am overwhelmed. My mind, trying to provide solace. Get a hold of yourself, Jassam.

He struck a match against the bricks and lit his cigarette. The soothing fumes filled his wrecked lungs. His nerves began to settle.

You told me you quit! You said you had to. Cassia's words rushed and petulant. The doctor wrote on your profile suss-suss-ceptteble for lung disease. Because of the mines.

He froze, rigid against the wall.

"Marked susceptible for lung disease," he quietly corrected.

Yes, susceptible.

Cassia? Is that really you?

Daddy, come back inside. I want to see you again. I can only hear you now.

Cassia, are you inside the temple?

Of course, I am, she giggled.

How?

The voice didn't answer. Doubts over his sanity returned.

I... I don't know, she finally replied. *I remember you gave me the owl before my flight. I wanted to bring it on board, but they made me put it in my luggage. The pilot announced there was a storm and to expect turbulence. I didn't understand what he meant until the plane began to rock and tilt terribly, Daddy. I got so scared! The lady sitting beside me held my hand. She was scared too! Then there was a loud crash. I saw fire!*

Are you in pain, Sweet-tears? Grief gripped his heart; his legs nearly gave out.

No. I... don't remember how I came here. Her voice fell silent inside Jassam's head. At last, she whispered, *It's quiet here. Very quiet. Cold and dark too, except for that circle thingy.*

Circle thingy?

"Jassam, can you come back in? Father wants to start the ceremony." Beyani held open the wooden double doors.

He nodded, stamped out the last of his cigarette.

Father was a small, portly man with white stubble on his chin that matched his silvery cropped hair. As they found their seats again, Father gestured to a young woman sitting at the piano. Soft, ethereal notes filled the chamber, but Jassam's mind reeled.

All through the brief burial ritual, he stared intently at the coffin. The owl stared back at him. He knew it was insane, but he grew positive Cassia could somehow see him through the little toy.

"Bow your heads. We shall send our prayers to Cassia, taken from us too soon." Father's words, hollow and practiced.

All of it, unheard by Jassam. Beyani nudged him with an elbow. She bent her head, eyes beckoning him to do the same. Jassam's breath came out harshly. He had been holding it subconsciously. He did as she instructed, but inside, he didn't pray. Only waited to hear Cassia again. Needed to hear her.

After a period of silence, Father walked from in front of the casket, held out his hand, and shook Jassam's.

"Father, I... I am going to take her owl."

Jassam stood and retrieved it before the man could answer. Father, for the first time showing true emotion, nodded in agreement. Jassam returned to the pew and continued his vigil.

"Please, take your time." Father beckoned the organist, and they left the room.

After a few moments, Beyani asked. "Where should we go eat?"

He didn't respond.

"Sir, are you hungry?"

"No," he waved his hand blindly at her. "Please. I need some time alone."

Beyani left the pew without a word. He worried he had offended her, but he had no patience for anyone other than Cassia. His fingers stroked the toy's small head.

Cassia? Are you… Are you there?

Yes. I'm glad you took the owl. I'll be able to come home with you now.

He frowned. His grandmother often spoke of gidims, lost spirits doomed to haunt the world and wander endlessly.

"Are you scared or angry with me?" he whispered.

No, Daddy. Why are you upset? What's wrong?

Guilt squeezed Jassam's heart again, his chest tightened until the confession poured forth.

I shouldn't have listened to your Aunt Lessnette. I should have kept you home with me, where it was safe. I sent you away because I thought you'd be happier. That they would give you things I couldn't afford. I wanted you to have a better life.

I know. Stop crying. I can't bear that!

He wiped at his face with the back of his hand, trying to catch his breath.

I am so sorry, baby. I love you so much.

I love you, too.

You said you see a circle?

I do. It's beautiful, like a rainbow filled with amazing colors and lights.

The circle is?

Her voice was hesitant. Uh-huh. Sort of. The circle thingy, it's like a window and through it, I can see this ocean. Like the ocean we saw with Mommy on her last birthday. Only it's filled with all these waves of color and twinkling stars. On the edge of it, I can see a white beach that stretches forever. I think there are people on it.

People? Who?

I'm not sure. Some are waving at me. Like they want me to come to them, but… I can't leave you, Daddy. I won't! Yet… it looks so warm there. Filled with those pretty lights. The more I look at the rainbow ocean, the more I can make out shapes. Animals and people are swimming together in the water.

Are you scared where you are?

She paused. *No. I just miss you.*

Jassam took a deep breath and tried to swallow his pain. *Then go, honey. Swim in the ocean. You love to swim. I know you want to.*

No, I don't. If I go… I don't think I can come back. I just wanted to tell you what I am seeing. It is so beautiful, Daddy! I wish you could see it.

Do you see anyone on the shore you recognize?

They are too far away. Her tone distracted and distant. She went quiet again for a long moment.

Cassia? Cassia!

There was no response. Coldness crept inside his heart and mind. He cried out, worried he had lost her all over again, even though he had told her to go. He brought the owl up to his face and stared deeply into its black eyes. Searched for any spark.

Oh, Daddy! I went closer to the circle! I could feel sunlight. And there were people calling to me and singing together.

Cassia, please don't stop talking to me. I… I have to hear your voice!

As long as you hold onto the owl, I will never leave you. Unless… Her voice trailed off.

Unless you go swimming? he finished her thought.

I think so. I want to swim. I want to feel that sunlight. It's so warm, yet different. It's…

Her words faded. His fingers squeezed the owl. He knew he was supposed to let her pass.

Like the warmth you felt when you were in Mommy's arms?

Yes! I won't do it. Her voice, close and sharp in his head. *I don't want to leave you. I can't lose you like Mommy.*

He had no words. Jassam knew he was being selfish, yet it was too soon. How could he bear to let her go? But if he didn't, was he cursing her to endlessly wander?

"Sir?" Father stood at the end of his aisle. "I am afraid I am going to have to ask you to leave. Rest easy knowing your daughter is in good hands. Trust us."

Jassam could only gawk at the man. He blinked several times before he shuffled out of the temple. Soon, he found himself sobbing behind the steering wheel of his old pickup, the owl clutched to his chest.

Daddy, please don't. I'm here. I'm not leaving you.

Oh, Sweet-tears, I am an old fool. I am not a good man or father. I know what you need but—

Yes, you are!

No. I am keeping you. Keeping you in the dark and cold.

I'll be brave, I swear, Daddy!

Jassam mopped at his face again, then placed the owl on top of the dash. An answer dawned on him. He smiled at the toy, sighed with weariness, and started the engine. It was late, the skies pitch black and starless. Only the streetlamps and his headlights lit the empty world around him. In another hour, he took the exit to Troddan River Park.

I know what I can do, honey. Hold on.

He guided the old Chevy into a parking spot facing several buildings and a playground surrounded by a sandy shoreline. Jassam dug the half-full prescription bottle from his glove compartment. He retrieved the owl.

Outside, he undressed and stacked his clothes on the hood. At the edge of the riverbank, he stepped into the rushing stream, his feet and legs soon numb. Jassam gulped down the pills. The empty bottle hit the water now rushing about his thighs.

I will take you to the ocean. You and me together again, Cassia. We'll swim. Take long strolls on the beach like we used to. Explore wherever you want…

Nonfiction

Machines of Endearment

GERALD WOOD

Imagine how life would be if horses and carriages were still our transportation. A regular fill-up would be oats. This thought came to mind on a recent visit to Martin Auto Museum in Glendale, Arizona. It was a nostalgic trip through time to a remarkable place filled with fabulous cars and memorabilia celebrating the history of automobiles.

Rows of vintage autos showed dramatic changes since the first horseless carriages rattled down dirt roads in clouds of dust! The attentive staff mesmerized us with stories about specific models and exhibits which amplified our experience.

Bright neon and stamped metal signs on the walls advertised vintage service products with some names remembered and others long forgotten. Numerous old-style fuel pumps stood tall throughout the building. Above-ground displays of gasoline in clear glass dispensers always fascinated me as a child.

They reminded me of a time when 'Service station' meant something different; when attendants greeted customers with a smile, checked oil levels, tire pressures, wiper blades, and cleaned windows at no charge while you waited for them to fill your tank.

The Martin museum's cars of the rich and famous evoked memories of movie scenes of yesteryear, with white-gloved ladies on the town with handsome men in stylish spats. The bright red Auburn 866 Boattail Speedster brought to mind road races ending in tragedy from the movie *"The Great Gatsby,"* based on the book by F. Scott Fitzgerald. Also on display were classy Packard and Cadillac four-door sedans for gentry, city slickers, and mobsters. Models came in any color so long as they were black.

In like fashion, Martin featured three former cars I once drove that prompted flashbacks to the roles they played in my life. A black 1928 Model A Ford with running boards resembled the one my brother and I shared as our first car for after-school jobs. We bought it for $100 in 1955 from our high school math teacher, who told captivating stories about his Model A in Algebra and Geometry classes. It became legendary because he never drove it to school. One day I asked him, in jest, if he would sell his car to me, and he said yes! We felt honored that our much-admired teacher chose us, as many students had asked before in vain.

When we proudly began driving this old car to school, girls giggled and asked us for joy rides that we gladly accommodated. At that point, we knew our money bought an unexpected benefit. Nights in town were fun times as we cruised back and forth on Main Street, our windows rolled down for waving, hollering, and acting like teenagers. We called it *dragging Main.*

Sounds of yesteryear came from our Model A's *oooga, oooga* horn, plus the *clickity-click* of red-spoked, narrow-gauge tires on our hometown's brick paving. A lever on the steering post made the engine *chug-a-lug, chug-a-lug, chug-a-lug,* as it slowed to a delightful speed.

Another Martin exhibit showcased a 1955 Chevrolet Bel Air like the one I bought in college. That pre-owned car was wonderfully reliable for driving to National Guard drills and for dating. A stereophonic sound system I installed for favorite hit-parade tunes made this '55 Chevy one of my favorites. It had the emblematic two-toned Cerulean Blue and Cream paint finish of the fifties.

Also on display was a popular 1964 Ford Mustang with a 298 V8 engine that reminded me of the one my bride and I bought with trade and cash. We saw it while driving past the Ford dealership's showroom, turned around to take a second look, and fell in love with that deep blue beauty.

Our final offer drove such a hard bargain, the Ford salesman—whose name was Price—said "No deal."

We drove away empty-handed and disappointed. As luck would have it, the telephone rang just as we arrived home. It was Price. *"Gerald, come and get your damn car,"* he said. My wife and I returned immediately, where he greeted us with a conceding smile and warm handshakes.

Universally loved cars like my Model A Ford, 1955 Chevrolet, and 1964 Ford Mustang are the envy of classic car buffs everywhere. Similar cars bring high bids at the annual Barrett-Jackson auctions in Scottsdale, Arizona, where I now live. When these old cars come out for Sunday drives, Rolls-Royces, BMWs, and Lamborghinis must share the road—and the limelight—with these curiosities from the past.

Changes continue to occur in automobile styling, safety, efficiency, and technology. All-electric and hybrid vehicles with self-driving capabilities are the latest advancements for urban and interstate travel. A fleet of driverless Waymo Jaguars is growing in greater Phoenix as alternate conveyances for cab service and Uber. These autonomous rides, in my opinion, prevent road-rage and accidents attributable to human judgment, or lack thereof.

Man-made machines, past, present and future, provide us with utility, pleasure, and progress. But memories make them machines of endearment.

Memorabilia

DONNA PARKER

We sit in groups, gather in coffee shops, libraries, and a few bars.
We sit and write down our stories.
        And wonder, will we finish? Who will read them?

We sit with our white hair, gray hair, and thinned hair.
Lives written on faces wrinkled and worn.
Revealing half forgotten loves and untold lies.

Hunched over laptops, tip tapping away, over leather bound journals
with carefully chosen pens and gnawed yellow pencils.

We reveal our memories. Imperfect at best.
Old ones telling old stories as old as time.
There are no new ones with these plots.
 Love, marriage, betrayal, revenge and loss.

Death becomes the theme; a red ribbon running through our narratives.
Our innocence, our youth, our families, one by one.
        They leave us.

Death the denouement of our lives which no one reads.
We all know the ending.

The Tailor

EILEEN SAUER

The last thing Elliott Farnsworth experienced was the horrific cacophony of shattering glass mixed with the screech of metal-against-metal. His beloved Mazda Miata was no match against the eighteen-wheeler. Had anyone witnessed the crash, they would have seen the briefest glimpse of something blurry and shimmery emerge, similar to the optical illusion of heat haze during hot weather.

During the crash, Spark 285912 was thrown violently from the entity known as Dr. Farnsworth, and found itself looking down with pity at what had been its home for 57 years. It turned away mournfully and began to rise, and the higher Spark 285912 rose, the more its heavy mortal veil of forgetfulness began to lift, in the way a hermit crab sheds its exoskeleton as it grows.

The artificial constraints of time and space fell away, and Spark marveled at this. *How could it have forgotten how small its existence in Dr. Farnsworth's physical plane had been?* As memories returned of what it *really* was (immortal), its terrain became more familiar, and its motivations.

Spark hadn't entered the physical plane to become mortal. Spark did so to experience what immortals could not: Joy. Only a mortal human can experience the ineffable sensation of holding the first newly invented iPhone, knowing the device would change the world. Fast forward a mere decade. "Oh, another iPhone release? Woo. Hoo. Yawn." Multiply that by infinity and, well, you get the picture.

Without the veil of forgetfulness, Spark could no longer feel joy. Spark knew what it must do to, well, *go home.*

It was time to pay another visit.

. . . .

"Hello!" exclaimed The Tailor in surprise. The neon sign proclaiming *Alterations Sew Wonderfully Precise* cast a faint green tinge on the entrance to the store.

"I wasn't done yet," lamented Spark, still mulling over the crash.

The Tailor sighed. "Spark, with over seven billion humans on Earth 9836, you are truly an old soul. I'd think you'd be an expert by now."

"By old soul you really mean slow learner, dear friend," grumbled Spark. "The living are funny. They hear 'the dead shall rise' and cook up some harebrained idea of a zombie apocalypse, when it's already happened, the dead have already risen. The only ones left recurring are us old souls because we're slow learners who can't move on from our love of the physical plane."

The Tailor eyed Spark thoughtfully, then stated resolutely, "It doesn't matter that you've always gotten what you've wanted; it's never enough. Let's make this the last go-around then, eh?" Eyeing the available garments, The Tailor finally selected one. "You've had it too easy. You need this one." He turned to see Spark's crestfallen expression.

"It looks so... plain," Spark muttered. The Tailor laid the garment on a worktable and spread it out to its fullest combinatorial explosion of possibilities. "Female? Not particularly attractive. Short. Not physically strong. At least born and raised in America, but not famous, rich, or influential. Comes into the world with powerful, intuitive skills, constrained by authoritarian parents. Could become anything from a kind-hearted wallflower who never reaches her potential to... what the heck, one improbable path leading to President of the United States!"

The Tailor nodded, delicately caressing the vibrant thread. "Unlikely, and the entity will die prematurely from a stroke if that happens."

Spark carefully soaked in the potential threads woven in all directions, the different destinies depending on choices made, and the resulting consequences. "This is really tough."

"But precisely balanced," The Tailor retorted, before softening slightly. "There are a few alterations that may help guide you in the right direction when you've forgotten."

"Such as?" asked Spark, hopefully.

The Tailor picked up a threaded needle, took in one side of the garment, then used scissors to cut away the excess. "There. You now have an aunt on your mother's side who is genetically the most similar to you, who does nothing with her life."

The Tailor repeated the operation on the opposite side. "You will be autoimmune and highly sensitive to pain at a time when people are unaware of the connection between gluten and autoimmune disease. This pair of alterations will make your life miserable, but with effort and discipline you will learn how to take care of yourself. You will learn what it means to be an outsider, to not belong. You will learn about limits, humility, and compassion."

"And you think this is an improvement?" yelped Spark.

"Within the dark alley, a knife fight begins," intoned The Tailor.

"You mean, when the student is ready, the teacher will appear," countered Spark, confused.

Bemused at the lapse, The Tailor concurred. "Ah yes, Earth 9836, not 9835. And," with a severe look at Spark, "when the teacher is ready, it seems the student will appear. Thanks to your hedonistic tendencies, a healthy percentage of the seven billion souls on Earth 9836 are related to you," admonished The Tailor, tapering another section, then hemming the garment. "This time, because of your parents' deep psychological scars, you will know from an early age that you don't want children."

"But why?" whimpered Spark, stunned.

The garment now finalized, The Tailor turned to look at the sumptuous fur coat Spark had draped on the counter. "I think you're done with Earth 9836." He scooped up the fur coat (it would need a thorough cleaning), and hung it on the rack of items to be processed. Carefully perusing the collection of available outer garments, The Tailor selected Earth 82745, a tattered trench coat with one loose and one missing button.

"Climate change. War. Black holes. Social inequity. Global pandemic. Inflation. Social media. AI. Children and pleasure have been forces too powerful; they've kept you tethered to the physical plane. With enough disincentives, we can eliminate those compulsions. This time, finish what you need to finish. If there needs to be a next time, you might have to return as a cockroach since that will be the only thing that will survive."

He laid the trench on the counter and spread it out, inspecting it carefully.

"When the student really *is* ready, the teacher will disappear," declared Orb 9385726 (a.k.a. The Tailor) with finality. "Complete your mission. Then and only then will you be prepared to meet The Architect."

Spark gasped. "I thought The Architect was just a rumor."

"Pshaw," spat Orb. "Do you think I was always The Tailor? I was once Spark 29384874. Who do you think transformed me?"

Spark 285912's head spun (figuratively, of course). "You mean to say, there is a beyond, beyond... *this*?"

"You think you're bored here, that there is no joy. You have no idea. You've been looking down with longing and regret, when you should be looking *up*."

"I wonder if there is anything above The Architect," pondered Spark.

"I don't know," The Tailor reflected. "When we are ready, only then does the next layer of the onion become visible."

The Tailor draped the garment and trench coat on Spark. The veil of forgetfulness became heavier and heavier as Spark returned to a new physical plane.

Gina's mindless doom-scrolling through Facebook stopped abruptly when she spotted a post from a clearly exhausted Zara lying in a hospital bed. Eyes closed, her best friend cradled a newborn, wrinkled with mousy brown tufts of hair, a snub nose, and mottled skin.

She knew Zara's decision to take anti-anxiety meds while pregnant was a complex one, but after 7/11 it had been necessary, given the gash in downtown Manhattan where three majestic towers once stood. Over 5,000 casualties – unthinkable. And doing this on a date mirroring the national emergency telephone number 7-1-1 – truly sick.

Her friend had flown there to attend a business meeting on the 101st floor of Tower 3, deciding to stay in the on-site hotel to save travel time the morning of the meeting. Miraculously, she overslept. After the first of three planes hit the towers, Zara didn't bother to grab her shoes; she simply ran, then walked six miles north in bare feet. It was two weeks before her husband was able to drive there to pick her up and return to Houston, Texas.

Gina peered closely at the photo. Was that a rash on much of the right side of the baby's face? Babies were supposed to look angelic, but this one... didn't. Not particularly. Maybe it will look better once it outgrows the prune stage. The caption on the post announced:

We're thrilled to share the news... It's a girl!
Nia Percy was born February 4 at 1:25 a.m., weighing 5 lbs. 9 oz.

120

NASA Releases the Pictures

PAM VAP

NASA releases the carefully chosen
images procured from the James Webb telescope:
a mountain range formed of dusty light,
another of giant star-dusted fingers pointing,
one image like a glorious kaleidoscope,
another a swirling spider web.

The poet is dumbfounded,
the scientist tingles, the student
is assigned an assignment,
social media quips pithily,
the priest wonders who are we
that you are mindful of us,
and the old woman carries her coffee
in a chipped mug out to the back porch
to stare at the pale morning sky
and imagines somewhere we cannot see
another star is born.

Nonfiction

My Spark Bird

JACKIE ANDERSON

I was hooked on birds the first time I saw the tongue of a hummingbird lick nectar from a blossom. For a few seconds, I watched this tiny bird hover near a flower. Its tongue flicked out and that small tube entered the blossom. It was the first time I looked through a good pair of binoculars. Those powerful binoculars opened up a portal to a whole new world and let me see, up close, something I'd never seen before. I have never forgotten the wonder of that moment.

This happened in October 2006 during my docent training program at the Desert Botanical Garden in Arizona. They hosted a bird walk on Monday mornings, so I joined in. Someone handed me a pair of binoculars. Plants stay in one spot, making them easy to observe and identify. Birds level up the challenge of observation because they hop, run and fly. I found the challenge exhilarating. I had signed up for docent training to learn about plants, but after my first bird walk, I discovered I was more interested in birds.

One of my first ventures into birdwatching had been years earlier, in 1992 when my 10-year-old son decided to identify all the birds in our backyard as part of a Cub Scout badge. I bought *A Golden Guide to Birds*; the first bird field guide I ever owned. I didn't own binoculars then. I gave my son a bag of birdseed and he threw it around the backyard. The birds arrived. I watched through the window as my son sat outside, looking first at the birds, then the book, then back to the birds. A few minutes later, he walked into the house with a disappointed expression on his face.

"All the birds are finches, sparrows, or doves," he said.

He had hoped for more variety, maybe even something exotic. He finished the project, earned his badge, and we both forgot about birds, believing there was nothing of feathered interest in our backyard.

A few years later, while homeschooling my two youngest children, we started a unit of study on the Sonoran Desert. I bought an Arizona wildflower guide and brought out our little Golden Guide to Birds. Orange and yellow wildflowers covered the hills near my Phoenix home that glorious spring. We spent almost every Friday hiking or picnicking in the desert. Together, we learned to identify globe mallow, brittlebush, and Mexican poppies while also attempting to identify some of the desert birds. It was exciting to see the noisy cactus wren, Gambel's quail families, and a roadrunner. I still didn't own binoculars.

My children went back to public school, but an interest in plants and animals of the desert stayed with me. It led me to the Desert Botanical Garden and, eventually, their birding walks. After that first look at a hummingbird, I was hooked. I took part every Monday and learned about Gila woodpeckers, gilded flickers, and red-tailed hawks. In the spring, the tiny walnut-sized quail captivated my heart.

It didn't take long to learn that a person serious about birds is called a "birder." The difference between a birdwatcher and a birder is a matter of intensity and dedication. While on vacation, birdwatchers might watch birds. Birders go on vacations in order to watch birds. Birders also spend thousands of dollars on binoculars, scopes, and cameras. I paid $250 for my first pair of binoculars, but the best binoculars can cost thousands. Getting my own binoculars took me to a whole new realm.

An introvert, the first thing I do when entering a room full of people is look for a corner in which to hide. I would rather have a root canal than talk to a stranger. But I found it easy to join the birders. First, because with binoculars held to my eyes, I could avoid eye contact. Second, I didn't have to talk to anyone about anything except birds.

I started a list of every bird I had seen in my life. Each new bird added to my list was called a "lifer." Some birders keep lists for their backyards, counties, states, and countries. These intense birders are sometimes called "twitchers," and they travel to exotic places all over the world to add birds to their life lists. About 10,000 species of birds exist in the world with a little over 1,000 found in the United States.

A "big year" is what birders call an attempt to see as many species as possible in a given year. This usually takes a great deal of money for travel and hiring guides. In 1973, Kenn Kaufman set the North American Big Year record and saw 671 bird species while hitchhiking around the country. Nineteen years old, he had only a few dollars in his pocket.

Most hard-core birders are men, but in 1995, Phoebe Snetsinger became the first person to see over 8,000 species from all over the world. Birding began as a hobby when she was a young stay-at-home mother, but over the years she became more obsessed and left her family for weeks at a time to travel to exotic locations.

I was only four months into my new hobby of birding when I heard about the National Audubon Society's Christmas Bird Count, or CBC. Volunteer birders sign up to count all the birds they can see in a day within an assigned area, often in teams. Of course, I signed up immediately.

A rookie birder, I was partnered with an expert birder. I barely knew the difference between gilded flickers and gila woodpeckers, but my partner could identify golden eagles and red-tailed hawks from miles away while driving. As she pointed out egrets and ibis, I wrote everything on a paper pad – this was before cell phones.

Driving through alfalfa fields we saw a farmer on a tractor, a cloud of blackbirds followed behind him. Some of those birds looked like they had been dipped headfirst into yellow paint. These yellow-headed blackbirds were mixed in a flock that included red-winged blackbirds. My job was to count not only the number of these birds, but also to separate the species. They kept flying up in the air and then landing again. *How could I avoid double-counting?* My birding partner taught me the patch method. I counted one patch, then estimated how many similar-sized patches of birds were there. Our count in the field that day: over 4,000 blackbirds.

It wasn't until my first CBC that I understood how intense birders can be. Before the Christmas Bird Count began in 1900, many families would have hunting competitions to see how many birds they could shoot on Christmas Day. Imagine sorting through that pile of bloody bird bodies. Frank Chapman, an ornithologist in New Jersey, came up with the idea of counting birds instead of killing them.

The competitive edge to a CBC has not changed in over 100 years. At the end of the day, all the birders in a 'count circle' get together to brag about all the birds they found that day. I have always hated any type of competition. In school, I was always last in any race, from running to potato sack races.

A heavy pit of anxiety grew inside as I listened to birders call out their findings on my first CBC. I tried to hide in the corner as I tallied my counts of mourning doves and blackbirds. Around me, birders compared notes on who had seen the most species and the rarest. I wondered if I had even been on the same count as these other birders who volleyed numbers and species like a ball in a tennis match. To some people, birding should be an Olympic sport.

Despite the fierce competition, I enjoyed counting birds that day. As we drove through fields and looked for birds in fresh haystacks, the smell of cut hay brought back childhood memories of living on a farm in eastern Oregon. Back then, I spent my days out in fields, either with my dad on the tractor or alone exploring. Along with cows and barn cats, wild birds had been my companions. Yellow-billed magpies hung out near our back door and tormented the cats who waited for dinner. They echoed my mother as she called my father.

"Jack, Jack, come in!" my mother yelled impatiently at the barn.

"Jack! Jack! Jack!" called the magpies in return.

In the spring, my mother wouldn't let my father take down the swallow's nest above our front door, even though bird droppings were everywhere. The adult birds guarded their nest (and that door), and dove ferociously at anyone who walked through it. Instead of using that exit, we watched the swallows raise a family, smiling as the last one flew away in the fall.

In the mornings of my childhood, I was awakened by the bright, bubbly song of a meadowlark. I learned to recognize their yellow breasts as they sat on the fenceposts. In late spring, when hay cutting season started, I often came home to the savory smell of a pheasant roasting in the oven. Pheasants build nests on the ground in spring and summer, and chose our alfalfa fields because they could hide among the plants. As they sat on those nests, they were often caught in the sharp blades of the hay mower. My father couldn't avoid decapitating at least one or two every year.

That feeling of being back in my childhood home is one of the reasons I do the Christmas Bird Count every year. Miles of walking, pushing through thick brush along dry riverbeds, may only uncover a few birds during an entire morning's walk. Driving along canals or through fields of alfalfa takes hours of focus. But finding a burrowing owl along the ditch bank or an irrigated field covered with egrets and herons makes the whole day worthwhile.

Today I use an app called eBird to record my observations. I use another app called Merlin Bird ID to help me identify a bird by sight or sound. Both apps are free, developed by the Cornell Lab of Ornithology. Scientists use the uploaded app data to aid in their study of bird migration patterns. Every time I use eBird to save my lists, I contribute to science.

I now own four pairs of binoculars, two cameras with a lens dedicated to wildlife, and a scope. The last time I counted, I had thirty-five wildlife field guides on my bookshelf. I have books dedicated to nests and eggs, warblers, hummingbirds, hawks, and butterflies.

I don't plan to do a big year like Kenn Kaufman. I am not obsessed with seeing birds all over the world like Phoebe Snetsinger. But I do go on vacation just to look for birds. For a little while, I forget I am only an average grandmother, and instead, I become a great scientist racing through the jungles of Southeastern Arizona. On one of my past birding trips, I jumped over piles of bear scat, searching for the elusive tufted flycatcher. Sometimes, I imagine I am a famous wildlife photographer, heavy camera slung over one shoulder, chasing after elegant trogons. A couple years ago, I found the trogons and accidentally caught them in the act of mating.

I also take vacations with my husband, affectionately known as a spouse of birder, or SOB. He stops and patiently waits in the car while I look for birds. A few weeks ago, I was visiting family in Texas.

"Grandma, look up!"

My granddaughter pointed to a flock of birds that had landed in the tree just over our heads, at least two dozen cedar waxwings, an elegant, crested bird with a black mask. They chittered above us as we marveled at them. After a few seconds, they left. I hope my granddaughter never loses the sense of amazement she felt at that moment.

I still feel that way every time I look through binoculars. Even my backyard is full of excitement now. I watch doves and finches, and I duck when hummingbirds zip by, barely missing my head. A spark bird is one that inspires a lifelong passion for birds. That hummingbird I saw in 2006 was mine. That spark changed my life and sent me on a journey of discovery and wonder.

JACKIE ANDERSON

Poetry

Transitions

LINDA ESPERANZA

Winter 2022

How do you know when you're satisfied with life?
Transitions make ambition strenuous.
Every now and then I feel, bare,
I don't belong anywhere.

Spring 2023

A full year since I've been back in my hometown.
I know why I returned yet; I'm still yearning.
I am searching for the "perfect" dwelling.
Now, what does that look like?

I survived my first year in a new career.
It's been difficult for many reasons.
It's been rewarding for the same purpose.
I am emerging professionally; is this settling?

Winter 2024

The air is cold and crisp, but I am warm inside.
Blood rushes as I reveal how I broke my own heart.
Survival mode isolating me at all costs.
Why does healing hurt?

Spring 2025

I've done so much to create—
this woman I love in the mirror …
A calmer nervous system: I am relearning
so much still. Is this my heart being all in, hopeful?

My gaze looks different in my reflection.
My eyes are bright, gleaming with enticing unfamiliarity.
Not distorted with guilt or fear.
Somehow ready for futures unknown.

LINDA ESPERANZA

Fiction

The Archivist of Small Things

G.B. CROISSANT

The town's Archive often smelled of rain-dampened wood, dusty books, and a hint of pine air freshener. Edmund sat at his small desk in the back of the building, jotting notes down in the ancient, leather-bound ledger. His fountain pen balanced between his fingers. The overhead light flickered sporadically. The room was silent except for the faint ticking of the brass clock on the far wall and the slow pattering of rain.

Outside, Edmund heard people walking by. He watched them through the window—umbrellas tilted beneath the lamplight. They looked serene and unhindered by their own pasts. Women smiled lovingly at their husbands. Children splashed in the pools of collected water in the street. But their faces were . . . indistinct. Blurred slightly by the fog, as though time itself refused to remember their details. He was in awe of their euphoric way of life, yet the sight unsettled him. In this town, joy seemed to be rehearsed.

All the objects that sat in the Archive's storage had once been someone's keepsake. An earth-bound memory. He could feel them behind him—the shelves leaning with their weight, whispering faintly when the wind pressed against the walls. While it saddened him to know that these memories would never be remembered, it was his sacred duty to help them forget. Once they were catalogued, the owner would be unburdened by the memory it held, whether it was a death or a marriage gone wrong. Sometimes they came to him hollow-eyed, clutching wrapped trinkets like their lives depended on it. When they left without it, they wouldn't know why they had come at all.

Lost in his thoughts, Edmund suddenly smelled something. Lilacs. Out of place in his tomb of forgotten treasures. He froze.

He rose from his dented chair and instinctively crossed to the window. A low fog had set in and swirled over the brick street. Underneath the sill, a small bundle of lilacs rested on a loose brick. Bright and fresh. It stood out vividly against the surrounding night, their stems beaded perfectly with droplets. Edmund stared in disbelief, his chest tightening.

His sister's favorite flower.

Tapping his thumbs together behind his back, he remained by the window, watching the leaves and petals tremble in the fog. Somewhere in the distance, a clock struck the hour—the Archive's own clock did not echo it. The silence that followed was heavy, as though the whole town had drawn in a breath and forgotten to let it out.

The rain hadn't let up for hours. By closing time, the town had finally gone still as it did every night. The wind carried no laughter from the pub down the road—only the dripping of rain pattered against the glass windows. Edmund felt safe in the dark, shrouded by the walls of the Archive. He crossed his arms and turned around to pack his belongings.

A light tinkling sound bounced off the walls. He looked down. A small marble hit his foot. Tilting his head, he carefully picked it up. Blues and greens mixed in the glass orb. A tug of familiarity gripped his heart, but no memories came forth. It pulsed, beating like an irregular heart, jumping in long pauses and short bursts.

Edmund sat down in his chair. He felt like he had lost this. But why was it here?

His open ledger began to tremble. In delicate, cursive handwriting that wasn't his, the ledger read, *Object #1149—Marble, blue and green swirl. Keeps secrets only the water remembers.*

A shiver coiled down his spine. He flipped through the previous entries—all his own, except this one. The marble reflected the dim lighting.

The rain poured harder on the Archive, masking the outside sounds of cars and people laughing. The marble pulsed again, harder and longer. A flash of sound—a girl's laughter—struck his ears. His eyes widened, and he tightened his grip on the marble. Edmund didn't have the heart to throw it across the room; it would feel . . . sacrilegious.

Edmund stayed long past closing time, his forgotten belongings hanging on the wall. The writing and the marble completely enraptured him.

The doorbell jingled. Edmund jumped to his feet. He hadn't heard the clocks chime the time. The cloud-garbled sun spilled through the water-stained windows. Rubbing his eyes, he slipped the marble into his pocket and opened the door, expecting someone to be waiting patiently on the stoop.

No one.

"You keep the things no one wants, right?"

Edmund slowly turned to see a girl, maybe ten years old, barefoot in the corner of the entryway. Her dark hair was unkempt, and her dress was well-worn, damp from the rain. She held a small picture frame, a pressed bundle of lilacs between the panes.

His eyes stung. That same hint of recognition hit him.

"Are you lost?" he stammered. "Where are your parents?"

She smiled faintly. "They left things behind, too. I'm sure I'll see them soon."

She placed the lilac frame on the counter's edge and walked back to the door. The hem of her dress brushed against his leg.

"Wait—what's your name?"

The girl paused, her hand resting on the knob, and turned her head slightly. "You'll remember it soon."

Too stunned and clammy to make any moves to stop her, she stepped out into the fog. He flung the door open to find an empty street. She had disappeared. He rubbed his eyes and returned to the counter.

The frame waited patiently. He reverently walked it to his desk and opened his ledger. Steadying his hand, he started the inscription: *Object #1150—Pressed lilac in plain frame. No signs of wear.*

The ink refused to dry as he took the collectible in his hands. He watched the ink swell and swirl on the page, creating new letters in different handwriting.

Remember the well in the orchard.

Edmund's chest tightened. The well had been sealed off for years, since . . . He pushed the thought away. It couldn't be her after all this time. She was gone without a trace, and no one had seen her again. He wiped a chilled bead of sweat off his brow. His hands shook.

Before he could bring himself to take the item back to storage, a drop of water splashed on the frame. He looked at the ceiling. It was completely dry. A shiver coiled around his spine. He looked from the ledger to the frame. The flower's petals curled up and down as if it were breathing.

Edmund burst through the door of the bookshop that was tucked in between the tailor and the church. The chime screamed in defiance of the rude interruption, echoing through the rows of dusty bookshelves. The smell of paper and damp carpet hit his nose, faintly sour.

Mr. Pellam sat asleep in the recliner by the teller, his glasses hanging on the tip of his nose, softly snoring with half his mouth open. The unofficial town historian and obscure history collector jostled awake at the sudden intrusion, sputtering and clutching his chest.

"Well, I say," he scoffed, blinking against the harsh lamplight. Seeing it was Edmund, he softened his anger. "Oh, bother, Edmund! I haven't seen you in weeks, and then you go and try to give me a heart attack?"

Edmund, still breathless, set the frame on the counter with trembling hands. The glass had fogged up from the humidity outside. From his coat pocket, he produced the marble, holding it out like a confession.

"I thought you had lost it," Mr. Pellam said quietly. The marble glinted and pulsed in response. "Have you been to the orchard yet?"

Edmund shook his head.

Mr. Pellam adjusted his glasses to their rightful place and examined the suspended browned lilac. His mouth pursed in thought. "That place has always been wrong," he said, after much consideration. He gestured with the frame emphatically. "You should have stayed away."

Edmund steadied himself, forcing the tremor from his voice. "You already know what happened, don't you?"

Mr. Pellam's bright blue eyes, dulled by years of constant study, lingered on the older man as if he were debating with himself. "She wasn't supposed to go there. None of us were. It was a dumb, childish dare that went too far, Edmund. You know that, right?"

Edmund's jaw tightened. "What's down there?"

Mr. Pellam absentmindedly wiped the mist from the frame. "What? The well?" He sucked in a long breath and sat back down. "It doesn't go down. It leads in."

"Into what?"

"Roots, memories. Things that should stay buried."

Edmund shivered in the heated shop. A faint sound rapped from the bookshelves, like a knock.

Mr. Pellam quickly cleared his throat, ignoring the sound. "We were kids," he said, rising to his feet. "The town—well, the town likes to forget. Why are you bringing this up now?"

A heavy silence settled over them for a few minutes. Mr. Pellam hadn't said *nothing* was down there. Edmund shifted uncomfortably, trying to find the right words.

"She came back."

Mr. Pellam's eyes widened, and a flicker of genuine fear flashed before being subdued by his professionalism. His hand shook slightly as he set the frame down gently.

"Look," Mr. Pellam broke the silence, "you can pull at these threads all you want, try to bring her back. But the town will unravel if you succeed. As the Archivist, I don't need to explain to you the importance of leaving things and being able to move on."

Edmund pressed his lips together. Taking the frame back from him, Edmund gave his old friend a nod and left without another word.

Edmund stood at the edge of the orchard, the edges of the frame between his fingers. The trees hadn't borne fruit in decades; their gnarled, brittle branches reached for the sky like pleading hands. Wind hissed through the hollow limbs, stirring the smells of rot and rain. The well was nestled further down the grove, swallowed by overgrown weeds. A scar on the town everyone pretended not to notice

A faint child's laughter drifted on the wind as he approached the well. He stepped carefully, remembering where it was from when he was a boy. Twigs crunched under his weight.

Crunch!

Edmund stepped back. An old, now-crushed teacup was underneath his boot. He recognized it from the collection in the Archive. The hair on the back of his neck prickled as he found more: a cracked mirror, a broken radio, and … lilac petals.

The marble in his pocket hummed in tune with the other treasures as if answering their call.

He reached the well and pulled hard on the rusted gate. It resisted for a few moments before snapping open with a metallic clang. Darkness vibrated within the gaping abyss below. It beckoned him.

Edmund stepped onto the ledge, held his lantern into it, and peered down. Nothing. Then steps appeared, circling down into the well's abyss.

He tentatively stepped onto the first. It held his weight. He took in a breath and descended.

With each step, the world above dimmed. It seemed endless. The farther he went, the more the walls of the well seemed to shift. Stone walls soon gave way to rotting wood. Then to tangled roots and earth. The stone steps were replaced with wooden planks. A patchwork of old objects was embedded in the walls: childhood drawings, broken pocket watches, bits of porcelain, and books half-consumed by the earth.

Finally, at the bottom, Edmund stepped into cold water. A chamber opened up around him, the light of the lantern not getting to the edges of the room, glistening off the slick rocks.

A shadowed figure stood in the middle of the chamber, unmoving. A silhouette of a dress and loose, long hair was visible, but no other features. Edmund held up his lantern and trudged forward.

"You came," the figure said, stopping Edmund in his tracks. The voice was older and feminine. Familiarity tickled his eardrums.

The water around his ankles rippled, lapping at his legs. The walls breathed, swelling with each breath.

"Why didn't you come back?" He tentatively stepped forward. The lantern swayed in his grasp.

"Someone must stay behind to guard the memories. Someone had to keep it asleep."

"What are you talking about? What's down here?"

"Not just down here." Her gaze flicked toward the walls, the roots that pulsed like veins. "Underneath everything. The town. The years. It feeds on what we forget. Our grief. Our shame. Our dead. That's how it keeps our world quiet."

Her silhouette wavered, and for a moment, he caught a glimpse of her face— his sister, young and bright-eyed. She was the same as the day she vanished.

"But the town doesn't truly forget anymore," she whispered. "You changed that. The Archive kept everything. You starved it."

His brow furrowed. "You called me here to feed it?

"No. To finish what we began." She floated slightly closer, still far enough not to be fully seen. "I called you here to help me. When it wakes, everything burning will rise. I cannot keep it at bay anymore. You need to free everything."

The walls shuddered a sigh, vibrating the embedded objects. The face of a pocket watch shattered. The marble in his pocket burned and sizzled through the fabric, landing in the water, hissing. The lantern's flame whooshed with the rolling winds that picked up, even under the earth's surface.

"It's waking up," she sang.

"Come with me," he said, pulling the lilac frame out of the satchel. "We can fix this some other way."

"I . . . we can't," she shook her head sadly. Her form flickered between old woman and girl, stranger to family. "There is no other way. The memories need to be revived."

Edmund, biting his lip slightly, took out the frame. It vibrated in time with the trinkets and roots. Why would she lie to him? It may have been decades since she had vanished, but she was still his sister. All the guilt he had accumulated over the years pressed into his eyes, a tear forming. He would have to trust her as much as she trusted him.

"I . . . I'm sorry for what happened," he stuttered. The tears fell. "I should've come back sooner."

She smiled reassuringly. "It wasn't your fault."

With a small sigh, he thrust the picture frame toward her. The glass split apart, and the petals dissolved into the air. The walls convulsed. The chamber tore itself open, allowing fragmented laughter, screams, and sobs to escape. Memories, long buried, spilled into the rising water, reaching like desperate hands.

But some of the words that poured out seemed to say *thank you.* Edmund's sister held out her hands, one reaching for him. She closed her eyes and allowed the light from above to envelope her. Lilacs bloomed from the roots and showered them.

Above them, the town stirred. People awoke from uneasy dreams in their homes and on the streets, to stare at the objects on their mantels. Old photos, toys, and letters—things they had long forgotten—returned to them. Every home, a small resurrection.

Edmund took her hand.

The sun fully breached the horizon. In the orchard, the well dried up. Ivy spread through the cracks. The iron gate lay on its side near the edge.

Edmund was gone.

The Human Question Mark

GAEA BAILEY

they stand bent as if to look at their own heart
making sure it is still there
listening to the eternal internal beat in wonder   wondering

they wear sweaters and sweatshirts
in the heat of the worlds broken thermostat
a cap to guard lice from their eyes or prevent a sunburned mind

as they reach for it   the something   with cragged hands
pushing scattered remnants of   today   yesterday   tomorrow
on borrowed-stolen wheels sure to be found one day
overturned next to a dirt soaked pack

they stand on thin ankles and move so slowly
(the evidence of progress unnoticed by those passing)
holding a cylinder   or   a banana peel with petals hanging
or an inhaler   savior of flat lungs   or a pipe to lift the mind to down

as i stare   wince   from the guilty coolness of my cars ac
incessant queries arise never to be asked   at least not of them
what happened here   was it the drugs of dis ease
or the weight of the world wrapped in despair
and now is it illness   insanity
or endless loneliness of the human condition
borne of unworthiness ground into the meat of self-loathing

or   is it my refusal to stay
to kneel on the cement   to utter the prayer
the wish to see their face
to seek their   forgiveness
to hear the blessings of their breath
to offer useless water without a straw
to help with fluttering hands that do not know how

hands   cover   my   face
as i bend forward to see if my heart is still there
a tear falls   theirs or mine?

GAEA BAILEY

Meet the Authors

Jackie Anderson | Nonfiction
Jackie has always felt a connection to nature, especially in Arizona, where she has lived for the past forty-one years. In a typical week, she can be found helping guide bird walks, hiking on a nearby trail, or playing with grandchildren. She counts among her greatest accomplishments raising six children and hiking to the bottom of the Grand Canyon twice. Writing a memoir has been the focus of her writing for the past ten years.

Lori Appleby Hoke | Nonfiction
Lori Appleby Hoke was born and raised in Arizona, but she has lived in other places including Mexico City. A self-appointed family historian, she draws rich storytelling content from those who came before her. Lori is a retired communications professional with a master's degree in English. Nature, travel, books, and conversations with her hive inspire her. Lori has been married to Robert for thirty-four years and learns the most from her daughters, Valerie and Lily.

Gaea Bailey | Poetry
Poet/author Gaea Bailey came to Phoenix from upstate New York nearly sixty years ago. Her work has been published by Moonstone Press, Phoenix Oasis Press, and others. She was co-owner of Lords of Art Town Studio & Gallery, served as review panelist for Phoenix Youth Arts Grants, hosts an online poetry critique group, and manages Old Hunt Road Press. She recently released a poetry anthology entitled *What is This? A Conversation Between 10 Poets*.

Derek Barton | Fiction
Derek Barton was born in northeast Indiana in 1970. The typical introvert kid; closer to books than people, but grew up with a fascination for horror novels (Stephen King, Dean Koontz) and medieval fantasy (Piers Anthony, R.A Salvatore). Since 2016, he has completed nineteen works of horror and epic fantasy on Amazon and Audible.com and published in five literary magazines. He moved to Phoenix in 1996 and married his wife in 2012.

Jordan Beckett | Fiction
Jordan Beckett has lived in Arizona for more than 30 years. A lover of short form fiction, she enjoys writing across multiple genres. Her work reflects her fascination with what it means to be human, in all its messy imperfection. She is currently at work on her first novel, which is a mosaic of stories set in the world of a fictional Chicago diner.

Tinamarie Cox | Poetry
Tinamarie Cox lives in Prescott Valley with her husband, children, and rescue felines. Her written and visual work has appeared in online and print publications. She has two poetry chapbooks with Bottlecap Press: *Self-Destruction in Small Doses* (2023) and *A Collection of Morning Hours* (2024). Her first full-length poetry collection, *Through a Sea Laced with Midnight Hues*, arrived in 2025 with Nymeria Publishing. Her second book, *A Numbers Game*, will be released in 2026.

G.B. Croissant | Fiction

G. B. Croissant is a part-time teacher, stay-at-home mom, and self-proclaimed "master of Latin." She has a bachelor's degree in creative writing with honors from Northern Arizona University. When she's not teaching English or toddler wrangling, she is trying to stay sane by sewing, writing, and attempting to read. She lives in Mesa, Arizona, with her husband, toddler son, three absurd cats, and a dog who pretends to be a cat.

Bonnie Danowski | Poetry

Bonnie Danowski is a fearless caregiver, advocate, author, artist, innovator, and speaker. Her husband Jim's multiple sclerosis created a passion to improve caregivers' lives. While with Valley Interfaith Project and the Franciscan Renewal Center, she co-wrote Arizona's Lifespan Respite Care bill, providing respite for thousands of Arizona families. Bonnie has received numerous awards from national, state, and local organizations. Much of her life is chronicled in her book, *The Path Beckoned: I Answered Yes.*

Julie Erfle | Nonfiction

Julie Erfle hails from North Dakota but has called Arizona home for more than two decades. She began her career as a promotions producer at KPHO-TV5 and 3TV before launching her own communications consulting firm, Erfle Uncuffed, in 2016. A former executive director of Progress Now Arizona and columnist for the Arizona Mirror, Julie is also a fellow with Leading for Change and the Flinn-Brown Arizona Center for Civic Leadership.

Linda Esperanza | Poetry

Linda Esperanza, based in Phoenix, Arizona, uses poetry and prose to process the world around and within her. She believes writing is a tool to become friends with her emotions. She loves epistolary poetry for such an experience. She hopes to promote mental health advocacy within her writing. Other creative endeavors include open mics, poetry videos and dabbling in zines. When she isn't writing or working, she is watching TV or connecting with her favorite people.

Tracy Holohan | Fiction

Tracy Holohan spent a good bit of her life teaching cartooning and animation to wildly creative and fun-loving college students. Then she spent a good bit more teaching math and science to sixth graders who taught her more about life than she ever taught them about anything. A resident of Arizona since she was ten, Tracy graduated from NAU in Flagstaff. She writes paranormal mysteries sprinkled heavily with the captivating personalities of her delightful students.

Nour Kandalaft | Poetry

Nour Kandalaft, a graduate student in Hydrosystems Engineering, blends her STEM background with a passion for poetry. Her writing explores themes of belonging, love, faith, and life's quiet moments. Originally from Lebanon and now living in Arizona, she finds in poetry an anchor through change from a heritage of mediterranean resilience to a present of discovery and growth through the desert.

Elle LeCarre | Fiction

Elle LeCarre grew up riding horses under the Arizona sun while developing a fascination with the intrigue of mystery novels. Completing her journalism degree from Arizona State University, she won the highest award from the Communication Workers of America for editing the monthly aviation magazine *The West Wing*. Elle is currently writing her first novel; a mystery combining a death onboard a commercial airliner, with a flawed but scrappy sleuth compelled to discover the truth.

Glen Loveland | Nonfiction

Glen Loveland is a queer writer and the Senior Career Coach at Thunderbird School of Global Management in Arizona. His work explores LGBTQ+ lives across borders, masculinity, migration, and work. A former HR leader who spent thirteen years in Beijing, he now calls the Phoenix metro home. His debut memoir, *Beijing Bound: A Foreigner Discovers China* (2025), traces chosen family and cross-cultural belonging. Glen mentors global students and writes candidly about identity, career, and community.

Ilana Lydia | Poetry

Ilana Lydia is a playwright, director, and former artistic director. Born and raised in Phoenix, Arizona, Ilana won her school's highest honor in philosophy as an undergraduate, the second female to have done so. Ilana likes to write fantastical feminism, the offspring of magical realism, and treating women as people. She is the founding Manager of Arts & Culture in Buckeye. IMAGE CREDIT, LAURA DURANT.

Donna A. Parker | Poetry
Donna A. Parker is an Arizona-based author who currently resides in Phoenix. Her short stories, magazine articles, and poems appear in various publications and anthologies. Her works as a playwright have been performed on college campuses. A long-time member of a dedicated writers' group, she draws inspiration from her decades of a well-lived life. Donna's insightful writing explores themes of connection, perseverance, and love in everyday life.

June Powers | Poetry
June Powers is a free verse poet from Philadelphia, Pennsylvania, now residing in Phoenix, Arizona. She has self-published three books of narrative poetry: *CHILD/ poems of consciousness, SOUTH/poems of passing through*, and *HEART/poems of love*. A member of the Arizona State Poetry Society, she enjoys writing about social issues, nature, love, and family, often intersecting these topics. She is currently working on poems that embrace the traumas of the human condition.

Jerald Riibe | Nonfiction
Jerry is a retired educator. He is a writer by passion if not prolific publication. Writing serves as his means to ponder both himself and the world. Each piece is an invitation for others to understand his perspective, but also explore their own, through the shared act of reading and connecting with words shaped by experience and curiosity. In 2020, Jerry and wife, Jody, became residents of the East Valley and claim Arizona as home.

Gayla Wigal Robinson | Fiction
Gayla Robinson grew up in Prescott, Arizona and has been living in the 48th state since the Kennedy administration. She found time during her busy career to take writing courses through the Maricopa Community College system. After retirement, she has continued to pursue her first passion—telling stories. When her attention is not diverted by two cats or her husband, she is working on a contemporary novel set in a fictional northern Arizona town.

Eileen Sauer | Fiction
A lifelong East Coast denizen (from Florida to New Jersey), Eileen Sauer moved to Phoenix, Arizona in December 2024, and has been exploring since. "What the heck is a haboob?!" She wrote *How Do I Become an Unstoppable Musician? Vol. 1* (of 3), and began writing fiction in 2023. She is a pianist, composer (evening classes at Juilliard), and former technologist, with a B.S. in Math - Computing from the University of Notre Dame.

Hope Spear | Poetry
Hope Spear is an emerging voice in the writing world. She was awarded a Poet and Author Fellowship with the Martha's Vineyard Institute of Creative Writing. Before becoming a writer, Hope spent years successfully convincing middle school students they were writers, and eventually even she convinced herself. She holds two degrees in education. Hope lives in Tucson, Arizona with the great loves of her life: tacos, her husband, and her three kids. In that order.

Eric Thurston | Fiction

Moving from Indiana to Arizona in 1980 activated Eric Thurston's curiosity for life. Living in a tiny room in downtown Phoenix, he shut down his shallow life for a year, read fifty classics, and wrote. Eric was permanently changed by that year, and left with a love of literature and a stack of journals. He was inspired to go to ASU, got married, raised kids, and taught special education. Always loving Arizona. Always reading and writing.

Pam Vap | Poetry

Pam Vap is rockhounding and writing in the Sonoran desert. She was awarded first place in the 2024 Princemere Poetry Contest and first place in the Cultural Integration on the High Plains poetry contest. She was also a finalist in the Lascaux Prize for Poetry, and an Allen Ginsberg Poetry Honorable Mention, among other awards. She has recently published in *Poetry East*, *The Lascaux Review*, *Presence*, *Patterson Literary Review*, *Abandoned Mine*, *Orison* and others.

Mike Williams | Fiction

Mike Williams is an up-and-coming fiction author. His voice is geared for fantasy and thriller, with a fearless attitude toward genre blending. From comedy to romance to horror, it's all on the table all at once. An Arizona resident for 20 years, he made a transition to Minneapolis with his boyfriend in March of 2025. Mike is currently working on a novella, "All is Fair", and a novel titled "Ride with Reaper".

Gerald Lloyd Wood | Nonfiction
Writer and artist, Gerald Lloyd Wood, now lives in
Scottsdale, Arizona, having lived in Tucson when he
completed all but his dissertation for the Ph.D in Higher
Education at University of Arizona. Aside from his scholarly
publications, his work appeared in *Frank Lloyd Wright
Foundation Quarterly*. He also wrote a weekly horticulture column in Mena,
Arkansas. Twenty-four of Gerald's stories about caregiving and dementia can
be found on the non-profit Meaning & Hope Institute's website.

Reader Advisory

Warning—spoilers ahead. Trigger warnings serve the important purpose of letting the reader know a piece of writing might contain distressing images or pertain to a sensitive topic. What follows is not an all-encompassing catalog of triggers, but does include common topics such as violence, assault, and suicide. *Inadvertently reading this list might result in the revelation of major plot points.* We encourage you to read on if you feel you might benefit from its contents. Otherwise, we recommend you skip the following pages to prevent revealing any information about the pieces within this anthology.

ALPHABETICAL BY TOPIC

Profanity
A Slip of Paper, page 17

Puberty
Angiosperms and Other Fruit-Bearing Plants, page 15

Self Harm
Arman Is Not Well, page 37

Sex
Angiosperms and Other Fruit-Bearing Plants, page 15

Sexism
Angiosperms and Other Fruit-Bearing Plants, page 15

Sexual Trauma
Angiosperms and Other Fruit-Bearing Plants, page 15

Suicide
A Slip of Paper, page 17
No Farewell, page 101

Trauma
Who's To Blame, page 63
That Sunday Dinner, page 27

ALPHABETICAL BY STORY

Angiosperms and Other Fruit-Bearing Plants, page 15
Aging, Mental Health, Puberty, Sex, Sexism, Sexual Trauma

With Thanks

To the **2025 authors**: This exists because of you. How amazing is that? Your willingness to write something curious, to take the chance on submitting, created this book. We are grateful for your talents and can't wait for the world to read your work.

To the **2025 community reviewers**: It takes a special kind of person to say 'yes, I'd love to volunteer to read a ton of submissions in a short amount of time and do it all through technology.' Thankfully, we found fifteen special people. You did it because you love Arizona's writing community, and you love great stories. Thank you so very much.

To the **2025 PHX Oasis Press anthology team**, you made this book a reality. You gave up your time and energy. You trusted there was a finish line even when we didn't have a map. You prioritized this project, and it shows. Special thanks goes to:

Leslie Cox, who managed our new Submittable system, all of our AI detection and editing software, and also copyedited, fact-checked, and helped refine our content advisory section. Our words are better because of your efforts.

Eric Boyd, who provided craft guidance, hosted workshops to help submitting authors polish their work, and answered all of our random late-night legal questions with his usual patient, upbeat manner. You know more about craft than the rest of us combined.

Mary Cornelius, who can probably host a workshop in her sleep after how many she curated in the beginning stages of the anthology submission process. You helped set the curious stage and taught authors how to lean into their strengths.

Cristina Scobee who orchestrated a new, blind, multi-stage review process involving community judges from around the state, ever focused on the end-goal of a cohesive, approachable, diverse, vibrant anthology. Your empathy and honesty know no bounds.

Felicia Penza, who crafted an unforgettable visual experience. From the outstretched, seeking hand, to the clean interior, you've created a special design. It hints at the entanglements of curiosity, leaving us with the feeling that just-out-of-reach answers will soon be revealed. Your ability to evoke emotions is impressive.

Derek Barton, who provided feedback across this journey, always focused on the author experience and how to help them shine. Derek played double-duty, taking on the role of community reviewer, as well as helping with a workshop. Your enthusiasm to support is unmatched.

And to **Sue Fulton**, who thought it was time to get curious, and goodness did the universe respond in the most unexpected of ways. Thank you for your mentorship.

Sincerely,
Tracy Skochil, Editor in Chief

About Phoenix Oasis Press

PHX Oasis Press is an oasis of inspiration and support for Arizona's aspiring, established, and I'm-not-really-a-writer writers. We offer low- and no-cost resources that help writers generate work, build skills, share their stories, and connect with Arizona's vibrant writing community. phxoasispress.com

www.ingramcontent.com/pod-product-compliance
Lightning Source LLC
Chambersburg PA
CBHW020152120726
47903CB00007B/2523